from
John & Astrid
18th March 1999

The Absent Child

Also by Patricia Fawcett

Set to Music
A Family Weekend

The Absent Child

PATRICIA FAWCETT

SCEPTRE

Copyright © 1997 Patricia Fawcett

First published in 1997 by Hodder and Stoughton
A division of Hodder Headline PLC
A Sceptre Book

The right of Patricia Fawcett to be identified as the Author of
the Work has been asserted by her in accordance with the
Copyright, Designs and Patents Act 1988.

10 9 8 7 6 5 4 3 2 1

All rights reserved. No part of this publication may be
reproduced, stored in a retrieval system or transmitted
in any form or by any means without the prior written
permission of the publisher, nor be otherwise circulated
in any form of binding or cover other than that in which
it is published and without a similar condition being
imposed on the subsequent purchaser.

All characters in this publication are fictitious and any
resemblance to real persons, living or dead, is purely coincidental.

A CIP catalogue record for this title is
available from the British Library.

ISBN 0 340 65807 X

Typeset by Palimpsest Book Production Limited,
Polmont, Stirlingshire
Printed and bound in Great Britain by
Mackays of Chatham PLC, Chatham, Kent

Hodder and Stoughton
A division of Hodder Headline PLC
338 Euston Road
London NW1 3BH

For my daughter Elizabeth

A special thank you to the staff of Barnard Castle Library for finding me so many books about adoption.

PROLOGUE

My darling Helen,

Tomorrow I say goodbye to you and I still can't imagine how I will feel when you're gone. I've been away from home for weeks, first at my great-aunt's and then here and so I've had lots of time to think. I go round in circles but the answer's always the same. This one. Adoption. It's for the best, they say. They all say that.

If only I hadn't seen you, held you, it would surely be easier.

Someone at The Children's Society suggested I might do this – write a letter to you to be placed in your file. They said that putting my thoughts down on paper might help. You might never read it of course because, when you're eighteen, you might decide you don't want to know anything about me and I can't blame you for that.

I'm trying to think of something profound to say but can't think of anything. There's not much to tell. I was nearly seventeen and still at school when I found out I was pregnant and my parents were shocked – that's an understatement – when I told them.

It was all a terrible mistake. My fault for being so naïve. Your father was nice enough, an uncomplicated friendly sort with a wicked sense of humour, the first boy who ever paid me much attention, to be honest. I suppose you could say I am a bit of a bluestocking, head buried in my books most of the time and it was a surprise to find out there was something more to life.

I met him on holiday, a week away with a girlfriend and her parents. I don't want it to sound as if I'm deprived but we've never gone in for holidays much in my family so it was something special. Blame it on the sun, the swimming, the late night dancing, the walks beside the sea, that sort of thing. It was all very romantic and he was persuasive, as I was ready to be persuaded. I think, for a while, I must have loved him. I hope he loved me too.

When the holiday came to an end we said goodbye and it was never serious enough for either of us to want to carry on with it. He doesn't know about you. Even if I did ever find him, and I'm not going to try, I wouldn't want to marry

• Patricia Fawcett

him. My dad wanted me to do that but it's not what I want. I have things to do, you see. Plans for the future.

Now I sound selfish. As if I'm only thinking of myself and making it sound as if you are just an inconvenience, a nuisance. Believe me, if there was some way I could keep you, I would. My parents, your grandparents, are nice people too but strict, especially my father. He's a religious man and it's hurt him a lot because he feels I've let him down.

There was never any question of them looking after you. That would have been one solution if they'd been willing to do that. However, it wasn't to be. That's why I was sent here to Wales, out of the way, in the hope that nobody would notice. They're so old-fashioned, you see, my parents, that's been the whole trouble. If it had been one of my friends, I'm sure their parents would have let them keep the baby.

Some day it won't matter at all, this sort of thing. Perhaps by the time you're eighteen and reading this, it won't matter at all. You'll wonder what all the fuss was about.

I love you so much, little love, it hurts.
I wish I could keep you.
I wish I could.
Tomorrow will be the saddest day of my life.
With all my love
Your mother.

Part One

1

Jenny Sweetman finished the letter, put the pen down and sighed. She tugged and twisted the long strands of her brown hair as she read it through. Her dark blue eyes were clear and bright and without tears. It still wasn't right. She couldn't get it right. All the other attempts lay scrunched up, discarded because they were too bizarre or too ridiculous. She'd always been hopeless at writing letters, mainly laborious thank you letters at Christmas and then the ones she'd written to her French pen pal. That had petered out because of the language difficulties. They couldn't express themselves properly. Just like now in fact. How could she possibly put it down in words? How could she begin to describe how she felt? How could she?

'Well . . . ?' Deborah's voice nudged at her. The two of them had become friends in the past few weeks, thrown together as they had been because Deborah was in the same boat, except it was worse for her. Her father was a vicar, of all things. She had really let the side down. Deborah reckoned it would take months if not years for her family to forget this one.

'How's the letter this time?' she asked.

'Awful, if you must know. Too sentimental,' Jenny said. 'There should be violins playing, it's so sugary . . . she'll fall about laughing at me. If she ever reads it, that is,' she added with another sigh.

'She won't laugh,' Deborah said. Her hair, mousy, or dark blonde as she preferred to call it herself, tumbled onto her shoulders from a centre parting. She was only sixteen, slightly built at that, but she possessed a determined streak and there was a stubborn look about the strong jaw and the defiant toss

5

of the head. At this moment she looked older than her years, her blue eyes streaked with worry. 'Can I see it, please?'

'If you want.'

Jenny shrugged, passed the letter over. Despite her misgivings, she thought she might have made a decent stab at it this time. After all, by the time she read this, Helen would be eighteen as she herself would be eighteen in October. She would have some inkling as to what it was all about. However, she felt herself flush with embarrassment as Deborah smoothed it out.

'It's a bit . . . you know . . . soppy. I mean . . . what can you say to them? What on earth can you say?'

'Oh Jenny . . . it's not soppy.' Deborah finished reading, looked up and smiled her gentle smile. Deborah was somehow disconcerting. Childlike one minute and very adult the next. 'It's lovely. Very moving. And I think it's right that you mentioned the father. She'll be so sad when she reads it. It will make her cry. Will you help me write a letter for Jacqueline? You have a wonderful way with words.'

'No I don't,' Jenny said at once. 'At least my English teacher doesn't think so. It's my worst subject.'

'Never mind what she thinks, you obviously can do it. I've tried to write a letter and I can't get any further than "Dear Jacqueline". I don't know what to say. She's only a baby and I can't think of her as being grown up.'

'I can't do it for you. That wouldn't be right. Just say what you think,' Jenny said, looking at the girl's worried face, 'that's all you can do. It's not compulsory. You don't *have* to put a letter in the file. It'll probably never be read anyway. We're just indulging ourselves, trying to make ourselves feel better. They might not want to know us, not when they're grown up.'

It was a hard fact to stomach but it had to be faced.

'True. I might not bother. See how I feel later on,' Deborah said, moving more easily in her chair now that her much discussed stitches were out. Jenny looked at the faraway expression and knew what was coming. A detailed retelling of Jacqueline's traumatic birth, finishing with an aggrieved question: 'How come you had such an easy time?'

Jenny managed a smile, crossing to the window to look out at the lavender-rimmed Welsh hills.

'Easy or not, I shan't have any more, Deborah. That's my lot. I've had it with babies.'

She might have added she wasn't exactly thrilled with men either. She thought briefly of the baby's father. Free as air, he was. He'd just gone on his own sweet way, none the wiser. Sometimes she felt she ought to have told him, maybe he deserved to be told but it was easier this way. She didn't want him going serious on her. Worse, she did not want to end up married to him, not at seventeen. Trust her to get landed in it after one mistake. Some girls had all the bad luck.

'I'm having lots more babies,' Deborah said, undaunted by her experience. 'When I'm married and grown up . . .'

They laughed. Deborah was doing her best to cheer her, especially today, the last day. The two of them were in desperate need of some cheering up. All in all, these last few weeks had been very strange for Jenny, the joy of looking after her baby tinged all the time with the knowledge that she would soon be gone.

It was ridiculous being palmed out to this place, some sort of private nursing home that her great-aunt had known about, that had once had vague connections with the Church and now had just a discreet wing for unmarried mothers, Christian girls in trouble, because these days it didn't matter quite so much. Not to most people, that is. Not in the seventies, for heaven's sake.

She and Deborah, coming from the backgrounds they did, were unlucky enough for it to matter a great deal. Her being here wouldn't fool anybody at home in Preston. Why would a disgustingly healthy teenager suddenly be in need of rest and recuperation at the home of a great-aunt in Wales? Her mother's desperate hint at some chronic illness, something pale and delicate, was laughable but understandable Jenny supposed under the circumstances. Her parents cared what the neighbours thought, especially her father. Righteous Reg they called him at the youth club. She'd felt obliged to defend him, but only half-heartedly because it was true, he didn't have much of a sense of humour.

She couldn't have picked a worse thing to have done. She often thought that if she'd failed her coming exams spectacularly, it wouldn't have mattered so much to them as this. She had told

• Patricia Fawcett

her best friend at school and it was a secret just waiting to be exploded. By the time she returned, everyone would know. Who would have thought it of her? Jenny Sweetman, that quiet little girl, the one who was brilliant at science. She would have to pluck up the courage to face them. She had made up her mind she was not going to discuss it at all. It was all done and dusted now . . . well, almost . . .

A regimental mass of red and yellow tulips were budding in the beds near the house, their petals gaspingly wide open in the afternoon sunshine, and the large expanse of grass was clipped and green after the first cut of the year, the sweet smell drifting through the open window. A few of the other patients, dressing-gowned, the chronically ill patients, were taking careful strolls with their visitors through the gardens. It was quiet and peaceful and had she been here for any other reason, she would have loved it.

Home in Lancashire was a terraced house with no garden. Her mother tried, potted out tubs and things in the back yard but, although there was a park nearby, it wasn't the same. Here . . . there was room to breathe. One day she would live somewhere like this, in the country, somewhere with views of hills. There was just something about hills she found very comforting and, just now, she needed all the comfort she could get.

Jenny leaned against the windowpane, no longer seeing the views. There was no point in stretching this agony out although she could have held onto the baby longer than this. Kept her for a few more weeks. Gone back to her great-aunt's for a while. But in the end it would be the same. She still had to hand her baby over. And it might as well be sooner as later.

The decision was made and tomorrow they would come, the people who were taking Helen away. They would probably drive round the back to the other entrance to spare embarrassment. Whose embarrassment Jenny didn't know. She would not be handing her over personally. Who in God's name could do that without falling to pieces? She would hand her over to an intermediary, a representative from The Children's Society, who were arranging the adoption, and that representative would then take the baby through the no man's land of the connecting corridor into the room where the adoptive parents would be waiting. It was all terribly civilised, organised so that there would be little chance of their bumping into each other. She had no wish to see them. She supposed they might be a little curious about her, what she looked like, that sort of thing. She was a little afraid that she would make a scene, clutch Helen to her and refuse to hand her over at the last minute. Then it would turn out very *un*civilised.

She had seen the white strained faces, the empty eyes, of the other girls when their babies had gone, and knew she would look like that tomorrow too. Deborah, she was sure, would cope better. Tomorrow night, they could console each other. Deborah was fighting it, pretending it wasn't going to happen but it was. Her baby, Jacqueline, was going too.

'What are you going to do when you get back home?'

'What? Sorry . . . I was miles away.'

She returned her attention to Deborah as, in the distance, came the sound of tea trolleys being pushed round and from the adjacent nursery, the sound of crying babies . . . feeding time at the zoo in a minute. There were just a few other equally disgraced girls here but they were mainly Welsh, talked often in Welsh, kept to themselves, and Jenny was not one to force her company on anybody.

'I'm absolutely full . . .' Deborah said, cocking her head at the sound, holding onto her breasts. 'It hurts a bit when she first starts to feed, then after a moment . . .' she sighed, 'it's wonderful. I'm going to miss it. What a waste, isn't it? All this milk. They'll be giving her a bottle, won't they? You should have fed Helen yourself, Jenny.'

'No fear. I don't care if I did get their backs up,' she said with that show of spirit that had not completely deserted her. 'It bonds you too much and I don't want to get involved any more than I already am. It would have been better if they'd knocked me out for a Caesarean and taken her away before I came round.' She saw Deborah's face and battled on. 'Oh yes it would. A lot easier. I would never have known what she looked like. She'll be gone tomorrow, for heaven's sake . . .' She turned away, defeated, as the tea trolley rattled in.

'What are you going to do then?' Deborah persisted, as they sipped their tea. 'When you get home?'

• Patricia Fawcett

'Go back to school and make sure I pass my exams,' Jenny said. 'Pretend it's never happened, I suppose. I don't think my father will mention it at all. My mother might but she's frightened of upsetting him. For a man who claims he's a Christian . . .' She paused and they exchanged a sympathetic glance. 'He hit the roof when Mum told him. Ranted on. It was a waste of time trying to explain. I haven't been . . . you know . . . what he called me. It was a mistake. It all just got out of hand,' she said, sniffing back the tears. She was so emotional these days, it took nothing to make her weep and that annoyed her too. Normally she kept a pretty tight grip on her emotions. It was ingrained in her. The Sweetman way of handling things.

'Don't tell me about dads. My dad went scarlet, nearly burst a blood vessel.' Deborah pulled a face at the memory. 'All he was bothered about was what the congregation would think when they found out. Everybody thinks I've gone to New Zealand to an aunt's for six months. Nobody believes it of course but my parents like to think they've handled it well.'

Jenny managed a smile. 'These aunts come in useful, don't they?'

'How my dad can stand in the pulpit and preach when he's lied through his teeth about this . . .' Deborah shrugged. 'Oh well, that's his problem. What next then? After you pass your exams? Get a job?'

'University I hope,' Jenny said, feeling a little embarrassed to be saying it. Deborah was, from all accounts, not considered bright enough for that and would be leaving school promptly, getting a job in a department store. Staying at home and trying to make amends.

Jenny knew she faced a fight, for her parents would like her to do something like that too. Neither of them approved of the idea of three years' study away from home at university. They had been lukewarm at her staying on into the sixth form and were totally mystified by her choice of subjects. In their opinion, Physics, Chemistry and Mathematics were such unsuitable subjects for a girl.

As far as they were concerned, any old job would do until she got married and had a family. Well . . . sugar and spice to that! They could take a running jump next time. She had complied with the decision to have the baby adopted because it suited her too. A baby and university were not compatible. She could not let her heart rule her head. What she really wanted, deep down, was just not possible. That's what she had tried to say in the letter, the letter to Helen.

She gave a half-smile as the other girls came in, followed by the first of the babies. Her baby. She could tell it was her baby even as the nurse lifted her gently out of the cot, even before she could see the baby's face. The shock of comically unruly hair told her.

The last time but three then. The countdown had begun. The last time but three she would be able to give Helen her bottle.

'Hello, little love,' she whispered, her voice obviously soothing as the baby looked momentarily startled and then relaxed. Jenny tied a bib round the little neck, adjusted her in her arms so that the legs with the white booteed feet were comfortable against her. There was a moment's anxiety as the mouth searched frantically for the teat then a greedy contented guzzling as she found it. There was the familiar baby smell of warm milk, talcum and soap. She had dark hair, a lot of it, straight and spiked. She *did* have her father's nose, quite distinctive for a baby. By the time she was eighteen, she would either have grown used to it or be angling for a nose job.

Opposite her, turned away for privacy, Deborah was feeding her child for almost the last time too, murmuring away to her, quite happily. It seemed sometimes that Deborah was refusing to accept the inevitable. When would it dawn . . . ? Or was she relying on a miracle, still expecting her father to forgive her? Still hoping they would relent at the last minute and take the baby home. A stay of execution was still just possible.

Jenny withdrew into her own little world, sounds receding as she concentrated firmly on the baby's needs.

'There . . . there . . . not so fast.'

She looked out of the window as the spring sunshine suddenly blitzed across the lawns, heard her daughter's joyous gulps, nestled the little body against her and savoured the moment.

Stephen Finch manoeuvred the little car down the narrow country road, finally able to overtake the tractor that had slowed them down. Just as well they had set off with lots of time to spare. It wasn't a matter of life and death of course if they were not exactly on time but he was anxious to show that they were a dependable couple, and somehow, arriving late for something as important as this was unforgivable.

'You've gone very quiet,' Stephen said, glancing at his wife. 'You've hardly said a word since we left Wrexham. Something wrong?'

Lizzie tossed her black hair back in that familiar gesture and gave a little snort as if he ought to know what was wrong.

'Well . . . ?' he asked impatiently. 'You seem to think I have a sixth sense. What the hell have I done wrong now?' He racked his brains as she remained maddeningly silent. 'I did remember to ask about the performance, didn't I? I thought you said it had gone well?'

'It did go well,' she said, 'except I'm just stuck in the chorus, hidden away at the back of the stage, as if I were just an ordinary singer. It's high time I was given my chance. I could have sung Marcia's role standing on my head. She moves on stage as if she's got glue in her shoes and she's so tentative too and that worries the audience. And, frankly, the tenor has a hard time looking as if he's desperately in love with her. She's fat, Stephen, and forty if she's a day.'

'Is that all that's bothering you?' he asked with a smile. 'You poor darling. Stop worrying, you've plenty of time,' he added, glancing at her and seeing she was not smiling in return. 'I thought you said you needed chorus work to gain experience. That you were in no great hurry to take on major roles.'

'Did I say that? When did I say that? I didn't mean it. You know me, Stephen, I'm always saying things I don't mean. I've waited long enough for my chance. The plain truth is my face simply does not fit, not in this company. I suspect the producer is sleeping with Marcia. That must be it. I can't think of any other reason why she continues to play principal.'

'Don't *you* get any ideas in that direction,' he said, smiling to show he was joking.

'As if . . . you big baby.'

She dug about at her feet for her handbag, whipping out make-up and perfume, spraying herself and him lavishly.

'The baby might not like that,' he said, feeling his eyes sting as the aroma exploded all around in the confined space. 'God . . . that's strong.'

'Don't you like it? It cost the earth and it's meant to drive you wild with desire. I thought it would really get you going,' she said with that delightful laugh of hers. 'If you must know, Stephen, I'm not sure how to tell you this but the truth is I'm having second thoughts.' She unscrewed her lipstick, trying to apply it as he ground the car up a steep twisting hill. 'Good lord, can't you stop it lurching? This is worse than behind the scenes at the Grand . . . Did I tell you there were ten of us squeezed into this cupboard of a dressing room, trying to get ready. Imagine it, struggling into those huge dresses. We complained of course, or rather I did on everybody's behalf, created a stink in fact but they'll do nothing. Disgraceful!' She replaced the lipstick in her bag, dropped it on the floor. 'When can we afford a proper car, darling? This is absolutely dreadful. When I'm famous, I shall need to exude a more glamorous image.'

'It's only a stopgap,' he said with a laugh, her slight sing-song accent still having the power to amuse and please him. 'Don't worry, I want something better than this too.'

He glanced at her as she began to brush her hair now, peering into the car mirror. She was never still, Lizzie. A fluttery, colourful butterfly, dizzying about from flower to flower, scarcely pausing to draw breath.

'Second thoughts?' he said, as it finally dawned what she'd said. 'What the hell do you mean? You can't have second thoughts. We'll be at the hospital in about twenty minutes. It's too late for second thoughts.'

'Twenty more minutes of this! I thought you said we were nearly there,' she said. 'I wouldn't have redone my lipstick if I'd known we still had twenty minutes to go. Where is this wretched place? Are you quite sure we're going the right way?'

'Quite sure. You're just on edge,' he said quietly, coming unexpectedly upon a crossroads and slowing to check the destination, having a moment's doubt himself about his sense of direction. 'On edge. That's all.'

'Don't tell me whether I'm on edge or not,' she said in *that* voice of hers.

• Patricia Fawcett

She lapsed into one of her silences and he let her, wondering if they were in for one of her monumental sulks. Sulk-wise Lizzie was in a class of her own. He decided to let her be, concentrating instead on the bends and the dips and the occasional bloody annoying tractor. God, this road was one of the worst he'd ever driven on. His estimated time of arrival was going to go up the spout at this rate.

'I'd forgotten what it's like in this part of Wales,' she went on after a while, in a more conciliatory tone. 'So countryish. It's such an age since I lived round here. If we had time, I could take you on a trip down memory lane.'

'Are you regretting it?' He swung the car round a corner and tried to fathom what the next signpost said. These damned Welsh names! He supposed he'd get used to it eventually now that they lived in Wales, albeit miles from here just across the border near Chester. He stole another glance at her, his wonderful flamboyant wife. She was right of course. She would have made a far better Carmen than the well-endowed Marcia, who was singing the principal role in the new production. With her flashing brown eyes, black hair and scarlet lips, not forgetting her slender body and the graceful way she used it, Lizzie would have been superb and the tenor would have had not a moment's hesitation in falling for her.

There was never a dull moment in the Finch household. Lizzie was constantly like this, up one minute, down the next. She'd try the patience of a saint, let alone a recently qualified architect. After five years of marriage, he was still madly in love with her. Lizzie's beauty and talent floored him but it had taken him a little while to realise that she was hell to live with. Artistic temperament he supposed. He had to make allowances. Artistic people like Lizzie had to be handled with care. Loving care.

They met over at Cardiff. He had been up from London where he was studying, several years into his course at the Architectural Association. It was a rare weekend away, an opportunity to see a rugby match with some student friends and they had swanned into this hotel, the gang of them, afterwards, for a drink. They hadn't known there was going to be a recital by an ensemble of young singers. That would have put them off in fact, for none of them was into opera.

Loud rude rugby songs, some kinds of pop music, but never opera.

'Bloody hell, Stephen . . .' one of his friends muttered, as they found themselves trapped there in the middle of the room, from where to attempt an exit would have resulted in a very undignified scrum. 'Hope it's not going to go on too long. We've got some serious drinking to do.'

And then Lizzie was there and suddenly and unexpectedly, for Stephen did not think of himself as the romantic sort, it was some enchanted evening time – a stranger across a crowded room and all that stuff he'd thought was pure invention. Utter magic. He was bowled over by the impact she made on him.

There she was, draped seductively in a long, very simple white dress with a red rose pinned to the shoulder. She stood quite still a moment as she waited for them to settle, a gentle smile on her face. Not too tall, glossily black-haired and beautiful. He supposed he fell in love with her there and then and she made it easy for him when he dumped his friends and made a beeline for her afterwards, animatedly chatting, looking up at him with those big brown eyes.

She wasn't the least interested in rugby, she told him, but she could see he would be. Rugby was such a virile sport, wasn't it? All muscle and mud. She had said all this without a trace of a smile, gazing up at him with those long-lashed eyes, quite delighting him with her look. The original flirt, Lizzie. In the space of a few hours, she had very effectively dangled the hook, caught him, and reeled him in. Not that he had put up much of a struggle.

By the end of the evening, he knew a great deal about her. She had trained at the Royal Northern College of Music, she told him, and then at the National Opera Studio. She was going to be famous one day and she said this so seriously that he did not dare laugh. She had calmed her Welsh accent a little but it surfaced from time to time and he thought it enchanting.

Within a few months, causing extreme inconvenience to family and friends, not to mention the difficulties of his completing his course when all he could think about was Lizzie, Lizzie, Lizzie, they were married.

In looks therefore, she was close to perfection, with a voice like an angel. A clear mezzo-soprano that had recently soared its way, albeit in the chorus, round a venue in Edinburgh. Before that, Glasgow and the week after next, the dizzy heights of Birmingham. She was rarely at home, at the modest semi-detached house they had bought, the house he wasn't entirely happy with but which would have to do until they could afford something better.

'Are you regretting leaving here, my sweet?' he asked her once more as the silence dawdled. It was a gorgeous spring day, the still-fragile sunshine gentle on the hills, the valley below green and moist. Born and brought up in Manchester, he'd always thought of himself as very much a town person, but just now, looking at the picture-postcard beauty of it all, he wasn't so sure. He'd quite like to wake up every morning and look at this. It was an instant shot of contentment in a way.

Lizzie laughed. 'I know you don't believe it, but you are *such* a romantic, Stephen. Country life does nothing for me. In fact, I regret nothing in my life except perhaps this foolhardy idea . . . this adoption thing. Stop the car, darling. We have to talk.'

'I can't stop here,' he said. 'It's too narrow.'

'Stop as soon as you can,' she said. 'You'll have to turn back. I can't go through with it so we have to talk. You'll have to telephone to tell them that we've changed our mind. I know it's going to cause an almighty stink but it's too important for us to go ahead with it if we have doubts.'

'I don't have doubts. Lizzie, for God's sake . . . we're due to be there at eleven.' He sighed his exasperation. He knew her of old. She liked to play this sort of dramatic scene from time to time. 'You really know how to pick your moments.'

'Of course I do. On stage, timing is all. That's why Marcia is so pathetic. She has no sense of timing.'

Irritated as hell, he pulled off into a field entrance.

Waited.

If they were late, he'd kill her . . .

'When did you fall in love with me?' she asked, smiling now as she looked at him. 'The exact moment, darling?'

'The very first moment I saw you,' he said on cue. They had had this conversation many many times before. 'One minute I was talking about the match with Jeff and Mike and the next . . . well, there you were. Looking absolutely stunning in a white dress.'

'It was beautiful,' she sighed. 'That gown. As I was singing, I saw you . . . towering over everybody as you were, it was hard *not* to see you. Tall, dark and handsome at that. I thought, Wow! That is the man I am going to marry. If you hadn't come to get me, I would have found a way of coming to get you.'

He reached for her hand, trying to curb his impatience. He was unsure where this was leading and time was marching on. It would look like they didn't care if they were late for their appointment.

'I'm sorry to do this to you, especially as it's going to cause a godawful fuss, but I don't think I can cope with a baby,' she said flatly, withdrawing her hand, fiddling nervously with her rings. 'I thought I could and I was bitterly disappointed at the way things turned out, but it was ridiculous to think of adoption. You were quite right, I should have listened to you. You should accept these things. If I'm not meant to have a baby naturally then I'm not meant to have one at all. And, after all, you and I are perfectly happy with just each other.' She purred her happiness, leaned across and kissed him. 'A baby would just get in the way, wouldn't it? It's much better just the two of us.'

Stephen sighed. He remembered the months of anxiety, the waiting, the endless tests, the time she spent in hospital, the final disappointment. The considered verdict was that it was highly unlikely Lizzie would ever be able to have children. Not absolutely impossible but unlikely. There was a blockage in the Fallopian tubes. Hopeless in one, less severe in the other. The consultant had tried to hold out a slender hand of hope but Lizzie had reacted fiercely. No more treatment. She was sick to death of treatment, of being prodded and probed and patronised. They would adopt. It was *she* who had decided that, for God's sake, and he had taken some persuading. Now, after they had gone through all the steps and were nearly there . . . literally, nearly there . . .

'We'll manage,' he said calmly. 'Other people do. I think all new parents must have second thoughts but you just have to get on with it. I know you're worried about taking a career break and that's why we're having a nanny. She'll take all the pressure off you. You won't have to run yourself into the ground.'

'But can we afford her?'

'Of course we can.' He looked at her. It was unusual for Lizzie to be concerned about money. She had a haphazard attitude to it, penny-pinching in some ways and wildly extravagant in others. To be honest, they could barely afford the nanny but things were improving financially all the time now. He was going places. He had big plans. He was no run-of-the-mill architect. He had talent too on the stage he played. He'd already outstripped his student friends, was on a far higher salary than they, in a more demanding job. Someday he and Lizzie would live in a beautiful house, something grand in the country, and he would drive something a helluva lot better than this old scrap heap of a car. Someday.

'You can carry on as normal,' he went on, sensing this was only cold feet, a temporary doubt. 'When we get home, get your bag packed and get yourself off to Birmingham or wherever. Don't you worry, Abigail won't be neglected. Mrs ... er ... the nanny will look after her.' Dammit, he'd forgotten the woman's name but she seemed a capable sort – middle-aged, friendly and sturdy. Lizzie's choice actually. Lizzie did not like beautiful women buzzing round him. Jealous as hell.

'Mrs Wallace ...' Lizzie said absently, diving once more into her handbag. 'Irene Wallace. That's her name. I do hope she'll be all right. She was very dowdy, wasn't she?'

'So?' He failed to see what difference that would make. 'She'll be fine. Off you go and Mrs Wallace will look after Abigail.'

'Abby. She'll be Abby.' Lizzie looked at him rather anxiously. 'You do like the name, don't you? You left it to me, darling. You came up with no suggestions of your own. No sensible ones, anyway. We have to be so careful with our surname. Lizzie Finch ...' she murmured, pulling a face playfully.

'Abby's a lovely name,' he said. 'Now, I think we'd better get on, don't you, or we are going to be very late.'

He patted her knee, regretting the gesture immediately because she bristled and gave him another of her disdainful looks.

'Just last-minute nerves, sweetheart,' he told her, and that remark was ill-judged too. Sometimes he felt as if he had to wrap his words in cotton wool before he uttered them. She was so damned quick to take the huff. He knew she had some reputation in her company for prima donna behaviour and, although he wouldn't dream of suggesting it, maybe that was why she remained where she was, firmly in her place where she couldn't hold them to ransom.

'I just hope we've got everything we'll need for the journey back,' she said when they were at last on their way again. 'All the baby stuff. We should have asked Mrs Wallace to come with us. What use is she twiddling her thumbs at home? What if the baby cries? I shan't know what to do. Do you think she'll be upset at leaving her mother? What if she takes a dislike to me?'

Apprehension, fear even, was etched in her voice, and Stephen tried in vain to soothe her.

'It's all very well for you but Mrs Wallace is the kind of irritating woman who's going to look to me for instructions and I don't know a thing about babies,' was the last thing she said before lapsing into a long silence, broken only as they came in sight of the nursing home which prompted another frantic diving-into-handbag session, and application of lipstick and powder and yet another drenching of perfume.

As they approached the square, rather forbidding building, Lizzie's mood soared and she was suddenly brighter, more confident, and it was he who had doubts as he drove round, as instructed, to the back entrance.

It seemed that both of them blew hot and cold on this, on such an important thing as this, and that worried him. They ought to have given it more time, relaxed a little and maybe a baby of their own would have materialised. Instead, Lizzie had insisted on starting this particular ball rolling and now it was too damned late. They were here and their baby was ready for them.

They waited in a pleasant anteroom, ignoring the coffee and biscuits set out for them. The preliminaries completed, they waited for their daughter to be brought to them. Lizzie was very pale now, composed, looking very much a mother-in-waiting but that could be her stage presence asserting itself. That was the trouble. He never knew for sure when she was acting. Lizzie was many things.

• Patricia Fawcett

At twenty-six, she looked younger. She was very fashion-conscious and had gone to some trouble today to look just right. The pleated wool Liberty print dress in subdued autumn colours skimmed the top of her high suede leather boots. A brown silk quilted waistcoat instead of a jacket. Dammit, he had gone to some trouble himself to look the part too. Conservatively clad in dark suit, plain shirt and tie. Respectable. At thirty, it was time he grew up and accepted some responsibility.

Even so . . . if Lizzie had been pregnant with their child, he would have had time to come to terms with the responsibility, as the child developed in the womb. He felt, even though it had taken some time to reach this final moment, that this had been thrust on him. In a few minutes, they would have their daughter, a fully fledged baby. He felt a great onslaught of butterflies in the tummy as he heard footsteps outside, reaching for Lizzie's cold hand, squeezing it and getting a little response in return, holding it firmly as the door opened.

'Here she is, the little darling. She's as good as gold, this one,' the woman said, frizzy-haired with a big toothy smile, carrying the white-shawled baby in her arms. 'Shall we let Mummy have her?'

She handed her at once to Lizzie, who reacted carefully with little apparent emotion so that the woman looked discomfited. Stephen, understanding something of what his wife was thinking, remembering the many many disappointments, leaned over and looked at the face half obscured by a fussy little bonnet, from which wisps of darkish hair escaped.

'Hello, Abby,' he whispered, suddenly choked with emotion himself. God . . . what a responsibility he was taking on! It dawned, too late, what an *enormous* responsibility it was. This little helpless creature was relying on him totally. Lizzie too, although he suspected strongly that he would have the lion's share.

Gently, he reached forward and touched the little cheek. Stroked it. The baby opened her eyes, rolled her head, and looked up, not at him, but towards the perfume-drenched Lizzie. Wriggled a moment, flailed her tiny hands. Was she remembering someone else? Another feminine presence?

He put that thought out of his mind as the final papers were produced for signature. Afterwards, it was he who held the baby as Lizzie dealt regally and theatrically with the goodbyes and thank yous to the staff. Despite the fact they must do this sort of thing regularly, Stephen was not slow to notice a few moist eyes and stiff upper lips. In his arms, the baby was warm but wary, frowning but not crying. She had blue eyes but then didn't all babies of this age have blue eyes? Dark hair like Lizzie.

Driving away from the house later, with Lizzie and Abby installed in the back of the car with the mountain of baby paraphernalia, he wondered briefly if she was watching from one of the windows. Abby's mother.

'How do you suppose she feels?' he asked. 'The mother?'

'Relieved, I should think,' Lizzie said, preoccupied from the rear. 'After all, it's what she wanted, isn't it? She couldn't have coped alone. We've done her a favour. Taken it off her hands.'

'Her,' he said irritably. 'She's our little girl now, Lizzie.'

'We'll have a boy next time,' she said, cheerful now that it was accomplished. 'In a couple of years maybe so that Abby will have a playmate. We'll call him Stephen after you. What do you think, darling? I must say The Children's Society have been very good about all this. Excellent organisation. Utterly charming and discreet. And we couldn't have hoped for a prettier child. Abby's really so sweet. Such a darling little nose.'

He said nothing. All this talk about another baby, a son. One step at a time. Lizzie was forever tripping off into the future, plans neatly tied up. He preferred to take it more slowly. After all, you never knew for sure quite what would happen.

2

Her mother, wearing her best navy suit, fussed her into the back of the car, climbing in beside her so that Uncle Harold, good old reliable Uncle Harold, was left alone in the front like a chauffeur. A very attentive one at that but then, in his profession as an undertaker, he was used to being attentive.

There was a twenty-year age gap between the two of them, her mother being the youngest member of the Walmsley clan, her Uncle Harold the oldest. Already sixty-one years old, he was, he insisted, in his prime and had no intention of retiring for many years to come.

'Have we forgotten anything?'

Jenny very nearly said, 'Just the baby,' but that wouldn't have gone down well, not when her mother was trying her very best to be cheerful. She did not look back at the ivy-covered house, knowing Deborah would be watching from one of the upper windows, a very forlorn, wildly upset Deborah. They would not see each other again, a mutual decision, for both of them wanted to forget this episode of their lives. A clean break was best. She would miss her, though.

'Are you all right then, Jenny?' Uncle Harold asked, once they were on their way. 'Got over it?'

'Shut up, Harold, and concentrate on what you're doing,' Christine Sweetman said sharply, giving her daughter a knowing look. 'Your dad would have come, love,' she went on as Harold fell huffily silent, 'but he had something on. Otherwise he would have definitely come with us. Wouldn't he, Harold?'

From the front, Harold grunted a reply of sorts and, in the back, Jenny tried to relax. She felt sick in fact. The effort she

• Patricia Fawcett

had made these last few hours, coupled with a sleepless night as she tried to put all thoughts of her baby into some hidden recess of her mind, was making her feel physically sick.

She closed her eyes, hoping her mother would stop talking a minute so that she could rest. Fat chance of course. Her mother would talk the hind legs off a donkey. She was quite like Jenny in looks, a pretty woman, small and dark-haired with blue wide-set eyes. She dressed rather conservatively but that was because of Dad. He didn't like women to be tarted up as he called it. It meant her mother wore little if any make-up but somehow, because she was normally so bright and cheerful and had such good clear skin, she did not really suffer as a result. Today though she was pale and would have benefited from a smudge of rouge, nor could she hide the sadness in her eyes. Uncle Harold, bless him, looked uncomfortable too, dragged along so that they didn't have to suffer the indignity of a tortuous train journey.

Jenny sighed, wondering if they – the adoptive parents – had brought the baby this way. Where was she now? It was time for her feed but they would know that. Some other woman would be holding her, giving her her bottle, calling her by the name they had chosen.

'. . . going on about it all the time,' her mother was saying as she surfaced, 'so I said to her, "Well, that's all very well, Janice, but there's many a good tune played on an old fiddle."'

'What? Sorry, Mum . . . I was miles away.'

From the front, her uncle began to sing the first stirring notes of 'Onward, Christian soldiers'.

They ignored him.

'Sorry, love, about you know what . . .' Her mother lowered her voice, awkwardly patted her hand. They weren't a 'touching' sort of family, never had been, and just for a moment Jenny wished they were. 'Never mind,' she added, as if the loss of Jenny's baby could be dismissed so easily, 'when we get home, we've got a nice surprise for you.'

'Surprise?' Jenny's voice was still dulled. 'What surprise?'

'No surprise if I tell you,' her mother said with a trilling laugh. 'And then, when you're feeling a bit more yourself, we'll go up town and I'll get you something new to wear. A new dress? Or even some of them platform shoes? We'll get round your father.'

Jenny nodded, watching the countryside whiz by, dreading returning home. It had to be done of course and she had to get back to school, catch up on things, but she was not looking forward to going back. Going back to being a child, their little girl, when she was now a woman, a mother. She turned to face *her* mother, tried a tentative smile. After all, she had been more supportive than Dad. If it had been up to her, she felt sure things would have been different. As it was, Dad's word ruled. It was like living in the last century with him.

Not so with Uncle Harold. For all his sober manner, he was surprisingly up-to-date and anxious to learn about new technology and everything. He, alone, was very keen on her pursuing a career in science.

After several abortive attempts, obviously itching to do so, he finally got his chance to have a private word when they stopped for refreshment and her mother disappeared into the ladies to freshen up.

'Don't let them two talk you into doing what you don't want,' he said, tapping the steering wheel with gloved hands as he talked. 'No give, your father. Turned out to be just like his father before him. I knew the family before your mother took up with him. Awkward lot, the Sweetmans. Your mother means well but she's under his thumb. Thinks the sun shines out of him.'

Impulsively, Jenny touched his shoulder, felt him jump at the touch.

'Thanks for everything,' she said softly. 'And don't worry, there's no danger of me being talked into doing something I don't want. I'm off to college if I get through my exams. I'm going to do something with my life, Uncle. After this . . . I've got to do something. I've let so many people down, you see.'

'No. You mustn't ever think that. You just had a bit of bad luck, that's all. Getting yourself off to university will be the best thing for you. If I'd my time over again . . .' he said, and she smiled a little, settling back in the seat. He was off. 'I'd have liked to be an inventor . . . something scientific like that. Mind you, love, I'm not complaining. Funerals is interesting. You can't plan. Nobody knows. Here today, gone tomorrow.'

He turned so that she could see his profile, the softly grey moustache, the sharp grey-blue of his eyes as he finally looked

• Patricia Fawcett

at her. 'Think on, Jenny. Any problems about college, grants and things, you come to me,' he said quietly, watching as her mother, heels clattering in her agitation, headed purposefully towards them. 'I've got a tidy bit put by and if you need any help, you only have to ask.'

'Them toilets!' Her mother shuddered as she climbed back in. 'They ought to be reported.' She adjusted her clothing. 'Sorry . . . I got held up. There was this woman who wouldn't stop talking. You know the type . . .' she laughed, smiled brightly. 'Come on, Harold, let's get off. Last lap.'

Harold started the engine and the first verse of 'Praise, my soul, the King of heaven', pulled out. Christine started a monologue about the Queen's Silver Jubilee celebrations. They were having a street party in Hargreaves Street and she had been roped in to be on the committee. She was doing some little cakes and jellies for the children. They were all chipping in with the bunting. They'd got fair enthusiastic about it.

Jenny found her attention wandering. The memory was proving hard to budge. It refused to go through to that hidden corner, lurked rather in her mind. The little warm body, the funny hiccups, the slightly cross-eyed look she had given her, trying to focus of course and not quite managing it. By now, she would be focusing her little attentions on someone else. Another woman. By now, she would be listening to another voice and gradually, perhaps even already, she would forget her. It would be so easy for her to forget.

The fields and villages were replaced by built-up suburban areas as they neared Preston. Uncle Harold, concentrating and strangely silent, took them through the middle of town, and home beckoned as he drove down the busy thoroughfare that was Plungington Road, past the shops her mother regularly used, before indicating a right turn.

As they waited for a break in the traffic, Jenny spotted a few familiar faces at the bus stop, knew this was going to be harder than she had thought as she saw them do a double take, forced herself to smile and wave but was relieved when the big car was on the move again.

'There's going to be a prize for the best dressed up street,' her mother finished as they at last turned into Hargreaves Street and bumped their way down between the parked cars. 'Home, sweet home,' she said with a sigh, as Harold stopped outside the crisply clean exterior of Number 14. 'I bet you're glad to be home, Jenny love.'

She patted her hand, smiled encouragingly.

'Thanks, our Harold,' she said, stepping briskly out. 'I'd give you something for petrol but I know you won't take a bean.'

'Quite right. And I won't come in either,' he said. 'You have things to talk about. Family matters.'

Watching the big car disappear down the street, Jenny followed her mother into the house. Her dad was sitting in the back room in his chair, smoking. He nodded at her absently as if she'd just been out on an errand but he did not move from the chair.

Her mother carried Jenny's case upstairs to her room, dumped it on the floor saying they'd sort it out later.

'Now then . . .' she smiled. Her face must ache today from smiling. 'I . . .' she stalled, flushed a little. 'What I mean to say, Jenny, is—'

'You never saw her,' Jenny interrupted, kicking off her shoes and sitting on the bed, noting that the room was freshly decorated. 'You never came to see her. I only had one visitor. Auntie came once.'

'I'm sorry, love. I couldn't,' her mother muttered, pushing at her hair, a few grey bits now amongst the brown. 'When you've no car, it's not easy. It would have meant two bus journeys at least. And to be honest . . . I couldn't bear it. I didn't want to see her.'

'She was beautiful,' Jenny said softly. 'A lot of dark hair but the nurse said it was very soft and she thought she might lose it and it might come back fairer. She might be blonde, her dad was. And I think she might have his nose,' she said, catching and holding her mother's gaze, seeing her own misery reflected there. 'Oh Mum, I wish I could have kept her . . . I wish . . .' She felt the tears flood into her eyes, blinked hard.

'If wishes were horses, beggars would ride,' her mother said crisply. 'Come on now, buck yourself up. You don't want to go down with your face blotchy. Have a wash, brush your hair and come down for your tea when you're ready.' She smiled. 'Do you like the room? We've done it up for you.'

Jenny nodded, barely able to take it in.

'It's lovely,' she said as her mother waited expectantly. 'Thanks.'

'We'll say nothing more about it, that little matter,' her father said over tea, which they took in the back room. The table was spread with a very white linen cloth, the best china out for some reason. 'Will we, Christine?'

'Least said, soonest mended,' she said, busying about with the dishes, obviously delighted to have Jenny back. 'She's learned her lesson, Reg. She's a good girl at heart.' She put two sugars in her husband's cup, stirred it and passed it over. 'Tell her then. Don't keep her in suspense.'

'Well . . .' He sipped his tea before exchanging a conspiratorial smile with his wife. 'I've got you a job, Jenny—'

'In his office. At Parkinson's in Guildhall Street,' her mother broke in quickly.

'Let me tell her, Christine.' He looked at Jenny, a subdued Jenny trying in vain to raise some enthusiasm for the delicious spread her mother had quickly put together. 'You're pale, love,' he said, as if noticing her for the first time. 'We'll have to get some roses back in them cheeks. Now . . . the arrangement is this. You'll be working for Mr Thorpe's secretary. You'll just be the junior, you understand. You'll have to make the tea to begin with and post the letters and things. Somebody has to do it but you're a bright lass and you'll soon move on to something better. They might give you a day release to study at the tech. Some accountancy qualification.'

'Mr Thorpe?' Jenny, tired, struggled to make sense of it. Her father was forever going on about him, his name spoken in hushed tones. 'The senior Mr Thorpe?'

'That's right,' her father said, helping himself to some tiny sandwiches. His fingers were stained with nicotine for he smoked a lot and, being away from the house for a while, she noticed the smell of stale smoke in the room as if for the first time. The ashtray balanced on the hearth was full. 'As I've told you many a time, he stands no nonsense but he treats you fair and square, Mr Thorpe.'

'Your dad asked him, you see,' her mother put in, 'asked if he could have a word. Private like. Asked if there'd be any chance of you getting in there. Told him that you'd got ever such good O levels and that you'd stayed on.'

'It's a grand office.' Pride in his work surfaced strongly. 'It'll be nice working together. We'll be able to take our sandwiches out onto the square if it's nice. Get a spot of fresh air. Looks like you need it,' he added. 'You're like chalk.'

'Tell her how much she'll be getting, Reg.'

'Ah . . .' He puffed out his chest. 'I did the best I could. Over a thousand a year. How's that suit you?'

'Good wage, isn't it?' Her mother dangled the plate of cakes towards her. 'Have a custard tart. Lovely, they are.'

'Mum . . . Dad . . .' Jenny shook her head and the plate was replaced. Deftly, her mother removed the cosy from the pot and turned her attention to pouring more tea. 'It's nice of you to have gone to all that trouble but I can't.'

'Course you can. It's all above board,' her mother said quickly. 'They were going to advertise for a junior clerk, weren't they, Reg? Your dad just jumped the gun, that's all. Saved them the bother of putting it in the paper and everything. You could say he did them a favour.'

'It's no trumped up job.' Her father's eyes were thoughtful. 'What's up? What are you looking like that for? It's the opportunity of a lifetime.'

She heard herself laugh, a touch of hysteria creeping in.

'I want more out of life than that,' she said, 'being a junior clerk in an accountant's office. Posting letters, making tea!'

'There's no need to be cheeky, our Jenny,' her mother said, her voice tightening. 'Your dad went to a lot of trouble. You know what that old Mr Thorpe can be like. He's from a very fancy family. Live out at Penwortham, they do, in a great big posh house.'

'I know it wasn't easy . . .' She smiled at her father but it backfired as his features set in that way of his. 'Honestly, I'm very grateful.' She pushed her chair back, stood up, feeling faint. 'But I want to go back to school and then to university.'

'We've sprung it on you,' her mother said after a moment, casting a warning glance towards her husband. 'You're tired. It was a long journey and Harold's a pain with that singing of his. Off you go to bed and we'll talk about it tomorrow.'

'Tomorrow, the day after, it won't make any difference,' Jenny said wearily. 'You can tell Mr Thorpe thank you but I can't take the job.'

'Now look here . . .' her father spluttered. 'I've taken just about all I can from you, madam. Showing us up like this. How do you think it looked at church? Me a churchwarden and all.'

'And he gave them lectures to the youth club on family life and everything,' her mother added darkly. 'Made him look a fool. There were mutterings. Still . . . if we stick together, we'll get through it. We're going to put it behind us,' she went on, giving him another warning look. 'I'll help you up to bed, Jenny love,' she said.

They'd done the bedroom in pink, two different wallpapers, one striped and one plain in a deepish rose pink with new pink curtains at the windows. They hadn't managed a new carpet but the old one didn't clash that much. The sheets and the candlewick bedspread on the single bed were new too. Also in pink, more a salmon shade.

'He means well,' her mother said, hanging up Jenny's old dressing gown on the hook on the door. 'We thought it would be easier for you. We thought it would be best if you didn't have to go back to school, face them. Not that there's any reason to go into details. It's no business of anybody else, but you know what folks are like round here. Sticking their noses in.'

'I'll get through it,' Jenny said, managing a smile at last. She was exhausted and the bed was comfortable, the pillows soft as she eased herself in. Her mother was instantly at her side, fussing with the covers, tucking her tightly in, very nearly swaddling her. 'I have to go back to school, Mum. Don't you see that?'

'I understand that you've been through a lot lately,' she said, the strain showing in her face. 'And you're not thinking straight. I don't want you to think I didn't care because I never came to see you down there. I've worried myself sick about you. Believe me, I've been thinking about you every minute, especially on the day you had the baby. I had that baby for you, I felt every twinge. I was on that phone every five minutes.'

Jenny nodded. She did not want to say how much she had

wanted her mother at that moment, then and later. How she had felt alone and unwanted. No point in twisting the knife.

'You'll meet somebody else soon enough,' her mother went on, 'and next time it'll be different. You can bring him home to meet us and you can get engaged, get a lovely diamond ring, and then you can get married. We can still have a lovely wedding. You can have a nice white dress. There's some folks who might tut but be hanged to them.' Her smile was very bright, her eyes too. 'Mrs Middlebrook knows what's what, love – Janice next door – but she won't say a word. Now . . . can I go back down and tell him you've reconsidered?'

Jenny stared at her in exasperation.

'No, Mum. Aren't you listening?'

'I'm listening to a lot of nonsense, all this talk about university. It's not for the likes of us, university. Let me tell you, your father practically went down on his knees to that Mr Thorpe.' The hurt expression in her eyes was hard to take. 'And what thanks does he get? You've a nerve, lady.'

The door did not quite slam behind her.

Home, sweet home!

Jenny sighed, snuggled down, listened to the voices below, heard the piano starting up. Something loud and angry. Oh God, he *was* upset! But honestly, what else could he expect?

That night, in the deep early hours when life stills, her father suffered a brain haemorrhage.

He died next day.

3

Abigail Elizabeth Finch was eight months old, chubby and happy, seemingly oblivious of the fact that they had already gone through three nannies. It was Lizzie's fault. Things were fine when she was away on tour, but as soon as she came home, all hell broke loose. Whereas Stephen let them get on with their job, Lizzie resented them, resented the influence they exerted over Abby, resented the way Abby clung to them or him in preference to her.

Refusing to accept that, by her continued absences, she might be in some way to blame for that, she seemed to go out of her way to infuriate.

Mrs Wallace, the first and by far the best in Stephen's opinion, lasted very nearly three months before bowing out, terribly upset to leave Baby but furious because she said Lizzie had accused her of professional incompetence. When he confronted Lizzie she had hotly denied it, saying all she had complained about was the woman's lamentable lack of style which had filtered through to her choice of clothes for the baby. What was the point in having a nursery full of baby clothes if the damned woman chose to use the same ones over and over again. It wasn't her fault if the woman had taken the huff. There were plenty more nannies where she came from. And it was really too bad of him to make such an issue out of it. Goodness . . . as if she didn't have enough on her plate. She was understudying in the new production and the last thing she needed was distractions on the domestic front.

The third nanny, officious admittedly, had resigned after a power struggle. Baby Abby, at this point, caught uncomfortably in the middle of all this toing and froing, became fretful for a while as a result. And then, having caused havoc, Lizzie simply swanned off again on some tour or other and it was back to the drawing board for Stephen in more ways than one. Trying to design at work and struggling to keep the fragile peace at home.

In the middle of all this came the unexpected news that Lizzie was pregnant. Abby would be just over a year old when the new baby arrived and he could have coped with that, particularly with a nanny's help, rather enjoyed the prospect of having two little babies around, in fact. What he was finding hard to cope with was Lizzie's reaction to her pregnancy.

'I should have sued that consultant,' she said, still on about it at five months pregnant. 'You were there when he said that it was unlikely – *unlikely* I repeat – I would ever be pregnant. Now what does unlikely mean to you and to most sane people? It means not likely. Doesn't it?'

'For God's sake, it's just a word. Your being pregnant is what we wanted.' He hesitated to mention the cost of the private treatment. The financial burden it had put on them. Money seemed the last thing they should be considering. 'Make your mind up, Lizzie. What in hell's name do you want?'

'How dare you? *You* made me pregnant,' she said, 'and, having done that, all you're going to do now is to carry on with your stupid designing. I'm stuck with having it. I'll have you know, Stephen, I've had to admit to it, own up to the producer. Had to turn down a semi-principal role. How can I do it? I'll be like a tent by then.'

'Most of those dresses are very loose,' he said with a smile, trying his damnedest to be helpful. 'Or the singers are . . . to put it bluntly . . . fat. You could get away with it, darling.'

'You know nothing about it. Nothing at all. Pregnancy will affect my breathing. My singing. You're not interested. You never have been. All you're interested in is yourself.'

She was pacing the room in her anger, perversely wearing a voluminous dress that drew attention to the pregnancy and, irritated to hell, he forced himself not to shout back. Miss Barton, the newest recruit, was getting Abby ready for her daily walk and he did not wish her to hear yet another row. She was good-hearted, Miss Barton, and she adored Abby, but she was a bit of a fiend for fresh air even in the middle of winter, which involved him going round shutting windows after her. He had learned by now there had to be some snag.

Stephen watched them leave, both bundled up to ward off the cold of the January day, and turned to look at Lizzie. He tried a smile on her but it did nothing. She looked terrific. A little flushed in her anger. Those gorgeous eyes of hers flashing. This performance would go a bomb in the theatre. She was blooming although he daren't bloody say that or he'd be for it. She was, at the moment, as volatile as touchpaper and he had caught Miss Barton eyeing her nervously, anxious not to do anything to upset and inflame.

'Should you be travelling next week?' he asked, thinking that she looked tired. 'Didn't the doctor say you should be taking it easy, that there might be complications? Why don't you take a short break, darling?'

'It's going to wreck my career soon enough, this baby,' she said bitterly, 'so it's not starting yet. I shall go as planned.'

'Look, sweetheart . . .' He was at her side, smiling. He had read a bit about pregnancy and it seemed that some women were affected like this. Pre-natal depression, he supposed. 'Just think how much we tried for a baby and nothing happened. Well . . . this is a sort of miracle, isn't it?'

'I had come to terms with it. Infertility. I planned another adoption,' she told him, shaking off his arm. 'It's worked so well with Abby that I planned a brother for her . . . but not yet awhile, for God's sake. It's going to be hell with two of them in nappies and everything.'

Stephen sighed, neglecting to point out that Nanny generally took care of things like that. On the work front, things were progressing well in his career and he was thoroughly enjoying his challenging job. The company in Chester was broad based and it meant he could dip his toe in every aspect of architecture. He would have a lot to offer someone else someday and next time he intended it to be a partnership and all that went with it. If it meant moving, so be it.

Everything rosy then except his marriage. He couldn't understand Lizzie. She ought to be delighted to be pregnant. Their very own child. Abby was wonderful, a little darling, but this one . . .

He felt guilty as he always did when thoughts like this intruded. This baby would not be any different from Abby. Abby was just as much theirs. Wasn't she? Of course she was.

'Once you've had the baby, you'll feel differently,' he said, not entirely sure whom he was trying to convince. 'Our family will be complete. Then you can really concentrate on your career.'

'That's true,' Lizzie said, smiling as her mood swung. 'It gets it over with, doesn't it? And you're right, a boy will make us complete as a family.'

She leaped up, a little too fast, dizzying herself, so that he had to reach out to stop her losing her balance.

'Careful,' he said, 'that's our baby in there.'

She looked down at the very small bump, circled her hands round it.

'So it is,' she said, as if it had only just occurred. 'This is our baby, Stephen. Our son.'

'Or daughter,' he said.

'Oh no . . . I hope not. Don't you see, that would be too difficult,' she said with a suddenly nervous laugh. 'I mean . . . we'd be forever comparing them. Two girls. One ours and the other not. Sorry,' she added hastily, 'I didn't mean that to sound as it did. Of course darling Abby's ours.'

Stephen managed a smile, thinking of his happy little blue-eyed daughter.

He looked out onto their patch of a garden, winter bare, the trees beyond stripped and bleak, the ground still covered in a sparkly frost. He shivered. He knew Lizzie didn't really mean it but he wished she hadn't said that.

4

Jenny, surrounded with her bags and boxes, waited patiently for her uncle to arrive. She had hardly slept, excitement keeping her mind active and unwilling to rest. She wished they were already there, that she had met people, that she was settled in her own room at college. She wished also, just at this minute, that she wasn't going.

'Are you sure you don't want to come with us, Mum? Don't you want to see where I'll be staying?' she asked, as her mother came through to the front room. She knew it was a waste of time but she felt she had to say it. One last attempt. 'We can squeeze you in the car. Uncle Harold said there'll be room.'

'You're determined to go through with it then?'

'You know I am,' she said. 'We've been over this time and time again, Mum. It's not as if I'm emigrating. I'm only going to Bath . . .'

'It's far enough. Why couldn't you have gone to Manchester? You got a place there too. At least you'd have been able to come home weekends.'

'Because,' Jenny sighed. She had explained it time and time again. 'Because I want to do the course at Bath. It sounds really good.' She attempted a smile. 'I'll be back in the holidays and we can write to each other every week. And telephone.'

'And then what?'

Her mother was very tense, even more so than she had been for the last few terrible months. She had taken her husband's death badly and, more than once, Jenny had been tempted to give in and put aside all thoughts of going to university.

'When you've finished, got your degree, you'll be off somewhere else, won't you? There won't be a fancy enough job round here for the likes of you, will there?'

'I'll have to see. There might be,' Jenny said carefully. 'That's three years away, Mum.'

Her mother sniffed. 'Do you realise just what your father did for you? Getting you that job that you turned your nose up at?'

Jenny tried another smile, to lighten things up a little, but it was hopeless. She'd never seen her mother quite so upset before. She'd seemed numbed somehow these last few months after Dad died, just going through the motions of living, paying very little attention to what Jenny did, showing no interest in school or exams, spending far too much time at the cemetery tending his grave. And now . . . looking at her now . . . it appeared that the stopper was at last about to be released.

'Of course I realise what he did for me,' she said quietly. 'It took a lot of courage for him to do that.'

'That it did. He had to humble himself with that Mr Thorpe, snotty so-and-so. He acted like he didn't know what Dad was getting at and in the end, as I've said before, he had to practically go down on his knees and you know what a proud man he was, your father.'

'I didn't ask him to do that,' Jenny pointed out, gazing anxiously through the nets onto the quiet street, willing her uncle's car to arrive. She had hoped, ridiculously optimistic, that her departure would go smoothly, that her mother would finally accept it. This, opposition to the bitter end, wasn't helping at all.

'Get yourself a job round here. It's not too late . . .' The hope caught at her mother, brightened her for a moment. 'You can cancel your place. It won't be wasted. They can give it to somebody else. They must have a waiting list.'

'No.' Jenny sighed, drew herself up, just an inch or so taller than her mother. 'I'm not giving it up. I've worked so hard for it. Managed to catch up on everything. It wouldn't be fair to my teachers or to the university. I can't.'

'Can't you?' Hope vanished and she bit hard at her lip. 'Well . . . you needn't bother coming back then.'

'Oh come on, Mum . . .' Jenny laughed, not believing it. 'There's no need to be melodramatic.'

'Melodramatic? Is that what you call it?' The voice was strange, different. 'I wasn't going to say it, I didn't want to say it, but I can see I'll have to. You've got a lot to answer for, lady. I tried to understand when . . . when *that* happened . . . but, as they say, it takes two to tango. You could have said no. You say he was a nice enough lad so you could have said no and that would have been that. I'm fed up of trying to make excuses. If we'd known what was going to happen, we'd never have let you go with that so-called friend of yours. Your dad had his doubts and I should have listened to him but I thought you had more sense than that. I trusted you. Good God, you were only sixteen. A child.'

'It was a mistake,' Jenny said, feeling her insides deflate at the rebuke. 'Aren't you ever going to let me forget it?'

'No.' She turned away, hunched. 'How can I? You killed him, Jenny. You killed your dad.'

'What? What did you say?'

She felt her heart thud, as, outside, a car, unmistakably Uncle Harold's, drew to a halt, the engine silenced.

'You heard. All that stress you put him through, getting yourself pregnant and all, it built up. And then, when you wouldn't have any truck with that job, he was going to have to go back in to Mr Thorpe and explain. Well . . . that did it. His head exploded. Never mind all them fancy names – when you get down to it, that's all it was.'

'Mum . . .' She looked desperately through the window but Uncle Harold was still messing about at the wheel. 'You're upset. You shouldn't say things when you're upset. Look . . . I'll ring you as soon as I get there. OK?' She moved towards her but stopped when she saw the dead look in her mother's eyes. 'You don't mean it. You don't know what you're saying.'

'I know exactly what I'm saying, madam.' The words were clipped, everything about her very still, controlled. 'If you go now, you needn't come back, that's what I'm saying. If you go now, then you're on your own. I shan't weep any more tears over you.'

By the time her uncle came in, splendidly casual for him in his light grey suit and pale tie, a dreadful silence had flooded the room, a silence which he was not slow to notice. He glanced at them both, but said nothing, taking his time to fill up the car with her possessions. Jenny helped, very aware of her mother's unbending presence. At last, the car was full, barely room for two let alone three. Uncle Harold had a final check in the front room and pronounced himself ready for off, discreetly disappearing so that they were left alone once more.

'Mum . . . ?'

One last agonised plea but it was a waste of time as, not looking back, her mother, her body stiff and proud, retreated silently into the other room.

Sitting beside her uncle in the car, Jenny did not look back either.

There would be no looking back.

What was the point of that?

5

Fourteen years on, they were still living in their now much extended house in Wales. Stephen, senses finely honed towards success, had satisfactorily served his wide-ranging apprenticeship and now worked in a senior position. He drove a flashy car, entirely his choice, for Lizzie did not drive and showed no particular interest.

They enjoyed spending money on clothes, holidays on the rare occasions their individual commitments did not clash, the girls went to an expensive private school, he'd managed to keep his hair when all around were losing theirs, and all should have been great.

But it wasn't.

Lizzie's career had not shot upwards quite as she had intended and that hurt. Lizzie blamed everyone else, particularly Stephen. It was no use pointing out that it hurt him, too, for God's sake, because she did not believe him.

He had followed her career with an intensity remarkable for someone who was so ignorant about the finer points of opera. For her sake, he had even tried to swot up on it so that he could make sensible contributions to the conversation at 'opera' dinner parties. He kept all her programmes, had to try to stop himself from boasting continually about her to colleagues. After all, not every man has a wife who can sing like an angel.

But singing like an angel was no longer enough. The truth was Lizzie was still as difficult and temperamental at forty and even the presence of two delightful daughters had not mellowed her. She still fluttered about looking for that elusive success.

Sometimes, it was as if she cared little about the girls and, to

• Patricia Fawcett

make up for that, Stephen had spoiled the pair of them rotten since day one. Now they were teenagers, they were both very good at exercising feminine wiles over him, but he did not mind. He was damned lucky to have them, proud of them, and he wished Lizzie felt the same, instead of acting as if they were not far short of a nuisance.

She had never been there for them when they were little, content to palm them off to Nanny and then, as they grew older, a succession of au pairs. She had missed out on all the really important moments – the first teeth, first steps, first day at school, that sort of thing. But that was Lizzie and, for all her faults, he loved her. And, for all her faults too, the girls adored her.

Sunday morning and Lizzie was away with her present travelling opera company playing a five-week season in the south-west. Plymouth tonight, weren't they? She was a semi-principal singer now, which as far as Stephen was concerned was pretty damned good, but it wasn't good enough for her, not with a company she herself regarded as inferior. And, at forty, although it was never said, she was running out of time to be discovered.

Stephen was having breakfast in the sunny room overlooking the garden, a tiny lawn surrounded by tired beds. A leisurely morning he promised himself and then, after lunch, he would pop up to his study and do some work. He worked less and less at the design board these days, rather to his regret, but he kept a close eye on his junior staff, made sure he knew exactly what was going on and spent a fair amount of his time rustling up commissions or out on site visits. He enjoyed and was invigorated by his work. Sometimes, with Lizzie frequently away and the girls doing their own thing so much more, work was his only consolation.

The Sunday papers were spread around him as he sipped orange juice and ate toast. Directly above, from Emily's room, a dull boom of a drumbeat thudded. Her music, the painful pop variety, was already switched on although whether she herself was at eleven thirty on a Sunday morning was in serious doubt. Emily was the slothful variety of teenager.

'Have you got the magazine supplement, Dad?' Abby asked,

popping her head round the door, a towelling robe over her pyjamas. She was usually the early bird. Her golden brown hair was tousled, lightened a bit by the summer sun. Blue eyes sleepy. Face clean, spot free at the moment and shiny. Barefoot, she padded and yawned her way into the room, flopping down opposite, giving him a hug first.

Darling Abby! He loved them equally, his daughters, absolutely equally. When Emily was born, just for a second as he had held her for the very first time, he was taken back to when he had held Abby, trying to recall if it had felt the same. It had. Emily was his, his and Lizzie's, but so was Abby. It was exactly the same. Well . . . almost, apart from the fact that Lizzie had gone through hell and back to have Emily as she constantly reminded him. It had been a difficult pregnancy, interspersed with grumbles and sulks, followed by a long painful labour.

'You can forget all about a son,' she told him when it was over, and, having been with her throughout, horrified at what she had suffered, he had done just that. He loved her too much to risk that happening again. It had unfortunately slightly taken the edge off their sex life.

Abby had known from the beginning she was adopted, almost before she could grasp what it meant. He and Lizzie bought a children's book on the subject, brightly explanatory, sat her between them and read it to her together. Looking back, Stephen realised it was one of the rare occasions when the three of them had done something together. They had turned the pages slowly while the little girl struggled to grasp what they and the book were saying. They worried for nothing. She accepted it with a smile.

Being adopted meant she was special and he remembered her running off to tell Emily *she* was special and Emily wasn't. Now it was, as the girls might say, no big deal. They told people they knew but there was no need to broadcast it to strangers.

Emily was, at thirteen, a miniature version of Lizzie, so like her that it still astonished Stephen. The same nearly black hair, the same deep brown eyes, the same coquettishness. In four or five years, the boys would be clamouring at the door. She was prettier than Abby and he hated himself for thinking it. Abby was charming and smiled a lot but her sharply defined nose robbed her of absolute beauty. No matter. She was a gentle quiet girl and he hoped, when the time came, she would find true happiness, something that had passed him by. She was a little lacking in ambition and his attempts to move her up a gear at school had failed. She was bright enough in her way but she just toddled along and wanted nothing more than to leave school as soon as possible and go to work.

It was an irritation to him and it would have helped if Lizzie had supported him on this one but Lizzie had few academic qualifications either so she just shrugged and said Abby could do what she wanted. They must not interfere. What was the point in trying to drag her off to university when she didn't want to go?

'School OK?' he said carefully. The fees were horrendous so it ought to be much more than OK.

'Great.' She poured herself some juice, reached for the magazine he had tossed her. 'Have you heard from Mum this week?' she asked.

He nodded, not wanting to admit he had not. When Lizzie was away, it was as if she were suddenly out of reach of the telephone. She said she liked to tune her mind to the singing, concentrate, and she could not do that if she was worried with domestic trivia. Irritated that phoning them was merely regarded as a domestic matter, he accepted it, not wanting to do anything to upset the performance. After all, nothing must upset the performance.

Afterwards, she would just turn up, usually unannounced, bubbling with enthusiasm if things had gone well, in the depths of despair if she'd hit a wrong note, in any case laden with gifts for the girls. When they were little, there were dolls and things. Now the presents were something more grown-up, clothes and make-up. She seemed to think that made it all right, made up for the emotional neglect.

Hell, it irritated sometimes, for hadn't he run round in circles to make sure they didn't feel neglected? It was, he reflected with a sigh, too damned late to change her now. Lizzie was Lizzie. She didn't have the same priorities as other people. She was an artist, for God's sake, but, if he were honest, he was getting sick of making allowances.

'Can we go to see her when *The Magic Flute* tours?' Abby asked, flicking through the pages languidly. 'I like that.'

'Course we can. I'll get your mother to arrange something special. Take you backstage. Would you like that?'

'Great.' She pinched some toast off his plate, fell silent, absorbed in the magazine, and he looked up as he heard her sharp intake of breath, seeing that she had gone quite pale, shocked.

'What's the matter? You all right, darling?' he enquired, wondering if it was one of these mysterious female things that had suddenly attacked her. At fourteen, she was growing up, no longer a child. Slightly built still but becoming curvier. Suffering the usual agonies of adolescence of course that he, dammit to hell, had to sort out because her mother was never here.

She said nothing, pushing the magazine aside, standing up, rushing out. Her feet thundered up the stairs and her bedroom door slammed shut. Considering she was a lightweight, she could make one helluva racket. From Emily's room, the drumbeat turned up a notch.

Not too concerned, used to teenage tantrums, he collected the papers together, contemplating half-heartedly doing something useful before lunch. A spot of gardening maybe, although he hated it. It was then, as he stretched lazily, the idea already losing its appeal, that he saw the article in the magazine, the one Abby had been reading.

A picture of Lizzie surely . . . he spun the magazine the right way up and stopped dead. Lizzie, accompanied in the photograph by a man. Sitting cosily beside him. The article in fact was about him, an up-and-coming young tenor at present doing a stint at the English National Opera. Simon somebody. Lizzie was mentioned in passing, referred to as the lovely, exciting mezzo-soprano Elizabeth Thomas, that being her maiden and stage name. No mention of Stephen. No mention of the small fact that she was married to him. No mention of her daughters. No mention of the fact that, at forty, Lizzie was very nearly old enough to be his – this tenor's – mother.

Good God!

And Abby had seen it . . .

Surely there was some mistake.

• Patricia Fawcett

The phone rang as he was debating whether or not he should go up and talk to Abby about it, to dismiss it as a mistake.

As he'd half expected, it was Lizzie. In a panic.

'Have you seen it?' she asked quickly and then, before he had a chance to reply, 'You have, haven't you? Oh Lord, it wasn't supposed to be in until next week. You can't trust these people an inch. They twisted Simon's words. He's quite furious. *And they quoted my age when I specifically asked them not to,*' she said, pausing as she perhaps realised the point of the call. 'I'm so sorry, Stephen. It isn't quite as it seems. I know it looks bad but we're not lovers . . . we're just good friends. I was going to come home to see you, to explain.'

'Explain what?' he said coldly. 'From what I see, there's nothing to explain. It's all there, Lizzie, in black-and-white. Abby's already seen it. If only I'd spotted it first, I would have hidden it from her. From Emily too.'

'All right. The truth. It happened so fast,' she said, her voice, that beautiful voice, not so sweet now, harassed and nervous rather. 'I never meant it to happen, darling, but you know how these things are.'

'No, I don't know,' he said, so angry and hurt that, if she were here at this moment, he might very well shake her. Damn the woman. Didn't she know he worshipped the ground she walked on? Didn't she know what this would do to Abby and Emily? Did she even care?

'I need space and time to think things over,' she said, 'Simon's asked me to move in with him and, although I don't intend to do that at the moment, it is an option I'm considering. He and I have so much in common. He understands about the music. You were always bored rigid when I talked about my work. Oh yes, you were, Stephen . . . It might be best therefore if we live separately for a while.'

He gave a short laugh. 'Don't we already?' he said. 'That's what's wrong with us, Lizzie. We're apart too much.' He was amazed how calm he felt. 'You might have had the decency to discuss this with me first. It's unforgivable that we should find out like this. Abby's very upset, but then when have you cared about Abby, or Emily for that matter? Dammit, I've had to be father and mother to them. You've never been around.'

'How dare you?' The voice hit the top angry note. 'It was your idea that I pursue my career vigorously and I can't do that by being at home and singing in the bath.'

'You could have compromised. You needn't have gone on every bloody tour.'

'You know nothing about it. If you're to get anywhere in this profession, you have to be there all the time. Availability is of the essence. If I'd known you were going to be so awkward about this, Stephen, I wouldn't have bothered to phone.' Her tone softened, a wheedling note creeping in, one he knew well. 'Please try to understand. I love him,' she said. 'I really love him.'

'Do you indeed. How romantic,' he replied, suddenly insanely jealous of the burly tenor in the photograph, the man whose name he would prefer to forget. He had the feeling they'd met once, at some performance or other. A broad-shouldered dark-haired man . . . Lizzie's type . . . who looked like he might run to fat one day. Stephen felt a perverse satisfaction at that for he had kept his lean shape, had no real trouble in doing so. This chap was only twenty-five, for God's sake. What was she thinking of? It didn't occur to wonder what the tenor was thinking of because, forty or not, Lizzie was still extremely attractive, looked years younger.

'What about the girls?' he asked, hearing but not listening to her as she, amazingly insensitive, extolled the man's virtues. Stephen interrupted her for he didn't give a damn if this Simon possessed a voice to rival Pavarotti. 'What about your daughters?' he asked again, controlling his own voice with difficulty.

'Really, Stephen, you seem determined to be as uncooperative as possible. I'll come home to see them,' she said, 'to explain. Children are remarkably resilient and it isn't as if I've been around all the time. It won't be much different for them. They'll go to school as usual, come home to you as usual. Come to visit me occasionally. They'll understand, darling.'

He nearly said, 'Don't darling me,' but it sounded pathetic so he said nothing, cold, icy cold, as he replaced the receiver. The bloody woman had dumped him.

He had a stiff drink before he talked to the girls, quietly and calmly, although there was a limit to how quiet and calm he

• Patricia Fawcett

could be when he was telling them that their mother was leaving them to live with someone else. There was no kind way of saying it, no way he could soften the blow.

'I hate her,' Emily said, when he had finished. She started to cry and Abby, big grown-up sister that she was, thirteen months older, put a comforting arm round her, soothed her with soft words, looking at him over Emily's shoulder, managing a sort of bewildered smile.

She even comforted him when Emily was gone, resting her head on his chest, telling him it would be all right. He patted her head as they consoled each other. Poor Abby. She deserved a happy home life. Would they have adopted her had they known this was to happen? He should have listened to Lizzie's doubts on the very day they collected Abby. They had damned well let her down.

It was a long time since he'd thought of the adoption. He and Abby talked only very occasionally of her natural mother and always when Lizzie was absent because she didn't like such talk. There wasn't much he could tell Abby. If she wanted, when she was eighteen, she could try to find her. She hadn't yet decided if she would bother. He wasn't sure what he thought about it, although he would support her if she decided she wanted to go ahead. Lizzie thought it was a dreadful idea but then Lizzie wouldn't be featuring much in Abby's life from now on, would she, even less than she had in the past.

He was on his own now, really on his own. He tried to analyse, when he was alone, what had gone wrong. He had thought they had a strong if slightly strange marriage, that they could cope with the separations and, when they were together, it was still, for him anyway, pretty good. Lizzie had learned to relax when she realised that Emily had been very much a one-off. She had given no indication, therefore, that she was tired of him – worse, bored.

Lizzie had once said she only came alive on stage. She had told him, not seeming to realise how hurtful it was, that singing was the most important thing in life. *She* was the most important thing to him but now he would have to let that go. Concentrate on the girls whilst she took off with him, the tenor.

His anger focused in his fist. God, if he were here now, that bloody tenor . . .

He and Lizzie could sing each other to sleep.

All Lizzie was fit for was singing and looking beautiful.

And making an almighty fool of him.

Part Two

6

At thirty-five, Jenny was an altogether glossier, more confident version of herself at seventeen. She now wore her hair, still the same rich brown colour, in a beautifully cut shoulder-length bob swinging heavily from a side parting and she enjoyed spending money on clothes. For work, the clothes were smart suits and a selection of silk blouses, unfortunately normally hidden under a laboratory coat which was hanging on a peg now as she waited for Trevor Cummings to appear.

'Don't shoot off at five,' he had told her earlier in the afternoon. 'I want a quick word with you before I go.'

It had peeved her slightly because she wasn't in the habit of shooting off at five in any case. She was at a level now where clock-watching was out of the question. It intrigued her though, Trevor's thrown-over-the-shoulder remark. What could he mean? He had looked cheerful enough so it must surely be good news. Promotion then? She supposed it was a possibility as she knew he had been keeping a keen eye on her and a few other people these past few months.

If so, it would probably mean a move to one of the other factories in the group, a move she would of course accept, although it would be a wrench to leave her little country cottage. She wouldn't say that to Trevor though. She would be blusteringly enthusiastic, raring to go. He had no time for people who quibbled about relocation. She recalled she had once told him that she would take the next shuttle to the moon if CWC offered her a promotion there. Joking of course but the point was not lost on him. She meant business and she knew, to her cost, that the brusque manner she often exuded came over sometimes as uncaring. Dammit, she wished she was accepted more, had some real friends instead of just acquaintances but that was the penalty she supposed of keeping her emotions in check.

'Sorry to keep you waiting, Jenny,' Trevor said as he bustled in, pulling out a chair opposite her desk. The office attached to a small laboratory was a mere cubbyhole and he had such presence he seemed to fill it. 'I'll come straight to the point,' he said. 'I want you to take over from John Harding when he retires next month. It'll be subject to an internal interview of course because we have to be seen to be obeying the rules, but take it from me, the job's yours. How about it?'

'Are you asking me to be Quality Assurance Manager here, at this factory?' she said stupidly, wishing Trevor wouldn't spring things like this on her. There'd been not a single hint. Everyone had assumed the QA job would be going to an outsider. 'Does he know?' she asked

'Does who know? Harding? It's sod all to do with him. He's going,' Trevor said with a quick grin. He was a ruddy-faced, grey-haired man in his fifties who wore slightly scruffy grey suits, striped shirts whose buttons were under constant pressure and usually a scarlet tie. An accident with a cricket ball in his youth had left him with a broken nose and a fierce dislike of any kind of competitive sport.

As Group Technical Director for Cedric Witcham Chemicals he had tremendous influence, gave short shrift to incompetence and had been ruthless in acquiring his team around him, hiring and firing with much the same enthusiasm. He didn't give a damn what people thought of him. In other words, he was a huge success. He was cagey about his private life but it was known that he was twice married, twice divorced, and thank God his relationship with Jenny, such as it was, had always been strictly business. Rumours had circulated for he was without doubt a ladies' man, but never involving her.

When she was looking for her first job, armed with a good degree in Chemistry and high hopes, she had initial doubts about applying as a graduate trainee to CWC, producers of additives and colorants for the food industry, because it meant moving back home to Preston. She had taken the job because she couldn't allow her domestic troubles to stand in the way of doing something she wanted, nor were there that many jobs going with such good prospects. In any case, it wasn't as if she intended to live within daggers-drawn, back-stabbing distance of her mother. That episode was well and truly done and dusted.

Over her years at CWC, she knew she had gained a reputation as a bit of a cool fish but she had learned it was best to keep business and pleasure separate. She was well aware that Trevor had 'favourites' and that she was one of them. So what? She might as well take advantage of it. Her present job was to run a small laboratory unit and she knew she ran it well. Even so, it was a big jump from that to Quality Assurance Manager, heading a department of eighteen or so. There would be a lot of people here who might have expected to get the job and Trevor's giving it to her would hardly win her new friends.

'Take over from Mr Harding?' she repeated, almost to herself. 'Me?'

'Yes, you. Don't sound so surprised. Now . . . let me tell you I've had to fight for this. Some of the buggers on the board are worried about what seems positive discrimination in favour of women in this outfit. Strictly between ourselves, Jenny. You know what a pushover I am for the fair sex. In the right place of course.' His smile flitted. Trevor smiled a lot, mostly insincere smiles she suspected. 'I told them you were one hundred per cent committed, that there wasn't a hope in hell of you buggering us up with maternity leave. I am right about that, I hope, Sweetman?'

'Absolutely, Mr Cummings.' She held his gaze, said what he wanted her to say. 'The job comes first with me.'

He nodded happily. 'Thought so. There'll be a company car of course as well as a substantial increase in salary. Other managerial perks.'

'That's wonderful,' she said, realising it couldn't have come at a better time.

She would be able to do up her country cottage properly at last without worrying too much about the expense. To hell with the expense now! All the long-term plans could be brought forward.

'Got to leave you,' he said, springing up and glancing at his watch. 'I've got a flight to catch. You'll have to be prepared for a

• Patricia Fawcett

bit of travel when you take over the job, popping down to head office for meetings, that sort of thing. Occasional trips abroad too if you're lucky.' He reached over, clasped her hand as she rose. 'Well done. You're the best man . . . person . . . for the job otherwise I wouldn't be recommending you. Don't you dare let me down.'

Jenny, aware that he'd held her hand a touch longer than necessary, wondered about that as he disappeared. She also wondered – and the thought irritated – if, at her tender age, she was really up to the job.

Hazelburn was a pretty hamlet in the Forest of Bowland, approached by several twisting lanes that crisscrossed in some mysterious fashion and boasted a collection of peculiarly contradictory signposts. Her visitors invariably got lost, having to ring her in the end from some phone box in the middle of nowhere.

It was a far cry from the poky flat in Preston that Jenny had used as her base when she first started work but she had planned the move carefully, waited until she could just about afford it, deciding that the joys of living in the country more than balanced the driving time it added to her day. After the stress of her job, it was a haven, a place to unwind and take stock.

The gable end of the cottage was the first thing you saw as you entered the village from the south side, a little white house amongst the more usual stone-fronted properties. Jenny approved of the hotchpotch, the wiggledy way the houses slotted into the lower slopes of the fell. This remote moorland with its lush green valleys was a constant surprise to her visitors who imagined Lancashire to be wholly industrial. The muck and brass and mills image took some dispelling. However, she was happy to keep quiet about it, so that it would remain unspoiled.

Its peace astonished her still. As she drew her curtains in the morning and looked out, all she could see were the patchwork of fields hemmed by hedges of blackthorn, hawthorn, holly and crab apple with the hills beyond, the hedges gradually replaced by dry-stone walls, sheep and the peat and heather moorland of the fell.

It was therefore, in her eyes, not far short of idyllic. The only fly in the ointment was the continued presence in the village of her erstwhile lover Ben Chambers.

Ben, as well as being incredibly handsome, was also powerfully successful, the sort of man women steal a second glance at when they think nobody's looking. He drove a silver Porsche with a personalised numberplate. Unable to see much beyond the good looks and the aura of power, she had allowed herself to be wined and dined and later very expertly made love to.

Everything was fine when he thought she was a successful career woman, university educated. Her accent did not betray her origins, and when he found out that she was from quite humble beginnings, his interest switched off instantly. The dumping was like a slap in the face with a wet rag. God . . . how he had humiliated her. It had so astonished her, the suddenness of it, that she had been unable to drum up some decent one-liners to knock him off his stride. Afterwards, she had felt like letting the tyres down on his beloved car but had decided he wasn't worth the effort. Looking back, she saw that she had been totally taken in by his undisputed charm, impressed by his attentive manner, unhappy even now to concede that his amusing chat-up line and prompt follow-on was faultless. She consoled herself with the thought that most women, including modern independent women like herself, were still almost comically willing to fall for that.

She was determined she was not going to let it affect her enjoyment of living here. If it bothered him, he could damned well move. Whenever they met, she was terribly polite, spoke only if he did, tried to ignore the chill atmosphere. She had had enough practice after all. She hadn't spoken to her mother in years either. She'd ploughed all her energy into the job and it needed all her concentration, leaving little time for anything else. Meaningful relationships, dammit, were almost out of the question.

As she crossed the little bridge that was the Hazelburn boundary, she saw the familiar big black car, Uncle Harold at the wheel, parked outside her cottage. Oh no! Bubbling as she was with the thrill of the new job offer, she'd forgotten all about him coming for tea. She swung her own car behind his, waving at him as she did so. His car was ages old but still in excellent condition, or fine fettle as he would say. A bit like the gentleman himself.

Once out of her car, she rushed round to his, giving him a quick kiss and a profuse apology that she was so late. He smelled reassuringly not of manly cologne but of cough linctus and chest liniment, pleasantly mixed with shaving soap.

'You look well, Jenny love,' he said, peering carefully at her with his pale rheumy eyes as if he hadn't seen her for years. 'I hope you're not dieting. You youngsters are too frightened of a little weight. A little plumpness in the face is very bonny, let me tell you. I can't be doing with scrawny women.'

'When you've quite finished . . .' she smiled as he followed her indoors. She was tempted to tell him about the new job but she refrained from doing so until the appointment was confirmed. He had a tea date with her twice a month, an old-fashioned ritual she was more than happy to comply with, and in between times they rang each other every week. He was pushing eighty now and long retired but still beavering about trying to smooth things over between her and her mother. All to no avail of course, but behind that rather severe exterior, he was the eternal optimist. She kept quiet about the hostility these days. People instantly took sides if she did mention it, irritatingly blaming her when they knew nothing about it. Nothing at all.

Her mother had meant what she said on the day Jenny left home to go to university. Meant every word. Jenny had tried for a while but her letters home remained unanswered, the telephone calls stiff and barely cordial and, after a while, she got the message. Mum hadn't even bothered to come to the graduation ceremony. Uncle Harold had, looking touchingly proud of her. She needed that to compensate for the fact that her mother was absent, that her father was of necessity absent. She needed someone from home to hug her and tell her what a clever girl she was. Someone in the audience rooting for her. Idiotic and childish but true. Uncle Harold had even offered his support if she wanted to pursue a further degree but she had declined. She couldn't let him do that. He'd helped her out enough already.

She was aware how ridiculous the feud was. When you belonged to a small family, it made it worse. The misery heightened at Christmas and birthdays when they exchanged terse cards. If Mother had other children to worry about, it wouldn't be so bad. If only there was someone she could talk to, a woman, someone other than Uncle Harold. Some things he just did not understand.

Damn it, she'd spent the last eighteen years feeling guilty.

Eighteen years . . .

Helen would be eighteen soon.

Leaving her uncle sitting comfortably with a cup of tea, she took off her working suit and changed into casual gear, annoyed to have had that memory intrude. Mostly, she succeeded these days in keeping it trapped but it could be triggered off, often by thinking about her unhappy relationship with her own mother.

The laboratory where she worked was on the outskirts of Preston and it only needed a slight detour to drive from work to her mother's house. Sometimes she was so tempted to take that detour, arrive unexpectedly at Hargreaves Street. Sometimes she wished they could make it up, go shopping together, meet for coffee, that sort of thing, but it had gone on too long now and it was increasingly impossible to do anything about it. What would she say after all these years? And she couldn't risk the possibility that her mother might still have that look in her eye . . . that accusing look.

One of them had to be big enough to say this is stupid, let's forget it.

One of them.

But it certainly wasn't going to be her.

Abby spent her eighteenth birthday moving house. Unfortunate and her father had been most apologetic but, because of complications with the conveyancing paperwork, coupled with deadlines at his office, it really was the most convenient date. She did not mind in the slightest, was delighted in fact that they were at last on the move from the rented accommodation in town that they'd been living in for too long now. It had been pleasant enough but had never felt permanent. She had frankly become impatient with Dad's patience. He was so determined to wait for the right house to come along that it seemed they would wait for ever.

• Patricia Fawcett

'I'll make it up to you,' he said now, for the umpteenth time, as they watched the furniture van disappear up the lane. 'I've got a table booked tonight for dinner. At the Dog and Partridge at Chipping. Highly recommended.'

'Stop worrying,' she said with a smile, more concerned with sorting out the piles of boxes that were scattered throughout the house. Giving a big sigh at the prospect of what was to come, she rolled up her sleeves. 'Let's get started, shall we?'

They spent the rest of the afternoon tidying up and unpacking and, by the time Emily was due to be back from school, they were more or less satisfied. Still a lot to do of course but it was beginning to look more like home. Curwin Hall, their magnificent country home. Dad had scoured Lancashire before he found it, talked to them at length before he took the plunge and bought it. He had worked in Preston for a while now, a partner in the company, and he deserved his dream. To live in the country.

Abby had lost count of the number of houses they'd looked over before they settled on this one, a disgracefully grand affair set in one and a half acres. Once he'd set eyes on it, there was never any question that they wouldn't buy it. A Manchester architect had been commissioned in 1876 to design the house in this exalted position using the fells as a backdrop and Dad thoroughly approved of that. The Manchester architect he decided was a man after his own heart, unafraid of a bit of grandeur, shameless in his finicky attention to detail. Frankly, he couldn't have done a better job himself.

Abby felt she would like it too once she had grown used to the space, although, just now, coping with being eighteen, a job *and* a new house was all a bit much. Emily was being awkward as usual. She had liked living in the house in town and was muttering dire warnings that she would probably fail her coming exams as a result of all the upheaval. Didn't Dad realise that moving house caused equal stress to someone dying on you? And another thing – she wanted to live somewhere where something was *happening*, for God's sake.

At nearly seventeen, Emily was sometimes distressingly pragmatic and the relaxed location and idyllic views meant nothing when she couldn't yet drive and had to rely on Dad or Abby for transport. She would be marooned here, she wailed, she might as well live on the moon for all the good it would do her social life. She'd never get boyfriends to traipse all the way out here.

Abby smiled as she thought of her sister. Emily was a hopeless case, still the sulky, awkward baby she'd always been. Pity they couldn't keep baby reins on her nowadays so that they'd know where she was and, more importantly, what she was up to. Emily was heading for a sticky end if she wasn't careful but Dad just refused to see it. Emily could do no wrong in his eyes.

Glancing at the clock, Abby wandered downstairs to the unfamiliar kitchen, found her father already there, busying about, making coffee. She went up to him and leaned against him, needing his comforting presence a minute. 'Happy birthday to you, happy birthday to you,' he hummed against her hair.

She laughed. 'Are you as shattered as me?'

'Absolutely.' He kissed the top of her head. 'Thanks for today, darling. You needn't have taken a day off. I could have coped.'

'I know . . . you always do.' She reached for her coffee, sank down thankfully onto a chair, 'Oh Dad . . . it's lovely here,' she said, knowing that would please him. 'I think we'll be happy.'

'Your mother would hate it,' he told her, grimacing as he said it. 'Sorry to remind you . . . she would have got over if she could have managed it for your birthday. I know she would. Pity she was needed for the rehearsals.'

Abby dismissed it, not wanting to discuss her mother's absence. The excuse was watertight. Mum's excuses always were but the fact remained that, if she had really wanted, she would be here. Eighteen was special after all. But then Mum had never been around much, even less since she and Dad had divorced of course. When they were little, she and Emily had looked forward so much to Mum coming home. Abby remembered the excitement of counting the days, particularly remembered the heavy scent as she was swept up briefly into her mother's arms. Remembered the beautiful shiny clothes. The gold jewellery. The dark glowing eyes. The scarlet lips and polished red nails. Have you got clean hands, darling? Don't mess Mummy's hair.

She looked across at her father, this big lumbering man whom she adored, and smiled. He had touches of grey now in his dark hair, handsomely distributed, and she thought, although maybe she was prejudiced, that he was still a remarkably attractive man.

'Do you want me to confirm that holiday for you yet?' she asked. 'Time's getting on and they're filling up, particularly for that resort.'

She didn't want to nag him but, even though she worked in a travel agency, she couldn't hold a booking indefinitely.

He laughed. 'Not yet. You know how it was going to be a couple of weeks away on my own? Rest and recuperation. Well, Clare's got it into her head that I've invited her to come with me and it's all starting to get complicated. She's worrying about the children and the damned cat as well and there are all sorts of convoluted arrangements about getting time off work. And then there's her mother of course. What if her mother died whilst we were away? Would she ever forgive herself? I tell you, Abby, it's beginning to sound like the holiday from hell.'

She laughed too. 'I'm just warning you. By the time you make your mind up, there might be nothing left.'

'Abby, darling, leave it please.'

She left it.

Dad got himself into such a tangle these days with Mrs Forrest. At first she had thought it nice for him to have someone else but now she wasn't so sure. It didn't seem to be going anywhere. She was nice enough, Clare Forrest, although Emily thought her a bit on the dippy side. What does he see in her? she asked. It's not as if she's pretty. She's nowhere near as pretty as Mum. But then, who was?

Abby's new bedroom, at the back of the house, overlooked the old paved terrace where wide stone steps led to the lawn and the rectangular flowerbeds, quiet at this time of year. Masses of old-fashioned shrub roses and herbaceous plants slumbered still but would be beautiful in summer. Her father might do something about a former grass tennis court which had been allowed to overgrow. That was the only thing that Emily was enthusiastic about, the possibility of tennis parties as in days of old.

It was, therefore, very much a formal garden, one that pleased her father's structured eye, a garden planned geometrically by the very same Manchester architect, no less, who had designed the house. Looking down on it from above, Abby admired and approved too.

She opened the window wide, sat on the window seat, and gazed out. Dad was undismayed at the size of the gardens, realised his limitations and had already engaged someone to come in and do them. The warm evening air, so fresh out here blowing unhindered as it did from the fell, wrapped around her and she breathed it in calmly. Above the hill line, clouds fluffed across the blue and pink sky. Downstairs, bringing her down to earth with a bump, she heard sounds of Emily's arrival home. Her loud voice. Laughter.

She knew she was ultrasensitive about it. Dad had always tried to be so fair, scrupulously fair, but she sensed there was something extra in his feelings for Emily. Emily just went her own sweet way, seemed to do things deliberately to irritate him, reminded him all the time of Mum, and yet still claimed that little extra share of his affection. Or so it seemed. Let's see what Emily thinks, he was always saying.

With a sigh, she pulled at her hair, making a face into the mirror. The hairdo was very modern, a new style to celebrate her birthday and official adulthood, but she now had doubts. She wondered if the severity of the club cut emphasised her strong nose. She was fed up to the teeth with her nose. She had once asked Dad about plastic surgery and he had laughed, probably not meaning to be unkind. What did she want plastic surgery for? He had said she was lovely as she was, which was a typical fatherly reply and no help at all. She would be a lot lovelier with a smaller nose.

Emily had no such problems. Emily had an adorable *retroussée* nose. Emily, when she wasn't being rude and unhelpful, was full of grace and confidence.

'Hi, Abby! You must have had a really grotto birthday,' she said as she barged in, tall and leggy and glossily brunette, her hair long and heavily straight. Dark brooding eyes. Very like Mum. She had the same butterfly mind too. 'That school of mine's crap,' she announced, dropping her bags on the floor. 'I don't care how much the fees are, it's still crap. I've told Dad but he takes no notice. And the bus journey's hell now, double hell. Imagine having to do it every single day. It's going to put years on me.'

• Patricia Fawcett

'Dad said he'd come and get you,' Abby pointed out. 'And it was you who insisted on going to school today anyway. You could have had the day off, helped us a bit.'

Emily shrugged, looking at herself in the mirror.

'I didn't fancy unpacking boxes.' She glanced at Abby's room admiringly. 'It looks great, doesn't it? So does mine. I'm going to turn over a new leaf, keep it really really tidy.'

Abby smiled. 'That'll be the day.'

'Guess what? I've just seen this fantastic guy,' Emily said, loosening her hair and fluffing it round her face. 'Wouldn't you just know it? Here I am, wearing school bloody uniform. He must have thought I was about twelve. Anyway . . .' her dark eyes danced, 'I've found out he lives in the village in that barn conversion so that's a boon. Makes this grotto place a bit more interesting. He drives . . . wait for it . . . a Porsche.'

'Wow! What does he look like?' Abby asked, exchanging a wide smile with her sister. Emily was man mad. At sixteen she had a string of discarded boyfriends already. Abby suspected it was mostly talk but it was difficult to be sure with Emily. Abby worried a little about it, had once tried to talk to Mum, ask her advice, but it had been a bad connection and they had aborted the call.

'What does he look like?' Emily considered the question carefully. 'I didn't get a close look,' she confessed. 'He took me by surprise, nearly knocked me down, screeched round that corner and flattened me against the wall. He must have been doing at least sixty. He is *really* something. I could feel the vibes through the car window as he drove past. We can ask him to our house-warming party. Bags I get first chance to chat him up. I saw him first.'

'House-warming? Don't push it, Emily. We haven't unpacked everything yet.'

'We must get one organised or we'll never get round to it. You know how busy Dad is. You ask him, it'll sound better coming from you, more sensible. We can combine it with an eighteenth party for you. It's a pity it's not a bit warmer. We could have had it in the garden, a barbecue or something, floodlights and things. When is he going to get that tennis court redone? Marked out and everything. Just imagine that. Strawberries and cream.

Lemonade. Wimbledon stuff. Really classy. Pity I can't play. I bet that Porsche guy plays. Ace after ace. I can just see him in white shorts.' She gazed into the distance dreamily.

'How can we have a house-warming? We don't know anybody here.'

'That's the bloody point,' Emily said, clicking her tongue in exasperation. 'We never will get to know anybody in this crappy joint unless we ask them to a party.'

'Stop swearing,' Abby said. 'You know Dad doesn't like you to swear.'

'Oh shut up, grumpy knicks, Dad's not here, is he?' Emily, totally unconcerned, pulled a packet of cigarettes out of her bag. 'Want one?' she asked, lighting hers not very expertly and beginning to smoke, trying unsuccessfully to look sophisticated.

'No and you shouldn't be smoking either. How can you afford them?'

'The ciggies? Oh come on, Abby, Dad's very generous with my pocket money,' she said with a wicked smile. 'I have to buy so much stationery these days for projects and things. Luckily he does not require receipts. He trusts me, you see,' she added, turning quickly away, having the grace to look a touch ashamed.

Abby sighed, wondered if now was the right time to bring up a delicate matter, decided it might as well be now while Emily was in a reasonable mood.

'I didn't tell Dad but Miss Ellis rang me last week. She wanted to speak to Dad but I put her off.'

Emily continued to smoke, looking at her through narrowed eyes.

'Go on . . . what did she want?'

'Have you been skiving off?'

'Oh *no* . . . so she did see me. One lousy afternoon, that's all it was. Wouldn't you just know it? I could have died when I saw her there. What the hell was she doing in the park anyway?'

'I assume she had a better excuse than you,' Abby said, nearly laughing aloud at her sister's indignation. 'Who was he? The boy?'

'I can't get away with anything,' Emily wailed. 'It's none of your damned business. Is there a spy network following me? You haven't said anything, have you? To Dad?'

'No. Of course I haven't,' Abby said. 'But if you keep missing school, I might have to for your own sake.'

'Jesus, Abby! Who do you think you are, my keeper? Loosen up a bit, for God's sake. I'm in the sixth form, it's not supposed to matter. It *wouldn't* matter at any normal school. Miss Ellis treats us like kids. Relax. Don't worry about me.'

Despite her irritation, Abby smiled at her sister's sheer exuberance. Emily was right. She should relax, let things be. It was her mother leaving that had done it. She felt older than her years sometimes, felt a responsibility towards Emily that she shouldn't have to shoulder. Poor Emily had taken it particularly hard, the divorce and everything. She had taken Mum's defection as a personal affront, worried for a long time that it was something to do with them, that they had somehow driven her away.

'When was it she last rang?'

'What?' Abby turned reluctantly away from the window, where she had been absorbing the softly setting scene spread before her. 'Mum?'

Emily nodded, suddenly subdued. 'It seems ages ago,' she said, 'and we haven't had a letter or postcard either. Why is it she's never in when we phone? Dad has told her we've moved, hasn't he? She does know this address?'

'And the phone number. She is busy,' Abby said, as always trying to buoy Emily up where their mother was concerned. 'We mustn't keep bothering her, not when she's in the middle of a season. She knows we're all fine. It's not as if we're children any longer. If something was wrong, she'd be on the first plane back.'

'You reckon?' Emily managed a smile. 'You've got more faith than me, Abby. Want to bet she won't make it home for my birthday either? I can't understand her. Can you? Imagine having an affair with him, that porky guy? How could she?' She seemed not to realise that the same question had been asked time and time again. And remained unanswered. 'How could she have left us, you and me and Dad? I don't care if he is a lot younger, Dad's heaps better-looking than him.'

'Get yourself changed,' Abby said, cocking her head as a

door downstairs opened. 'That's Dad. He's taking us out for a meal later.'

'Oh good. That's another thing about that grotto school of mine. The meals are obscene.' She shuddered at the thought. 'He's not asked that dippy Clare woman to come, has he? God, that's all I need after a really lousy day at school. She's so pathetic. Her eyes fill with tears if you mention her ex, or her cat or those kids of hers, or her scatty mother. What *is* her problem?'

'She's not coming. It's just the three of us,' Abby said. 'A birthday treat.'

'Fantastic.' Emily hastily stubbed the cigarette out on a convenient surface, wafted the smoke away at the sound of footsteps. 'Don't you dare breathe a word,' she whispered as there was a knock on the door.

Abby broached the subject of the house-warming party after their dinner, a quite delicious meal. Even Emily had perked up, having eaten everything put in front of her. She was now stuffing herself indelicately with mints, having decided there were no young men about who might be eyeing her up.

'A house-warming party? If you like,' he said, looking from one to the other of them. 'Do you want one, Emily?'

'It sounds quite a nice idea,' she said demurely, successfully managing to make it sound as if it were Abby's suggestion. 'If it's a warm night, we can have an outdoor party.' She smiled at her sister. 'You can organise the eats, Abby. Get some caterers. If you like, you can leave me to deliver the invitations.'

'Thank you,' Abby murmured with a smile. Honestly, Emily was incorrigible.

The matter seemed to be worrying Dad.

'If it's what you two want, I'll go along with it,' he said, 'but who will we invite? I suppose I could ask people from work. And Clare . . .'

There was a little silence.

'Don't you worry about that. Leave the invites to me,' Emily told him. 'We'll ask the entire village. With a bit of luck, the really boring fuddy-duddies won't come and we'll be left with all the interesting ones.' She shot a knowing glance towards Abby. 'That's anybody under forty,' she added playfully.

'Less of that.' He smiled none the less as he called for the bill.

'Thanks, Dad.' Abby tucked her arm into his as they went out into the now coolish evening. Emily, temporarily forgetting she was supposed to be a sultry sixteen very nearly seventeen, almost skipped ahead of them. 'That was a lovely surprise. And thanks for the watch. It's gorgeous.'

He squeezed her arm. 'You're welcome, darling,' he said. He gave an embarrassed little cough. 'I want you to know I'm very proud of you, my grown-up daughter.'

The moment seemed right for a special speech from her too. There was so much she wanted to say to him. They didn't often talk seriously to each other. He clammed up a bit when she tried to talk about Mum. And he was terribly embarrassed if she tried to bring up the subject of her natural mother.

She wanted to say thank you for everything, for being such a super dad, for always being there when she needed him, and most of all, she wanted to say how lucky she was that *he* had adopted her. She couldn't have wished for a better dad. She also wanted to reassure him, to say that it didn't really matter about Mum. Mum was like that. She couldn't help it.

But they were already at the car and it was too late.

7

'If it was up to me, I'd pack it in tomorrow,' Christine Sweetman said, in a confidential aside to the woman on the next stall. She eyed the massed array of ornaments, mainly glass, that occupied their own. 'These all have to be put away and then brought out again every time. What a carry-on! You should see the pile of boxes we have *and* the newspaper. Still . . .' She smiled at the woman, a stranger, not one of the usual table-toppers. 'It's my brother, Harold, you see. He enjoys it, enjoys the socialising. It's his only hobby and you have to humour them, don't you, when they get older? It makes him a bit of extra money, not that he's short of it. You should see his house up near Sharoe Green Hospital, a great big detached. He's a bachelor, our Harold, only ever had himself to think about.'

'Is that him?' the woman asked doubtfully. 'Him with the white hair?'

Christine nodded. 'Lovely head of hair, hasn't he? It runs in the family, a good head of hair. See that overcoat he's wearing? Beautiful quality that. One of his best funeral coats. Must be ten years old, that coat. He used to be an undertaker,' she added, lowering her voice respectfully. 'Taylor and Walmsley out at Ribbleton. Remember them? He's the Walmsley bit of it. Harold Walmsley. He didn't retire until he was nearly seventy. They sold off the business. Neither of them had a son to carry it on. Shame really. I mean to say, it's a good business to be in. Trade never falls off. Another hot summer like last year and they'll be dropping like flies, you mark my words. Sees them off, the heat.'

'I suppose somebody has to do it. He looks the right sort. A

• Patricia Fawcett

bit miserable.' The woman sniffed, rearranged the knitted items she had brought along, a right motley collection. Baby garments, tank tops and sad-looking understuffed toys. 'Slack today, isn't it?' she went on, taking a glance round. 'Not exactly bulging at the seams. I thought this was supposed to be busy. Where is everybody?'

'It's like this sometimes,' Christine said. 'You get your off days. I blame the weather. First time you've been to this one then?'

'And the last if it's always as dead as this,' the woman said. 'I'll be starting the car boots as soon as the weather picks up. I'd rather be out in the fresh air.'

'We do car boots too,' Christine said. 'In fact, look at this . . .' she fumbled in her handbag for her diary, 'up to our eyes we are for the whole summer. It's hard work fitting it all in because I go out to work,' she went on, waiting for the woman to ask what she did, supplying the information when there was no interest shown.

'I work in a supermarket,' she said, 'one of them out-of-town ones. Stacking and pricing and check-out relief. Part time, a few hours Monday, Wednesday and some Saturdays. They wanted me to do Sundays when they started on that lark but I said no. Told them it was against my principles and then they don't fuss. I mean to say . . . there's always a car boot somewhere on a Sunday. Still . . .' she heaved a sigh, looked to the woman for some sympathy, 'it's a handy little job and it gets you out. I'd go spare if I was on my own all the time. And you know what they say – it's not work that kills but worry.'

'That's a fact.'

Christine glanced at her with exasperation. She was one of them sorts you couldn't hold a decent conversation with. She looked round the church hall a minute as more people drifted in, realised their mistake, and drifted out again. Dead loss this place. She'd half a mind to get Harold to cross it off their list. When she thought of all the little jobs she could be doing at home . . . She gave another heartfelt sigh and decided it was worth persevering with her neighbour as there was nothing else to do.

'I lost my husband, Reg, eighteen years back,' she went on. 'Brain haemorrhage.' She paused, this time getting a murmur of sympathy. 'Such a shock it was. I mean, you don't expect it, do you? When you go to bed, you expect to wake up, not to wake up in a coma. Still . . . he wouldn't have wanted to suffer. To linger. He was very religious, was Reg, so you have to think of it that way. Gone to his maker, that's how he would see it. Although, to be honest, that's not a lot of consolation to them that's left behind.'

To her irritation, the woman, without so much as an excuse-me, got up and went to get herself a drink from the scouts who were providing the refreshments today.

Christine turned her back on the garish knits. She'd talked practically non-stop since they'd got here and she was getting nowhere. Some people! If she expected her to keep an eye on her stall, she could forget it. She had enough to do, lumbered with looking after their own. Harold was no use. In fact, he tended to put people off. Gave you the creeps sometimes, Harold, but that was because of seeing what he had seen of course. Not for the faint-hearted that profession of his. She frowned, trying to catch his attention, but he was now talking with some animation, still wearing his winter overcoat. Harold was a great believer in never casting a clout till May be out. Felt the cold, he did. Once he got going though, chatting, he was like a child let out of Sunday school.

'As I was saying . . .' she said as the woman returned, carrying two cups. 'Oh thanks. Do you want paying?'

'My treat,' the woman said. 'Talking makes you thirsty, doesn't it? Thought you might fancy one. They're not sugared. Is that all right?'

Christine nodded. 'That's what he went for,' she said with a laugh, 'quarter of an hour ago. Look at him, talking nineteen to the dozen. For God's sake, don't get him talking about funerals or you'll never hear the last of it. The tales he tells. Makes your hair curl. I never knew what they had to do. I just thought they dropped the body in the coffin. Believe me, that's not the half of it.'

She fiddled with her hair as she spoke, smugly noting the other woman's lank greyish locks. Christine had her hair tinted auburn nowadays to cover the grey. Just because she was in her fifties that was no excuse for letting herself go. She was proud of her shape too, never strayed much from the size twelve she had

• Patricia Fawcett

been twenty years ago. She spent a fair amount of her wages on clothes and, because of her slim figure, she could get away with short skirts, not too short mind, and high heels. When you'd been given good legs, it was a shame to hide them away and, because of her height, she felt frumpish wearing that mid-length and flatties. She bought most of her clothes in town at C & A, suited her to a T they did but sometimes she bought stuff off the market. These black leggings were off the market, a bargain at £3.99.

She wore casual clothes for the table tops, warm clothes because church halls and whatnots were not noted for their extravagant heating. Today, the slightly imperfect leggings were tucked into her winter boots and she wore a sloppy big-patterned jumper pulled right down over her bottom. If she did gain the odd ounce, that's where it ended up.

How they'd started on glassware, she couldn't remember but it looked nice on the stall, sparkled, and Harold spent hours at the sink before they came. He did most of the stock buying, rooting bargains out at jumble sales and charity shops. A good snooper round, Harold. A good eye for a bargain. He'd never bought anything yet that they hadn't sold on at a profit.

'How much do you want for that vase?'

She perked up and looked at the young man who had enquired. It didn't do to put price stickers on all the items, just a few to show willing. You had to weigh up your customer first. You could spot a dealer a mile off and he wasn't one.

'Doesn't it have a price on then?' she asked with a laugh. 'Wouldn't you know it? My brother's supposed to have done that. Want something doing, do it yourself.' She exchanged a knowing glance with the woman on the knits stall before returning her attention to the prospective buyer. 'A fiver, love. How's that suit you?'

'A fiver?' He picked it up and turned it upside down as if he knew what was what.

'Beautiful vase that,' she said, playing to the gallery as a small number of people, constituting an audience, gathered. 'Came from a big old house out at Garstang when they sold up. Stick some spring flowers in that and it'll look a treat. You'd pay twenty pounds and more in the shops. It's a bargain. Best quality. They don't make glass like that any more,' she finished fiercely.

'Four fifty,' he said, digging in his pockets for change.

She hesitated only a moment. A bird in the hand . . .

'All right, love, you've twisted my arm.'

She wrapped it carefully in newspaper, and pocketed the coins. Well at least they'd earned enough today to pay the cost of the table and more. She watched the lad disappear, clutching his purchase, and rearranged the items to cover the gap. They'd got a bad spot today, right at the entrance. People tended to walk right past, eyes ahead. She'd have a word with the organiser. After all, it wasn't fair when they came regular. The regulars should have the best position. Casuals like this woman next to her should make do with what they could get.

'Have you any family?'

'What?'

She stared at the woman, who was drinking her tea. She pulled a packet of sandwiches out of her bag, silently offered Christine one. Christine smiled vaguely and refused. She didn't care for the look of them and you never knew what state other people's kitchens were in. Her own was immaculate. You could eat your dinner off her kitchen floor.

'I have four kids,' the woman said, tucking into a doorstep of a sandwich. 'Two of each. John's twenty-four, an engineer, just got himself married. Jason's twenty-two, works in a shop. Margaret's just turned twenty-one, she's engaged to be married and the wedding's going to cost me a fortune – six bridesmaids would you believe, a reception and that evening disco they all have. My youngest is Julie. She's only seventeen. Lovely-looking lass, even though I shouldn't say it. Long blonde hair. Slim. She could be a model if she had a mind to.'

'Really? How nice.'

Christine finally caught Harold's eye across the room, indicated he should get himself back over here.

'How many do you have?'

Christine's withering look was lost on her. For crying out loud . . .

'I have a daughter,' she said quietly, seeing she was not going to get away with no reply.

• Patricia Fawcett

'Just the one?'
She nodded.
'What does she do then?'
Christine ignored that. Thank God Harold was heading back.
'My brother's taking over for a while,' she said with dignity, 'So if you'll excuse me . . .' She slid between the stalls as Harold reappeared. 'You and your talking,' she said sharply, 'leaving me to look after things . . .' She allowed the rebuke to settle. 'I've sold that vase,' she whispered, 'that one you bashed in the sink this morning.'

'Nothing wrong with it,' he said quickly, 'not as I could see. Oh . . . you've already got your cup of tea.'

She left him to it. Let him deal with the knit woman whatever her name was. Nosy so-and-so. What business was it of hers how many children she had?

She went to the ladies to freshen up. She applied another layer of the bright pink lipstick she used and a dusting of powder. Her blue eyes stared back at her, just a little swimmy. That woman had upset her a bit, asking about Jenny. She usually kept all thoughts of Jenny firmly shuttered away. She had no wish to be reminded of that madam. Of course she sometimes popped up uninvited in her dreams but there was nothing you could do about that.

That was the trouble when you only had the one.
One chance only.
And look how she had fouled up.

8

'Take a seat, Jenny. Good flight?'

Trevor smiled, lowered himself into his chair. Behind him, through the wide window, there was a panoramic view of the city, rooftops bathed in a soft morning glow. Unused to it, Jenny found her attention drawn to it, was hard pressed to keep her mind on the business in hand. It was a one-to-one meeting with Trevor, anxious to brief her on a three-day seminar he wanted her to attend in Amsterdam on the company's behalf.

Alone, thank God. His memo on the subject had been ambiguous and she had worried on the way down that he might be coming with her, a cosy weekend away with a perfectly legitimate business excuse. She was relieved to have misinterpreted it and a little ashamed too. She ought to credit him with a bit more guile than that. However, she knew she would have to watch him none the less. It was always the same. She had a knack of attracting the wrong men. Somewhere, someday . . . she hadn't given up hope yet even if she was amused by the juvenile idea of there being a Mr Right lurking on the horizon. Fat chance.

'That's all clear then.' Trevor's voice was clipped. 'You'll just be a run-of-the-mill delegate this time but hopefully, in the future . . .' He let the pleasant promise stand before lighting a cigarette, not asking her permission. 'So, Sweetman, what's the verdict?' he enquired. 'On the QA job?'

'It's difficult,' she said carefully, 'but then I didn't expect it to be easy. It was left in . . .' She hesitated, unwilling to criticise her predecessor.

'A bloody shambles eh?' he laughed. 'John let things go, didn't he? Just as well he's gone; he can get on with the most important thing in life now, the golf.'

'I don't know about that,' Jenny said, uncomfortable still, 'but everything does need tightening up. It's all become a bit slaphappy.'

'And . . . ?' He waved a hand irritably. 'I sense a problem. For God's sake, spit it out. We'll get nowhere if you act coy.'

'The staff are suspicious of me,' she said, trying hard not to let him see just how much that hurt. 'Weighing me up, I suppose. Some of them, particularly the women, think I'm too young and inexperienced. They don't seem to think I'm up to the job.'

He chuckled. 'Then it's up to you to show them otherwise,' he said, his hands restless on the big bare desktop. 'How are your two section heads reacting to you? They're more important than the lab staff.'

Jenny told him. The two men were obviously annoyed that she had got the job. Both of them had fancied their chances but one was approaching retirement age himself and the other, Len, was far too slick a customer. Trying to get started on the right footing, she had called each of them into her office for a private word.

She remembered Len tapping the door and entering immediately, checking his watch as he did so, trying to look bored. He unsettled her. He had insolent grey eyes, heavy unkempt eyebrows, a blue-black chin even at the start of the day and an awful lot of curly dark hair, worn long on his collar. He worked alone more or less, having lost most of his staff following a streamlining operation instigated by the man opposite.

He now supervised an audit system, personally inspecting their suppliers' quality control systems, visiting their laboratories, so that CWC could accept deliveries of raw materials without the need for further testing. With five hundred raw materials involved in manufacturing the Preston factory's five products, he was kept busy. He was out on inspections most of the time so, as he pointed out, she had been lucky to catch him.

'So he wants to be left in peace, does he?' Trevor said thoughtfully, when she had finished. 'He's in the last chance saloon, that bugger. Let me tell you, Jenny, we'd have sacked him a few years ago but some silly sod fouled up the evidence and he'd have had us for wrongful dismissal. He's a loser so you'll have to watch him. If anything goes wrong, he's bloody clever at passing the buck. Upwards. Or downwards. He doesn't care as long as he saves his own skin.'

So her hunch had been right. She did not feel unduly concerned because she was pretty adept herself at saving her own skin. It was a purely technical problem and she would solve it. What worried her more was the personal aspect. She wanted them to like her. Simple. It wasn't too much to ask, was it?

Trevor took her out to lunch. Still talking shop for which she was grateful. She hoped she was wrong for she could do without complications in her private life but the worrying feeling persisted that Trevor was latching on to her, manoeuvring her into an impossible position before pouncing.

She'd caught the look he gave her on more than one occasion and she wasn't a complete innocent, far from it. She knew exactly what it meant.

Oh God . . . that would really mess things up if he started getting ideas.

The company car, her own choice, a dark blue BMW, was still like an expensive new toy and she was childishly thrilled with it. She parked outside the cottage, stilled the engine and sat a moment, delighting in the new car smell of it, wondering if that swine Ben Chambers had noticed it yet. It didn't quite match up to the Porsche of course but it was more than good enough for her.

She had to sort through some estimates this evening for improvements to the cottage, rather boring essentials, things that she could go ahead with now she could afford them. In addition, she had brought work home and, in trying to shut the car door, one of the files slipped her grasp and fell onto the narrow verge. Almost in slow motion, she watched as a couple of sheets of paper fluttered off in the freshening breeze.

'Shit,' she said, comically dallying as she debated what to do.

'I've got them, it's all right—' the sound of running feet before a young girl appeared, clutching the papers triumphantly, waving them aloft. 'Are they important?'

• Patricia Fawcett

'Not that important but I wouldn't have wanted to lose them.' Jenny smiled as she took them from her. 'Thanks.'

'That's OK. Want any help?' she volunteered as, foolishly, Jenny attempted to off-load four heavy files, her briefcase and a carrier bag of groceries simultaneously.

'Thanks again. Could you carry this for me?' Jenny said, handing her the groceries and leading the way through the tiny porch, filled to the brim with pot plants, into the tiny cottage.

'Wasn't it lucky I just happened to be passing?' the girl said cheerfully, following her into the kitchen, depositing the groceries on the table. 'Isn't this just fantastic? Beamed ceilings and everything.'

Pleased, Jenny showed her the living room, delighted and amused by the reaction.

'God . . . look at that fireplace! And I really love pine furniture, it's my very very favourite. It looks great. When I've got my own place, this is exactly the sort of thing I'll have. You should see our furniture at home. Dad likes *big* furniture. Colossal stuff.'

'The cottage is seventeenth century,' Jenny told her. 'It has its drawbacks, continual problems with the plumbing mainly, but I wouldn't swap it for anything. Would you like a coffee? It won't take a minute.'

'I'd love one,' the girl said, smiling broadly. She was wearing a bottom-skimming denim skirt, thick black tights and clumpy shoes. Big dark brown eyes surrounded by sooty lashes shone in her pale face. Quite obviously a lot of laughter bubbled inside her. That and a hint of rebellion. Jenny bet her parents despaired. Boys must buzz round her like flies.

'My name's Emily. Emily Finch,' she said, artlessly following her into the kitchen as Jenny busied with the coffee, 'My dad's called Stephen and he's an architect and my sister's Abby. She's just eighteen. I'm seventeen . . . well . . . almost. My mother left us four years ago. She went off with this geeky guy ages younger than her. They're both opera singers. She's a terrific mezzo-soprano. It's always really irritated her that I can't sing. Anyway, they live in California now, sing in Los Angeles or somewhere. I've got some of her programmes at home. I'll bring them round sometime for you to look at. What do you think of the village? Oh, I suppose you love it . . . I think it's a bit of a dump. I'm the youngest person here, unless you count a couple of babies at that cottage by the pub. Twin boys.'

Jenny smiled. Emily had obviously wasted no time in doing an inventory of the village's inhabitants.

'By the way, in case you're wondering who I am, we're the people who've just moved into Curwin Hall.'

'I imagined you must be,' Jenny said, a little taken aback at the depth of information imparted in just a few minutes. She didn't often meet youngsters like this and it made her feel her age, dammit. 'We've been watching all the toing and froing of the workmen with interest. Plumbers. Builders. Decorators. It's been the talk of the village for weeks. We knew that somebody must be moving in fairly soon. It'll be nice to see it occupied again. It's a very beautiful house.'

'It's Dad's dream house. I'm not that keen. I like brand-new stuff. If he'd wanted, he could have designed us something really fantastic, bang up to the minute. Anyway . . .' she drew breath, 'I might go to see Mum soon if I can persuade Dad to pay for the trip. My sister works in a travel agent's in Preston so I could get a discount. It costs a lot though, even with that.'

'I should think it does. Your father will have to be extremely generous.'

'He is,' Emily said, taking the cup of coffee. 'Thank you. I can wind him round my little finger. All I have to say is that it's desperate that I talk to Mum. Female stuff, you know. He gets a bit hot round the collar when you start hinting at things like that.'

Jenny laughed, couldn't help it.

'Poor man,' she said with feeling. Coping alone with two nubile young women couldn't be easy.

'So . . . what do you do then?' Emily asked with unembarrassed directness, not waiting for a reply. 'That's a terrific car you drive. What with that and that Porsche I've seen cruising around and Dad's Mercedes,' she rolled her eyes, 'it's real executive stuff round here, isn't it? Are there any locals?' she asked, again leaving no time for Jenny to answer. 'I'm hoping Dad'll buy me something really great to drive when I've passed my test. Abby just wanted a little car she could park easily but then she's like that. No style, my sister.'

• Patricia Fawcett

'So you're going to learn to drive soon?' Jenny watched her with amusement. Oh God, it seemed for ever ago that she was that age. She had not enjoyed being seventeen herself, not under the circumstances. Quickly, she pushed that thought from her mind.

'Too busy. Studying for my exams,' she said. 'Dad thinks I should be poring over books the whole time. You wouldn't know I was practically seventeen, the way he thinks I should have no social life. It's one party after another because a lot of my friends are coming up to eighteen but Dad pulls this face when I want to go. I don't know why he bothers. It's a waste of time. I haven't a hope in hell of passing anything.' Her forced laugh didn't fool Jenny. 'Why worry? Life's too short. Something will turn up. I can always be a model although I'm probably too fat.' Her quick smile was quite disarming. 'Did you say what you did?'

'I'm sorry.' Jenny drew breath, on behalf of Emily as much as herself. 'I'm Jenny Sweetman and I'm an analytical chemist. I work for CWC – Cedric Witcham Chemicals, that is. The factory's near Preston, the Longridge side. We're involved with making things for the food industry.'

'Wow.' Emily seemed overawed. 'You don't look scientific. I mean . . . all the people I know who are doing science are real nerds.'

Jenny smiled, not in the least offended. 'We come in all shapes and sizes,' she said. 'It's pretty routine stuff most of the time although now I'm in management it's a bit different.'

Emily, having finished her coffee, fished in the floppy fabric bag she had with her, and produced a card.

'Invitation,' she said, handing it over. 'To our house-warming party. Dress informal,' she added. 'Will you be able to come?'

Jenny glanced at it. 'I hope so,' she said, 'but I can't guarantee it. It depends if I'm away on business or not.'

'Hope you can,' Emily said, standing up to go, hesitating a moment. 'Do you think he'll be able to come? The guy who drives the Porsche? What's his name by the way?'

'Ben Chambers,' Jenny said brightly, heart sinking a notch. 'I have no idea about his social diary,' she added, feeling sure she was giving something away as she caught Emily's expression.

She had the uncomfortable feeling that Emily knew what was what.

She hoped to goodness the child did not have any designs on Ben. Ben Chambers might be a number-one bastard but she didn't think he'd stoop to sixteen-year-olds. She'd give him the benefit of the doubt on that one.

They sounded as if they might be a nice family and she looked forward to meeting Emily's father – Stephen hadn't she said? – and her sister, Abby. She would make a special effort to be available for the party.

9

Harold was trying to worm his way into moving permanently into her house in Hargreaves Street. Christine knew that but she was keeping him at arm's length. She had no trouble fending off any number of hints he might make. Reg wouldn't have approved. He and Harold had never quite hit it off.

Two separate houses. One person in each of them. It did seem daft when you thought about it but Christine couldn't make her mind up. At his age, it seemed crackers to be thinking about moving. As he often said, he could be dead next year and nobody would bat an eyelid when it happened. He reckoned he'd had a good enough innings, seventy-nine not out. Naturally enough, for someone with his professional experience, he'd already made the arrangements for his funeral. Church service, hymns already selected, followed by cremation with a nice commemorative plaque at the crematorium, one that she could put flowers in. He'd thought of everything, Harold.

She'd always thought he would be buried like Reg but then it was such a personal thing, wasn't it? And not something she was entirely comfortable discussing. There was room for her beside Reg or on top of him, she wasn't sure, but somehow that idea appealed to her less and less as the years passed. She might opt for a simple cremation herself without a separate church service, although that would make poor Reg turn in his grave. He'd had no time for unbelievers.

Harold's Victorian house was grander than hers but harder to maintain with all those draughty rooms going to waste and that big expanse of garden. She never had understood why he'd taken it on but then he used to have big ideas when he was younger. As

• Patricia Fawcett

for her little house . . . there was nothing wrong with it, cosily sandwiched in the middle of the row. A neat little terrace of Accrington red-brick houses just off the Blackpool Road and she could be on Moor Park in a few minutes when she fancied a walk. They'd done the street up, new paving and whatnot, parking bays, stuck a few little trees here and there, brightened things up a treat. Who needed a garden? Gave you a bad back, gardening. She had her yard and she kept a few tubs there in summer. She didn't care as long as there was room for her deck chair so that she could sit and sun herself on hot days. She liked a tan. Made you look healthy, a tan. Stuff what they said. They were always on at you to stop doing something or other. Got on your wick, they did. Look at Reg – he had smoked like a factory chimney all his life and then died of a brain haemorrhage.

Remembering, Christine sighed as Harold turned the car into the street and parked in the slot outside her door, the last notes of the hymn he had been singing fading as he did so. They'd been to a community hall today for the table top and there'd been a good turn-out. Harold switched the engine off, fiddled about a minute with this and that and waited. They sat a moment in silence which she knew she would be the first to break. He had the patience of a saint, Harold. Slow metabolism he once said. He was the sort who'd live to be a hundred. What is the secret of living to be a hundred? they'd ask him. Singing hymns and being a pain in the neck to my sister, he'd say.

She glanced at him irritably.

'Well?' she asked. 'Are you bothering to take the stuff home or shall we just leave it in my front room wrapped up? We have that giant car boot next week.'

'As you wish.'

Exasperated, she clicked her tongue. He drove this car like he was still in a funeral procession. Two speeds. Slow and dead slow. He was always followed by a queue of traffic.

'Do you want to stay for tea?' she asked. 'It's only tuna sandwiches and some cake. Oh, and I've got a lovely piece of tasty Lancashire and cream crackers. And maybe a slice of my apple pie.'

'Thank you, Christine, I will partake,' he said, a twinkle in his eye. 'I never can resist your pie.'

She snorted. 'It's true what they say, the way to a man's heart is through his stomach.'

The front door opened immediately into the sitting room, the room that used to be called the parlour, that she rarely used. A softly green room, dominated by a hefty multi-cushioned three-piece suite in green Dralon with gold fringing and a few pieces of dark polished furniture. A very tasteful green and cream striped Regency wallpaper and a good quality fitted carpet also in green. It was a little chill for she never lit the fire in here except on Christmas Day and she didn't have central heating. Reg would never entertain it. That dry heat was bad for your chest he used to say. She and Harold went through it, the furniture showroom, without a second glance, into the back place.

Another three-piece suite, pink this time, with space for the old piano that Reg used to play and she hadn't the heart to get rid of, and, sitting importantly on a modern corner unit, the new television set. The gate-leg table was to one side, seldom used now because it was such a nuisance making the room for it when it was extended. They'd used it when there were the three of them.

All in all, the room was a bit cluttered, she supposed, weaving her way through, but it was cosy. They used to have a real fire but, when Reg died, she soon got fed up with that and got herself a gas one. Real flame effect in a lovely wooden surround. Reg would never have agreed to it. Cleaning out the fire everyday and resetting it was one of life's little rituals. He'd loved his routine.

Bending down, she switched the gas full on because she felt cold after the stint at the community centre, left Harold sitting in the swivel rocking chair that was fast becoming his and went into the little kitchen to make the tea.

She washed and dried her hands, listened out for him starting up the singing and sure enough it only took a few minutes. The Twenty-third Psalm. One of his favourites. He had a lovely deep voice, Harold. Very tuneful.

'What did we make today?' she asked, popping her head round the door and interrupting him.

'About forty pounds,' he said solemnly. 'Got rid of some stuff we've had hanging about for a long time too. I'll have to be thinking of replacing some stock.'

• Patricia Fawcett

She let him carry on counting the money and retired to the kitchen, spreading doilies on the plates, cutting the wafer-thin sandwiches into neat triangles. Tuna and mayonnaise. And egg and cress. A couple of nice chunks of cheese and some pickles. She cut three slices of the chocolate cake Harold liked and a couple of generous portions of her home-made apple pie. He could have a spot of cream with it if he fancied. There, now all there was to do was make a big pot of tea. She whirled round and there he was in the doorway, hovering. Sneaked up on you sometimes, Harold, looking hushed and expectant. It was all the years of having to be sober and serious, sympathy was etched into every line in his face. She remembered how he'd been a tower of strength when Reg died. He'd been a credit to his profession and no mistake.

'I thought we might have a talk,' he said, 'whenever you're ready.'

She gave him a look. He had a long face, quite a prominent chin, and was proud that he'd not lost his hair as most of his acquaintances had. The droopy moustache had come and gone over the years. She was fond of him, she supposed, in a way, although whether she could stomach him living here, day in and day out, with all those macabre recollections of his was another matter. Some things she'd just rather not know about.

She often wondered why he'd never married. He would never talk about that. There had been one young lady over fifty years ago who had ditched him very nearly at the altar and married somebody else. A butcher from the Co-op and even now she didn't like to mention the Co-op, not to Harold. It had caused a rare old family rumpus, had that. Their mother, Lily, had not been the faint-hearted type, far from it. She had to be restrained from going round and leathering the lass for doing that to her poor Harold. The air round their little house had been blue for weeks with the cursing. The frocks had been made and everything. Christine remembered being put out herself because, at six years old, she was looking forward to being a bridesmaid.

'Now you listen to me, Harold, it has to be thought through carefully,' she said to him, once they were sitting down, eating. 'We don't want to make a mistake, not at our age.' Nor, to be honest, did she want to be lumbered with looking after him if he took bad, but she wasn't about to say that.

'As it is, it's nice to have you visit – lovely – but you do go home afterwards. We have to ask would we get on each other's nerves? There isn't a lot of room in this house, you'd have to sell off your furniture, and how would two of us manage in that kitchen? You can't swing a cat round in it and you know how you like to do a spot of cooking. We'd be falling over one another, wouldn't we? Admit it now.'

He smiled, a rare occurrence. He still had his own teeth and was proud of that too. Big and yellow, they were, and he looked quite different when he did get round to smiling.

'I've always admired your frankness, Christine love,' he said. 'However, on this occasion, I didn't have our proposed accommodation arrangements in mind. I know you like to keep abreast of what's happening so I thought you'd like to know that I've been to see Jenny up at Hazelburn and she's got some news.'

She bit into a sandwich, placed the remainder of it neatly on her plate.

'Jenny? Our Jenny?' she repeated foolishly, taken by surprise. 'Oh you have, have you? And how was she?'

'She's been promoted,' he said. 'Quality Assurance Manager now. Twenty or so under her. Company car as well and, when she goes down to London, the company pays for the flight. Imagine that! Reg would be tickled pink she's done so well.'

'Hmmm . . .' Christine pursed her lips. 'I suppose you could say she's done well for herself,' she conceded reluctantly, 'even if it is a queer job she does.'

'Scientific,' Harold said with a satisfied nod. 'Very commendable, Christine. I know you both wanted her to go into an office, get married, but it wasn't to be, was it? Let me tell you, she looks ever so well these days, and she lives in a right bonny little village. I'm partial to that Forest of Bowland, a grand place.'

'Don't start trying to butter me up,' she told him with a sniff. 'She let us down and there's nothing more to be said. After you know what, we did our best to make things right. You've heard it a thousand times but it still needs saying. Reg set his heart on her working at the office, went to all the trouble of asking his boss, and then, when it's arranged bar the final shout, what does she do but say no. It made Reg look such a fool. Ungrateful madam.' She gave a small shudder.

'Don't you dare look at me like that,' she went on firmly, in her stride now. 'You know nothing about it, our Harold. You've never had children of your own.' She was sorry to have to say it but he needed telling sometimes. 'All the upset, one thing after another, I blame that for Reg going so sudden. You hear about all this stress, what it can do. The plain truth was he couldn't face going into work and telling that Mr Thorpe.'

Harold frowned. 'No,' he said, his voice as calm as ever, 'you can't blame Jenny for that. Stress doesn't cause a brain haemorrhage. Don't forget it was a bad time for her, coming as it did just after she'd given up her baby and all. She was as upset as you.'

'You could have fooled me. She can be selfish.' She eyed Harold closely, knowing she was fighting a losing battle. Soft devil. Jenny could twist him round her little finger. 'So what's it like then? This fancy cottage of hers? Not good enough for her to live round here, is it? Her with her university degree and all.'

He sighed, twiddled his moustache. 'It's grand and no mistake. Only little but she's done it up nice. Bit of a garden at the back although she's not much of a gardener.'

'Can't expect her to be good at everything,' Christine said, irritated at the remark. Harold thought nobody could look after a garden like him. That was another thing. He'd have to say goodbye to that if he came to live with her. He wasn't getting his hands on her tubs, not under any circumstances.

'Why can't you let bygones be bygones? The child only wanted to do the best she could,' he said. 'What's wrong with that? Some parents would be proud. Most parents would be. I never did understand you and Reg taking on about it.'

She ignored that.

'She's nearly thirty-six and what has she got to show for it?' she asked, firing on all cylinders now. 'I don't hold with career women. She should have got herself married. I could have been a grandmother by now,' she went on, feeling herself soften at the very idea. 'There's some lovely little frocks in Marks & Spencer for babies. All my friends are grandmas by now,' she added, aware it sounded daft. Childish. 'If she would shape herself

The Absent Child

before it's too late ... Too busy now to think about that although she wasn't too busy then, was she? How could we keep it a secret? Something like that? It made him a laughing stock, Reg, him so pious and everything. And I couldn't face them at the hairdresser's for weeks. My hair was a real sight by the time I did pluck up courage to go back. Nobody mentioned it. Not a word. But they all knew. There were looks.' She drew a deep shuddering breath, the memory sharp and intense.

'Are you still thinking about that?' he said gently. 'That's water under the bridge, love. It's a long time ago.'

'It's yesterday.' She held his gaze before pushing the apple pie towards him. 'Want cream on it?' she asked.

10

Stephen had had a couple of lightweight affairs since his divorce – never anything remotely serious – and it was becoming an irritation that his relationship with Clare Forrest was in acute danger of becoming serious if he didn't put a stop to it. He blamed the confusion fairly and squarely on himself for he had allowed Clare to mistake his intentions.

It had all started when he was under particular pressure at work, angling for new contracts abroad that, in the end, had proved extremely lucrative. His mind half on his work then, he had scarcely noticed the acceleration of the 'dates' with Clare. He had known her for a long time, in a casual way, knowing her ex-husband Roger rather better, for he and Roger went back a long way in architectural circles. They had studied together at the Architectural Association in London, qualified at the same time as Associates of the Royal Institute of British Architects. Roger had swanned off thereafter to somewhere in the Home Counties, and he and Lizzie to Wales.

Following on from that, he and Lizzie, Roger and Clare, had met up at various dos and Roger left her shortly after Lizzie left him so that's how it started. A mutual misery. The girls quite liked her, Stephen thought, although they didn't say much. Frankly, there was little about Clare to dislike for she was a very agreeable woman. Irritatingly agreeable. No sparks with her. Compared to Lizzie, she was like a damp squib. When he moved to Preston, she had moved too, ostensibly to be nearer to her mother, although he ought to have seen through that.

They couldn't continue as they were, going nowhere. If Clare was expecting something of him then he was sorry but it was out of the question and it was time he told her so. He would have done it before but she was so damned emotional and he hated tears. Lizzie had known the power of tears.

He was meeting her for lunch shortly and then they were driving over to the coast to visit her mother at the nursing home. God, what a social calendar he had! He glanced out of the window at a softly blue sky with just a few fluffs of cloud, discarding his jacket as a result. The dark slacks and pale blue Pringle sweater would do admirably for nursing home visiting. Clare's mother would not approve of course. Dammit, she had told him off once for not wearing a tie, told Clare off for not wearing stockings on a blistering hot day last summer.

Smiling at the memory, he picked up his car keys and went downstairs, calling to the girls that he was off. His footsteps echoed across the tiled hall, acres of it, and he took a final delighted glance at it as he closed the door. The novelty of living at Curwin Hall had not worn off yet and the pleasure he felt in it was very satisfying as he tried to see it as others might see it when they came to this house-warming party the girls were thrusting on him.

One thing was sure, Clare would never set foot in this place, for he knew she was itching to do so, reduced to throwing out unsubtle hints now. Dammit, he would tell her today. And next time, for there would surely be someone else, he would tread more carefully. He couldn't imagine being without a woman for ever. He needed a woman. Someone like Lizzie. Or rather, not quite like Lizzie.

'There's more tissues in the glove box,' he said tersely as they approached the nursing home. The nearer they got, the louder Clare wept. He regretted that he was not in the mood for being sympathetic. Frankly, she had got on his nerves over lunch. For a start, never mind what she said about being just good friends, she had held onto him in the restaurant in a most proprietorial manner.

'I'm sure Mother would be pleased, aren't you? If she really knew what was going on, that is,' she said now, between little sniffs.

'Pleased about what?' he said, determined to be bloody awkward for the entire day.

'About us.' She controlled her voice a little. 'I'm quite sure she would give us her blessing. She likes you, Stephen.'

'She thinks I'm Roger half the time.'

'She likes you,' Clare persisted. 'And I do believe the boys are at last coming to terms with it. With you and me. And after all, Roger's got himself settled with someone else so it's high time I forgot him. And the same applies to you,' she finished, laying a hand on his knee. 'Lizzie's gone and you have to face up to it.'

'Can we talk about this later?' he said, forcing a smile. 'We're here.'

Gaining admittance to the nursing home was akin to getting into Fort Knox. Getting out again was another story. The receptionist/nurse was new and greeted them with a smile.

'You've come to see Mrs Colclough?' She looked down at her list. 'Ah yes it's Mr and Mrs Forrest, isn't it?'

'Well . . .' Clare blushed, pushed at the hair that was forever falling in front of her face. 'This is my . . . er, um . . .'

He grinned, held out his hand to the somewhat bemused young woman.

'Stephen Finch. I'm a friend of the family,' he said, coming gallantly to the rescue.

Clare looked up at him gratefully, even though he had been sorely tempted to say something outrageous. Boyfriend would have upset her. Gentleman friend smacked of something dubious. Partner was too bloody politically correct. Lover . . . ? He smiled to himself at that. The nearest they'd got to that were a few panicky sessions in Clare's bed when the kids were out for the evening at a friend's. Clare had worried sick. Worried that they might come home early. Worried even when the damned cat started to scratch at the door. Urged him to hurry up and that had been the kiss of death of course. He did not want to hurry up when he made love to a woman. He wanted to take his time so that they both enjoyed it. Hadn't it always been that way with Lizzie? Or rather, it had been that way in the early days. They hadn't raced against the clock. He couldn't think now why he and Clare had bothered. It wasn't as if either of them had much enthusiasm for it and

• Patricia Fawcett

Clare had none of Lizzie's charms, her warmth or her sense of fun.

Mrs Colclough was in the residents' lounge, a high-ceilinged elegant room decorated in shades of green, heavy velvet curtains framing the long narrow windows. Stephen followed Clare through, hoping to God the old dear would be a little more *compos mentis* today. The nursing home catered specifically for the needs of aged people like Clare's mother so that a great many of the occupants were in a similar bewildered state. Memory needle well and truly jammed. Short-term memory non-existent but older events recalled in startlingly vivid detail. As Clare said, you had to look for the humour in the situation or you would weep. Which didn't of course stop her.

'Do sit down,' Mrs Colclough said graciously. 'How are you today, Roger? Where's your jacket?'

'In the car,' he said, exchanging a quick glance with Clare as they perched opposite the old lady. He had given up long since on the explanations. It was easier to play along with it.

Clare, bright-eyed now with not a tear in sight, twittered on. The usual. Nothing of interest happened to Clare from one week to the next. She was something to do with insurance although he'd never been sufficiently interested to fathom just what. The chat moved on to the boys, dour individuals too, both of whom seemed to regard him with great suspicion.

The old lady listened, a half-smile on her face, although Stephen wondered just how much was getting through to her. If any of it. Looking round the room, at the largely blank faces, he felt a depression settling on him. It always had this effect. If only there could be some quick and easy switch-off when you'd reached the end of your useful days. What was the point of existing like this? It was an uneasy no man's land between life and death. They were all playing the waiting game here. Every week there was one face missing, a new face to replace it.

'Forty-eight and you're eighty-four, Mother,' Clare's voice broke into his thoughts. 'You'll be eighty-five in June.'

'Oh no. That's not right.' The old lady looked disconcertingly at him, as if she could read his mind. 'She's wrong, isn't she? I'm older than that, aren't I, Roger? I must be . . .' the concentration was immense, 'sixty-nine, I think. Is that ginger cake?' She leaned over and picked up a piece, wrapping it in her handkerchief with painstaking care. 'I'll have it later,' she told them with a smile, placing it in the big old shiny leather handbag that accompanied her everywhere.

Wondering what else was in the handbag, he exchanged a helpless glance with Clare. The old lady chatted on, muddled thoughts about long-lost family members, and they let it waft over them a minute until she became agitated and insistent, requiring an answer to a question.

'Mother's speaking to you. Asking what you do for a living,' Clare said, and Stephen returned his attention to Mrs Colclough, looking into the surprisingly alert eyes. It was difficult to imagine what scrambled thoughts were going on underneath the tightly permed white hair. She was prettily made up, with lipstick and a covering of face powder, her nails manicured and painted pale pink. Smelling of something flowery. Wearing a flowery frock. The corridors smelled of flowery disinfectant. The nursing home was called Rose Head.

'I'm an architect, Mrs Colclough,' he told her, his attention straying to a couple opposite who visited regularly too. They had the right idea. They rarely exchanged a word with their aged relative, merely dealt the cards as soon as they arrived and had a few hotly contested rounds.

'An architect? What a coincidence.' She beamed, clutched Clare's arm with delight. 'Fancy you knowing two architects. She's married to one. He's called Roger as well, Roger,' she added and, as there was no sane answer to that, Stephen said nothing. His charade smashed, it was wiser to say nothing. If he got out of here alive, he vowed, he was never coming back. This was it. The last time.

Clare wept again on the way home. She was riddled with guilt of course. A painfully slim lady with a fine-featured face. Big disappointed eyes and very fine, unruly blonde hair. Lizzie had always been so neat, sometimes wearing her hair swept severely off her face, a style only beautiful women could get away with.

'Of course you can't possibly look after your mother,' he said, by means of consolation. Dammit, he did feel sorry for Clare. 'It's out of the question. Because she doesn't know who she is half the time, you'd have to keep her under lock and key. How could you do that? Imprison her? You have a full-time job and a family to look after and you couldn't cope. Could you?'

'No. You're quite right.' She sighed, momentarily relieved. 'I always want to bring her home with me but it's an absurd idea. Thanks for coming with me, Stephen . . .' She leaned slightly towards him as he drove and he rued his indecision. She was going to take it hard. Tears were definitely on the agenda.

'It's a good home,' he went on, still feeling a need to console. 'Your mother's very happy there. She's clean and comfortable and well fed.' He paused, wondering if she realised how awful that sounded. When she made no comment, he pursued the point vigorously. 'Under the circumstances, it's the best possible solution. For you and for your mother. You can see the staff care.'

'Yes they do. They are very kind.'

She blew her nose hard and then lapsed into what he felt was a worried silence and he was happy to leave her to it. Frankly, much as he sympathised, he had enough problems of his own. He felt badly about spoiling Abby's birthday and was especially irritated at Lizzie for missing it.

It would have been difficult for him, Lizzie staying, but it would have been worth the small sacrifice on his part for Abby to see her mother. Lizzie ought to have tried. Her career should have taken second place on this occasion. He was under no illusions. She probably wouldn't make it for Emily's birthday either. In that sense, she showed no favouritism. Treated both of them equally badly.

'Here we are then. It's seemed such a long journey today.' Clare started to unbuckle her seat belt as they turned into the road where she lived. A pleasant leafy avenue of solid semi-detached houses. 'Can you come in a minute?' she asked with a smile. 'The children are out. Cricket practice followed by tea at a friend's. They won't be in until later.'

He nodded, not happy. He couldn't stand many more Saturdays like this. The truth had to be faced. He had been using this poor woman and, by the sin of omission, had led her to believe that she meant something to him.

It was hard to understand what he did wrong. Here he was, undoubtedly successful in his career, dynamic, decisive, reliable and here he was, too, unbelievably naïve and crass when it came to dealing with women. Lizzie had knocked his confidence in this damned department.

'Sit down and I'll make coffee,' she said, showing him into the sitting room. 'Bobby will entertain you.'

They eyed each other suspiciously, he and the cat, a snowy heap of fur but, mercifully, the cat decided against gracing him with his presence, remaining curled on the cushion of the most comfortable-looking chair. Stephen looked round the room, a bit untidy like the lady herself, a lived-in room, so full of clutter the gracious proportions were dwarfed. Catching sight of a family photograph on a bookshelf, just Clare and the children, Stephen sighed.

He liked Clare but, sometimes recently as he'd come to know her better, he thought he understood why Roger had upped and left. There was no fun in Clare. No joy. She was destined to be more or less miserable all her life like so many of the tragic heroines in Lizzie's operas. A wistful aria would have gone down a treat this afternoon. Lizzie had been wonderful with them. She had known how to wring out the emotion to the last drop. She had a quality in her voice that could make a man weep.

'Stephen . . . there's something I have to say,' Clare began as they drank their coffee. She had plumped, not for the sofa beside him, but, rather to his surprise, a chair opposite. 'I think it's been building up for a time but I've been trying not to . . . not to acknowledge it, I suppose . . . and I feel a bit of a fool now, making all these assumptions and everything when you've never said a word.'

'About what?' he smiled, warming instantly to her embarrassment. 'You're upset,' he said. 'You're always upset on Saturdays.'

'I want to call it off, Stephen,' she said, flushing beetroot, blowing at the hair that had wafted across her face. 'Before *you* do . . .'

That made him sit up.

'But . . .' he struggled for sense, 'this afternoon you said—'

'I know what I said.' She was calm, much more in control than she had been all day. 'And then, at the nursing home

• Patricia Fawcett

I got thinking. Yes I know I talked all the time but I wasn't concentrating on that. I was looking at you and thinking. Thinking about Roger. Mother kept calling you Roger, mistaking you for him and it suddenly dawned . . .' she bit her lip, managed a rather beautiful smile, 'I wished that he'd been there with me. Sorry . . . I still love him, Stephen. Isn't it pathetic? If I can't have Roger then that's it. Anything else would be second best. And I don't want second best. I'm not doing this for the children. I'm doing it for me. You do understand?'

'No. Not quite.' It took a moment to say it as it dawned that she was offering him a way out.

'You still love Lizzie,' she told him softly. 'Oh yes you do, Stephen.'

'I still keep tabs on her but that's because of the girls,' he said, wondering why he was denying his feelings. 'I still talk about her because she's part of my life. Poor Lizzie. She'll never do what she wanted to do. Not now.'

'She always had a big opinion of her own talent,' Clare commented, probably not meaning to sound unkind. 'Personally, I thought her very good. She had a wonderful presence on stage, you found your eyes drawn to her. Roger was always terribly impressed too.'

Stephen nodded, ridiculously pleased.

'I wish she could have reached the top of her profession, for her sake. She always wanted to sing a principal role at one of the major opera houses. That was her dream. I wish she could have done that. She would have been absolutely superb. I would have been so very proud. The girls too.'

Clare smiled. 'See what I mean?' she said. 'Admit it, Stephen. You still love her, don't you?' The smile was a little tremulous now.

'I don't know,' he admitted. 'Maybe you're right, Clare, about you and me. It wasn't going anywhere, was it?'

She shook her head, turning as the gate crashed open and the boys ran full pelt up the path into the house and up the stairs.

'Oh, I didn't expect them back for ages,' she said. 'Just as well we weren't . . . you know . . .'

She smiled and for the first time almost, it was a genuine smile.

'Just as well,' he said, returning her smile. 'Well . . . if you're quite sure that's what you want, I'll leave you then.'

'Let's stay friends,' she whispered, as she kissed him goodbye.

11

'Mr Harding didn't usually bring documents for typing so late in the day,' her secretary said, not even bothering to disguise the sulky tone.

Without a word, Jenny dropped the files on the girl's desk. If she heard anyone else mention the dearly beloved departed, she would scream. They were short-staffed. Len was off ill, and seemed to have annoyingly and perhaps deliberately arranged things so that nobody knew for sure what the set-up was in his unit. That would have to be sorted out and fast but she hadn't the time to do it herself. The truth was this lot were a shiftless bunch and if she was to do the shaking up, she would not win any prizes in a popularity contest.

The phone was ringing when she got back into her office and she snatched it up, her irritation showing in her voice.

'Caught you at a bad time?' Trevor enquired. 'You sound bloody pissed off.'

'I am,' she said sweetly. 'I'm getting damned little co-operation, that's why. And I could do without that directive about smoking that's just come through. There are mutinous mutterings afoot. Practically all the lab staff smoke – they seem to think they have a God-given right to spend time in the rest room, smoking.'

'I'm sorry about that. It's the way of the world, Jenny, and they'll have to learn to live with it. I have to, for Christ's sake, when I come up. It doesn't do my nerves any good either.'

'It's unpopular and, because it's come just now, it looks as if I've initiated it, doesn't it? John Harding, bless his sainted memory, would never have dared.'

• Patricia Fawcett

She jabbed a pencil on a pad, broke the lead, tossed it down. Laughed suddenly at her own bad humour.

Trevor laughed too. 'Pin the notice on the board and sod them. No technical problems then?'

'Not as such.' She sat back, tried to calm herself.

She was due at this house-warming party at Curwin Hall tonight and feeling as she did, tense with work worries, she was not looking forward to it that much. She would be rotten company.

'I shall be at the meeting on Tuesday, Trevor,' she told him, consulting her diary. 'Is that what you need to know? I did ask Rose to confirm but she's probably not got round to doing it yet. She's complaining. It would seem I'm giving her too much work.'

'Do her good. She had it too easy before. Harding's got a lot to answer for. Will you be staying over at the usual hotel?'

'I will. Just the one night,' she said, as somewhere a little warning note sounded. 'I'll catch the morning shuttle next day.'

'Good. Maybe we can meet for dinner?'

'Dinner? Just the two of us?' She instantly regretted the enquiry but it was too late. It was said.

'Hell, no. There'll be quite a gang of us. We'll sink four bottles of wine at least.'

If he was amused at her assumption, he did not let it show and, embarrassed at her gaffe, she was grateful for that.

Curwin Hall with its tall, clipped yews and balled gateposts was half hidden from the road, splendidly positioned as it was on the lower slopes of the fell, the hills beyond a perfect natural enhancement. On the market for some time at a staggering price, it deserved to be lived in again and was already happily casting off that hint of neglect that had threatened. The lawns were cut and someone had taken a hoe to the shabby flowerbeds. The evening air, still quite warm after an unseasonably sunny day, smelled sweet.

Halfway up the curving drive, Jenny, clattering along on higher heeled shoes than normal, hesitated a minute as the house had a very quiet look about it, but, as someone might have seen her from one of the upper windows, she hadn't much choice but to plough on and commit the worst crime of all. Arrive first.

'Oh good, you could make it,' Emily said, pulling her inside and closing the door. 'You're early. Nobody else is here yet.'

'Oh dear . . .' Jenny said, fighting an impulse to use a stronger expletive. She slipped off her coat, handed it to Emily, taking in, in a single fascinated glance, the magnificent red-carpeted elegant staircase. 'I lost the invitation and couldn't remember what time you'd said so I . . .' She stopped, realising she was making matters worse by twittering on, as she caught sight of the man who must be Emily's father coming to greet her.

They shook hands and Emily, wearing a very short velvety skirt and skimpy luminous green top, grinned at them both.

'Jenny lives at that white cottage, Dad, right at the beginning of the village,' she said. 'One of the villagers told me it's supposed to be haunted.'

'Is it?' Jenny looked at her in astonishment. 'It's the first I've heard.'

She was glad she'd worn the smart black dress with some discreet jewellery, fiddled a little more than usual with her hair so that it was in an elegant topknot with wispy bits at the side. She was very conscious of the man beside her, aware that he was looking at her, aware what the look meant. If Trevor Cummings had looked at her like that, she'd have clocked him one and be hanged to the consequences. A little unexpected tingling and the beginnings of a smile warned her that she was reacting like a silly schoolgirl. Just because he happened to be very attractive and had a wonderfully firm grip and a devastating smile was no excuse. She'd been caught that way before. Most recently with that prize shit Ben Chambers who would no doubt turn up this evening to grace them with his presence.

'Ghosts?' He smiled gently at his daughter, a fond father smile. 'Emily always picks up on stories like that,' he said, leading Jenny through to what he called the drawing room. She looked round with interest. She had never seen the interior of the house and was every bit as impressed as she thought she would be. With the huge squashy sofas, heavy drapes and appropriately large pieces of furniture, it was both gracious and traditional, thank God, for, hearing that he was an architect, she had worried that he might do something fearfully modern to it.

'Drink?' he asked, crossing to a small table on which there was a sherry decanter and glasses.

'Thank you. How are you settling in?' she asked as he brought it to her. 'You and your daughters?'

'Very well,' he said, sitting opposite. His shoes, she noted in passing, were highly polished. He was rather formally attired, in a beautifully cut suit and crisp white shirt. 'Have you met Abby yet, my older daughter?'

Jenny shook her head. 'No, but I've heard about her from Emily.'

'Oh, have you?' He sighed, smiled. 'You must forgive Emily. She never stops once she gets started. What exactly did she say?'

'I get the impression, although I could be quite wrong of course, that Abby's a different sort of girl,' she told him. 'Quieter? It doesn't surprise me. Sisters are often different, aren't they?'

'They are indeed. Our girls are anyway.' He cocked his head as footsteps clicked outside. 'That's Abby now. You'll see for yourself.'

She came into the room, wearing a simple mid-calf-length blue dress that seemed a touch old for her. She had blue eyes and her hair was not so dark as her sister's, surprisingly fair in fact. The only resemblance seemed to be in the smile, a similar smile that reached her eyes.

'It's nice to meet you, Miss Sweetman,' she said, coming across and shaking her hand. 'Emily's given out invitations to everybody so we don't know for sure who's coming. The buffet will feed the five thousand just in case.'

'Some people from work are coming along,' Stephen explained, a little apologetically, 'but I've warned them they must not talk shop. Ah . . . that might be them now.'

His disappearing to welcome them meant Jenny and Abby were alone a moment.

'Emily's very impressed with you,' Abby said, helping herself to an orange juice. 'Impressed at what you do for a living.'

Jenny smiled. 'Is she really? I find it very interesting but it won't appeal to everyone. Science never does. In fact, it bores most people rigid. What do *you* do, Abby?' she asked, before she remembered that Emily had already told her. 'Oh, it's a travel agent's, isn't it?'

'In town. I enjoy it. I've just booked someone on a round-the-world cruise today. It's to celebrate their ruby wedding anniversary. Isn't that wonderful?'

'Wonderful,' Jenny agreed. 'Maybe I'll pay you a visit sometime, if I can get myself organised for a summer break. I'm afraid I can't stretch to a round-the-world cruise; it'll have to be something more modest.'

'Whatever, I'll be pleased to see you.'

Abby whirled round as people came in, chattering. For a moment, Ben Chambers was hidden in the group but, as they dispersed, he was revealed in his full puffed-out peacock splendour, wearing that smirk that passed for his smile. Jenny caught his glance and sighed her irritation. She might have known. He wouldn't pass up the chance to have a peep in this house, although with his own sleekly modern views on interiors, she didn't think he would approve of the quiet charm of this.

During the evening, which passed pleasantly enough, she caught Ben looking at Abby a couple of times. Dammit, surely not . . . ? Abby was only eighteen, a baby in Ben terms.

She also, worryingly, caught Abby looking at him, prettily flushed. Abby probably suffered all the problems associated with having a sister who was prettier and more confident than she. For a moment, Jenny wondered what it would be like to have a sister. Someone to confide in, to talk to, someone to have a quiet grumble with. It would surely have helped her with this stupid thing with Mother.

She hoped Stephen Finch didn't notice her looking at *him*. They didn't actually get to speak to each other again, not properly, not alone, but as she watched him skilfully dispensing his duties as host, she knew she would enjoy getting to know him. He seemed charming and confident but not in the slick way Ben was. He was, she knew already, just a nice uncomplicated sort of man. They were on the same wavelength. Why on earth had his wife left him?

She must be mad.

* * *

• Patricia Fawcett

Abby had had a few boyfriends but mostly they had been about her own age and, she now realised, dreadfully naïve. Because she was a more serious person than Emily, she preferred older men, was more at ease in their company. And as for Ben Chambers . . . well, Emily was right for once and she felt absurdly pleased that, despite all the eyelash fluttering and chest sticking out, Emily had made no great impact on him.

Ben had homed in on her instead. Very charming and attentive and she had, in the space of a few hours, learned a lot about him. At over six feet tall, blond, lean and agile, he appealed to her physically, and just from talking to him she got the impression he was definitely going places. With his father shortly due to retire because of ill health, he more or less ran the family business. He had been to university, graduated with a degree in Economics and, since then, he had been working in the business, something to do with printing and graphics, learning the ropes. The company had stagnated a bit in recent years but he intended to do something about that. Plans were afoot for large-scale expansion.

The Chambers family had money and he had used an inheritance from an aunt to buy the barn in the village and have it converted a couple of years ago. He also had a small flat in town that he sometimes used mid-week. He kept fit by working out at a gym, went on several holidays a year, skiing in February, a golf break in summer and somewhere hot in September. He seemed mildly amused that Abby worked in a travel agent's, seeming to assume, quite wrongly, that she did it merely to earn herself a little pocket money.

She began to tell him something about herself, but as she sensed him losing interest, did not pursue it. She would not rush it. But she felt a little glow kindle within at the way he was monopolising her, and, at the end of the evening, when he asked if she'd like to accompany him to the ballet next week, she had absolutely no hesitation in agreeing.

'How old is he then, this Porsche guy?' Emily asked, peeved, as they cleared away when the guests were finally gone. 'Honestly, you might have played a bit harder to get. You just have no idea how to deal with men. He was all over you, Abby. Go on then, how old is he?'

The Absent Child

'He's thirty,' she said, checking Dad was not within earshot. 'And I don't know what you're talking about. I did nothing to encourage him at all.'

'Thirty? Jesus! He's too old for you. He'll be thinking of getting married, settling down, having a family, really grotto things like that,' Emily said with a frown. 'Has he asked you out again?'

'He might have,' Abby smiled. 'Stop fishing.'

'Fishing? I'm only thinking of your own good,' Emily said crossly. 'He looks like he might take advantage. You're so innocent.'

'Not *that* innocent,' Abby murmured, refraining from going into details, smiling at her sister instead. 'Listen who's talking. You're the one who's going out with a brainless hunk.'

'Who told you that?' Emily asked, undismayed. 'OK, I admit Rick's not exactly blessed with brains. No conversation, but sometimes you don't need conversation, do you?' She grinned, tossing her hair back in that familiar gesture. 'I'm only going out with him to make everyone else jealous. The entire school fancies him.'

Abby smiled, thankful that, in the meantime, Ben had been forgotten.

She looked forward to the ballet and especially she looked forward to being with him once more.

12

Janice Middlebrook, Christine's next-door neighbour, looked after her little grandchild whilst her daughter, Catherine, went out to work. It had spoiled things a bit, upset their routine. Janice was widowed too, of a similar age to Christine, and they enjoyed each other's company. They used to have long uninterrupted chats at their frequent morning get-togethers, all the gossip, but since Shane had come along, first as a very fractious baby, then a troublesome toddler and now a thoroughly clumsy child, it was one long hassle.

'He's never still, from getting up to going to bed. At it all day long,' Janice said with a sigh. She was a harassed-looking woman, with short silvery hair and big glasses with fancy red frames. She favoured sparkly jewellery and, it had to be said, she was a bit on the flash side. Glittery patterned sweaters. Green pearl eye-shadow and an overabundance of mascara. Tastewise, Christine thought her a touch common, but her heart was in the right place.

'Look at the knees of them trousers,' Janice went on. 'Our Catherine just can't cope. She's had him at the doctors asking if they couldn't give him something to quieten him a bit, make him sleep.'

'Like a knockout pill?' Christine suggested.

Janice looked at her oddly. 'Of course not. The doctor said give him hot milk and read him a bedtime story. I ask you, he won't sit still long enough to listen to a page. He doesn't go to bed until midnight and then he has two hours if they're lucky. Our Catherine hasn't had a decent night's sleep since he was born. Hyperactive, that's what she thinks it is only you can't get a straight answer off that doctor of hers.'

• Patricia Fawcett

'Hyperactive? Is that what they call it nowadays?' Christine asked, watching Shane like a hawk. He was a slight, sickly-looking child and viewed the world through innocent-looking round spectacles. Just plain naughty, that's what she would call it. All these fancy words! Janice had no idea how to handle him. If it was her, if he was her grandchild, there'd be none of this nonsense. None of these tantrums he was forever having. None of this arguing back. Nor this constant bribery. Janice ought to have shares in whoever it was made Smarties. All he really needed was a good smack on his bottom except you weren't supposed to do that sort of thing nowadays, not with that European whatnot.

'Mind you, we wouldn't know what to do without him, would we, precious? Who's Grandma's little sweetheart then?'

Janice smiled fondly at him, tried to cuddle him but he wasn't having it and wriggled loose, kicking out and slipping her grasp. Rubbing her shin, she made do with ruffling his hair, her smile a touch forced. 'Although, between you and me, Christine, I don't think Catherine means to have any more.'

She said this quietly in a confidential aside so that Shane wouldn't hear. After all, as Christine had been at pains to point out to her before, little pitchers have large ears.

'Doesn't she? I'm not surprised.'

She whisked the teapot away before he knocked it off the little table, the smallest one of the nest she kept beside the piano. His glass of Ribena was balanced, nearly full, beside Janice. If she had a pound for the number of times he'd spilled his blackcurrant drink, she'd be worth a fortune. Lucky the carpet was plum-coloured or he'd have been for it.

'One's quite enough, if you ask me.' She might have added it was, however, putting all your eggs in one basket but she didn't.

'Like in China,' Janice said sagely. She thought she knew it all. She was red-hot on the television news and documentary programmes. Watched the lot. 'They have a one-child policy there. Do you know you have to apply for permission to try for a baby? Imagine! You can't have more than one. If you do, God only knows what happens. They do say that girl babies . . .' she lowered her voice but seeing that Shane had suddenly

• 110

developed an interest in the chat, she shook her head instead, thankfully not pursuing it.

They suffered a momentary diversion anyway as Shane, whose concentration span was five seconds or so, abandoned his Action Man helicopter and sped off to play the piano or rather bang on the keys. Christine watched, lips pursed, waiting for Janice to tell him off. Reg must be turning in his grave, for hadn't he loved that piano? He had had a light touch and had stroked his fingers lovingly over it far more often than he had done to her. He'd been happier, bless him, with inanimate objects. Sex had always been a bit of an ordeal for Reg. She'd not minded. Learned to live with it. She'd rather have a decent cup of tea anyday. All that huffing and puffing.

'Stop it, our Shane,' Janice called out lightly, totally relaxed in the chair. 'If you're a good boy, Auntie Christine will let you watch the telly. He likes the morning programmes,' she said with a smile, as the playing abruptly and thankfully ceased. 'He'll watch anything. Proper little telly addict he is.'

She said this with a certain amount of pride and Christine sighed. If she had a grandchild, she'd do things she used to do with Jenny. Take her for walks. Talk to her. Read to her. That little vision nudged into her mind, the one she tried to forget, Jenny as a little girl. She'd known what was what before she went to school. Known how to write her name. How to fasten her coat. How to tie her laces. How to tuck her vest properly into her knickers and wash her hands after going. To say please and thank you without prompting. From the word go, she'd been the star pupil. She'd been such a good quiet little girl although how she'd latched onto that science was a mystery. It wasn't as if she and Reg had been that way inclined.

She sometimes wished . . .

'Our Harold went to see Jenny the other week. Out at Hazelburn where she lives,' she found herself saying. Janice predated Jenny. Janice knew what was what but had always been very discreet about it. She never brought the subject up herself but was happy to talk about it if Christine did.

'I haven't been up that way in years,' Janice said, looking thoughtful. 'What does she do now? Catherine's husband said there were one or two changes pending in management. I did tell you he works at CWC, didn't I? Mind you, it's a big place so he'll probably not know your Jenny.'

Christine agreed. She hoped not.

'She works in a lab, Harold says. I can't remember what she calls herself.' She eyed Janice shrewdly. 'Does he like his job then? Your Catherine's husband?'

She shrugged. 'Doesn't say a lot. Between you and me, I can't say I've ever got through to him properly. He's too busy doing up that house of theirs. God knows why they ever bought it. A ruin, it was. A shell. I told Catherine but would she listen? Give me a new house anytime. I always wanted a new one.'

'I'm happy enough with what I've got,' Christine said with a sniff. It didn't do to want what you couldn't have.

'So am I. That house of Catherine's though . . .' she shook her head, 'they'll never get it finished. He never sits down either, Shane's daddy. I think that's where he gets it from. Catherine won't hear a word said against him and I suppose he's been a good husband. Don't worry, I never mention Jenny. It doesn't do, does it, with you and her being . . . well . . . not speaking like.' She joined Christine in a heartfelt sigh. 'You should talk to her before it's too late,' she said quietly. 'Suppose something happens to her. You'll regret it the rest of your life, believe me.'

She smiled quite kindly, anxious like Harold to be the instigator of a reunion. 'It's not as if it was about anything in particular. Just a few words you didn't really mean. I wouldn't let Catherine not speak to me. I mean to say, it caused a bit of an upset when she wanted me to look after you know who . . .' She indicated the back of the child's head, as he held the helicopter in a hover position before dropping it with an almighty crash onto the table.

Christine held her tongue as Janice yelled at him before continuing with a sigh, 'Well, thank you very much, Catherine, I said, bang goes my bit of peace and quiet in my old age. But I said I'd do it. She didn't want to leave him with just anybody and what else could I do? She needs the money.'

Christine switched the television on, sat Shane on the pouffe in front of it so that he could watch a phone-in session to an agony aunt.

She sighed and shook her head. 'I know you're right but I can't forgive what Jenny did to Reg, upsetting him like she did and then him taking ill right after and everything. You know what he was like.'

'Salt of the earth,' murmured Janice.

'Never away from that church. I used to go with him, support him you know, but, to be honest, my heart was never in it. Don't get me wrong, Janice, some of them church folk are very chirpy. Lovely, some of the ladies in the flower guild. But it affected Reg different. Never speak ill of the dead as they say but it made him pious and that's a fact. He couldn't do with loose behaviour either. Took after his mother. Lavender had a face like a wet weekend in Scarborough. Do you remember Lavender?'

They laughed and she tugged at her skirt, realised she wouldn't have worn one as short as this if Reg was here. She supposed she'd blossomed out a bit since he'd gone. He would go daft if he could see the colour of her hair.

'Marriage was sacred to Reg,' she continued brightly. 'They even got him to give the youngsters some talks on it. He took them talks serious. So you can imagine what it did to him when Jenny went and got herself pregnant.'

She glanced towards Shane but he was preoccupied, already off the pouffe, running a little tractor round the edge of the rug. She firmly believed in the innocence of childhood. They tried to make them know too much nowadays. Flummoxed them. There were some things you had no need to know until you got married.

'She tried afterwards,' Janice said awkwardly, 'tried to make up for it. She was determined to go back to school, wasn't she? And it must have been hard for her facing up to everybody. And I can't begin to understand how she must have felt, giving up the baby like she did. I couldn't have given Catherine up, not once I'd set eyes on her. Not for all the tea in China.'

'There was no choice,' Christine said in exasperation. 'I could have forgiven her that maybe after a while but not her going off to that university. She could have got herself a job and she owed it to me to stay round here. She should have got herself married like everybody else and had another baby. Oh no . . . that's not good enough for her. Jenny has to have a *career*.'

• Patricia Fawcett

'The way of the world,' Janice said. 'Whatever will the next generation be doing?'

'There won't be much of one at the rate they're going. They do say that having children is going out of fashion. We don't need rules like in China. We do it ourselves.'

They tut-tutted before lapsing into reflective silence and then, as they came out of it, they realised simultaneously that the present phone-in caller was discussing in unembarrassed detail the peculiar sexual habits of her lover with the world at large. Shane, his spectacles sticky and smudged, was quiet for once, the tractor tipped up and abandoned, picking his nose, inches from the screen, listening soberly and intently to the advice being offered.

Hastily, Christine reached for the off button.

13

From his upper office window, Stephen had a clear view over the tree-tops of Winckley Square and found it a pleasant diversion, the constantly changing beauty of nature soothing him. It was Saturday and he was alone in the office, taking the opportunity to catch up on a few things. It was an office rule, instigated by himself, that they always wore suits, none of this nonsense about casual dress on Friday, and he therefore felt odd to be here dressed illegally in jeans and a sweat-top. The weather had taken a turn for the better and everyone seemed suddenly cheerfully determined to make the best of it as, according to the forecast, it promised to be short-lived.

It also felt odd not to be meeting Clare for lunch and driving over to the nursing home. He had not actually missed her and, on her behalf, felt a touch ashamed of that. Her brother was now fulfilling his duties and acting as her chauffeur so he needn't feel guilty on that score.

Enough . . . he pushed the papers aside, tidied up, dropping some notes on his secretary's desk for Monday. He would drive home now and spend the rest of the day relaxing, see what his daughters were up to. Emily was supposed to be revising although he had his doubts about that.

As for Abby . . . Abby had been a big hit with that young man who had come to the house-warming – Ben somebody or other – and had been out with him already a couple of times so you couldn't accuse the fellow of wasting any time. She seemed happy enough so he let his own misgivings ride. He had no idea why but there was just something about the chap he didn't quite like, but if he spent his time

• Patricia Fawcett

worrying about his daughters' boyfriends, he was on a loser to nothing.

Abby was eighteen now, an adult, and she was old enough to know her own mind, old enough for a sexual relationship if that's what she wanted. Embarrassed as hell, he had tried to talk to her about it, irritated because Lizzie should have been on hand for that. It would have sounded better coming from her mother. As it was, they'd just ended up in a confused jumble, Abby blushing, and he talking in such convoluted circles that he'd not known what he was on about either.

Thinking about Abby and Ben and the house-warming reminded him of Jenny Sweetman. She was a lovely-looking woman with sleek dark hair, a nice smile and a very pleasing direct way of looking at him, not flirting à la Lizzie, but promising something none the less. He wished he had had the time that evening to chat to her some more. Not chat her up, God no, just talk to her, find out a bit more about her. She was a helluva lot younger than he of course but surely he was not mistaken about that little note of interest in those widely spaced blue eyes of hers. Or was it wishful thinking . . .

Grabbing his briefcase, he set off through the square to pick up the car and there, strolling towards him in a pale yellow summery dress, was the lady herself.

'Why, hello. Fancy meeting you here,' he said with a smile, as they stopped inches from each other.

She seemed momentarily confused, taking off her sunglasses and shading her eyes against the quite spectacular midday sun.

'Hello, Stephen. What are you doing here?' she asked, and, relieved of the sunglasses, he noticed the deep cornflower blue of her eyes as if for the first time. She had eyes the same colour as Abby.

'I work here,' he said, pointing back to the office, 'over there. I've just been catching up on things and now I'm off home. What are *you* doing here?'

'A little nostalgia trip,' she told him with a pensive smile. 'I came in intending to do some shopping but it's so hot in the shops and I thought I'd take a walk to the park instead. Get some fresh air. My father was always telling me I should get some roses in my cheeks. He loved it here too. He used to work just round the corner. An accountant's office in Guildhall Street. It doesn't seem to be there any more.'

'Really? Mind if I join you?' he asked, the impulse too strong to ignore. 'I've nothing planned for the rest of the day and I'd quite like a walk in the park myself,' he added, feeling he had to justify it. 'We must take full advantage. This might be the only sunny day we get all summer.'

'Pessimist!'

She smiled her assent and he quickly deposited his briefcase in his car before they strolled out of the square and along to Avenham Park. Very much a Victorian's idea of grand parkland, with a broad expanse of grass dipping into a bowl and stretching towards the River Ribble. Nearer at hand, the flower garden with its wooden bridge spanning water, altogether Japanese in character, was ablaze with colour as the ever strengthening sun burned down. Stephen was glad he had taken Abby's advice and worn casual gear this morning for, initially at breakfast, he had appeared, without even thinking, in his suit.

The sweatshirt was too warm and he pulled at it to give himself some air as they stopped to admire the garden, commenting, as if they were seasoned gardeners, on one or two plants, before Jenny admitted with a laugh that her own well-intentioned cottage garden had been a disaster the previous year with everything coming up in the wrong place.

Stephen made his confession too, that he was more than happy now to leave it all to a gardener, that he didn't actually know one plant from another let alone how to care for them. Their gardening limitations thus revealed, something in common established, they smiled and walked on.

'What do you do exactly?' she asked after a while, breaking a silence that had not been uncomfortable. 'I know you're an architect, Emily told me, but what kind of buildings do you design?'

'I've done the lot over the years. House and office. But our partnership has been specialising recently in designing large-scale sports complexes,' he told her, 'and we've managed to get a contract for some out in the Middle East. It's meant canvassing for extra staff to complete it in time. It's the jewel in the crown, as it were. The big time at last,' he finished with

• Patricia Fawcett

some satisfaction. 'I may have to spend some time out there soon, overseeing the projects.'

'How interesting!' she said, and, to her credit, she made it sound as if she meant that. 'It makes my work sound terribly boring.'

'Not at all,' he said politely, listening as she briefly outlined what she did. God, it did sound boring to him but he could tell she was committed to it and he admired that. He stole a quick approving glance at her as they walked under the bridge taking them into the adjoining Miller Park, making their way towards the ornamental fountain, the spout of water silver in the sunlight. They sat awhile on a bench, watching some children leaning over the edge searching for goldfish, and listened with adult smiles to their excited chatter.

'I used to do that when I was little,' Jenny said with a sigh. 'It seems no time ago. Where do the years go, Stephen?'

He laughed. 'Yes, you are incredibly ancient, aren't you?'

She laughed too.

'What I mean is . . . when I come back here, my childhood memories are sometimes so vivid. That's what comes of always living in the same town, I suppose. Apart from the years at university, I've never left. For instance, I remember . . .' she did not finish the sentence, but lapsed into silence and he let her, sensing that something troubled her, something she was unwilling to discuss.

'Childhood memories are special, aren't they?' he said after a moment, easing the way for her. 'To be treasured. I had a happy childhood and I hope to God Lizzie and I have given our daughters some happy memories of their childhood, things they will remember in later life.'

'I'm quite sure you have. They both seem well-adjusted. Emily's very breezy, true, but that's just her age and the pressure she's under with her exams. Don't worry, she'll be OK. And I think Abby's charming. You have two lovely daughters,' she said quietly. 'You're lucky, Stephen.'

'Lucky? I don't feel it. Lizzie left me, remember?'

'No, no. Sorry, I didn't mean that.' Her voice was pained at the idea. 'I didn't mean to remind you of that. And it really is none of my business. Emily told me about your wife,' she added as an afterthought. 'You know Emily. I could hardly tell her to shut up. I think she just wanted to let off steam, to talk about it and I happened to be there. I'm afraid she was a little indiscreet.'

'I'm sorry. I'm a bit touchy about it,' he said, smiling to show he was not mortally offended. 'We've been divorced for a while and sometimes, even now, I can't quite believe that. It was such a shock. She'd never given a hint. Everything seemed fine or at least as fine as it ever was. Percentage-wise we, the children and I, didn't feature greatly in her priorities. She was away from home a lot and that takes something out of a marriage.' He paused, wondering if he'd gone too far.

'I'm so sorry,' she said, at his side, her eyes hidden now behind the damned sunglasses. 'It must have been such a difficult time for you all.'

'She loved us in her way,' he continued quickly, anxious to make that clear, 'but, when it came to the crunch, the singing mattered most. Lizzie has this enormous talent, you see. I wish you could hear her sing.'

'I'd love to. I'm afraid I don't. Sing.'

'Neither do I,' Stephen said, 'at least not since I met Lizzie. He sings. The bloke she went off with.' He was not sure she knew about that but knowing Emily, she probably did. He also regretted the bitter tone. Dammit, it was time he learned to live with it. He had to stop playing the part of the aggrieved husband. It was bloody pathetic and he hoped to God Jenny didn't think he was angling for the sympathy vote.

'Relationships can be so cruel, can't they?' she murmured. 'I've had my share too of unhappy relationships.'

She whipped the glasses off, looked sideways at him, smiled.

He took her meaning. She was warning him, so gently, that she was not ready for another, not just now.

'I'm still not over Lizzie,' he said, anxious to let her know how he was fixed. 'If she walked through the door tomorrow, I'm not sure I wouldn't take her back.'

There! That had made it distressingly clear.

'Shall we walk back?' she said, standing up and dusting herself down.

Her smile was beautiful.

It was also relieved.

14

The restaurant was in the cellar, down some steep stone steps. Softly lit at that, sickly pink, perfect therefore for an unsuspecting soul to catch a heel and make a spectacular entrance. Carefully, worried that she might rip the hem of her new cream dress with unfamiliar heels, Abby followed Ben down the steps, holding onto his hand.

She had never been here before but Ben was instantly recognised by the head waiter, who approached them with a smile and a flourish.

'Table for two, Mr Chambers, as you requested.' He flashed a smile at Abby, took her jacket and passed it to a minion. 'If you and the lady would follow me.'

There followed an unfortunate furore about the table. Apparently Ben had asked for a particular table and was not going to be palmed off with another. Dismayed at the way he occasionally treated people like dirt, Abby had no choice but to wait with a smile on her face as a flurry of activity followed before they were at last able to sit down.

'They get away with things like that if you let them,' Ben said, smiling at her, quite unperturbed, reaching for the menu. 'Steak for me,' he said, without bothering to read it. 'Where's the wine list? Good God, they're slack tonight.'

Debating what to have, Abby felt quite nervous. Sometime soon he, she too, would want things to progress beyond the gentle kissing stage. And, before anything happened, she felt she must tell him that she was adopted. She had not meant to keep it secret, goodness no, but it was such a private thing and not something she blurted out at first acquaintance, not to someone she might never see again. But now, if they were about to become lovers . . .

She ordered a chicken dish for her main course, the homemade soup to begin with. Smiled her appreciation of the elegant room as they waited.

'Something's been puzzling me,' he said, reaching across the table and holding her hand. 'What the hell do you work in a travel agent's for? Bit of a humdrum job, isn't it? Why in heaven's name did you have to leave school at sixteen? Why didn't you stay on? Go to university?'

'Because I didn't want to,' she said at once. 'It was my decision. I wanted to get out into the real world, if you like. Earn a living.'

'Your father should have insisted you stay on and finish your education,' he said, pausing as their starters arrived. 'That all right for you?' he enquired as she started on her soup.

'Fine,' she assured him hastily, even though it was bland to the point of nothingness. She did not want another scene. 'I like my job,' she went on, wondering why she felt ever so slightly defensive.

His laugh was brief. 'Working in a travel agency? You can do better, Abby,' he told her. 'You'll be telling me next that you're an old-fashioned girl, all you want out of life is to get married and have babies.'

She laughed too, not sure if he was teasing her. Or testing her? 'I want that too . . . eventually,' she said, wondering how to qualify it or if indeed she ought to.

'How long have we known each other?' he asked. 'It seems ages and I still don't know anything about you.'

'You do,' she protested. 'You know a lot about me. You know my parents are divorced. You know that dad's an architect and that my mother lives in Los Angeles.'

'Ah yes, the opera singer.' He paused, tasted the wine, pronounced it admirable, watched carefully as the waiter poured.

'You've met my father and my sister, Emily,' she went on, feeling his attention wandering, trying to grab it back. 'I'm so glad we came to live in Hazelburn. Isn't it beautiful?'

He nodded. 'It's not bad. Pretty unspoiled. I should have no trouble selling the barn in a couple of years. Damned good investment. Sounder investment than that place of yours. People are reluctant to take on monstrosities like that these days.'

'It's not a monstrosity,' she said, insulted. 'It's lovely.'

They continued their meal in relative silence, Abby doubly irritated now that he should dismiss Curwin Hall, their home, in such a manner. Over dessert, he brightened, talking of work and golf, for which she tried to display some enthusiasm although she didn't feel much. As soon as she started to talk about her work, though, he made no such reciprocal effort, switching his interest off in a very evident manner. It made her cross but it had been a very expensive meal and she determined to make one last attempt to salvage the evening.

'You've set me thinking, Ben,' she said, over coffee. 'I might try an Open University course.'

'Open University? Better than nothing, I suppose. Infinitely better than some of these so-called new universities. Who's kidding whom? They will always be second-rate. Polytechnics in fact.'

'Some of the courses are excellent, much more geared to actual jobs,' she said, and then, seeing his face, 'so some of my friends tell me.'

'Assuming you started a course . . .' He smiled and it looked like he was humouring her. If she'd been that sort of girl, she might well have thrown the last of her wine in his face. But she wasn't and she couldn't. 'What would you read, darling? What subject?'

'History,' she said without hesitation. 'It fascinates me. We have loads of books at home.'

'History?' A sigh and a sneer. 'And you talk about the job market? That equips you for nothing except perhaps teaching and, in my opinion, that's not a job worth having any more, not with the delinquents around these days. In heaven's name, why History?'

'Why not?' she asked, feeling an anger rising. God, what was the matter with him tonight? He seemed to be going out of his way to irritate her. In addition, he was being boorish and unpleasant. The sooner this evening was finished, the better. Their relationship, which she had begun to think promising, was obviously over before it had properly begun. There had to be something else as well as the looks.

'History bores me to death,' he said. 'I like facts and figures not some waffle about the past. What's past is past. When you get down to it, why should we need to know? People should stop dwelling in nostalgia. It does no good, harm more likely. The past festers. We should start with a clean sheet. History should be abolished.'

'That's a very sweeping statement,' Abby said coldly, 'and if I may say so, an ignorant one too. What a silly thing to say! Of course it affects the present,' she went on, rapidly collecting her thoughts on the matter, hearing her voice shake with intensity, keeping it low though as there were people at nearby tables. 'What's gone on before is desperately important. Don't you see? Don't you feel something when you visit an old building, a castle? Don't you feel voices speaking to you? Don't you feel that atmosphere? I certainly do. Surely it does something to you? Surely you . . .' She stopped as she caught a glimmer of a smile on his face.

'Got you.'

His follow-up grin was unrepentant, his voice triumphant. 'Beyond that ice-cool-maiden exterior of yours, I knew there was real fire, Abby, but I was wondering if I'd ever find it. Emily was right. She said you were mad keen on history. You were really taken in, weren't you? Thought I was a complete Philistine?' He was still highly amused, at her expense she felt. 'Shall I ask for more coffee or have you had enough?'

Quite enough. She had had quite enough. Stony-faced, she managed the basics of politeness. 'No more for me, thank you.'

He clicked his fingers at the waiter, barely glanced at the bill before placing a gold credit card and a five-pound cash tip on the plate.

Abby rose to her feet, feeling foolish and furious that he should treat her like a child. Her stalking out, up the steps, was spoiled by tripping on them. She banged her knee on a sharp edge, felt her tights tear but carried on, ignoring the pain, desperate to keep control. And then she had to wait fuming at the top until he had retrieved his card and collected her jacket. The waiting did nothing to soothe her anger. Seething, she sat beside him in the car. She would have preferred to make her own way home but it was a ridiculous gesture as it was such a nuisance by bus and she thought she'd missed it in any case. Ben had made a fool of her and worse, she had fallen for it. What had Emily been saying to him behind her back?

'I didn't realise it would upset you so much,' he said as he drove. 'I thought you'd be able to take a joke. That's all it was – a bit of a game. I couldn't resist teasing you, my darling.' His laugh was short. 'You should have seen your face. You really are quite passionate about history, aren't you?'

'It was a childish game,' she said, realising too late that she was acting as she did with Emily. Emily was right. She should loosen up a bit but she'd never liked to be teased. Hated it in fact. However . . . she sighed and, although she felt the teasing had a faintly nasty edge to it, she would give him the benefit of the doubt. Perhaps he had just made a mistake.

Relaxing a fraction, she rubbed surreptitiously at her hurt knee. 'I suppose, if I'm honest, Ben, I do feel I've let myself down a bit,' she said after a moment. 'I would have quite liked to go to university but things were difficult when I was sixteen. Dad had come to rely on me by then. He's never really recovered from Mum leaving us. He's such a love, Ben, I didn't want to leave him. Emily's so scatty and she needs me to look after her.'

'Abby to the rescue!'

He drove so fast he made her uneasy but she could hardly ask him to slow down. Dad drove fast too but she felt safe with him. Ben was impatient, cutting in on people, overtaking on blind corners, slamming his brakes on at the very last second, that sort of thing. Once on the lanes heading towards home, it was even worse as he shot along at breakneck speed. She hung grimly onto her seat, determined she was not going to be dippy, as Emily would say, and ask him to slow down. 'You will come in for a nightcap, won't you?' he asked as they shot over the bridge, past Jenny Sweetman's pretty little cottage. 'You don't have to report in to your father first, I hope?'

'No I certainly do not,' she told him, glancing in the direction of her own house as she stepped out of the car outside Ben's barn. It was impossible to see Curwin Hall from here in fact but even if it weren't, there would be no problems. Her father understood such things. He allowed her a private adult life. He worried, she supposed, but he had said, in the most ridiculously convoluted way possible, that it was OK so long as she looked after herself and was not promiscuous.

Abby had been briefly in Ben's house a couple of times before, liked the way it had been cleverly converted, but was not quite so taken with his taste in décor. He had paid an interior designer a fortune, as he had been at pains to point out, to decorate and furnish it and Abby thought he ought to ask for his money back. Masculine verging on the austere. Painfully bare surfaces. No knick-knacks. Navy and cream striped sofas. Chrome and glass elsewhere. Not a single cushion or ruffled curtain in sight. No plants or flowers. Curwin Hall was spacious too, but somehow it managed to be cosier than this. That was it. This place did not feel like a home. The ghost of the working barn it had once been lingered a little and made her uncomfortable.

Ben disappeared to make coffee and Abby perched on the nearest sofa, taking the opportunity whilst he was out of the room to look at her knee. Wow! A gaping hole in her tights, a nasty graze and a bump with bruising already establishing itself nicely. The throbbing was also gaining momentum.

Ben returned with a tray. Jacket discarded, tie loosened. All smiles. Abby allowed her skirt to fall over the wounded knee, waiting as he flicked a switch to close the blinds at the windows, switched on a couple of the lamps to cast a soft romantic glow. Abby looked around, uncomfortable with the open-plan set-up. She preferred doors, some privacy. A spiral chrome staircase led up to a galleried bedroom, the enormous bed clearly visible. Music, the easy-listening variety, pitched low, wafted from unseen speakers. She wondered just how expert he was at seduction. At thirty, he had presumably had more practice than she. She had had just one serious boyfriend, a relationship that had fizzled out in a friendly enough fashion. At least they had been novices together whereas Ben . . .

'You're quite safe with me,' he said, reading her mind. 'You needn't look like that. Just coffee and an apology and then if you really want me to, I'll escort you home. Walk you round.' He handed her a cup of coffee, settled himself on a chair opposite. 'I hope you'll stay though for a while. I want you to stay, darling.'

The Absent Child

She smiled what she hoped was an enigmatic smile.

'I can't believe myself tonight. I behaved like a . . .' He raised his eyes heavenwards or, more disturbingly, in the direction of the bedroom. 'It was unforgivable. I am sorry. So very very sorry. The whole thing set off on the wrong foot with the business about the bloody table. Believe it or not, you look so beautiful tonight, and I feel such a responsibility towards you that it made me quite nervous and I act like that sometimes when I'm nervous. Will you forgive me? If you don't, Abby, I will have to do something to punish myself. Something dreadful. Sell the Porsche even . . .' he grinned. 'Well?'

'You're forgiven,' she said, after the briefest pause. 'Just don't do it again.'

'Certainly not.'

Feeling uncomfortable that he had managed to win her round remarkably easily, Abby sipped her coffee and looked across at him.

'So you've been talking to Emily recently?' she asked, not daring to glance towards the staircase, refusing to be rushed.

'Ah yes, Emily. Vivacious, I think that's the word. I met her the other day in town. Didn't she tell you? Quite by chance. She told me she was skiving off school incidentally.' He flashed a smile. 'Whoops! I wasn't supposed to tell you that. Promised her I wouldn't. I didn't actually recognise her but she reminded me who she was. I took her for a coffee and we had a chat.'

'What did you talk about?' she asked tightly, wondering if Emily had spilled all the family beans. Once she got going, she was unstoppable. Damn her if she had told him because then it would look as if she were trying to hide something.

'This and that,' he said, stretching out his legs, his face partly in shadow in the dim light. 'She told me all about your mother. She sounds a very interesting lady. My parents are thrilled actually. My mother, you see, adores opera. I've told her all about you and she's awfully impressed, Abby, because it's not every young lady who has a mother who's an opera singer and a father who's a successful architect. I do believe Mother's done some discreet checking on your father. Sorry about that. His business she concludes is most satisfactory and she can't wait to meet them both. How on earth did your parents get together? Such

• Patricia Fawcett

an interesting contrast, aren't they? My mother fully approves. Two excellent professions.'

'Approves?' Abby queried, wondering what he meant. Mrs Chambers sounded rather formidable. She didn't know whether to be amused or appalled at the idea of her checking up on Dad. The almighty cheek of it!

'You'll have to forgive her but she's a bit of a snob,' he said with an easy smile. 'I've disappointed her a little. As you know, I've had a chequered past, three fiancées already, I'm sorry to say, and my fiancée but one was the daughter of a furniture salesman. Mother never got over it, gave the poor girl hell. I think it was a relief when it broke up. That wasn't the reason of course,' he added with unnecessary haste. 'I wouldn't dream of letting Mother dictate my choice of partner. No . . . the truth is we were incompatible.'

'We don't worry about things like that, in my family,' Abby said, wishing it didn't sound so smug but she felt she needed to make the point. 'It's what people are like deep down that counts surely?'

'I agree. I couldn't agree with you more. I'm not like that at all,' he said. 'Believe me, Abby, Mother will adore you when she meets you. I'm being unkind. She's not so bad as she sounds. We must allow her a few idiosyncrasies. You'll like her when you meet. They're on a cruise at the moment so we'll have to put that off.'

Abby nodded, unconvinced.

'Emily seems a lot younger than you,' he went on, offering her more coffee, which she refused. 'I know she's only a year younger but it seems more than that. She smokes too. Did you know? I suppose she thinks it's sophisticated. And she never stops talking. I came away from our meeting exhausted.'

'Did she divulge any family secrets?' Abby asked, trying to keep the question light-hearted but feeling herself grow hot with embarrassment. Somehow, this time, it was bothering her, having to tell him she was adopted. But she couldn't put it off much longer, the time was now.

'Family secrets? Do you have any?'

'It's not really a secret,' she said, 'but there is something I should have told you earlier, Ben. We hardly ever think about it.

I'm lucky it's never been what you might call a big deal. However . . . I really ought to tell you. It's quite important.'

'Oh Lord, not now . . . I don't care what the hell it is, it doesn't matter.' He came across, sat close beside her, pulled her towards him. 'I've been wanting to do this all evening,' he said softly as he kissed her. A small kiss on the lips and then on the very tip of her nose. 'You're so lovely, Abby. Very worried but lovely. Isn't it time we got to know each other better?' He was stroking her hair as he spoke, looking deep into her eyes and she was mesmerised by the look. 'Haven't I been incredibly patient? I've been so wary of trying to rush you, sweetheart. I'm very conscious that you're so young. Not that it matters of course. Why the hell should it matter?'

'I've got a hole in my tights,' she said ridiculously as his hand slid under the folds of her skirt. 'And I banged my knee on those steps at the restaurant.'

'Why didn't you say? You poor sweet . . . and it was all my fault, wasn't it?' He looked at the messy tear, the bruised and scratched skin, and frowned. 'Good God, that looks terrible. Shall we bathe it and then I'll kiss it better.'

She smiled.

Forgave him.

Wrapped her arms round his neck as he kissed her.

And it was much much later that it occurred to her she still hadn't told him.

Oh well, it could wait.

15

Christine kneeled at the graveside. She removed last week's withered offering, poured in fresh water and stuck today's flowers in the pot. Made a bit of a fuss about arranging them nicely. Spring flowers. Daffodils and whatnots. Not very exciting ... still, they added a spot of colour.

She came out of duty more than anything else. She was convinced that, if Reg was up there watching her, and he was bound to be, wasn't he, then he would know if she missed her regular visit. The truth was Reg had sometimes been a bit of a tartar. Stubborn as a mule. Her mother had told her as much but at nineteen had she taken any notice? Of course not. Marry in haste, repent at leisure, as they say. Her mother had never taken to Reg.

He'd been good-looking when he was young. She'd worked in the Empress Cinema at the time as an usherette and she'd met Reg at a Saturday night dance over in Blackburn. She'd gone with the girls for a bit of a laugh and Reg had been there with his pals. When they'd found out he'd had an office job, got paid monthly, wore a suit for work, and it was rumoured he'd had a bob or two in the bank, all the girls had been after him. The fact that he hadn't had much of a sense of humour hadn't seemed to matter. Some of the girls had been a bit coarse and she'd sensed right off he didn't care for that sort of talk so she'd watched her Ps and Qs.

He hadn't been quite so religious then. That had come later with a vengeance, a fervour that had flowed through his veins much more freely than any passion for her. All the fun, what bit there'd been, had been squeezed out of him once he breathed

• Patricia Fawcett

religion. She'd never been able to reconcile herself to that. Surely God didn't mean you to be miserable as sin the whole time? He meant you to enjoy life . . . didn't He?

The Church had come first with Reg. He'd been there every minute God sent. Parochial meetings. Bible discussion groups. Choir practice. He'd been in charge of the youth club and had helped edit the magazine. He had been there more than the vicar it seemed and because it had been commendable, not like he'd had a bit on the side or anything, then she couldn't have complained. But, as her mother might have said, it had been a bit of a bugger.

Mother had relished a good old-fashioned curse so it had not been surprising that she and Reg had never really got on. Reg had thought her vulgar and once he had even managed to make Christine feel ashamed of her own parents. He ought not to have done that and it made her uncomfortable thinking about it. You ought never to be ashamed of your roots. She supposed Jenny must be. She'd never said as much but she must be.

She looked quickly round the cemetery, rows and rows of graves gloomy in the morning chill. After a brief spot of unseasonable sunshine, they were back to normal. There was nobody about but Christine did not mind. She found it peaceful, the cemetery, a nice place to be.

'I might not see you next week, Reg,' she murmured, keeping her voice low but needing to say the words out loud to him. She laid her hand on the dark grey marble, top quality, a special offer from Harold. Well, when you had a brother in the trade, you expected the best. It had been a wonderful funeral and there'd been a beautiful wreath from work with Mr Thorpe senior coming along himself. Harold had done her proud and taken care of all the arrangements personally. Just as well because she had been in a right old state. It had taken her all her time to keep from blubbing and showing herself up.

The church had been crammed full and the vicar had given him a beautiful sendoff. There'd been a touching write-up in the church magazine, praising him to the heavens. One of the flock had even composed a poem and some of the big lads from the youth club had helped carry the coffin. Reg would have been tickled pink at all the fuss.

The Absent Child

'I've got so much on it's unbelievable,' she went on. 'It's these car boots I told you about. They've started in earnest and Harold likes to get a good pitch. Once you pick your spot, it's more or less yours.' She patted the stone, glancing down not daring to think what he would look like now. 'Harold's got this daft idea he wants to come and live with me but I mean to say, love, would it work out? Me and him? You know what he's like. Once he starts reminiscing – all that talk about dying and everything – it gets up folks' noses, that does. And them hymns . . .'

A spot of rain, just the one, splashed on the grave and she looked up at the grey sodden sky and shivered. The heavens were going to open any minute now. She was ready for off but before she went . . .

'Our Jenny's got a promotion,' she said, and on the grave top, one of the pinkish pebbles suddenly moved as if there were a corresponding movement far below. 'It was Harold who told me,' she added hastily. 'I haven't been to see her. Nor will I. Not after what she did to you. She shouldn't have upset you like that. And then, when I wanted her to give up that university and stay at home, keep me company, would she? Not likely. She could have got a job up town no trouble, her looking so smart and everything. She wouldn't. Said she couldn't. She had that look on her face. You know the one I mean.'

She stopped before she started going on about it too much. He knew all about it. Hadn't she told him the details just after it happened, him fresh in the grave then? She'd never really let him settle.

The tears bubbled up as they always did when she was here, and she sniffed them away. So, he might have been rigidly righteous with no sense of humour but nobody was perfect. She'd been able to rely on him. Money on the table every month for her to sort out. No two ways about it, he'd have put himself in front of her bullet without a second's thought. He had thought the world of her and of Jenny, although he hadn't been one for soft words. Undemonstrative, you see.

The Sweetmans were all the same. Miserable lot, especially that mother of his. Lavender Sweetman . . . such a beautiful name. If ever a woman had been blessed with the wrong name!

• Patricia Fawcett

Going round to that house of theirs when she and Reg were courting had fair put the dampener on things. Lavender had eyes in the back of her head and if Reg so much as put his arm round her, Lavender was there, tutting. She blamed Lavender for Reg not being able to let himself go.

'So ... Reg love ... as I was saying ...' she crumpled the tissue that had been round the flowers and crunched it in her hand, 'I'll be back soon and I'll see if I can bring some nice carnations then.'

She rested her hand a moment longer on the ice-cold stone, her eyes still pricking. The flowers shone against the dark of the grave.

She walked through the cemetery, quickening her step as the heavens finally opened and the rain started in earnest, just catching the bus back to town.

Occasionally, if she felt up to it, she got the photograph album out. The wedding pictures of her and Reg and the rest of the family. Lavender in shocking pink and her mother looking odd in a smart two-piece without her pinny.

Jenny at seven months, seven years, seventeen ... she favoured the Walmsley side of the family, thank God. The Sweetmans had always been old before their time on account of their not smiling much. Jenny hadn't even had a boyfriend as such at sixteen and that had begun to worry Christine a bit for it was easy for girls to feel left out if their friends had boyfriends. So in a way, she supposed, she had been responsible for what happened. It was she who insisted Jenny went on holiday when she had the chance. She and Reg never went in for them. A couple of days at Southport maybe, but Reg was anxious when he was away from home and, wherever they went, they had to be within bell-ringing distance of a church so that he didn't miss morning service.

A holiday by the sea then, for Jenny, seemed a lovely idea. The south coast, one of them resorts with a pebble beach. She was going with her friend Rosie and Rosie's mum and dad so no harm would come to her. Reg had taken some persuading but, once he realised there would be a chaperone, albeit Rosie's brassy mum, he relented.

The Absent Child

If only...

So off they went and Christine worried a bit at home. She ought to have realised something had happened when they returned although Jenny said not a word. She showed them the photos including one of a tall blond lad with his arm round her shoulders. Jenny had blushed and not volunteered any information about him so, realising she was embarrassed, Christine had not asked. It never occurred to her that Jenny had done what her friend Rosie had not done with a boy who very quickly vanished off the face of the earth.

How could she have done it? At sixteen?

If she lived to be a hundred, she would never forget having to break the news to Reg. It took two weeks to pluck up the courage and in the end Jenny, in one of her awkward moods, threatened to do it herself. It had taken them a while to put two and two together because Jenny's periods had always been a bit on the funny side and at first they'd assumed it was just that, a bit of irregularity. Then, when she suggested it might be a good idea to go to the doctor's, see what he had to say, Jenny had come right out with it and confessed that there was just the chance... It turned out she was four and a half months gone already, hardly showing an inch, and even if Reg had consented to an abortion, which he hadn't on religious grounds, it would have been much too late. The damage was done and they had to live with the consequences.

'Now, Reg, you've got to promise me you won't get mad,' she had said, taking him through to the front room to impart the news whilst Jenny waited, white-faced, in the back. 'Our Jenny's had a bit of bad luck...' She remembered the look on his face as it dawned. Then he had gone quiet, struck dumb she supposed, and when he finally did speak to Jenny, he reduced her to tears with his acid condemnation of her conduct. The family conference with Jenny sitting there like stone was an ordeal. She had so wanted to go across and put her arm round her, tell her it wasn't the end of the world but of course she couldn't. She and Reg had always maintained a united front.

• Patricia Fawcett

The rest was history, their family history.

Rosie's mum had to be told and she had come round, mortified. Hand on heart, she wouldn't of course breathe a word to anyone, especially not Rosie. She felt responsible she said but she hadn't realised what was what. She had never thought that Jenny and that young man were ... you know. She'd thought Jenny too well brought up for that. That had been hard. The quiet triumph in that woman's eyes. Her Rosie, breasts bulging out of her blouse, eyes all knowing, was still intact. Would you credit it?

Christine sighed. Her granddaughter, her only granddaughter, would be a young lady now. Eighteen. Oh how she had been sorely tempted to make tracks to that nursing home and bring them both home. Stuff what the neighbours might think. But it was out of the question. She couldn't go against Reg and his principles.

She slipped her coat on and picked up her bag. She fancied making an early start, going shopping to take her mind off things. Shane was being dropped off by his mother as she went out. Christine smiled and had a quick word with Catherine. Catherine looked a lot like Janice but had less patience it seemed with Shane.

'He's been a right little sod this morning,' she said to Christine as Shane banged fit to waken the dead on his grandmother's door. 'He's had a complete change of clothes already and it's only nine o'clock. And he's broken his spare glasses. I'll have to see the optician *again*.'

'Boys will be boys,' Christine murmured. 'When does he start school?'

'September. Roll on.' She pushed wearily at her hair, smiled. ''Bye then.'

Once on the bus, Christine smiled at the encounter. Poor Catherine. He might be a little handful, that Shane, but blood was thicker than water and Janice thought the world of him. To be fair, there were times when he was a little love. Times when he smiled with that childish innocence that tore her heart. Kiddies were a joy and what she wouldn't give for a grandchild of her own. With Jennifer forty in five years' time, she'd have to get her skates on. Forty was too old for a first baby no matter what they said nowadays. A baby would do it of course, provide the incentive she needed to make things up.

Yes . . . it would be nice if they could be on friendlier terms.

On any sort of terms.

Nice. But about as likely as pigs flying.

16

Abby was in love. Walking on air. Ben was hinting at marriage and she was already trying to think what she would say when he finally proposed. She had no qualms about being his fourth fiancée. Fourth time lucky! She would have to prepare herself for meeting his family, particularly his awful-sounding mother, but she wouldn't be marrying his family, would she, she would be marrying Ben.

He was not perfect but then nor was she. She determined there would be no more repetitions of that embarrassing scene in the restaurant. He had to learn to behave better than that but she could put up with his little faults. Minor irritations. She would work on him and erase them gradually once they were married. And, at last, she had told him that she was adopted and he didn't mind. How silly of her to have worried about it. She had been sly, although she preferred to think of it as deviously feminine, choosing the moment carefully. They were in bed at the time, the colossal bed up in the gallery, and, glowing as she was from the aftermath of lovemaking, she was imagining moving in here, living with him, having his child. She had planned to tell him now and it was indeed exactly the right moment.

'It's not a big deal,' she said brightly, as a starting point, her voice singing into the happy silence, trying to say what Emily might say. 'We never really think about it much at home but the thing is, darling . . . I'm adopted.'

As there was no reply from him, just a definite intake of breath, she continued gently, propping herself on one elbow, facing him, 'Mum and Dad adopted me when I was a baby because they thought they couldn't have children of their own and then –

• Patricia Fawcett

you've guessed it – Emily came along a year later. Mum got more than she bargained for, two babies instead of one.'

'I see.' After a pause, he continued to stroke her shoulder, rather absently, and she carried on, needing to get it off her chest now that she had started.

'It was a while before I understood what it really meant. They were so anxious to be open about it that I think they told me too soon. Confused me a little.' She smiled, remembering. 'To be honest, Ben, and I wouldn't say this to anyone else, Mum was never the maternal type . . .'

'Which mum?' he asked, his voice quiet, very calm and controlled.

She laughed nervously. 'I've only got one mum,' she explained. 'The . . . the lady who gave birth to me isn't my mum. At least, I don't think of her as my mum.'

'I'm amazed. My God, you certainly know how to take the wind out of my sails.' He smiled, shaking his head as he digested the information. 'Adopted eh? Emily didn't say a word.'

'That's a surprise. It's just the sort of thing she might blurt out,' Abby said, pleased that he was taking it so well. She reached for a wrap, insinuated her body into it without getting out of bed, smiled again.

'Do you want to talk about it?' he asked. 'I'm listening.'

'There's not much to tell. I was born in Wales, one of those unpronounceable places – we have family connections with Wales you see. Mum is Welsh. As for my natural mother, well, all I know for sure is that she . . .' she hesitated over the words as she always did, 'she was very young and not married. I know it doesn't matter much now but it might have then. I don't know.'

'Aren't you curious about her? About your real father too? Can't you insist on knowing who they are these days?'

'I could find out if I wanted now I'm eighteen. Or rather, I could try. It's not always straightforward trying to trace someone. People move. Change their names. That sort of thing. If she's decided she doesn't want to be found then it's going to be very difficult if not impossible. Mum and Dad wouldn't mind, I think, but I'm not sure I want to. There are a lot of things to consider.'

'You are amazing, Abby. I would want to know if it were me,' he said fiercely. 'I couldn't rest until I knew.'

'Ben . . . can I tell you something?' She waited for his nod before continuing. 'The reason I'm hesitating is that I'm frightened of finding out. What if we don't like each other? Wouldn't that be awful? She might have another family and not want to know me. She might have two heads . . .' She sighed, the silly attempt at light-heartedness not fooling either of them.

'Frightened?' He kissed her lightly before flinging the covers back and reaching for his robe. 'Frightened or not, it's something you should do, Abby. Find out. You owe it to yourself.'

Alone later, in her own bed, she thought about what he had said.

She was curious sometimes.

On balance though, it was best she did not know.

That way, her dreams could not be shattered.

The kitchen, in keeping with the rest of Curwin Hall, was very smart country-house, laid out in a horseshoe shape with an island unit in the centre. Copper pots and pans and bunches of dried herbs hung from a rack above, and Abby hoped they would be an inspiration as she struggled to prepare what was to be such a special dinner.

Emily was no help. She was sitting doing nothing at the table, books spread out before her. Suddenly, she let out a squeal of annoyance, holding out her hand as Abby whirled round. 'Look at that. Smudged. I spent ages doing them too. Frosted pink.'

'Don't you dare start doing your nails in here,' Abby warned, seeing Emily rummaging in her bag. 'I don't want nail polish remover stinking the place out.'

'Oh shut up. You don't want this. You don't want that. You get on my nerves, Abby. You're worse than Mum ever was. She never gave a toss what we did.' She stood up, hitching up the folds of her ankle-length skirt and adjusting the stockings and suspender belt underneath. 'I hate wearing stockings,' she said, 'but tights are even worse. About as sexy as Clare Forrest. Thank God that's all off. I can't think what the hell he saw in her.' She thumped down again into the chair, made a great thing of turning the pages of her book, sighing hugely. 'I don't know

• Patricia Fawcett

why you're in such a tizzy,' she went on, as Abby, fingers sticky, simultaneously turned the pages of a cookery book. 'Unfreeze something. You can always lie and say you made it.'

'It's not beyond me to cook a decent meal,' Abby said. 'I've been doing it for ages or hadn't you noticed? Meals in this house don't appear as if by magic. We don't employ a cook.'

'Ask Dad. Dad would get somebody in to help if you just asked. You're such a martyr all the time. Decent meals, did you say?' Emily laughed. 'All I can say is it must be getting serious with Ben if he's invited to dinner with Dad too. Is it?'

'Maybe,' Abby said carefully. 'By the way, I'd rather you didn't keep *accidentally* bumping into Ben in town, in the middle of the day when you should be in school. How many times is it now?'

'Just the once,' Emily said, indignation at the fore, 'and I don't have to answer to you, Miss bloody Prim. I met him quite by chance. Outside Debenhams, if you must know. We did bump into each other, honestly, and he insisted on buying me a coffee and cake at Brucciani's. I could hardly refuse, him practically being family and everything ... Don't worry, I am not going to steal him from you. He's fantastic-looking, I grant you, but miles too old for me. Too old for you too,' she muttered under her breath. 'He'll be proposing before long. I'm not getting married. Ever. I'm going to be like Jenny. An independent woman with a fantastic highly paid job.'

'Doing what?' Abby popped the dish into the oven, washed her hands.

'I don't know. But whatever it is, I won't be scratching round for money. I intend to have a career.' She didn't actually say 'unlike you' but it was implied. Abby smiled, refusing to rise to the bait.

'Not if you don't pass your exams, you won't.'

'Oh, sod off, Abby. I know I've got to pass the bloody things. And I don't know how to. I just go into a complete panic.' For a moment she looked quite desperate, 'It's going to be a total disaster. I can feel it in my bones. Oh Abby, I wish Mum was here.'

Abby sighed, and went over to put her arms round her sister.

'We'll talk about it later, you fool,' she said. 'You will not fail your exams. You just need to apply yourself, that's all.'

She felt Emily's thin frame shudder, knew she was trying hard not to cry. She wished suddenly that Mum were here too. Mum would have said something outrageous to make them laugh. Mum hated anyone being down in the dumps. Mum never took anything really seriously. Perhaps she should drop a line to her, induce her to take an interest in their welfare, offer some advice. On the other hand, who was Mum to offer advice? Trailing halfway round the world in search of love.

A little deflated, Abby went upstairs to get ready for dinner.

17

Jenny was keeping Trevor at bay. Just about. She had managed to make sure that they were never alone, off company property as it were. If they met at the hotel she usually stayed in when she was down in London, it was as part of a wider group, not difficult because CWC tended to use the same hotel. At work, it was easier to keep things brisk and businesslike. It was, however, a bit of a worry, because she didn't know how he would react if, or rather when, she gave him the brushoff.

Sack her . . . ? God no, he was wiser than that. Wiser and much more devious. He wouldn't do anything to risk her claiming unfair dismissal but, as Technical Director, he had the power to make life extremely difficult, and worrying about it was making her tetchy. However, as there were no meetings scheduled for the next couple of weeks, she could relax a bit, get on with her own work without hindrance.

She buzzed Rose.

'Is Len in this morning?'

'No, he rang in first thing to say he'd be at . . . just a minute . . .' there was a rustling of papers, 'Ettybridge Chemicals,' she said with a clear reluctance, as if Jenny were trying to catch him out. She was not. She merely wished to know where he was. 'They are one of the suppliers, Miss Sweetman,' Rose added, as if speaking to a moron. 'He inspects them regularly.'

'Ettybridge Chemicals?' Jenny jotted it down. 'They supply – what is it? Just refresh my memory, Rose.'

'Acetic anhydride,' Rose replied, 'an essential ingredient for the Cedrox process.'

'I know what it's essential for,' Jenny said sharply, waiting for the usual fond reference to John Harding which, rather to her surprise, did not materialise. 'I'm well aware, Rose, that Len has to spend a lot of time travelling round taking samples,' she went on, smiling down the phone and hoping it was transmitted, 'but I do need to know where he is.'

She stopped short of a direct criticism, not wanting to show Rose just how irritated she was at Len's attitude. Cavalier was putting it politely. The man was so laid back, he might as well bring a bed into the lab, conduct his business from there. 'Perhaps you might ask him to pop in for a quick word when he gets back?'

'It won't be today,' Rose said. 'But I'll pass on the message, Miss Sweetman.'

'Thanks.'

She got down to work, trying in vain to put domestic thoughts aside, but much as she tried, they persisted in intruding. She wondered about it, her and Stephen. Early days of course but was it the start of a precious new relationship? The meeting in the square and the walk in the park had led to a very gentle sparring. He had been anxious to press upon her the fact that he still hankered after his wife. Just as she had felt it necessary to point out that she was still a little fragile from previous disappointments. Rather desperately fencing round each other then. Why would they do that?

There was no rush. He was older but not so that it mattered, as it mattered with Trevor. Trevor was all things, too old, too fat – she felt ashamed of minding that – and altogether too bloody-minded. Quite simply, he very nearly repelled her physically. She could no more go to bed with him than . . .

Now Stephen on the other hand – for all his professional poise, and he had a good deal, she detected a gentle warmth within, a longing for happiness, a desire to forget what had been a somewhat stormy past. A mirror image of her own feelings in fact. She must tread carefully. See how it went. She was a firm believer in fate. If it was meant to be, then it would be.

A knock on the door startled her and, guiltily, she returned her attention to work.

'Come in, Rose,' she said, as the girl entered, carrying a sheaf of papers. 'Is there a problem?'

'Alan's gone for lunch but he asked me to show you these figures,' she said, handing them over. 'Apparently there's been a problem with one of the polyamide batches.' She waited, dark hair in a neat pigtail, her spectacles swinging from a gold chain round her neck, as Jenny perused the data.

'Did Alan make a comment?' Jenny asked when she had finished. She made a note that he was querying a funny viscosity data which immediately suggested to her that water might have accidentally got into the reagent. Definitely not good news.

Rose slipped on her glasses and consulted her notes.

'He said that the raw materials data is OK so we'll have to put it down to a variable test result. It happens sometimes. He's not too worried but he thought you should be informed out of courtesy. He's available this afternoon if you want a word.'

'OK. Thanks.'

Preoccupied, Jenny took up the notes again as Rose left the room. Call it intuition if you like, but she had a sharp feeling that something was not right. She was not buying the 'variable test results' theory. She hoped Alan wasn't trying, somewhat pathetically, to cover up. She would have a word with Alan, yes, but she knew in her heart that the problem lay ultimately with Len.

What in heaven's name was he up to?

And, more importantly, would she outmanoeuvre him before he dropped her in it.

'Hi!' Emily careered into her as she locked the car. 'How are you? I haven't seen you for ages. I've had a really grotto day myself. I feel totally depressed.'

'Mine's not been too brilliant either,' Jenny muttered. 'Problems galore! Like to come in for a coffee?'

'Thanks. I wanted to talk to you anyway,' Emily said, barging in after her, wearing a long see-through summery skirt in a black and white print, wraparound scarlet top and sandals, her dark hair bushier than usual. That combined with the soulful eyes giving her a gypsy look. 'About Abby.'

'Let me get the coffee on then I'm all yours,' Jenny said, going through to the little kitchen. Looking out of the window she saw that the early summer flowers in the garden, unruly and straggly last year, suddenly looked a bit more in control, with quite distinct patches of colour, pinks and yellows and creams amongst the greenery. God knows how they had sorted themselves out for she had done nothing except look at them in some desperation, wondering which ones to heave out. They must have heard her thoughts, decided to make one last glorious stand for survival.

'Do you know anything at all about this Ben Chambers guy?' Emily asked, as soon as they were back in the living room, coffee and biscuits before them. 'He's the one with that marmaladey coloured hair and that really fantastic smile,' she grinned. 'The madman who drives that silver Porsche,' she added, just to make it absolutely clear, as if there could possibly be another man in Hazelburn matching that description.

'Ah . . . him!' Jenny smiled, giving herself time to think. She was rapidly turning into a mother substitute for Emily and, funnily enough, she didn't mind. It was obvious that Emily missed her mother very much and had turned to joking and swearing as a safety valve, poor love. It disturbed Jenny to think that, under the blasé exterior, the girl might be desperately unhappy.

'Why I ask is because I'm beginning to think he's a bit creepy,' she went on. 'Looks aren't everything, are they? It's got to be looks plus something.'

'Quite right,' Jenny said cheerfully. 'Or you might get by with just the plus something. You're learning, Emily.'

'Ben looks you up and down. You know? I had been trying it on I suppose but suddenly it wasn't fun any more. I didn't like it.' She looked very young and vulnerable, uncertain of her reasoning. 'Oh . . . I can't explain. And he's so bloody shirty with people. He kicked up a fuss in the café when I was with him because they hadn't cleared the table. I could have died on the spot. The girl was doing her best. Everybody looked.' She clicked her tongue with exasperation at the memory. 'I'm worried about Abby. She's easily taken in. She's not had much experience with men. She's only ever had two proper boyfriends and you should have seen them. Juvenile or what! She has no idea at all.'

'I see.' Jenny tried to keep her amusement hidden.

'But if *I* tell her what I really think about him, she'll think I'm just being bitchy. It would be much better coming from you. She'll take notice of you. The trouble is she's getting serious, I think. She spends a lot of time with him, sneaking in at all hours. It can only mean one thing, can't it? They're sleeping together.'

'It's nice of you to be so concerned,' Jenny said. 'But I don't think you should worry too much,' she added, not wanting to own that she was more than worried herself if Abby was getting deeply involved with Ben. 'Look, why don't you ask her to come and have a chat with me sometime? Believe me, boyfriend trouble happens to the best of us.'

'Not to me,' Emily said cheerfully. 'I finish with them before it starts to get serious and soul-searching. I've just given this guy the boot.' She grinned. 'He was terrific in the looks department but up here . . .' she pointed to her head, 'he was seriously brain-challenged. He made me look like Einstein. Men are a pain, aren't they? I think I'll be like you and stay single.'

'My being single isn't entirely through choice.' Jenny felt obliged to point this out. 'It's just the way it's worked out.'

'Is it? You mean you haven't met Mr Right yet?'

'You could say that.' Jenny smiled a little. 'It didn't matter once but now . . . well, I wouldn't be averse to settling down. Must be something to do with my age. And before you ask, I'm coming up to thirty-six.'

'I wasn't going to ask,' Emily said indignantly. 'Oh by the way, Dad said he'd met you the other day in town?' The question was lightly tossed, the meaning behind it not quite hidden. Curiosity burned deep in those dark eyes of hers.

'Yes, we did meet. On Saturday. Quite by accident. I was just taking a walk and he'd been working at the office. I'd forgotten he worked in Winckley Square. It was so nice, that lovely sunny day, that we decided to take a stroll in the park,' she said, wondering why she needed to explain.

Emily seemed satisfied. 'You're from Preston originally, aren't you?' she asked. 'Is that your dad? The one who sometimes visits?'

Jenny laughed. There were precious few secrets in Hazelburn.

'My uncle,' she said. 'My father's dead. My mother . . .' she hesitated but Emily was listening intently and she couldn't get out of it, 'my mother still lives in Preston,' she said, 'although we don't see each other much.'

'I wish my mum lived so close,' Emily said wistfully. 'I sometimes fancy a chat but whenever I phone it's always the wrong moment. If it's not the stupid time difference, she's just out to a performance or something and has to hurry. Then she always forgets to ring back when she promises . . .' She bit her lip, suddenly looked all of fifteen.

Jenny smiled reassuringly. She was hungry and needed to slot a meal into the microwave. She had just had a bite at lunchtime and her stomach now rumbled its protest.

'You want me to go?' Emily, oddly perceptive, stood up at once. 'Why didn't you say? I'll tell Abby that she can come round if she wants a chat, although I bet she won't. She thinks she can sort out her own problems. Thanks for the coffee, Jenny.'

Jenny watched her disappear up the lane, tall and slender and so very young. Worries pressed on you so at that age. Helen would be just a bit older. Funny to think that. If Helen wanted now, she could start to make enquiries, initiate a trace. If she did, then it was all in the file – the letter and further current information as she did not want there to be any problem in tracing her.

Who knew? There might be a letter or phone call any day. She knew she had to prepare herself for the possibility but did not know how to.

18

'It was a grand building, that old town hall,' Harold commented, looking in the general direction of it. 'Damned sight better than that box of a thing . . . carbuncle, isn't that what Prince Charles would call it? Remember the town hall?'

Christine grunted a reply of sorts. Shivered as the sun, reluctant from the word go today, disappeared behind a bank of clouds, making the temperature plummet and her spirits with it. Harold had one of his moods on. On his high horse.

'A crying shame it was when they knocked it down. Sixties of course – demolition happy – streets and streets just disappeared and what did they replace them with? Blocks of flats, that's what. Slum clearance they called it. People just booted out and stuck anywhere. They wouldn't do it nowadays. Nowadays they'd renovate . . . but it's all too late.' He sighed. 'It was a grand old building,' he repeated.

'There's still the library and we've got the Guild Hall now,' Christine said, jigging him out of his misery. 'And that town hall wasn't all it was cracked up to be. It used to be full of pigeons. They used to sit all over the ledges. Pigeon muck all over. Remember *that*? People used to sit on them seats and eat sandwiches. I ask you, some people. Good riddance, I say. You can't stand in the way of progress. I'm not one for sentiment where old buildings are concerned.'

'Ah yes . . . I agree you can't stand in the way of progress. However, when it comes to buildings we're talking architecture, Christine. A different ball game – that's the current expression. Architecture, you see, is about environment . . .' He coughed, had to be patted soundly on the back as he

• Patricia Fawcett

went crimson and threatened to expire and mercifully the point was lost.

'Stuff that environment rubbish, Harold. It's too cold to be worrying about things you can't change,' she told him. 'That wind's fair whistling up my skirt.' She wrapped herself cosily into her big cardigan. 'I'll be catching that cold of yours by the time we've finished. I told you it was only early for car boots. It's perishing today.'

Harold sneezed without any warning, an Everest of a sneeze that sprayed germs like an avalanche over the stall, drawing forth icy stares from the two customers who were eyeing the wares.

'So sorry, ladies,' he apologised, giving one of his funny half-salutes. 'Caught me by surprise, that one.'

'You want to take care,' one of the ladies said, looking accusingly from Harold to Christine as if it were her fault. 'You want to look after your dad,' she went on. 'You have to be careful colds don't settle on their chest at their age. Before you know where you are, pneumonia. That's what saw my husband off.'

Perhaps feeling sorry for him, the other lady bought a large glass fruit bowl that had been conspicuously gracing their collection for many months past.

'Beautiful bowl, this,' Christine remarked with a smile as she wrapped it. 'It came from a house sale out at Longridge. Classy house, wasn't it, Harold? One of them big old stone ones.'

'The wine glasses came from the same house,' Harold said, pointing them out. 'Set of six. Perfect. They entertained on a lavish scale, that family. Money no object. You can just see the dinner parties, can't you? Beautiful frocks. Fine china. Wonderful food. These glasses filled with wine . . .'

Sales pitch perfected, they waited until a decision to purchase them too was arrived at. No haggling either. It perked Christine up a bit. She was feeling fed up if the truth were known because, unwisely maybe, she had packed in her job after a row with the supervisor about how high they could reasonably stack the baked beans. The customers would need a set of steps to reach them and Christine had felt it her duty to point that out. Toffee-nosed madam, that supervisor . . . just because she had double glazing and a fitted kitchen and one of them funny bubbly baths, you'd think she was somebody.

The Absent Child

Christine was therefore now out of work and at her age it wouldn't be easy to get something else. Still, no use crying over spilled milk, as they say, and she could manage because her living expenses were fairly minimal and Reg had provided for her. He had been careful with money and had ploughed a small inheritance he'd got from Lavender into what had proved a good investment. It provided her with a bit extra. Dear me no, Reg hadn't been a financial assistant for nothing.

They had kept their aspirations on an even keel. No point in moving to a bigger house if that would make things tight. No point in owning a car when the buses were so handy. No point either in having another baby when they could provide all that was necessary for just the one. Another child would have stretched the budget. She would have liked another baby but she understood Reg's point of view. Jenny never wanted for anything.

No, it wasn't so much the money from the job she missed as the companionship. With Janice fairly frizzled these days looking after that Shane, and most of the other ladies in Hargreaves Street going out to work, it was a bit lonely. She needed somebody to talk to.

Harold sneezed again and blew into a big white hanky. Christine glared at him and reached for the flask of coffee with the tot of rum in it. The way that sun had burrowed itself under them clouds, they needed it. It would sulk away all the rest of the afternoon by the look of it. God, it was like winter!

'I've picked up some holiday brochures,' Harold said suddenly, and she looked at him, quite shocked. 'From the travel agent's,' he said as if she didn't know where such things could be found.

'What for? You never go on holiday. What's brought this on?'

'Old age,' he said, 'and the inclement weather. I have a yearning to see something of the world before I pass on and I want some sunshine. I wouldn't have this cold if the sun was shining. My old bones are in need of drying out so I have enquired about what is called a package holiday.'

'You mean you want to go on holiday now?'

- Patricia Fawcett

'Precisely. As soon as we can organise it. I told the young lady she could expect to see me again tomorrow. I always knew them passports we got would come in useful one day. I trust, Christine, that you will come with me as my travelling companion?'

'I can't,' she spluttered, wondering why she couldn't. She had no job to go to just now but go on holiday with Harold . . . ?

'When we get back to your house, we will peruse the brochures,' he said firmly. 'Next week we could be in Greece.'

She looked at him, jolted into action. 'Or Majorca. Janice used to go there. Or Tenerife. They say that's nice.'

'Wherever,' Harold said with a smile. 'I will go wherever you choose providing it is hot. I will of course pay.'

'You'll do no such thing. I'm paying my whack, Harold. I'm not accepting charity.' She frowned as he sneezed once more, mightily. 'Hell's bells. Can't you stop that? People are looking.'

'Thank you for your sympathy.' His nose was red, eyes watering. 'Shall we pack up?'

Christine didn't need asking twice.

Hot soup and a big pot of tea. Chairs drawn up round the fire.

'This is the life,' Harold said, dunking bread in the soup. Frightened that he would end up with pneumonia, she had insisted he put a blanket round his shoulders until he warmed up. 'I think we'll wait until the weather bucks up before we do any more outdoor boots. We'll catch our death.'

'We'll wait until we get back from holiday,' Christine said, reaching for the glossy brochures, fired with enthusiasm now. 'Oh Harold, just look at this . . . Sorrento – it looks lovely. Do you ever see sea that colour here?'

'We could have a cruise,' Harold said, 'if you prefer . . . although if anything happens to me, I wouldn't want to be buried at sea on any account. My arrangements are all in hand. I did mention the arrangements?'

She gave him a look. And how!

'I'd rather keep my feet on dry land,' she said. 'No. We'll go to a hotel with a swimming pool and chairs you can sit on.' She cheered up at the thought. 'I'm glad you thought of this, Harold, it's just what I need. A break. And when I get back, I can think about getting myself another little job.'

The Absent Child

'I will have to tell Jenny,' he said thoughtfully. 'She's expecting me next week as usual. We'll have to cancel our tea date.'

'Tea date! You and your tea date. I don't suppose it's ever occurred to you to take me along too?' Christine asked, feeling her mood tighten as it did whenever Jenny was mentioned.

'Would you come if I did?' he asked amiably enough. 'Nothing would give me greater pleasure than to bring you two foolish ladies together again. When I think of all the problems in the world, and there are many, we allow a little family tiff to dominate our lives.' He gave her a big brother look. 'Would you come if I asked you, love? Many a time I've lain in bed at night thinking about how things might have been. If only you could have got Reg to bend a bit. You'd have had a granddaughter, Christine, and you wouldn't have lost your daughter either.'

'Fine words butter no parsnips, Harold.'

'Stop that,' he said. 'You and your daft sayings. Think about it, Christine. Before it's too late.'

A little subdued at the sharpness of his tone, she returned her attention to the brochures, her excitement dulled.

'Promise me you'll try when we get back,' he went on, more gently. 'It's not worth harbouring grudges, love. When I think about how things might have turned out for me through no fault of my own . . .'

She remembered the nearly wedding, their mother's indignation. The lovely satin dresses advertised in the paper for sale. Poor old Harold! He must have loved her a lot because he'd never looked at another woman. She still lived around here too, hard-faced madam, although her husband was long gone. There hadn't been any children.

'If it was up to me, I'd go to see her tomorrow. But it's Reg,' she said helplessly. 'I can't let Reg down.'

'He's gone,' Harold said through half-closed lids.

He leaned back in the chair, adjusted the blanket, his face blotchy from the cold, his silvery thatch of hair in some disarray. 'If you want to believe all that about him looking down at you, watching over you, then you're doing yourself no favours. Dead is dead. And I should know. Many a time I've sat there alone with a body – just me and it, it stiff and cold – thinking . . . wondering . . . food for thought, Christine.'

• Patricia Fawcett

'For God's sake, Harold, I've said I'll think about it. And another thing, if I do go on this holiday with you, I want no mention of funerals. People don't want to know about that when they're on holiday.'

'I was only trying to point out that you can leave Reg out of the equation, love. You were a very good wife to him so you've no need to reproach yourself, but he's gone. You have to think about Jenny now and if I had Reg weighed up right then he would have forgiven her long since. I know he had a stubborn set to him but he thought a lot about her and she was his only daughter after all.'

'I know. You're probably right. He did love her, Harold. He was ever so proud of her, really. He was so pleased at the thought that she'd be working with him. If only he could have gone then, at that moment, he would have died happy.' She gave a little sound, remembering that. 'As it was, he died unhappy, worrying about tomorrow.'

'He picked the wrong time to pop off,' Harold said. 'That's what went wrong. Churned both of you up.'

'I don't want to talk about it any more, Harold. Do you want anything for pudding?' she asked. 'I can rustle up some jam sponge and custard.'

'A dose of cough medicine would go down a treat.'

'Maybe I'll go to see her after the holiday,' she said, trying to sweeten him up a bit because he did look bad, bless him.

Harold opened his eyes, looked at her.

He wasn't fooled.

• 156

19

Stephen felt it churlish to have doubts about Abby's young man when she was so obviously infatuated. Ben Chambers was having a good effect on her for she seemed bubbly and extra pretty these days, dressing with a new-found confidence too. Stephen particularly liked the pale green softly draped trousers and matching top she was wearing this evening and at last, the blunt hairstyle had settled on her rather nicely.

The meal was superb, quite worthy of the panic and resulting shambles in the kitchen, and Abby played the part of hostess perfectly, flitting about unobtrusively from course to course. The big circular table in the immense dining room was set for three, Emily having made her excuses tonight. Through the french windows, the finely cut lawns stretched towards the boundary wall, the wide border beginning to reveal some of its summer secrets. The gardener came in three or four times a week, his affection for the old place already showing in so many ways and the garden was returning the affection.

'You two go through to the drawing room,' Abby told them as they finished off their desserts. 'I'll just clear away.'

'Leave it, darling,' Stephen said, but she was quietly insistent and it dawned a little belatedly that she wanted him to have a private moment with Ben. He wished Lizzie were here because he wasn't sure how serious these two young people were. He had the impression from certain glances that they exchanged that they were lovers already . . . That thought did not lie easily on his shoulders but, God knows, he had to be sensible.

He had telephoned Lizzie some time back to ask how they should deal with this sort of thing, when it arose, and she laughed away his worries. Don't come the heavy-handed father, she had warned him, or you'll make it ten times worse. Relax and let things take their course. The girls are practical and sensible, she had said confidently; they are perfectly able to look after themselves.

He hoped to God she was right about that.

'So, I find myself very interested in what you do for a living, Ben,' he said politely, once they were sitting comfortably in the drawing room. Neither of them smoked but Stephen did pour them each a whisky. 'And the plans that you outlined for the business seem very sound. However, do you think it's the right time for expansion?'

'It's exactly the right time.' Ben stretched out long legs, sipped the whisky. 'My father's totally against it I must admit but I've managed to convince the rest of the board. He was out on a limb and climbed down. It's caused a bit of family division, I'm afraid.' The smile was rueful. 'He's resisting me taking over. He's had two heart scares but we're having a hard fight to persuade him that I'm capable, more than capable, of running things. Whilst he's away, on a long cruise, I'm getting things moving.'

He leaned forward intently. He was all business, Stephen conceded, but he knew that if he came to him for a job, he wouldn't get it. Call it instinct but he didn't damned well trust him.

'We've been lacking direction these last few years. What the company needs in fact is a good kick up the backside. We could stay small,' he went on, 'small and insignificant. Or we can go for it. You must have faced the same dilemma?'

'Not quite,' Stephen said quietly. 'We didn't expand until we had the orders in our pockets. You're talking of expansion first, capital expenditure, and then going after them. Risky. What if the orders don't materialise?'

'You sound just like my father,' Ben said, the smile broadening. 'He's scared, Stephen, scared of failure.'

Stephen didn't recall inviting him to use his Christian name but said nothing. He wished Abby would get herself back in here before things turned sour.

'He's frightened of upsetting people on the shop floor,' Ben went on, undaunted. 'My plans will mean reshaping and that means losing staff of course. God knows that's not going to make me popular but I'm managing a business. An injection of new equipment will mean fewer hands. It's just got to be faced. You can't carry dead weights in a business, can you?'

Stephen smiled politely, wondering what this man saw in his dearest gentle Abby. Or more to the point, what did she see in him? Couldn't she see through him? She deserved much, much better than this. He saw Ben Chambers as a selfish man and he wanted Abby to have a man who cared for her much more than himself. Like he had with Lizzie.

'You obviously don't approve.'

'Of what? Your business methods? I wouldn't presume. I know nothing about printing, Ben. I'm an architect.'

'Quite right. Each to his own. I wouldn't dream of trying to design a building either.'

There was a small silence. Uncomfortable. This man opposite wasn't working up to asking for his daughter's hand in marriage was he? Did anyone do that sort of thing any more? If he does, what the hell will I say? wondered Stephen.

'Abby tells me she normally does the day-to-day cooking and looks after the house,' Ben said suddenly. 'She said that you dispensed with the services of a daily help when your wife left home. You used to have a housekeeper as well apparently.'

'Ah yes, the good old days! My wife did tend to employ people as if we were the aristocracy,' Stephen said lightly, wondering what in God's name it had to do with him. 'Abby thought we could manage on our own—'

'Did she? How old was she at the time?'

'Nearly fifteen. Why?' Stephen felt his anger rising and by God when he lost his temper, he lost his temper.

'I simply wondered why you allowed her to dictate to you at fifteen?'

'I beg your pardon. I think that's my business actually. It was important to Abby that she felt useful and if I may say so I know her rather better than you.'

'Do you? We know her in different ways, that's all.'

His eyes glittered and Stephen realised at last what it was he didn't like about him. That easy smile of his never reached his eyes. He had cold eyes. A chilly grey like a northern ocean. His dear, sweet Abby couldn't be in love with this man, could she?

'If Abby had come to me at fifteen and told me she intended to leave school as soon as legally possible, stop her education, so that she could become a drudge—'

'She's hardly that,' Stephen interrupted, keeping his voice even with difficulty. 'We have all mod cons, as they say, things to make life easier. She has a job she likes, her own car, and she does no more nor less than a lot of other women do. She never complains.'

Ben laughed. 'Oh no, she wouldn't. She's not the complaining sort, is she? Didn't it occur to you that she might want to go to university, read History? You scuppered her chances of doing that. My father would never have allowed me or my sister to drop out like that. Of course there was never any question of my not going to university. My family have supported both of us all the way.'

'I am trying to understand why you are taking this attitude,' Stephen said, mindful that Abby would hear if he raised his voice, mindful too that it was discourteous to have a slanging match in his own home. 'And I suppose it must be because you love her or think you do. Believe me, if I thought for one minute that Abby was unhappy then I would support her too if she wanted to leave her job and go to college. However . . .' he smiled with a supreme effort, desperate to cool the situation, 'although Abby is interested in history, she is not what I would call academic. She always said she didn't want to go on with study. Emily's the same.'

'Emily's in the sixth form working towards university, surely?'

'Only because we don't know what the hell to do with her. I've resigned myself to her not getting good grades. We'll have to have a drastic rethink come September.'

'I apologise if I sound critical,' Ben said, with a gracious tilt of his head, 'but your attitude towards Abby is so alien to me. You see, my family have always been so keen on equality for both of us. My sister and myself were treated exactly the same. No favouritism.'

'Nor is there any favouritism in ours,' Stephen said. 'Quite the opposite. We've always gone out of our way to treat the girls the same.'

'You would say that of course.'

'What exactly are you getting at?' Stephen drained his glass, set it down. To hell with this pussyfooting around! 'Come on, out with it! If you're criticising the way I've brought up my daughter, you've got a bloody nerve, Ben. When you're a father yourself,' he paused, hoping to God Abby wouldn't have a share in it, 'then you can tell me how to do things. Until then, let me tell you that fathers do not take kindly to advice.'

'But you're not, are you? If we're being nit-pickingly correct here.'

Stephen stared, unsure he had heard right. 'What the hell . . . ?'

'You are her adoptive father,' Ben said, a sort of triumph in the voice, a cold calculation in the eyes. 'It's not the same thing at all, is it? Actually, Mr Finch, it's rather thrown me. I should have been informed earlier. I find myself a little irritated that Abby chose to wait some considerable time before she told me. I'm having to reconsider my position and in fact, the more I think about it, the more I realise how fortunate it is that I had not already purchased the engagement ring. Mother was very keen on the match, looking forward to meeting Abby, but at the time we were under the impression, the *false* impression, that Abby was the daughter of an architect – yourself – and an opera singer. I now discover that, to put it bluntly, her real parents could be just anyone.'

'You bastard,' Stephen breathed the word, ready to throw him out but Abby chose that very moment to breeze in, make-up freshly applied, a little flushed, looking happy and gorgeous.

'That's all done,' she said. 'Have you had a nice chat?' She stopped, caught the atmosphere. 'Something wrong?'

'No, darling.' Stephen, stunned, attempted a smile, rose from his seat. 'If you'll excuse me, I have things to do. I'll be in my study if you need me.' He kissed Abby as he passed, holding her close a moment. His precious daughter.

He closed the door.

• Patricia Fawcett

Slammed an angry fist against his chest.
This would break her heart.

'Of course you can have a word,' Jenny told him, laughing. 'You don't have to make an appointment. Come on through to the garden.'

Stephen followed her into the cottage, liking its cosy neatness, although he felt a little hemmed in by its size. She had been sitting on a wooden bench on the little paved terrace, enjoying the gentle early evening sunshine.

'I thought you said you were a rotten gardener,' he said, admiring the colourful clutter of it. 'And you've got hanging baskets too.'

'Oh yes. The works. I get them made up for me and then all I have to do is remember to water them.' She was looking at him enquiringly, obviously curious to know what was the matter but not rushing it. 'Would you like a cool drink?' she asked.

'Thanks.'

He waited, trying to stay calm, his thoughts still in turmoil although it was a couple of days since the disastrous dinner.

'Emily pops in quite a lot,' Jenny said, bringing out a jug of orange juice. 'She reminds me of a girl I used to know, someone who was always the life and soul of the party. It's a shame that youthful exuberance gets squashed, isn't it? Oh to be seventeen again . . .' Her expression changed momentarily and he might not have noticed had he not been looking intently. 'I know she's worried about her exams so, for what it's worth, I've been trying to help her a bit with her homework, trying to encourage her. She lacks organisation, that's all. Whether I'm getting anywhere or not is another matter.'

'Thanks for trying. I don't seem to get anywhere either,' he said with a grimace. 'She's started smoking, you know. Thinks I haven't realised. I'm trying to play it down, hoping it will pass. Lizzie's always been so laid back about what they get up to and I'm terrified of playing the overbearing father.'

'You? Overbearing?' She laughed, sat down cosily beside him. She was wearing a blue denim skirt and white embroidered top, very little make-up, her hair loose. He preferred it that way. 'You can tell me, Stephen, if there's something wrong,' she said. 'I'm told I'm a good listener.'

'It's Abby,' he said. 'She invited her boyfriend over for dinner the other night and I'm afraid, between the two of us, me and him, we've cocked things up for her . . . Sorry, but that's what it feels like.'

'Ben Chambers?' she asked thoughtfully. 'Is she still going out with him?'

'Was,' he replied. 'She hasn't admitted it – maybe the bastard hasn't got round to telling her yet – but I know from speaking to him that, as far as he's concerned, it's over.'

'She's better off without him,' Jenny said quite heatedly, so that he looked at her in surprise.

'You don't like him either?'

She shook her head. 'I don't want to go into details, Stephen, but no I don't.'

'I see.' He smiled, not quite seeing but reluctant to probe further. 'Abby's looking pretty miserable. I'm very sensitive to her moods, Jenny, and it hurts me when she's hurt. I had a feeling all along it wouldn't work out with him but what can you say? You have to let it run its course.'

'You should stop worrying,' she told him. 'She's a sensible girl and, believe me, girls prefer to sort out their own problems. They do not go a bundle on parental advice. I speak from experience,' she added ruefully, and he wondered again about her background. Something was wrong there somewhere.

'You're right, I suppose. I have to relax more, let them get on with it. And God knows, I don't want her to accuse me of interfering.'

'You'll have to let her go one day, Stephen,' she said after a moment.

The sun lowered in a sky that was streaked with pink and they sighed, the scent of a nearby plant drifting their way. The silence here was so palpable, it bordered on the religious. He felt it powerfully and he knew she did too. She was, despite her scientific leanings, a sensitive soul.

'You'll have to let both of them go.'

'I know that.' He reached over and took her hand, held it a moment before letting go. 'It happens to every dad. But it's not

• Patricia Fawcett

just that, Jenny. You don't quite understand the position. I hate to see Abby upset because she's always been so special to me.'

'Naturally. Your first-born.'

'That's it, you see. Abby's our adopted daughter,' he said.

He had seen many reactions to those words over the years, one or two regrettably approaching Ben Chambers' version, but he was surprised to see Jenny's.

She was so taken aback that for a moment she swayed as if she was going to pass out, paled too.

'You all right?' he asked anxiously.

She nodded. 'I'm getting cold. Shall we go indoors?'

Puzzled at the sudden change in her, he followed her. What had he said? Oh God, the last thing he needed now was to upset Jenny too. She meant something to him. He wasn't sure yet of his feelings but he knew she meant *something*.

20

Jenny recognised it finally for what it was: the precious start of a relationship that promised much. Slowly does it then. They had touched a few times, in passing almost, and there had been the odd meaningful glance. She was starting to look for them and she was becoming enveloped more and more in a romantic glow. Falling in love time. Dammit, she should have more sense by now. Was she still as much of a fool as she had been at sixteen? Surely she was past that?

Before the brief blitz with Ben there had been one or two others, never anything really serious, but this time it was different – good – and she felt a bit worried for it was too soon, much too soon, for thoughts like this. She would be wise to snuff it out before anything happened. True his girls were grown-up, not dependent on him but nevertheless they were part of him, as was his ex-wife, this Lizzie he kept on about. She still featured a lot in his life, in his thoughts, even though she was far away these days. Oh why did she always end up with men with strings attached? Either that or boorish bastards like Ben. Oh for a nice uncomplicated bachelor or widower with no children. This way, and she knew it was selfish, this way she couldn't really have Stephen for herself. It was Stephen plus the encumbrances.

So Abby was their adopted daughter and, once Jenny had recovered from the shock, she had listened intently to the story. They had thought they would never have a child of their own, adopted Abby, and then almost at once, because the pressure was off, presumably, Lizzie had conceived, not entirely deliriously happy as a result. If he was honest, Stephen

• Patricia Fawcett

supposed that was the start of the problems in their marriage. Jenny understood why he needed to be extra loving to Abby. It was a way of covering up his guilt.

For a moment, as he said the words, it was as if someone walked over her grave. It had caused an instant memory jarring of her own baby. Sometimes she imagined she had succeeded at last in smothering all those old longings but of course she had not. She would do anything to avoid holding babies and her friends assumed she was strictly non-maternal. She never explained.

Eighteen years ago . . . his features were dim now as memories faded but if she really tried she could conjure them up. A tallish fairish man, boy really, with a nice sense of humour, the face itself blurred. The one photograph was gone, mysteriously disappeared, but she suspected it had been torn up and thrown onto the fire – for her own good of course so that she wouldn't brood. She imagined the flames licking it until it was reduced to layers of white ashes. Gone for ever. Like him.

The memory could not be destroyed though, not completely, and as it swam into view once more, she could remember the dark blond hair, blue eyes and the big strong nose.

Quite like Abby's.

Abby was at a loss to understand what had happened. Why the sudden cold shoulder? The silence from Ben was complete.

She could pinpoint the moment exactly. After the dinner party something had happened between him and Dad and Dad wasn't saying anything either. When she'd walked into the room, you could have cut the air with a freezer knife. She had felt her father shaking with anger as he kissed her and, although he did his best to hide it, he had that look on his face that she knew very well, that suppressed anger look. They'd made themselves scarce when they were little, she and Emily, when they'd seen that look appearing.

As for Ben, he couldn't wait to be off and their ensuing conversation had been suddenly strained. He had complimented her on her cooking which, after the effort she had made with her appearance, was the last thing she wanted to be told. His kiss goodbye had been light and the 'I'll be in touch' had rung untrue even then.

She wished she could talk to Mum about it but she was never in when she tried to telephone and in any case it wasn't the same as face to face. If this was the brushoff from Ben, and it surely was, then it was pretty spectacular coming as it did when he had been hinting at an engagement, mentioning dates for going to visit his parents, as soon as they returned.

Damn it, she would go and see him and ask what had happened. He owed her an explanation if nothing else. They couldn't leave it like this, not when they lived so close. She was damned if she was going to hide from him, scared to catch his eye if they met. Decision made, she marched round, indignation bubbling, wearing old jeans but reluctant to take the time to change in case she lost her nerve, noting his car was in the drive so he was definitely in. Bouncing up the drive, she knocked loudly on the door, her anger on show immediately.

'Oh, it's you,' he said. 'I thought it was the bailiffs at the least.' The smile was a little late. 'Come on in.'

'I'm here because I haven't heard from you,' she said, sitting down without being invited to. 'Not a phone call or anything.'

'I've been busy.'

'That hasn't stopped you from seeing me before,' Abby said, strangely calm now that she was here. In tight jeans and sloppy sweater, he looked great as usual, however, he was shifty as hell and it was obvious to anyone with the slightest degree of sensitivity that it was all over. It was a terrible embarrassment to him that she was here now. But she needed to know why. She did know why in fact but she wanted him to have to say it, the slimeball that he was, she wanted to squeeze those words out of him. She wanted him to own up to being the same supersnob as his mother.

'You're right. I don't normally let work interfere in my private life. Things have changed between us, Abby. I was going to explain.'

'Really?' She kept her voice pleasant and light. 'You can tell me, Ben. I can take it. You don't have to treat me like a child.'

'Very well. If you insist.' He chose not to sit down, hovering by the window instead. 'We've been a little premature. Rushing

• Patricia Fawcett

things. It's what you girls, particularly you younger girls, seem to expect nowadays. I often feel it's a pity that the old romance has gone out of a courtship. We should pursue things at a more leisurely pace. Now, if you're not in bed together after the fourth date, there's something seriously amiss.'

'I'm sorry, I don't quite understand . . .'

'Come on, Abby, don't act dumb. Of course you understand. You're not a child and I can personally vouch for that.'

His laugh was at her expense and she wondered with a clarity that amazed how she could have possibly thought herself in love with him. He was arrogant, smug and egotistic.

'You might have had the decency to tell me it was over,' she said, glad she was able to control the tremble in her voice. 'Isn't that the gentlemanly thing to do? You needn't have bothered with the excuses. I think I understand all too well what they are.'

'Don't get stroppy with me,' he said. 'Surely you didn't think it was serious? You didn't expect wedding bells and all the trimmings, did you?' He snatched at the short pause. 'Oh my God, you did Abby . . .'

She couldn't admit that she had had a brief vision of white lace and flowers and, indeed, all the trimmings. Dad escorting her up the aisle, so proud of her, Mum there in all her splendour being persuaded later to sing for them, even Emily fed up in a bridesmaid's dress. As she stared at Ben's smiling face, the disgrace was complete. Annoyingly, she couldn't immediately think of a quick quip that would cut him down to size.

'No hard feelings I hope, darling? Put it down to experience, eh?'

He escorted her across what seemed like miles of humiliating floor to the door, held out his hand which she did not take. 'Shame you never got to meet my parents. My mother was looking forward to meeting you at one time.' He opened the door, attempted to smile her out.

'Was she indeed! I can't say the feeling was mutual,' Abby said. 'My being adopted was too much for her to take, was it? And you too? And you haven't even got the guts to admit it. You can't bear to think there's a chance my real parents might be very ordinary people indeed.' She controlled a sudden upsurge of feelings on their behalf, people she had never met. By her very stillness, she forced him to look at her. 'Oh my, what a lucky escape I've had,' she whispered.

'My regards to your . . . er . . . father.'

She noted the hesitation. Knew exactly what it meant.

'Oh sod off, Ben,' she said, throwing the remark cheerfully over her shoulder as she flounced off. Mum had made some splendid exits in her time but even she couldn't have done better.

21

Christine had to pack for Harold too. Harold had no idea. He had no casual clothes either and she'd had to drag him to the shops to buy some. He had protested of course, not at the expense but at the waste of time. Christine insisted. He was not sitting sweltering on a hotel terrace in a suit, stiff shirt and tie. He was not showing her up like that. It was a pain in the neck trying to sort him out with some nice lightweight shirts and shorts and, to be honest, he did look a right pickle in them with his knees.

Still, when in Rome . . .

She had some new stuff herself, rapidly and painlessly purchased, and she was taking her black swimsuit. Not that she would be putting so much as a big toe in the pool because she didn't like swimming, made her eyes itch. She was going to do nothing but sit on a lounger and sunbathe and maybe read a nice book. That was her lot. Harold could go on the optional excursions to his heart's content but she was not budging.

Having successfully sorted him out, she was left with precious little time to do her own packing. She would have to get her skates on if she was to be ready and thank God for Janice. Janice loved ironing, said it was therapeutic. Therefore, she stood at the ironing board, steam iron poised, happily going through a pile of blouses and skirts as Christine fretted and fussed about what to take.

They were accompanied by Shane giving a virtuoso performance on the piano. Somewhere, vaguely, there were the remnants of a tune. His concentration on this occasion was commendable. He'd been going at it hammer and tongs for all of five minutes, little fat fingers fair flying over the keys.

'Shut up, sweetheart, there's a good boy. You're giving Grandma a headache,' Janice said with a smile. 'Do you think we should take him for lessons?' she enquired of Christine. 'He seems a natural.'

Christine ignored that. Of all the things Shane might be, a budding pianist was not one of them.

'Is your Catherine all right?' she asked instead. 'She looked a bit peaky last time I saw her.'

'Ah well . . .' Janice paused in mid-steam, looking warningly towards the child. 'She's expecting again,' she muttered. 'Caught out. Furious she is with him, that husband of hers. He was supposed to be seeing to things.'

'Oh dear.' Christine put on a sympathetic face, rolling up underwear and cramming it into her suitcase. 'She'll be carrying on working though? Getting that maternity leave?'

Janice shook her head. 'Not a chance. She had such a bad time with him, bless his little heart, and it looks like it's going to be just as bad again. My God, is she sick! Morning, noon and night. Sick as a dog. She's packed her job in already, told him where he could stick the extra money. It was just for luxuries. After all, it's not as if they really need it, not with Len having a good job and everything. I told you he works at CWC, didn't I? Senior sort of job like your Jenny.'

'But they've taken a lot on with that house they're doing up, haven't they?'

'He does a lot of it himself. He does very well for days off,' Janice said. 'As I said, he has a senior job and they more or less leave him to his own devices. Lucky for some, eh?'

Shane, the concert over, unfortunately had taken it upon himself to help Christine with her packing, stuffing wrong things into wrong corners. Reluctant to tell him off, Christine looked round for a diversion but Janice's alert eyes had noticed.

'Leave them alone, sweetheart,' she said. 'Auntie Christine's going on a big aeroplane tomorrow and she's taking that with her.'

That set him off, roaring round the room with his arms held out like wings. They smiled and Janice leisurely completed the pile. 'There. That's finished. Any more?'

'Thanks, Janice.' Christine straightened up, her back a bit stiff and smiled. 'Fancy a cup of tea?'

It was a relief frankly when Janice went with Shane getting on her neves more than usual and she made herself a second cup of tea, a quiet one this time, taking it through for some reason to the front room. Funny how they'd never used this room, not as a room should be used.

Christmas they'd come in here. The tree stood in that corner, the same old tree, one of them that folds up when you've finished with it, green and silver, and the same decorations, year in year out. Things Jenny had made at school. All carefully packed away now in that big box in the loft. Now that she was alone, she never bothered. Just stuck a few pieces of holly and tinsel behind the pictures. The sherry and her homemade Christmas cake on the sideboard in case any of the neighbours popped in.

A quiet little girl, Jenny. She'd liked dolls and playing in the Wendy house at nursery, all the things you weren't supposed to let little girls play with these days in case it got them started on the wrong foot.

Sitting in the chair, the one by the window that she'd always sat in, the painful vision returned. Jenny, hair pulled back into a ponytail, playing with her presents, Reg in one of his cheerful moods, stuffing himself with chocolates, smoking a special Christmas cigar, maybe even having a glass of sherry. He had loved Christmas. He'd really come alive at Christmas. And for once she hadn't minded all that traipsing to church.

Just the three of them on Christmas Day itself. Here in the sitting room with a big roaring fire and the tree with its lights twinkling.

Harold was right. She should take the bull by the horns and put a stop to all this nonsense. She should go to see her. She could go this afternoon, get there in time for Jenny getting home from work, take her by surprise. She'd worry about getting back afterwards. She wasn't sure how she'd get to Hazelburn but Harold had said something about an occasional bus. She troubled about it as she tidied up, completed the preparations for the holiday. Harold was calling for her first thing in the morning and they were driving to Manchester Airport, leaving the car

• Patricia Fawcett

there. They'd neither of them been up in a plane and she was looking forward to it. Wouldn't it be wonderful then if all this – this thing with Jenny – could be got out of the way before they went? She'd enjoy her holiday a lot more if it was sorted out.

But what would she say?

Jenny . . . hello, love, it's me.

That was daft.

I was just passing and I thought . . .

That was even dafter. How could she be just passing on the only bus of the day?

Would Jenny have forgotten the last words? *She* remembered them for they might as well be ingrained in her heart but Jenny might have forgotten.

Harold phoned as she was getting ready but she did not tell him she was planning to catch the bus or he'd insist on coming to get her and driving her there himself. She did not want him interfering.

'Can I go through the check list again?' he asked, and laboriously they went through it together. Documents, the foreign money, sunglasses, his old camera, phrase book, etc. And another thing, he said, if he died suddenly whilst over there, he wanted to be sure she knew what needed to be done. There was no need for her to panic.

'I won't panic,' she told him sharply. 'But it won't half spoil my holiday so you'd better not.'

Finally he put the phone down, reminding her he would pick her up at six o'clock prompt. They would arrive fifteen minutes *before* the earliest checking in time. No plane would be delayed on account of their late arrival. In over forty years of funerals, he was at pains to point out, he had never once been late.

She caught the bus with minutes to spare. It went up hill and down dale and took God knows how many hours but it was scheduled to stop at the crossroads in Hazelburn at five thirty. Harold said Jenny usually got home about sixish so she wouldn't have long to wait. She supposed she should have rung first. Harold said she went away quite a lot on business and hadn't she just been to Amsterdam? Serve her right if she wasn't in then, serve her right for being impulsive.

She worried on the bus about what she would say. A woman

with a tartan shopping trolley and blue-rinsed hair got on at Longridge and came to sit beside her. Christine smiled at her, made room, gave her chance to settle.

'I'm going to Hazelburn,' she said, as the bus shuddered off. 'I've heard tell it's a lovely little place.'

'It is. Nice church there,' the woman said. 'I used to clean at the big house there, Curwin Hall. Then he died, Mr Muncaster, and I lost my job. Couldn't blame him of course. Not with him dying. There's new people there now. Just moved in not long since. A man and his daughters. Divorced they do say.' She lowered her voice but nobody else was listening. 'An architect they say, up in Preston.'

'I come from Preston,' Christine said, pleased she had found someone to talk to, to while away the time. 'My brother, Harold, used to be in funerals. Taylor and Walmsley out at Ribbleton. He's the Walmsley. And my husband . . . well, I—'

'Oh, there's my stop coming up,' the woman said. 'Nice to talk to you. See you again.'

Christine doubted it very much. She smiled as the woman got off the bus, sorry that she'd had to go just when they were getting acquainted.

Alone again, she brooded once more. She dreaded seeing the same look in her daughter's eyes that she remembered. The look of a stranger. If it was still there then her journey would be a waste of time. And another thing, she didn't know how she was going to square this with Reg. She'd have to tell him. After the holiday.

What fools they were. Jenny had lived fairly near these last few years and they'd never tried to get in touch. Never once. Wasted years. They could have done things together, just like Janice and Catherine. Jenny could have come for Christmas and, if there'd been a man, he could have come too. After all, Jenny wasn't that young any more. You couldn't expect her to live like a nun.

'We're here, love,' the bus driver called, now that she was the only person left. She didn't know how these country routes paid now that everybody else had cars. 'Where do you want dropping?'

'Anywhere will do,' she said, smiling her thanks. 'Can you tell me the time of the bus back?'

• Patricia Fawcett

He looked at her as if she'd gone crackers.

'Well now, that'll be a bit of a carry-on. You might be able to catch the Garstang bus,' he said, consulting his timetable, 'but it doesn't come through here. You'll have to walk to the next village – four or five miles – and then pick it up at the pub. Just after seven. As near as dammit.'

'Thanks very much.'

She felt absurdly like tipping him, remembering herself in time, stepping out into the quiet, watching as he drove off. She breathed in the country air – fresh, granted, but tinged with manure from the farm she was standing beside. So this was it, this was what all the fuss was about.

The little village street straggled away from the farm towards a green with a stone cross and a church, the hills in the background, quite pretty she supposed if you liked this sort of thing. Jenny's was the white cottage at the end of the street, Harold had said, you can't miss it and she had a big blue car. No sign of it yet.

She walked on, her slingbacks not so clever on this pitted surface that passed for a pavement. She supposed she couldn't expect anything else in the country. If she had to walk five miles to catch the bus back, she'd be on her knees and she had to be ready for six tomorrow, up at five that meant.

She clattered on. There was a lovely big house that she glimpsed through a fancy gate, a big posh house with clipped bushes and flowerbeds. And then, round the corner, at the end of the village there was the white cottage with tubs and hanging baskets. That was its name, The White Cottage.

She slowed as she walked past, peeped in the windows but not so anyone would notice. Not that there was a soul about. She'd go spare if she lived here. She knew she was forever grumbling about Janice and Shane but they were better than nothing. And the quiet was deadly. All she could hear was her own breathing. A bit ragged because she'd got herself into a state.

She hesitated a moment before she knocked on the door. Waited. She'd known even before she knocked that there was nobody in but she gave it one more knock for luck before she turned away.

She'd wait in the church. Wait for Jenny to come home.

Appropriate for she could talk to Reg, as it were, at the same time. Explain.

Inside, it was quiet and cold. Big for a country church and a bit dusty. She put a fifty-pence coin into the donations box, slipped into a pew at the back and prayed to God to give her strength to do what she had to do. Slotted a bit in at the end to the effect that she hoped the weather wouldn't break while they were away, not in Italy, because they were really looking forward to it and Harold especially needed his bit of sun. And then finally, love to Reg . . . something like that.

Every few minutes she popped to the door to check if the car was there yet. It began to occur to her after an hour that this had been a very silly thing to do. Jenny was working late or maybe she was away somewhere.

If Christine was to catch that bus back, she'd have to get a move on for she had no idea how long it would take to walk to the next village, not in these shoes. Coming out of the church, she felt tears welling up. Stupid she was. And there was no way she was walking five miles. Five *miles*!

There was a phone box, a proper red one, nearly opposite the big house. She would ring Harold, get him to come and fetch her. Face the music then.

She willed Jenny's car to come, waited a moment in the phone box, coins poised, as a car did appear. A flash silver thing with a man driving. Disappointed and distressed to the point of despair, she phoned Harold and, when she heard his reverent tones announcing his number, had never been so relieved in her life.

22

She sounded like she was in the next room, not another continent.

'Do you know what time it is?' Stephen asked, sitting up in bed, trying desperately to rouse himself from his slumbers. He had always slept like a log, never had a problem with it, not even when the girls were babies, nor in those difficult days when Lizzie left.

'Oh no, I forgot again. I forgot it's different for you. Are you in bed?'

He nodded, ridiculously, into the mouthpiece.

'Alone?'

'Yes, alone,' he said, coming to a little. The room was softly lit by the lamp at the bedside. His bedroom, and it was very much his choice now that he slept alone. Heavy dark furniture and a plain bedcover. If Clare – God forbid – had ever come to live here, it would have been all-frills-go from the outset. That and unbelievable clutter.

He sighed, plumping up the pillows into a heap he could lie against. The green numerals on his clock glowed. Hell . . . he had an important meeting tomorrow and he needed to be razor-sharp for that.

'Hello, Lizzie,' he said, and couldn't help a little smile. 'To what do I owe this pleasure? You don't often ring me.'

'Not often enough. Don't be sarcastic, darling. You don't ring me either. There's no need for a complete news blackout. Are you settling in that mansion of yours? Abby wrote to tell me you'd moved. She says the house is absolutely enormous with huge gardens. Emily hates it. Really, Stephen, did you have to move house on Abby's birthday? It was most inconsiderate.'

'It couldn't be helped,' he said with a sigh. He was not up to an argument, not now. 'What do you want, Lizzie?'

'Do I have to want anything to ring you? After all, you are my ex. We are still friends, aren't we? I'm always telling people how lucky we are to have had such an amicable divorce. It's rare you know. Most of my friends are spitting fire at their ex-husbands. But we remain friends, don't we?' The plea was in her voice, the very descriptive voice, and he could see her expression, the way she had of looking at him through lowered lids. 'And we still have the girls, our joint responsibility.'

'You should ring them more often,' he told her, refraining from stating the obvious. That she had very effectively opted out of her share of the responsibility when she took off with that tenor of hers. 'Abby's very down at the moment. Boyfriend trouble. She wanted to talk to you about it.'

'Whatever for? What could I tell her? Who is he, this boyfriend?'

'Someone from the village. A lot older.'

'That shouldn't matter at all, not if he was the right man,' she said firmly. 'Age is not important.'

'Obviously not.'

She laughed. 'Still a bit touchy, aren't you? You never understood, Stephen, that the thing with Simon had nothing at all to do with age. It was a purely physical thing and I'm not ashamed of saying it. You and I had drifted apart, admit it, and although Simon and I did everything we could to prevent it happening, it was hopeless. Fate. He was a very persuasive man.'

Still a bit sleepy, he nevertheless caught the past tense she was using.

'Is it over then? Have you two split up?'

'No . . . well, yes. It was all very civilised. We decided, quite agreeably, to go our separate ways. He was starting to pile on the pounds, poor soul, and this appalling diet was making him very bad-tempered. Worse, he had to wear a corset on stage and it was affecting his performance. He was starting to move badly.'

'Really?' He couldn't help the triumphant sound. He knew it. He'd known it all along. So, the tenor was being given the heave-ho now, was he? 'What are you going to do?' he asked.

'Do? I have no idea. I'm not suicidal, darling, if that's what you're thinking. I could have my pick of any number of men if that's what I wanted. Luigi is still snapping at my heels but he's too short, poor darling. My plans are a little vague but I think I may go to New York when my contract ends. The climate's not so good but it's all happening there.'

'Might you be coming back here?' he asked, finding himself gripping the phone as if there were no tomorrow. He didn't know what he wanted her to say. It would cause all sorts of problems if she did come home.

'Do you want me to?' The purr was in the voice and for a moment he couldn't say a word. The clock ticked solidly and he stared mesmerised at the glowing figures. 'I ought to come home to see my daughters,' she continued as he made no reply. 'Especially Abby if she is fretting about this man of hers. How is darling Emily by the way?'

'Worried about her exams.'

'Silly girl. Exams are never worth worrying about. Emily is beautiful and that counts for so much more than exams.'

'Tell that to a prospective employer,' he said, exasperated at the way her mind worked.

'Don't be such a bore,' she said with another laugh. 'I am due a vacation and I will try to get over. No strings though. I don't expect a reconciliation. I'm not sure I want one.'

'Nor I,' he said stiffly. 'I'm thinking of the girls. It would be nice for them. They miss you, you know. And Emily would love you to be here for her birthday.'

'But I missed Abby's so it might look as if I was showing favouritism,' she said, knowing how his mind worked. 'Perhaps after her birthday . . .'

They moved on to talk about her work and the wonderful Californian climate but it was not long before they had exhausted the small talk.

'I'll let you get back to sleep,' she said. 'Good night, darling.'

He remembered other times she had said that. Happier times.

'Good night, Lizzie,' he said as he replaced the receiver.

* * *

He wondered if it was worth telling the girls in the morning, raising their hopes when, knowing Lizzie, she would never turn up. In the end, the ungracious triumph he felt about Simon won the day.

He told them over breakfast, the usual scrambled affair as they fought against time.

'He's left her!' Emily shrieked. 'Did you hear that, Abby? What does that mean? Is she coming home?'

'No, no,' Stephen said quickly, 'they left each other apparently. Don't forget we're divorced, darling. She wouldn't be coming home permanently. As far as I know, she's intending to stay in California. If she does move anywhere, it will probably be New York, not back to England.'

'Can I go to see her? Now that porky face has moved out?' Emily asked, snatching a piece of toast. 'If I go now it won't get in the way too much with my studying. If I leave it any longer, it will get in the way. Don't you see? Abby can come with me. Can you fix us up with cheap flights?' She turned on Abby, who was busy piling dishes into the dishwasher.

'Hang on . . .' Stephen laughed, caught Abby's affectionate glance at her sister, 'you're not going anywhere, Emily Finch, until you've finished your exams. After that, who knows? Let's see how you do in those exams first.'

'That's bribery,' she spluttered, licking buttery fingers. 'Tell him, Abby. Isn't it just awful that he has to resort to that? All we want to do is see Mum.' She fixed pleading eyes on him, so like Lizzie in that split second that he had to take a deep breath. 'Look at the time . . .' she gave up, annoyed. 'Is anyone going to give me a lift or have I to wait for that crappy bus?'

'Emily! Don't let me hear you say that again. It sounds disgusting from you.' Stephen fixed her with a stern look, half amused at the way she buckled under the gaze. A closer glance at those innocent eyes confirmed his suspicion. 'Are you wearing eye make-up for school? Is it allowed?'

'Of course it is. Relax, Daddy.' Emily kissed him. 'I'll get my things and you can drive me in. I like arriving in style in the Merc.'

'What else did Mum have to say?' Abby said when they were alone. 'I hope you didn't tell her about Ben.'

'I did mention it,' he said, dismayed that it mattered. 'Didn't you want me to?'

She shrugged. 'It's just that I really wanted to tell her myself.'

'Sorry . . . I didn't think. She sends her love,' he said, realising she hadn't. 'She said it was probably for the best. Ben wasn't the right man for you.'

'I know that,' she said impatiently, 'but it frightens me, Dad, that I nearly made a terrible mistake. Why did you get married to Mum? What made you decide it was the right thing to do?'

'She decided for me,' he said. 'She swept me off my feet.'

They laughed.

'You mustn't take it to heart, darling,' he said, following her into the hall as she prepared to leave. 'Anyone who thinks that way about adoption is just plain ignorant. I could have—' he stopped, realising he was giving it away.

'Then he did say something to you?' Abby asked, pouncing on it. 'About you not being my real father?'

He couldn't avoid an answer as she was looking at him with those lovely trusting eyes of hers.

'Something like that,' he said, unable to produce even a small smile. 'Come on, Emily,' he yelled up the stairs as they heard crashing sounds above, 'I haven't got all day.'

Abby gave a strangled laugh, came over and kissed him.

'Dad . . . you're not upset, are you? How dare he say that to you?' she said. 'If I met my real father tomorrow, what else would he be but a stranger? You're my dad and you always will be.'

The anger blazed momentarily in her eyes.

Warmed his heart.

Emily wearing her version of a school uniform thundered down under the weight of several bags, with what looked like hiking boots on her feet. A dash of lipstick and perfume too if he wasn't mistaken. Lizzie's smile. A feeling of great affection settled on him.

He loved them, these daughters of his.

23

Another few minutes and Jenny would have been out of the laboratory on her way to the admin building. It was cutting it fine but she decided she had time to take the call that Rose put through.

'Jenny? Bill Johnson here. How are you? Long time no see.'

She smiled into the receiver. 'Hello, Bill. How are things with you?'

'Fine. No problems. Well – not many. Time for a quick chat?'

'Quick,' she said, glancing at her watch. 'I'm due in a meeting soon.'

She had known Bill since they were at university together. Kept vaguely in touch. Their career paths had followed similar patterns although he worked for a company based in Scotland.

'Still at the same place?' she asked.

'Yes. Fifteen years now. Congratulations on the job by the way. I spotted your appointment in the Institute magazine. Big step up for you but no more than you deserve, you clever old thing.'

'Thank you, sir,' she said with a little laugh. 'It's not easy though, especially when everybody expects you to have all the answers.'

'Same here. We've had a panic this week and I've never got home before nine. Sara's going daft.'

'How is she? And the children? Three, isn't it?'

'Three and a bit,' he said, 'another one due. The two oldest have got Scottish accents.'

'How lovely!'

She checked her watch. She didn't want to hurry him but . . .

He seemed to sense it, changed his tone. 'Down to business.

• Patricia Fawcett

I'm killing two birds with one stone, Jenny. Congratulating you on the new job and picking your brains too. I'm on the lookout for an alternative supplier for acetic anhydride. Can you recommend anyone? We've got quality problems with our current source.'

'We get ours from Ettybridge, Bill,' she told him confidently.

'Hell. So do we.'

'And you've got problems?' She pulled a notepad towards her, began to doodle on it, suddenly puzzled and a little worried.

'We certainly have. That's what the panic's been about. If we get just a trace of water it fouls up our process.'

'Same here. Expensive business eh?' She continued to doodle, drawing a frame round the picture, her mind working overtime.

'And how. Hundreds of thousands of pounds worth of dud product. Unrecoverable at that.' He sighed. 'My neck's on the block over this, Jenny, although I think I'm over the worst.'

'What do Ettybridge propose to do about it?'

'Wholesale panic on there as well. I think it's just a blip on their part. Chance in a million, you know.' There was a short pause. 'Glad I rang, then. I wouldn't like you to get tripped up when you're new to the job.'

'Thanks.' She smiled. 'Nice to speak to you again, Bill, and don't forget to let me know when the new baby arrives.'

After her meeting, she called in Len and Alan, her senior Quality Control Officer, but Alan arrived alone smiling an apology on Len's behalf.

'Back lunchtime I think,' he said. 'You never can be sure with him.'

'Where is he exactly?' She sighed, having the feeling she'd been through this before. 'He's supposed to log in with Rose.'

'I can check for you. Andersen's, I think.'

'Can he be contacted there or is he flitting about from department to department so that nobody can be sure where in hell he is?'

He looked at her oddly. 'I'll root out the number for you,' he said. 'Do you want to give him a call?'

'No. Sit down, Alan.' She frowned her irritation. Len was a loose cannon and all hell could break loose if what she was beginning to suspect was true. 'You remember we had some quality concerns about polyamide some time back? You checked Len's raw material sheets and everything seemed OK? Incoming batches already verified at the suppliers and so on.'

He nodded. Eyes wary.

'I'd like you to retest the reference samples for the last six months.'

He stiffened in the chair. 'Christ ... sorry, but don't you realise what's involved in that? Remember we've got rid of most of the raw materials staff and I haven't got the people to spare.'

'Find them,' she said shortly. 'Pull people off non-essential work and get them to retest the acetic anhydride. Work overtime if you have to. I'll square it with Mr Cummings.'

'Len won't like it,' he said. 'It's his area of responsibility. His baby. It'll look like we don't trust his figures.'

She did not flinch, caught his look. Something told her, deep down, Alan would not be too dismayed if Len was finally hooked.

'Just do it, Alan.'

'Very well.' There was the ghost of a smile. 'Len won't like it,' he repeated. 'Those sample sheets are sacred to him.'

'If he asks, refer him to me. This is potentially very serious, Alan,' she said, knowing she didn't really have to tell him that for he knew already. 'One of our processes could be in great danger of being . . .'

'Cocked up?'

She smiled. 'Of being contaminated I was going to say. Can you let me have that phone number for Len? I'll see if I can catch him there.'

A few minutes later, armed with the number, she was in contact with Andersen's QA manager. The man was mystified.

'I haven't seen him personally for months,' he said. 'I'll check for you but as far as I'm aware, he telephones now and then but as an inspection is no longer deemed necessary for every batch—'

'He hasn't checked your samples for some time then?'

'Well, no . . .' A certain cageyness crept into his voice. 'I understood that CWC were happy enough to accept our own figures without the need for a further check. There isn't a problem, is there?'

'Not with your product,' Jenny said. 'I'll get back to you later on this. Thank you very much for your help.'

After they had concluded their conversation with a few more pleasantries, Jenny sat and thought a minute, then buzzed Rose.

Trevor was in the States on business. Some sort of whistlestop tour. Not back for two weeks his secretary told her. If it was an emergency he could be contacted.

Jenny declined to leave a message. She was being a bit hasty in any case talking to him until she had really dug out the dirt. Len must be on the fiddle. It was patently obvious. But he was, as Trevor had warned her, a sly customer and, if she wasn't careful here, she could end up shouldering the blame. Well, sugar to that – she would not weep any tears if she had to recommend Len's dismissal.

It worried her though and she drove home with the nasty business whirling round in her mind. The weekend was looming and she had nothing planned other than a long soak in the bath when she got in.

Abby Finch, though, effectively knocked that idea on the head, turning up as Jenny stepped out of her car. She was wearing shorts and a loose top and an air of nonchalance that didn't fool Jenny. Nothing would fool her today, her senses were on high alert.

'Could I have a word?' she asked. 'Emily said it would be all right. If it's not convenient now, tomorrow will do.'

'Now's OK,' Jenny said, not wanting to put her off. 'Come on in . . . you're looking very well,' she added carefully, drawing back the curtains in the little sitting room so that the light flooded in. 'It keeps things cooler,' she explained with a smile. 'Hasn't it been gorgeous today?'

'Great,' Abby said. 'People are going daft, booking holidays here, there and everywhere. Peak of the season of course. Have you decided on anything yet?'

Jenny shook her head. 'Too busy at work. I'll probably leave it now until September, then I might take a last-minute booking somewhere.'

The Absent Child

Abby smiled and Jenny, still in her working suit, slipped off the jacket and sat opposite her.

'What can I do for you?' she asked.

'I rang Mum but it was a bad moment,' Abby said with a sigh. 'She was in the middle of something. She promised to call back but . . .'

'That's the trouble with phones,' Jenny said, somewhat desperate to lift Abby out of her gloom. 'I had a boyfriend once who always rang just as I stepped into the shower. He seemed to have a sixth sense.'

'Can I ask you something?'

'Of course.'

'If you were me, Jenny,' she began, choosing her words with care, 'would you want to know who your natural mother was . . . if you were adopted, that is. You do know, don't you, that I am?'

'Yes,' she said brightly. 'Your father told me. He's very proud of you, Abby.'

'I know and that's part of the problem. If I did find out who she was, it wouldn't change the way I feel about him or about Mum but I'm not sure he understands that. I suppose I need to know because sometimes I feel incomplete. Yes, that's it . . .' she said, as if it had occurred for the first time, 'incomplete. There are too many unanswered questions. What would you do? Would you want to know?'

'I . . .' she hesitated, that little seed of doubt within filling up as she looked at Abby, saw the straight firm nose . . . saw *his* straight firm nose . . . the blondish hair . . . *his* blondish hair. She couldn't see any resemblance to herself unless it was in the rather earnest manner, the quiet determination that Abby obviously possessed. 'No,' she said, 'I would leave well alone.'

'Why? In case something's wrong?'

'Exactly. It would be a big mistake. As you've pointed out, you already have a mother.'

'She's not here,' Abby said, reasonably enough. 'She's never here. Since I was little, she's just turned up now and again.'

'Not many mothers are perfect. Mine isn't,' Jenny said, seeing it as good a pointer as any. 'We haven't spoken for years. She more or less threw me out. She wanted me to give up university and stay at home to be with her after my dad died. I couldn't do it. Sometimes I feel terribly guilty.'

'My mother's too far away even to have a tiff,' Abby said with a little smile. 'She phones. Sometimes. She writes long rambling letters all about California. Sometimes.'

'You feel that she's abandoned you?'

'It's happened twice. I've been abandoned twice.'

'Hardly. The first time . . . well, you don't know the circumstances, do you?' She wondered if she could risk a little probe. 'Where were you born? And how was your adoption arranged? Through an agency?'

Abby did not answer, her mind elsewhere.

'I don't want Mum and Dad to think I'm being disloyal if I do this,' she went on. 'But I don't want to do it behind their backs either. Once I've found her – if I find her – then we'll see.'

Jenny felt she had a notice pinned to her chest saying, 'Look no further, Abby. Here I am.'

'I'm sure she loved you,' she said, feeling foolish to be saying it. 'Your natural mother. It must have been a very difficult decision for her.'

'I don't know how she could do it,' Abby said. 'I've never had a baby but I suppose I'm quite a maternal type. I really look forward to having one someday and I can't see any circumstances where I would give away my baby. Can you?'

Jenny laughed but it sounded hollow even to her. 'It seems incredible, doesn't it? But young girls can get desperate. I know it doesn't matter now but it might have then.'

'If I was pregnant now, Dad wouldn't mind. He would be surprised and it would be such a nuisance,' Abby said. 'Nobody would mind except me because it would be Ben's and I don't want his child.' She stopped, blushed. 'I am eighteen,' she added, a little indignant in the silence. 'Old enough.'

'Ben Finch is a bastard,' Jenny said, exchanging a little uncomfortable smile with her. 'I speak from experience.'

'He didn't . . . ?' Her eyes widened. 'Heavens . . .'

'He's only a few years younger,' Jenny said, irritated that Abby's reaction was making her feel about a hundred, 'not so that it would matter.'

'No. I didn't mean to suggest it did.' She dropped her gaze, embarrassed. 'It was him who set me thinking in fact. He said I ought to be curious and I am curious. She might be sitting there waiting for me to get in touch now that I'm eighteen. It would be nice to meet her, to talk to her.'

Where the *hell* was this child born? Realising it might sound odd if she asked the question yet again, Jenny knew she would have to leave it, find out from Stephen maybe.

'Promise me you'll think about it very carefully,' she said at last. 'Remember there's not just you to consider. There's your father. Your mother. And Emily.'

'I will think about it,' she said. 'I am thinking a lot about it. It's driving me mad, trying to decide.'

'You were eighteen in April, weren't you?' Jenny asked suddenly. 'What date was that?'

Abby told her.

As a piece of the jigsaw slotted neatly into place, Jenny threw caution to the wind and asked again whereabouts in Wales it was.

'Somewhere in South Wales. It's on my original birth certificate. I had a different name too but I don't know what it was. Isn't that strange? It makes me feel really peculiar to think of it. I can't think of myself as anything other than Abby,' she said with a smile, apparently not in the least suspicious. Why should she be? As far as she was concerned, there was nothing to link the two of them. Nothing.

Jenny's work worries faded into the distance as she watched Abby leave. Damn it to hell! Just when she and Stephen had been getting on so well, just when she was beginning to have fond feelings for him, stupidly thinking about the future . . . the possibility of a future together.

Two halves did not necessarily make a whole. Just because the birth date was right and she had been born in Wales . . . there must have been lots of babies born on that day in Wales. But how many had been adopted?

If there was the remotest chance of Abby being Helen, then Jenny had to stop her from finding out.

For Abby's sake.

For Stephen.

And for herself.

24

'Did you have a lovely time?' Janice asked, inviting her to sit down. 'I've missed you these last two weeks. Missed our little chats. Haven't we missed Auntie Christine, Shane? Never got a postcard.'

'Didn't you? We sent one. That foreign post is hopeless. We had a lovely time, thanks.' Christine smiled, showed off her tan, handed Janice the presents. An ornament – a fat brown toby jug, some monk or other, the sort of thing Janice liked – and a little white tee shirt for Shane with 'Capri' printed on it. Shane was persuaded to give her a kiss in return. A kiss accompanied by a globule of snot. Christine retained her smile, carefully wiping her mouth.

'You should have seen our Harold,' she went on. 'Took to it all like a duck to water. He loved his shorts . . .' she laughed, 'and his panama hat. As for his legs – you can guess, can't you? I couldn't get over him, Janice, how he took to it like he did. He sat with me by the pool, sunning himself. He ate everything they put in front of him, all that pasta and stuff. He went on all the excursions. To Pompeii and everything. Anyway, there he was, up till all hours, dancing. It went down a treat with some of the old dears that he used to be in funerals. One in particular . . . he could have got off, you know, if he'd a mind too.'

Shane joined wheezily and uncomprehendingly in the laughter. He had a cold – runny nose, cough, eyes streaming. He would have been better in bed but he wouldn't stay there, Janice said, so she'd let him get up. He was sitting, bleary-eyed, by the fire in Janice's front room in his pyjamas and Postman Pat dressing gown, Batman slippers in red. It was a warmish day and with

193 •

the heat of the fire the room was like a furnace. Janice was a great believer in sweating colds out.

'Soon passes though, a holiday,' Janice said, handing out chocolate biscuits. 'Now be careful, Shane, don't get chocolate on that lovely dressing gown or Mummy will be cross. Now then, let's see . . . what's been happening while you've been away?'

'How's Catherine?' Christine asked.

It was taking some doing to get back into the old routine. All that sun out there and nothing to do. The heat of the sun and such a blue blue sky and dazzling sea. The beautiful scenery, nice hotel, good food. That ice-cream parlour with them lovely waiters in pale pink jackets. Made her feel special, they did, but then there was something about Italian men that appealed to her. They knew how to treat a lady. They had style. The women too were really smart.

'Catherine's all right,' Janice said cautiously, making room, just about, for the new ornament beside the clock on the mantelpiece. 'Bit off colour last week so she has to take things easy. It's going to be him all over again, I can feel it in my bones. Two of them,' she added with a sigh. 'Can you credit it?'

Christine looked at the little boy. Poorly, bless him, he was a bit easier to tolerate. He sniffled now and Janice reached for the tissues. 'Blow your nose,' she said firmly. 'Big blow. No, *blow*, Shane.' She smiled at Christine. 'Heard anything from Jenny at all?' she asked suddenly, much to Christine's surprise. 'I wouldn't ask, only it turns out that our Catherine's Len works under her. Did you know? Don't you worry, I shan't breathe a word but isn't it a coincidence?'

'I tried to go to see her before I went on holiday,' Christine told her after a moment's hesitation. 'I made a right mess of it. She wasn't in, you see, and then I had to get Harold to come and bring me home. He was that mad, Janice, because we were going off next day and he was wanting to have an early night. Anyway, I needed a tot of brandy when I got in, I can tell you. Fair shook me up it did, making all that effort and then her not being there. I should have rung her first. I don't know why I didn't.'

'You are daft,' Janice said with a fond smile, 'you and Jenny both. Len says she's very efficient, calls her that new boss of his, keeps them all on their toes. But then, she was always a bit like that, wasn't she?'

'Like what?' Christine asked. Sometimes Janice could be a mite bitchy. You'd think the sun shone out of Catherine. Perhaps mercifully for their future friendship, Shane caused a diversion by having a spectacular coughing fit. Janice decided she was putting him back to bed with a hot-water bottle and no arguments. Christine sipped her tea whilst Janice carried him up. Clutching his new tee shirt, which he'd really taken a fancy to, he'd managed a little forlorn wave and Christine felt suddenly sorry for him. He'd calm down before long. It would just be a passing phase.

So Jenny kept them on their toes, did she? Christine felt a moment's pride. Just like her dad. If Reg had had a bit more education he could have gone far, but it had held him back, pegged him down. Pity that. If Jenny had been a boy it would have been different. They'd have wanted a boy to do well so that he could support his family but it wasn't the same for a girl. Well . . . not round here anyway. They mostly got married and went part time.

That reminded her. She must go to see Reg this afternoon, tell him about the holiday. She would not be mentioning that fiasco about going to Hazelburn on the bus. No point because she hadn't seen Jenny.

Next time she would phone first.

Easy enough.

All she had to do was pick up the phone and punch the buttons.

25

At work, things were brewing up nicely to an almighty showdown and Trevor was still in the States. He had rung Jenny a couple of times but the calls had been tense and technical so she had declined to mention the problems in the laboratory, preferring to break the news to him face to face when he got back. Although it was very much business talk when he did phone, it always ended with a very personal goodbye, his voice subtly changing, so that she didn't know quite how to handle it. If he had been anyone else, she would have pre-empted what was to come, told him frankly to forget it, but Trevor being who he was . . .

Worried as she was about that and about Abby, she almost wished she had not issued the invitation to Stephen to come for a quiet dinner. What was the point of encouraging their friendship along when it couldn't go anywhere? If Abby was her daughter, and she was starting to think there was a slim possibility she was, then how *could* it go anywhere? It was altogether too bizarre.

That didn't stop her enjoying the meal though, for Stephen was good company, and by the time they had finished, they felt free and easy with each other, their conversation wide-ranging and sometimes, cheerfully, they agreed to differ.

'Thanks for talking to Abby,' he said at last. 'I hope to God my daughters aren't being a nuisance to you. It's because Lizzie isn't around now, you know. They need an older woman to talk to.'

She nodded. She did know. Outside, rain pattered onto the window and it was quite dark for the time of evening. She switched on lamps, sat opposite him with her legs tucked under her.

'Lizzie was Welsh, *is* Welsh,' he said with a smile. 'We lived in Wales, just about, for fifteen years before I moved to Preston.'

'The girls don't have Welsh accents,' she pointed out, 'not at all.'

'You don't have a Lancashire one,' he said. 'Lizzie still has a bit of her accent left, with just a spot of American thrown in now. One or two words. It's particularly obvious over the phone.' The hesitation was minimal. 'She rang recently. Out of the blue as usual, in the middle of the night. She always claims she forgets the time difference but I think she does it deliberately to try to catch me out. In the morning, I wondered for a minute if it had been a dream.'

'A pleasant dream?' she queried with a smile.

'Well . . . yes, I suppose.'

'Do you miss her?' she asked gently.

He didn't quite answer the question. The Finches were quite good at not answering questions, Jenny thought.

'She wasn't around much,' he said instead. 'Always off somewhere. As she used to say, it was essential in her profession. That was the root of the problem.'

'You have to be together,' Jenny said thoughtfully. 'You have to come home to each other as often as you can.'

He nodded. 'Why have you never married?' he asked. 'Or is that too personal a question?'

'It's just not happened,' she said. 'I'm not complaining, Stephen. I quite like living alone. I like my job – most of the time – and I need my independence.'

'Ah yes . . . why is it I always get myself involved with independent ladies?'

She was unsure about the *involved* bit. She noted the subtle change in the voice but, whereas in Trevor it worried her like hell, in Stephen it was somehow reassuring that he did somehow care for her.

'Either that or someone like Clare,' he said. 'You never met her but it was all a bit complicated. Lizzie and I knew Clare and her husband. It never felt right. I always felt Roger's presence very strongly and I suppose she felt Lizzie's.'

'I'm not surprised,' Jenny said. '*I* feel Lizzie's presence and I've never even met her. You talk about her a lot, Stephen.'

'Do I?' He seemed astonished. 'Do I really? God, how boring for you. I'm so sorry. I didn't realise.'

'It's all right.' She laughed at his discomfiture. 'If you find it therapeutic, it's OK by me. I'm happy to listen.'

'No it damned well isn't OK,' he said. 'Mention of Lizzie is banned from this moment on. Forgive me, Jenny. From now, we only talk about ourselves. You and me.'

'Stephen,' she sighed, 'please . . .'

'I know. You just want to be friends,' he said easily enough. 'I'm not rushing you. That's fine by me too. We've got all the time in the world.'

He rose and came over to her, crouched down beside her chair.

'I'm pretty hopeless at this,' he said softly. 'Lizzie . . . damn it, sorry . . . well, it was easier in those days. I was young and brash and the thought of rejection never entered my head. Now I'm getting older and I keep thinking, what the hell must this woman think of me? I'm ages older than you, sweetheart.'

She smiled at the endearment, touched his arm and he did not draw away.

'That is not a consideration,' she said. 'I don't want a man just now, that's all. It takes me a while to recover from a relationship . . .' she thought briefly and angrily of Ben, 'especially when I made a complete fool of myself last time.'

He leaned over and kissed her, very lightly, on the lips, nuzzled her nose, and for a dizzying moment she was tempted to hold onto him.

'I understand,' he said. 'I'll give you time.'

Oh no he did not understand, she thought later, as she sat alone in the dark. He did not understand at all. How could he? He thought she was just being cautious but that wasn't the half of it. She didn't know how she would tell him the truth. That Abby, his daughter, was very likely her daughter too.

It was bound to drive them apart. The situation was just too difficult to live with.

26

The situation was critical. It was only by sheer chance that their products had scraped through the quality check. No thanks at all to Len. The simple truth was he had not been doing his job.

Trust Trevor to arrive for a visit the morning after the misdemeanour was finally unearthed, the result of Alan's painstaking efforts to hand. Len was still aggressive, complaining bitterly, according to Rose, insisting everything was OK. Jenny was not yet ready to discuss it with Trevor, not before she had had it out with Len. She would be fair and give him the opportunity to explain himself before she took it further.

'How are you doing?' Trevor asked, breezing into her office, accompanied by a whiff of expensive cologne. 'I've had a wonderful time over there. Made some very useful contacts.' He smiled his smile, looking rather debonair today in what must surely be a new suit and a plain cream shirt, spoiled unfortunately by the ubiquitous presence of the red tie. 'Everything all right your end?'

'Fine, thanks,' she said, knowing she ought to say something about the trouble brewing but wisely refraining. She did not need Trevor to do her dirty work for her, hauling Len in and shouting the riot act. 'I shall be at the meeting on Friday next. I've asked Rose to confirm.'

'Good. Look forward to that. Now . . .' he glanced at his watch, 'it's twelve thirty. Can I take you out to lunch?'

She hesitated and he smiled, adjusting the cuffs of the new shirt. 'Come on, I'm not dining in the bloody canteen. Let's go into town. Is there a decent restaurant?'

'Lots,' she said firmly, 'but I can't spare much time, Trevor. I am very busy.'

'Working lunch,' he said with a frown. 'It's not a bloody social invitation. I have things to discuss and we can talk over lunch.'

Impatiently, he waited while she told Rose where she was going and what time she would be back, and grabbed her jacket.

She drove him into town, took him to a pub she knew, where they could hide away in a discreet corner. He was a little too cheerful today, perhaps the result of his transatlantic trip, and she knew she had to be on guard. She had not liked the proprietorial way he had put his hand on her waist as they squeezed through the door of this place. Throughout the meal, he had, as promised, talked about work but it was all pretty routine stuff, things that could have waited.

'I'm up here for a few days,' Trevor said, pushing his plate aside. Uncharacteristically he had left most of his food. 'I was wondering if you'd care to join me for dinner one evening at the hotel? And *that*, Sweetman, is a social invitation. Dining alone is bloody miserable. I could have dined with Eric Earnshaw from accounts who's been staying up as well, but I'm buggered if I fancied a candlelight dinner with him.'

Jenny smiled a little, continued to toy with her salad. She couldn't fail to notice the extremely shifty look on his face. This called for some delicate handling and she had to get out of it somehow, but the practicalities of doing that without offending him escaped her for the moment.

'Dinner? When exactly?'

'Tomorrow?' he suggested, and Jenny felt the tension in him despite the jocularity, knew with a horrible certainty, that it meant a lot to him that she say yes.

'Sorry. I have something on tomorrow,' she said brightly, struggling to come up with just what exactly. 'Aerobics,' she said after a moment, remembering that someone from work had asked her to go. 'It's time I got myself fitter. I need to firm up.'

'What for? You're OK as you are. More than OK. I hate skinny women.' A leer, never far away, surfaced. 'Can't you put it off?' he asked irritably. 'Exercise causes more harm than good, believe me. That bloody jogging I did last year nearly saw me off. I started getting palpitations and at my age you can't take chances . . .' He stopped, probably wishing he hadn't said that. Admitted to an age-related problem.

'I can manage Wednesday,' she said, and could have cut her tongue off. Why the hell had she said that? Just because he'd sat there with a little-boy look of expectation on his face was no damned excuse. Was she going soft? Sooner or later she would have to tell Trevor that she didn't actually fancy him one little bit. It was cruel to do this – build up his hope – and it was also dangerous because Trevor had been known to drop 'favourites' like a ton of bricks for less and to harbour quite bitter grievances. She needed his protection. The way the CWC hierarchy formed, everyone needed a protector.

'Wednesday it is,' he said with a grin. 'Look forward to it.'

'Me too,' she said, matching his quick smile.

'Right.' He rubbed his hands together, dug in his pockets for cash. 'Back to work, I think.'

What was the matter with her? She wasn't normally so wet and weak-willed. She'd really sorted him out, hadn't she?

She pushed her plate away. A very heavy feeling had settled in the pit of her stomach.

Abby grabbed a bite and tried not to tut her annoyance at Emily, who had her books sprawled all over the kitchen table as usual. Why was a mystery when she had a perfectly good desk in her room.

'Do you want a sandwich?' Abby asked. 'You've had nothing to eat since you got in.'

Emily shook her head. 'Couldn't eat a thing,' she said. 'My stomach's churned up.'

Abby eyed her suspiciously. She hadn't had any breakfast either. She hoped Emily wasn't getting any daft ideas about dieting. That's all they needed, an eating problem. She resolved to keep a check on her, a surreptitious one, of course.

'I'll never pass these exams. Never, never, never,' Emily said suddenly, flinging her pen down. It slid across the table and onto the floor.

'Pick that up,' Abby said, deciding attack was the best way of lifting Emily's spirits. 'All you have to do is get on with it. You never do a stroke. It's no wonder you're behind everybody else. You just don't apply yourself. Sitting there staring into space isn't helping a bit.'

'Lecture over?' Emily enquired with a sweet smile. 'Anyway, grumpy knicks, I am doing something. I've got a work plan. Here . . .' she dived into her bag, pulled something out, 'Jenny helped me to compose it. See, it's a countdown to the exams, all divided off into sections. The pink shaded bits are the things I've already done. The big deal is I've got the whole of Sunday free. The rest of the time I've only got to cram a year's work into my head.'

'That looks impressive,' Abby said, glancing vaguely at it. The writing was neat, large and confident, certainly not Emily's. 'Shouldn't you be getting started then?'

'Jesus, Abby, give me a break.' She retrieved the pen and took a deep breath, pulling one of her books towards her, looking at Abby thoughtfully. 'You're not serious about the Open University thing, are you? God, I can't imagine anyone choosing to study.'

'I don't know. Maybe. It was Ben, he just got me thinking, that's all. I know he talked a lot of drivel but maybe he had a point about that.' She hesitated before continuing. 'As a matter of fact, he got me thinking about something else too . . . he kept on at me to try to trace my mother, my natural mother.'

'What the hell does it have to do with him? Cheeky sod, I'd have told him where to get off.'

'I did, as a matter of fact.' Abby smiled, remembering.

They fell into a subdued silence for a moment and then Emily sighed.

'Don't start it all off,' she said quietly, showing the sensitivity she was at pains to conceal most of the time. 'Please don't. It'll be a terrible mistake. You don't really want to know, do you?'

'I can't make my mind up.' Abby looked at her sister, wondering what Emily would do if positions were reversed. 'Jenny doesn't think it's a good idea either.'

'Well, then . . .' As far as Emily was concerned, that was it. The seal of absolute approval. 'Promise me you won't.'

'Promise? Why should it matter so much to you?' Abby asked, genuinely puzzled. 'It won't affect you at all.'

'Yes it will. You might find out you've got another family somewhere, other sisters . . .' She blushed, avoided eye contact. 'I don't want to share you, Abby, with a load of strangers. You might like them more than you like us.'

'As if that would happen, you fool,' Abby said, a sudden great affection for Emily bursting forth. Poor Em. She did take things so much to heart. She might be awkward and a big worry but Abby loved her for all that.

A smile flitted between them tinged with embarrassment.

'In any case,' Emily went on, trying to cover it up, 'not everyone's got a sister like you. Insufferable. Nagging. Workaholic. Boring as hell. Dresses like she's thirty if she's a day. Most of my friends have got normal ones.'

Abby laughed, swiping her one with a wet cloth.

She tried the number in the States once more when Emily had gone.

'Mum . . . it's me.'

'Darling! Now this time I've got lots of time to speak to you. Sorry about before, Abby, but I was just dashing out and I would have missed my appointment. And since then, it's been incredibly hectic. Rehearsals. More rehearsals. Parties. The usual round. Terribly boring people but fearfully influential. You have to be *seen*, sweetheart.'

'That's OK,' Abby said, smiling as she heard the familiar busy lilting voice. 'How are you, Mum?'

'Very well. How are you?'

'Fine.'

'Good. That's that sorted out then. What's this I hear about a boyfriend? Your father tells me it's been rather traumatic for you.'

'I'm over it now,' Abby said, realising with some surprise that she was. 'He wasn't worth the hassle.'

'Oh, you've realised that! Men never are. I'm sorry to be cynical but you will find that out as you grow older. The trouble is we do rather need them around – or at least I do. I don't actually enjoy women's company very much. There's so much jealousy in this profession but the men are generally sweeter. Talking of men, how is he? Your father?'

• Patricia Fawcett

'OK, I think. He's very busy at the office. It's these Middle East contracts.'

'Really?' Mum had always been bored to death with Dad's work. 'Still seeing Clare Forrest?' There was an irritation in the voice. 'I never could stand the woman myself. Twitchy, don't you think?'

Abby decided it was best if he told her himself so she kept a discreet silence, listening as her mother began to talk about her work, what she was doing at the moment.

'I'll send you copies of the programme and the reviews, darling,' she said. 'Would you like that?'

'Yes, please.'

'I am resting my voice just now because I have a hint of a sore throat. Colds are the bane of my life, sweetheart, but California's an awful lot better than England. Or Wales.'

'I'll be quick then,' Abby said, anxious not to make things worse for her. 'When will you be coming home?' she asked, not daring to ask about Mum's tenor as her mother had not mentioned him at all. 'Emily misses you so. Me too.'

'I can't promise anything,' she said. 'If I do come home, where do I stay? Your father will be horribly embarrassed if I stay with you. I could always book into a hotel, I suppose.'

'No you couldn't. We've got lots of room. You'll love the new house,' Abby said. 'The village is very pretty.'

'I'm sure it is although I'm hardly into village life. After LA, I don't think I could stand it for long. I like bustle, Abby, activity, life. Lots and lots of vibrant people all around.' There was a pause and Abby sensed she was looking at her watch. 'I'll write you this enormously long letter, darling, telling you all the news at this end. I hope you and Emily will visit me sometime when she's finished those wretched exams.'

'Mum . . . ?' Abby twisted the flex of the phone in sudden anxiety. 'Can I ask you something? It's about my adoption. Suppose I wanted to find my natural mother . . .' she sighed, hearing the ominous silence at the other end, 'would it matter to you? I am curious, that's all.'

'Of course it's up to you. You're eighteen, an adult,' her mother said, voice strained, all laughter gone. 'We would never try to dissuade you if that's what you decide although . . . if you must know, Abby, I *would* try. I think it's an enormous mistake. Can of worms, you know? It's best you don't pry. Think of her. She will have put it all behind her now. It's not fair to her to drag it all up again. And, after all we've done for you, it does seem just a teeny bit ungrateful on your part. Do you see?'

'Yes. But it's still my decision,' Abby said, feeling quite miserable at her mother's lack of enthusiasm. 'You can't stop me.'

'No . . .' The anguish was there and remorse. 'We've spoiled things for you, haven't we, darling – your father and me? Mostly me, I suppose. I never meant to disappoint you and Emily but these things happen. Love between a man and a woman is a very strong emotion. The strongest.' Her voice caught. 'Look what you've done. You've upset me now and that will only make my throat worse. I shall be croaking by matinée time.'

'I'm sorry.' Abby glanced at the clock, the solid tick reminding her ridiculously that this call was costing her dad a small fortune. Transatlantic and transcontinental. Prime time. 'Write to me, Mum,' she finished, suddenly tearful. She wished her mother were here, giving her one of her scented hugs. Empty words. They were better than nothing.

'I love you, Abby. Goodbye, darling.'

She put down the phone. Sniffed. Her mother could transmit emotion very powerfully whatever the distance.

On or off stage.

27

Shane was still coming to Janice's to get him out of Catherine's way while she put her feet up for a few hours. He had recovered his health and it was all systems go as usual. He was kitted out this morning in a little football outfit. North End colours, of course. His face was scrubbed, his glasses shining.

Christine duly admired the football strip, was rewarded with an unexpected little kiss from him. Unprompted at that.

'Bless his little heart,' Janice said with delight, her diamanté earrings swinging as she looked from one to the other. She was wearing a blue denim blouse with puffy sleeves and sparkly sequins on the yoke, tucked into white tight trousers that ended just above the ankle. At her age, she ought to be careful with skin-tight pants. High-heeled slingbacks completed what Christine thought was a particularly tarty ensemble. Oblivious, Janice went on happily, 'He's been such a good boy this morning, Auntie Christine. That bad do seems to have knocked the stuffing out of him. He's very quiet, a little angel.'

Christine eyed him suspiciously. She wouldn't go so far as to say that.

'Not fixed up with anything else then?' Janice asked. 'Didn't you get that job at Richard's?'

'No,' Christine said shortly. 'Turned out it wasn't my cup of tea anyway. I'm in for a few more. I'm not desperate,' she added, catching Janice's sympathetic look. She didn't want anybody feeling sorry for her. 'If our Harold comes to stay then I'll have my work cut out looking after him, the old so-and-so.'

'Is he coming then? I thought you'd made your mind up it wouldn't work, you and him?'

'He is my only brother. The only one I've got left.' Christine gave her a look. Janice could be a bit hard-faced sometimes. 'We got on quite well on holiday. If you can keep him off death and that singing of his, he can be quite entertaining. But you're right,' she said after a moment's contemplation, 'if he came to live here, we'd get up each other's noses. Sure as eggs is eggs.'

'If he does sell up, move in with you, he'll have a lot of money coming his way,' Janice said. 'I suppose it'll all be coming to you eventually.'

'He'll leave it to charity if I know him. I don't want his money,' she said. 'I have quite enough, thank you. Reg left me well provided for.'

'So did Clive. I'm not short of a bob or two,' Janice said, not to be outdone.

They gave a collective sniff.

'Between you and me . . .' Janice glanced at Shane, but he was engrossed in doing something quiet for once, jamming pieces into a jigsaw, 'they've taken on more than they can chew, Catherine and Len. Great big mortgage. Brand-new cars. One each, I ask you. And now they've only got one wage coming in. Lucky he's got a good job. I told you he works at CWC, didn't I?'

'You did,' Christine said wearily. She could see where this conversation might lead and she was not in the mood for discussing Jenny, not after what happened before the holiday. She hadn't rung her yet. Something was holding her back. Fear of a rebuff, she supposed. She needed to hold on to some hope. In the dream she had, Jenny always rushed towards her without a minute's hesitation but Christine always woke up before she actually held her.

'She's not liked, I'm sorry to say,' Janice went on, undeterred. 'Your Jenny. They used to like the old boss, a Mr Harding. He was a nice chap, Len says, keen on golf. He just more or less let them get on with it. But your Jenny's forever sticking her nose in. Wants to stop them going for a smoke now. I mean to say, for them that smokes that's serious.'

A quick ratatat on the door was never more welcome. Harold staggered in, complete with boxful of tricks. He had just been to the auction rooms and acquired some new stock.

Mindful that it was mainly glass and Shane and glass were not compatible, Janice beat a hasty retreat.

Carefully, Harold unpacked it: a complete tea set, perfect nick; some glass items – sugar bowls, jugs, that sort of thing. Things that would look a real picture on the stall. Cheap but pretty stuff that always sold.

'I want to talk to you, Christine, if you've a minute.'

She didn't like the sound of that. She was going to have to tell him straight that she didn't want him to live here. She hoped he wouldn't take it badly because she didn't want to alienate him as well as Jenny. She might end up with nobody family to talk to and it was different talking to family. Things could be said. In theory.

'Stay and have a bite,' she said with a smile. Butter him up a bit before she dropped the bombshell. 'I'll do us a nice poached egg on toast.'

He carried the crate of stuff through to the kitchen for washing, left it. Watched as she prepared the meal, got under her feet, started to sing 'O God, our help in ages past'.

She ignored him as best she could, setting out plates and cutlery.

'Being my age makes you think,' he said after a while, abandoning the third verse.

'Don't you start getting morbid,' she said. 'As I've told you before, you're the sort who'll live to be a hundred. You'll have your picture in the *Lancashire Evening Post* and a telegram from the Queen.'

'Maybe I will. But you can't help starting a countdown. And so . . . I might as well be doing what I want to do. Make the most of the few years I've got left.'

'Now listen, Harold, I've given it a lot of thought,' Christine said, waving a knife aloft, awkward to be saying this. 'It's nothing personal but it's just that I've got used to living on my own. I have my own little ways.'

'You listen to me,' he said with that rare smile of his. 'You have the wrong end of the stick, love. I have decided to sell my house, yes, but I am not coming to live here. Not with you.'

'You're not?' She juggled with hot toast a moment, reached

• Patricia Fawcett

for the butter, checked the plates were warm. 'Where are you going to live then?' A thought struck her, astonished her. 'Not with Jenny?'

'Certainly not. I wouldn't dream of imposing on her. I am going to purchase a small property abroad, possibly Italy. I shall live out the remainder of my days in the sun. I was very taken with it, the leisurely pace of life.'

'You can't do that,' Christine said with a laugh, carrying everything through. 'Come and eat this while it's hot . . .'

'Why can't I do it?' he asked as they ate, plates balanced on trays on their knees. The eggs, peppered, were perfect. 'I have been making enquiries. There are quite a number of small country properties available. It will be a cash purchase. I have quite a tidy sum put by and there'll be the money from selling the house.'

'But, Harold, you don't know anybody there. You can't speak Italian.'

'I would make friends. I would learn the language.'

'At your age?' she asked gently. 'That's a tall order. You're being daft. Impulsive. What's got into you?'

'Boredom,' he said. 'I cross the days off the calendar and what do I look forward to? A new country will give me a new lease of life. You can always come with me if you want. It's time folks were more European-minded. We have to stop thinking about them and us.'

'No fear.' She shuddered. 'I don't like it when I don't know what people are saying. Fair puts you at a disadvantage. It was beautiful for a holiday but not for always.'

'My house is going on the market this very day,' he said briskly. 'I have to sell it before I can proceed.'

She smiled her relief. That could take for ever and a day but she wasn't going to tell him that. He probably expected somebody to come round tomorrow with a wad of notes.

'I shall miss the car boots,' he said as he helped her clear away.

'Miss them?'

'When I'm living in Italy,' he explained. 'I don't know if they do that sort of thing there.'

Christine smiled to herself. She would humour him. The poor

The Absent Child

love had got hold of this daft notion and she would humour him. There's no fool like an old fool and no mistake.

The thought of Harold living and breathing in Italy was mad. What would happen if he passed on there? She was surprised he hadn't thought of that. One of his clients had once popped off while on holiday and Harold had had to deal with all the red tape. Bamboozled you, the Italians, with red tape. Getting that body back had been the devil's own job.

No, they wouldn't be able to make head or tail of him, the locals.

'So . . . I'll be able to come and visit you then,' she said, as he helped her tidy up. 'All I'll have to do is get the train down to London, go down that tunnel, and then a foreign bus at the other end. It'll take me about a week to get there. Nothing to it.'

'Sarcasm does not become you, Christine love,' he said, rolling up his sleeves and sinking his arms into the soapy water. 'My mind's made up.'

She picked up the tea towel and frowned at him.

In some ways, he reminded her of Reg.

He had been a stubborn so-and-so too.

28

This time, for the first time, it was just the two of them and Jenny bitterly regretted accepting Trevor's invitation to dinner. She had toned herself down as best she could, wearing a simple beige dress with an orangey chiffon scarf draped around it. Trevor was wearing a double-breasted dark suit of excellent quality that, on anyone else, would have looked superb.

'Order what the hell you like,' he said, as they sat studying the menu. 'It's all on expenses. We'll order a top-notch wine too. Sod it. The company can afford it.'

Amused at that, Jenny nevertheless ordered a modest dish, not actually very hungry. She would give him the benefit of the doubt, she decided. Maybe Trevor just wanted company because it was pretty lonely being stuck in a first-class hotel on your own and room service never appealed to her much either.

Outside of the office and shop talk, she wasn't sure they would have much in common, if anything. She let him ramble on a while about politics, fairly general stuff, keeping a polite smile on her face until it dawned on him that he was boring her.

'You don't know much about me, do you?' he asked. 'And I don't know much about you. You keep your private life pretty damned private, Jenny. I've been married twice,' he said, when she did not rise to the obvious prompt. 'Did you know that?'

She nodded. 'I have heard it mentioned. I'm sorry . . . what went wrong, or is that too personal a question?'

'Not at all. It hurt at the time, a helluva lot. Good thing I had the job because it really got me down. Matter of fact, I came pretty close to a breakdown.'

'I understand,' Jenny murmured with a smile. She didn't

• Patricia Fawcett

quite, in fact, because, of all people, she wouldn't have targeted Trevor as being particularly sensitive.

'As I see it,' he went on, unstoppable now that he had got started, 'they were both too wrapped up in themselves, my ex-wives. Neither of them was the sort of woman you could confide in. In my line of work . . . well, of course you know the way things are . . . it helps to be able to talk to someone about it, to get an impartial view, even if they know bugger all about it. In fact it's better if they don't know anything about it. Don't you agree?'

'Yes, I suppose I do, although as soon as you start going technical, people switch off.'

'Quite. You and I, we understand each other. We know the ins and outs of the business, how things tick.'

'Hm . . .' She wasn't sure where this was leading but knew she would have to be careful what she said and how she said it this evening. She felt he was fencing with her, testing her reaction and, if she were to come out of this without deeply offending him, it would be a miracle. Coming out to dinner was the first mistake. He had made a special effort, freshly shaven and everything, and she did like him but that was all. That really was all.

'I asked you for dinner because I wanted to talk to you,' he said at last, as they waited for their main course. 'It's hellish difficult because I've nobody to talk to these days, not about this sort of thing. As I said, my wives weren't the sort of women who listened. You strike me as a particularly good listener.'

'Do I?' She smiled at that.

'I need to talk to a woman,' he went on with a frown, 'and if that sounds sexist, I'm sorry. I do my best, Jenny, but it's a minefield for us men these days. Every time you speak, you put your foot in it. Offend the ladies.'

'Is it work?' Jenny asked. 'A problem?'

'You could say that,' he said, the hesitation unusual in him. 'A problem at work.'

'Well then . . . ?'

She wondered if she had got it wrong. He hadn't asked her here tonight because he was trying to get her into bed, but for another reason.

She watched him closely as the waiter arrived and there followed the usual flurry as he served them.

'This looks delicious,' she said, giving him time to come to grips with whatever it was that was bothering him. He had rather a haunted look in his eyes, one that she had never seen before. Was he ill? Was that it? He hadn't got some terrible disease, had he, something that was killing him? She hoped not. She didn't know how she would deal with that, how she would be able to comfort him. If at all.

What on earth to talk about? She didn't want to talk about the problem with Len, not yet, not until she had come up with some ideas of her own. Rather desperately therefore, she latched onto telling him about her cottage and the village where she lived, amusing anecdotes about Uncle Harold, and then, delving deeper, about the time she had been at university in Bath. By the time they had finished and moved into the lounge for coffee, she was exhausted with her efforts to cheer him up.

'Mind if I smoke?' he asked, as they sat in a little private corner behind some plastic potted plants. 'Addicted,' he grumbled with a little smile, and then, out of the blue, he came out with it. 'They want rid of me, the bastards. Early retirement.'

'Oh . . .'

'That's taken you by surprise, hasn't it? You didn't think I was that old, did you, Sweetman? Well, let me tell you I don't feel that old, Jenny.' The look he gave her was strange to decipher. 'What do you think about it? Me being retired?'

'You don't seem very pleased,' she said carefully.

'Should be. I've got a bloody good deal. Too good to refuse. I've been with CWC for forty years.' He exhaled blue smoke towards the ornate ceiling. 'I started when I was seventeen in the despatch department. Callow youth. Scraped my way up with my bare knuckles. Got all my qualifications part time. Worked my arse off in those days. Still do, as a matter of fact, can't get out of the habit. So, all in all I have no complaints. Given the golden handshake I'm getting, it's the honourable thing to do. It's high bloody time I made way for someone else.'

'You don't want to go, though?'

'I don't know what the hell I want,' he said, and his eyes were suddenly frightened. 'It scares the shit out of me. Everything I

• Patricia Fawcett

do is geared to work. My whole life centres on work. I've no other bloody interests. Without work . . . I think I'll be gone in six months.'

'Gone where?' she asked stupidly before it dawned. 'Oh God, Trevor, what nonsense. Look . . .' she sat up as straight as she could in the absurdly uncomfortable chair, 'you have to get a plan organised for your retirement. Organise your day at home like you organise your day at work. Make sure your days are full.'

He flicked ash vaguely towards the ashtray, smiled at her. 'What I really need is a wife,' he said, 'a new wife. New interests. With the lump sum I'll be getting, we'll be quids in. We can go on holidays, any number. She can have her own car, spend what the hell she likes on clothes . . . she won't even have to work although, if she's the kind who needs to, we can get round that. Come to some arrangement.'

Jenny regarded him calmly. Sipped her coffee.

'I don't suppose . . .' He smiled again, a genuine smile she felt. 'No, no, of course not. Just a joke, Jenny. Forget I said it.'

She wasn't sure about that, about it being a joke. If she had shown the slightest interest, he would have turned that around.

'When do you go?' she asked. 'And if you don't mind me being cheeky, who's taking over from you?'

'All business, aren't you?' he muttered. 'I'll be gone pretty soon, date not yet fixed, but I can't answer the other question. It won't be you, if that's what you're hinting at.'

'Of course not. I'm not ready – yet,' she said with a laugh, attempting to lighten the mood. 'Come on, it's not the end of the world. You ought to be delighted. It's not as if they've booted you out without a pension. If you like, I'll help you organise your retirement plan.'

'Plan?' He stubbed out the cigarette, a very final move. 'What plan? What is there to plan? What time I get up? What time to walk the bloody dog?'

'I didn't know you had a dog.'

'I don't. Figure of speech. I do have a cat so it will give me more time to spend with it. Quality time together. I can learn moggy speech.'

'It happens to everyone, not just you,' she told him sharply, trying to jig him out of this depressed mood. 'You should have prepared for it, Trevor. You of all people. Didn't you organise a seminar last year about this, for people about to retire?'

'Yes but, Christ, it wasn't meant for *me*, Jenny. I imagined I'd work for ever,' he said quietly. 'I had it in mind to die in the lift. Between floors. I would be discovered lying there when someone pressed the button, having expired between decisions. Still in the bloody thick of it. What a way to go! Preferably a decision that only I knew the answer to, leaving the lot of them in the shit. Serve the buggers right for all the things they've done to me over the years.'

She smiled with him.

'Is it for general release yet?' she asked. 'Or am I supposed to keep mum?'

He put a finger to his lips.

'Glad I told you,' he said. 'Even if you can only come up with stupid ideas about organising my day. Don't worry, I'll work something out and if I don't, I can always jump off a bridge.'

'I wish you wouldn't say things like that,' she said awkwardly, 'even as a joke.'

'Who said anything about a joke?' He fumbled for his cigarettes again before deciding not to bother. 'It's an option, that's all. And I believe in studying all options before coming to a decision. You're the same, aren't you? You're not telling me that you haven't had to face up to awkward decisions in your time – and we're not talking chemistry now.'

'I made a very important decision once,' she told him after a small silence, 'and to this day I don't know if it was the right one. But I have to take the consequences to the grave.'

'Ah . . . a man?' He had recovered his spirits a bit, was looking more like his old self. 'Enough said. Thanks for listening, Jenny. You are a good listener, quite maternal in fact. That's what I needed tonight, a bit of mothering.'

It occurred to her as she left that he would not have been averse to a bit of loving too. All this doom and gloom – she had not been prepared for it, would have coped better with a good old-fashioned pass, for, during the course of the evening, she had worked out what she would say, the kindest way to say it.

• Patricia Fawcett

Without offending him, she could have told the truth.
He appreciated straight talking, did Trevor.
She would have told him.
She much admired him. She had always admired him.
But sorry.
There was someone else.

She talked to Len next day, asking him to come to her office, and tossing the incriminating papers across the desk at him.

'Alan's team have been working flat out on these,' she told him, 'rechecking. You've not been doing your job, have you, Len? God knows where you've been when you were supposed to be at various suppliers. I've checked with them personally. Some of them have seen you, true, once in a blue moon.' She sighed her exasperation. 'You're not a complete fool. Surely you realised you wouldn't get away with it?'

'What do you mean?' he asked, a faint flush above the dark stubble of his chin. 'I don't know what you're talking about. Mr Harding never had cause to complain.'

She ignored that. 'Don't waste time with excuses,' she said. 'You haven't answered my question. What have you been doing?'

'There's never been a problem,' he said, still aggressive. 'I might have occasionally used old data but I resent the implication that I've been doing it all the time. Has there ever been a major production problem as a direct result of my samples? When in the last five years? Never is the answer.'

'Whether or not there has been a problem is irrelevant,' Jenny said, thinking that if she'd been wearing her chiffon scarf as a chic accessory to her lab coat, she'd have throttled him with it. 'You don't seem to realise how serious the situation is. I regret doing it but I have to report up on this.'

There was a heavy silence that she was determined not to be the one to break. Rose had instructions not to disturb her and Jenny knew the whole lab was agog, rumours rife. The general consensus seemed to be he had got away with it for too damned long. John Harding, bless his sainted memory, had turned a blind eye.

'Oh come on, Miss Sweetman,' Len gave a twisted smile. 'Give me a warning this time. A written warning if you like. You have my word it won't happen again.'

'I can't do that,' she said, pointing to the file that lay before her. 'You've had your written warning already, following on several verbal warnings. You know as well as I do that this time it has to go before the Technical Director.'

'Not Cummings?' he groaned. 'He's had it in for me ever since I came. I'm for the chop this time if he gets wind of it.'

'I'm sorry,' she said stiffly, 'it's clear cut. I have no choice.'

'For God's sake . . . please . . .' His shocked eyes stared at her and inwardly she flinched. 'You can't. My wife's pregnant, we have this house to do up, we have a little son . . . You're a woman, can't you show a bit of compassion?' He stopped suddenly, probably regretting the pleading.

Jenny avoided looking at him, trying to make it easier.

'I'll keep you informed about what is to happen next,' she said. 'That's all for the moment.'

She did not look up as the door closed quietly behind him.

29

Abby had an afternoon off work and had spent it shopping in town. Feeling a bit under the weather, she cut the shopping short and returned home and was now, a little guiltily, watching some afternoon television.

It was Oprah Winfrey having a heart-to-heart as usual with a studio full of people anxious to discuss their worries. It was squirm-making stuff but strangely fascinating. Abby sat glued to it, the subject matter near to her own heart.

Adoption – that was the theme today and there were the usual heartbreaking stories, and a couple of really embarrassing meetings between long-lost sons and daughters and their natural mothers. Lots of hugs and tears. Rambling explanations. Excuses really. Abby shifted uncomfortably in her seat. If ever there was a message for her, it was here. It was surely fate that she had just happened to watch.

Hastily, she switched the set off as she heard Emily come in. A very cheerful Emily, who amazingly volunteered to make them a coffee and did so, bringing it through, still all smiles.

'What's the matter with you?' Abby asked, quite taken aback. 'You're in a very good mood.'

'I've had an absolutely fantastic day,' Emily said. 'We had some tests and, guess what, I scraped passes in the lot, every subject. It's paid off, all my hard work.'

Abby spluttered her indignation. 'Hard work? You could have fooled me. You must have been doing it in secret.'

'Of course,' Emily said airily, 'I do a lot of things in secret. Just like you.'

Abby did not rise to the bait. All those people hugging and

crying together on the screen was still in her mind. For all she knew, her natural mother might have been watching the programme too, wondering if Abby would ever try to find her. Somewhere, she felt a great pull on her emotions as if the woman was tugging at her, sending thought messages, urging her to try.

'I've decided I might as well have a proper go at them, these exams, so I'm making a fantastic sacrifice. I'm finished with boyfriends,' Emily announced, comically intense. 'Until the exams are over, that is, and then I'm going to have a terrific party.' She paused, face thoughtful as something occurred. 'I've been thinking. You don't suppose there's anything going on, do you, between Dad and Jenny?'

'I don't know. Don't start trying to matchmake,' Abby said, a little wearily. Dad could find his own lady if he wanted to, though she wasn't entirely sure he did want to. The trouble with Dad was he still adored Mum.

'I like her. She's OK, isn't she? Not boring at all even if she is scientific. She's got a bit of style, miles better than Clare Forrest, anyway. Can you imagine having her two dippy sons as brothers? That thin ginger one fancies his chances with me. He's a real one hundred per cent plonker.' She shuddered. 'She's a good listener.'

'Who is? Jenny?'

'Of course Jenny. You didn't think I meant Clare, did you? She's too busy feeling sorry for herself to listen.'

'She is a good listener. We talked, me and Jenny, about my being adopted,' Abby said. 'I got the feeling she wasn't in favour of me trying to trace my natural mother.'

'Neither am I. It's a mad idea. I'd have thought one mother was enough for anybody. Particularly one like ours,' she added.

'She seemed very concerned about it, in fact,' Abby went on, recalling the conversation with Jenny. 'She wanted me to promise not to take it further without consulting her again. I can't think why she should be so interested.'

'It's because of Dad,' Emily said. 'She's involving herself with us because she knows she's going to have to if she and Dad get hitched. She'll be our stepmother, won't she?'

'I hate that word. If anybody looks less like a stepmother . . .'

The Absent Child

'Wicked stepmother,' Emily said with a laugh. 'I think she'd be great but I tell you one thing: Mum will go daft. She'll hate it if someone else takes over.'

'She can't have it both ways,' Abby said, fed up of defending her mother's actions. 'She can hardly complain after she went off with Simon-the-tenor, can she?'

'Will you try?' Emily asked, after a moment. 'Try to find your natural mother?'

'You don't want me to, Mum doesn't, Jenny doesn't either. There's only Dad who's offering any support,' Abby said with a sigh. 'It puts me under pressure. All I want to do is make contact, see who she is, that's all.'

'How? How will you do it?'

'There are ways and means. I've been making enquiries,' Abby said, feeling herself flush. She hadn't meant to be secretive but . . .

'The Salvation Army can help sometimes but they say the best thing will be to contact the adoption agency first. They have my records, you see, and they should be able to find out my original name and my mother's name too. They might have her address even and other information. They will do an initial search for me if I decide to proceed.'

'What if she's moved? The odds are she will have in eighteen years,' Emily said, determined to be pessimistic. 'She might have got married, changed her name, left the country . . . died even,' she added. 'Well you have to face up to things, Abby. It's not going to be all roses.'

'Nobody said it was easy,' Abby said, 'but it's a start. I'll have to go for counselling to make sure I understand the implications—'

'Counselling! Jesus! That would be curtains as far as I'm concerned. If ever I was offered counselling, I'd tell them where to stuff it.'

'It's meant for the best,' Abby said tightly, remembering the pleasant voice on the end of the telephone. 'They'll make the first contact to smooth the way. They'll find out her reaction, whether or not she wants to see me, and then they'll maybe give me a telephone number so that I can call her myself, although I think I'd rather write. And if I have problems, I can always try Norcap. I can put a letter in their magazine, register on their contact list, just in case she reads it.' She stopped, Emily's pessimism catching at her. 'I know. It's a long shot, I suppose,' she added miserably.

'And if all else fails, you can always go on *Surprise, Surprise.*'

'That's right. Take the mickey. I might have expected it of you. No encouragement.'

'You're not going to let it rest, are you?' Emily said, her expression showing she was finally resigned to it. 'Don't build your hopes up too much. You might not get on. Have you thought of that? You'll be strangers.'

30

'I don't know what you've got one of them things for,' Christine said, looking round the other stalls, embarrassed. 'At your age.'

Harold ignored her, finishing his call on his mobile telephone, lurking near the car so that, infuriatingly, she could not hear what was said.

'It's extremely useful,' he said. 'It means you can keep in touch anywhere, anytime. Another five years and you'll have one too. They'll be commonplace.' He held up his hand as Christine protested. 'The trouble with you is you're too frightened of change,' he went on, much to her irritation. 'Sometimes I find it hard to understand that you're twenty years younger than me. If it was up to folks like you, our Christine, there'd be not one change from one Preston Guild to the next.'

'Nobody else has one,' Christine muttered, 'nobody that I know. You're a terrible one for gadgets. Who do you need to keep in touch with at all hours?'

'The estate agent for one,' he said, unperturbed. 'I like to be on hand to field calls. That is the term they use. Nothing must put people off. Selling a house is not easy nowadays.'

'I'm glad that's dawned.'

Christine sighed, looking up at the sky. Thank God, the clouds were clearing and it looked like it would be nice once it got started. They had a good pitch here where they could see what was happening all round. They had the stuff set out on two trestle tables and they'd been here since eight o'clock. That woman had never reappeared, that nosy one with the knits but then she hadn't looked a stayer. This morning, as the sun finally blazed forth and church bells pealed in the distance, she and Harold were sandwiched between two old hands.

A woman in a short flared skirt selling old gramophone records. Dozens of them. And to their left, a shifty-looking bearded chap selling tools and car bits. Where he'd got hold of them, Christine shuddered to think but it didn't do to ask questions. She and Harold were all above board anyway.

'So, who was that then?' she asked him because he had maddeningly not ventured any information. 'On that daft phone of yours? The estate agent?'

'On Sunday morning? No, it was a private call. I intend to renew the acquaintance of several old friends prior to taking up residence abroad. However, talking of estate agents, someone is interested in viewing the house,' he said, 'this afternoon. Four thirty. Do you wish to be present?'

'Why? It's not my house,' she said huffily. 'You know me, I might say the wrong thing, put my foot in it.'

They waited as a family – mum, dad, two children and a dejected-looking dog – paused, stopping to examine the display.

'That's what they call a claret jug,' Harold pointed out knowledgeably to the man who had picked it up, 'complete with two glasses. If you look closely, you will see they are engraved with flowers.'

'Came from a country house out at Ribchester,' Christine put in, sensing his interest. 'One jug and two glasses. Complete set.'

'How much do you want, love?'

The man had a hard face and she left the negotiating to Harold.

No sale. The chap offered a price, take it or leave it. Harold left it.

'What's the matter with you?' she hissed as the man departed. 'You're losing your touch.'

'I'm not letting them go for fifteen pounds,' he said thoughtfully. 'Did you notice how he homed in on it rightaway, that jug? Put them away, Christine, and if he comes back tell him they've gone.'

Christine clicked her tongue. He was always on the lookout

for that elusive item that was worth a fortune. If it was up to her, she'd have been happy to get that fifteen pounds because, to be honest, they didn't look anything special. Washed-out colour. Harold would be poring through the price guide when he got in.

Sure enough, the chap did come back and, true to form, Harold had disappeared in the meantime. Christine feigned astonishment.

'Would you believe it?' she said. 'Right after you'd gone, they went.'

'What did he get for them?'

'I don't rightly know,' she said faintly, 'I was serving somebody else.' She was sure she blushed and she wouldn't half give Harold what for when he turned up. It flummoxed her, too much lying.

'I hope you're not serious about going abroad,' she told him as he drove her home. 'Everybody thinks you're crackers.'

'Sitting in the sun. Siesta. Wine and good food. Quiet pace of life. Oh yes . . . I am crackers. I only have a few years left, Christine, and I might as well make the most of them. Would you deprive me of that?'

'But you'll miss me,' she said helplessly. He'd always been like this: once he got a bee in his bonnet, he wouldn't shift. 'Haven't we had a lovely day today? And we have sunshine here sometimes. Look at me,' she stuck her arm towards the wheel, 'see . . . I'm fair pink. Bucked my tan up nice, today has.'

'If you don't want me to go, Christine, then you must say so,' he said. 'I would only reconsider my decision under those circumstances. If I thought it would upset you too much then I might revise my plans.'

He dropped the stuff off at her house before zooming off, showing an unexpected turn of speed, anxious not to be late for his prospective buyer. Christine left the boxes in the front room, behind a chair where they weren't too obvious. She was fed up. She was finding it hard to admit to Harold but the truth was she didn't want him to go. She had never thought for a minute he was serious.

All those years of living with Reg had made her bottle up her feelings. She dreaded anything happening to Harold. Her other brothers had died fairly young and she missed them too but not like she would miss Harold. Because he was so much older, he'd always seemed more like a dad than a brother, especially when their dad died. How she'd turned to Harold then. He was the only link left, the last of the Walmsleys. With him gone, the line was finished.

She tried to prepare herself for it, Harold popping off, but that didn't make it any easier. She'd show herself up at the funeral she just knew it. She'd never get through all them hymns he wanted to have, hymns he was always singing, especially not the Twenty-third Psalm. That had been one of Reg's favourites. She only had to hear the first line and she was off.

As well as that worry, there was the business with Jenny still to be sorted out. She hadn't plucked up courage yet to go again. Harold had gone daft at her taking the bus and, to be honest, it had spoiled the start of their holiday with him going on about it.

She should have stood up to Reg. They should have brazened it out, Jenny having the baby. Daft her going off to Wales when everybody knew anyway. Waste of time but Reg had been adamant. She could have brought the child up herself, on Jenny's behalf. Looked after it when Jenny went to university.

She should have stood up to Reg, told him what for. Instead, she'd just knuckled under and done what he wanted.

Reg Sweetman . . . he had a lot to answer for.

'Harold's got this barmy idea of moving to France. It started off with Italy but he's changed his mind,' she told Reg when she went to see him later in the week. She had got over her irritation, and spent a long time arranging the carnations she had brought him. 'What do you think of that? French people are different,' she mused, finally satisfied with the colour mix. 'I know that you have to be careful what you say nowadays, with that European whatnot and everything, but I'm only telling you. They're bound to be different, stands to reason – all that funny cheese and wine. They don't get any decent food inside them. No, Harold won't last five minutes,' she went on, 'that's if he ever gets there, that is. I can't see it. What would they make of him? And, I ask you, does he expect me to go traipsing over there every week? I don't like the ferry and I wouldn't go under that tunnel thing for a gold clock, and as for flying . . .' she bit her lip, remembering. 'I was getting on all right and then Harold goes and says that he feels a bit cooped up like he's in a coffin in the sky – sorry, love – and that was that. Made me ever so nervous, I couldn't touch the food. Lovely it was . . . considering . . . in little plastic trays.'

She was whispering, the words barely audible, but her voice carried on the warm summer breeze when there was no other. It echoed. Christine paused, feeling the pleasant warmth on her back, looking up at a gently fluffed sky. It was a beautiful day, the trees in full leaf, the sun filtering through the greenery, ending up dappled on the dark stone, the traffic a distant murmur not intrusive at all. Looking down at the grave, running her hand along the smooth surface, listening to the powerful silence, made her realise that Reg couldn't feel the sun any more.

Couldn't see the flowers.

Couldn't hear her either.

The inscription was clear, white letters picked out bold and bright.

Reginald Anthony Sweetman. Aged forty-five years. Beloved husband of Christine, loved and loving father to Jenny. Called to Eternal Rest.

And that was that when you got down to it. So much for the eternal rest. She couldn't keep bothering him with her troubles because he was no help at all. Suddenly feeling foolish, she patted the grave, before walking briskly away, without a backward glance.

31

She'd been seeing a lot of Stephen lately and it was brewing up to something special. She knew it. He knew it. They were just taking their time, that was all, tormented still by past mistakes.

'Did you enjoy the play?' he asked, as he drove her home.

'And the meal. Thank you, Stephen.' Jenny reached across and touched his arm. 'I had a lovely evening. After all the hassle at work recently, it's a relief to forget about it for a while.'

'Have you sacked him yet? That bloke?' he enquired. 'Thank God I've never been called upon to do anything like that.'

'It's one of those things,' she said, aware that she had been a trifle indiscreet in discussing the matter with him although she had been careful not to mention names. 'If you have the job title, you have the job responsibility too.'

'Correct. But it doesn't make it any easier, does it?'

'Not when he practically pleaded,' she admitted. 'But I had to look at it from a broader sense, Stephen. Things could have gone badly wrong and that might have affected hundreds of jobs, not just his. He either didn't consider that or he didn't care.' She wriggled a bit in her seat, uncomfortable with the conversation. 'Let's talk about something else,' she said. 'How are the girls?'

'Fine. Emily's getting down to it at last, would you believe? As for Abby . . . she's a bit preoccupied lately, something on her mind I think, probably this adoption thing. Incidentally, she's going ahead with it. Going down to see a counsellor to discuss it, to take it one step further. Lizzie's furious.'

They were back in Hazelburn and Stephen drove carefully through the gates of Curwin Hall, parking on the gravel in front of the entrance. The garden was especially beautiful, beds

233 •

heaving now with summer shrubs and flowers, the hills beyond the house a pale golden green tipped with purple, the sky a pastel wash of misty blue and pink, with just a few wispy clouds, an artist's afterthought.

Jenny sighed her delight and, suddenly, something in the gentle scene reminded her of another grand house, another beautiful garden with hills in the background. More soberly, she followed him indoors into the cool. It was very quiet, which she queried because Emily's taste in music was of the multiple-decibelled variety.

'The girls are out,' he said, a little embarrassed she thought. 'For the weekend actually. They've gone to visit an old friend of ours down in Wales. Should I have mentioned it, that we'd be alone?'

'It's OK.' She smiled. Now was the time to beat a hasty retreat if she wanted to before things became any more complicated. She wanted to stay. She also wanted to quiz him a bit more about Abby and the circumstances of her birth. Dammit, she had to know for sure before she made a complete fool of herself. If Abby went ahead, then she might very soon be getting a telephone call herself from the counsellor. What in heaven's name would she do then?

She had to wait until they were sitting cosily together on the sofa in the sitting room before she pressed on further.

'You said Lizzie was annoyed,' she said, 'about Abby trying to trace her natural mother? What about you? Do *you* mind?'

'I mind a bit,' he said sadly. 'And I'm only telling you this, Jenny, because I . . . I trust you. I'm worried for Abby. I can see all sorts of difficulties but if she wants to do it then I'm going to help all I can. It's the least I can do.'

'She's so lucky to have you,' Jenny said with a sudden rush of affection for him.

'And I'm lucky to have you,' he said unexpectedly, reaching and holding her hand.

'But in my opinion,' Jenny ventured, trying to stay calm and in control as she felt the pressure of his hand on hers, the gentle movement, 'I still think she should consider this very carefully. She might regret it deeply. Tell me, Stephen . . .' her earnestness made him remove his hand and look at her enquiringly, 'do you know anything at all about the mother?'

He shook his head. 'Lizzie didn't want to know, frankly. She thought it was for the best although we've been aware for some time that this was on the cards when Abby reached eighteen. It makes us feel helpless because although Abby has the right to look for her mother, what rights do we have as adoptive parents? None. To be honest, I'm afraid we might lose her. Lose her a little. Lizzie says she doesn't want to share her with anybody, although as Lizzie's chosen to live God knows how many miles from her, she's got a bit of a nerve to say that.'

'Try not to be bitter, darling,' Jenny said quietly. 'That won't help.'

'I know and I am trying. Sorry. All we can guess about her mother is that she was young and unmarried, of course. Sad, isn't it? That she was driven to do that, give up her child. I often think about her, what she must have felt just then.'

She knew the moment was drawing nearer. She had to tell him. If they were going to become lovers, and they surely were, she had to tell him.

'Stephen . . . can I tell you something very painful? Something about my past?' she said, trying not to notice that his arm had slipped around her, that her head was now nestling comfortably against his shoulder, that his breathing was certainly quickening, that hers was too, that he was gently running fingers up her bare arm, up and down. 'It's not something that I tell—'

'No,' he said sharply. 'I don't want to know. Whatever it is – *whatever* it is – it doesn't matter to me. We've both got pasts. We should forget them. What matters is now. Me and you.'

'But this is—' she broke off as he tilted her chin and kissed her, a long long kiss. His eyes were full of love for her and, to her astonishment she realised she had never seen that look before in a man, not quite, but then who was to say how she looked herself. She felt a deep longing for him, a powerful physical longing and a desire to please him as well as herself.

'I don't expect you to have led a completely innocent life,' he murmured against her hair, 'not a woman as beautiful as you. But I really do not want to know about other men.' He was stroking the back of her neck and, dammit to hell, that had always done things to her.

'Some things might matter,' she muttered indistinctly, knowing full well she was going to chicken out because she didn't want to spoil this moment, spoil what was to come. Why tell him when she was probably worrying about nothing?

'Know something, my darling?' he whispered as he drew her to her feet, questioned with his eyes before leading her out. 'You remind me of Abby sometimes. She has exactly the same look on her face when she's worried. You've no need to be worried. No need. You are my darling and I'll take great care of you.'

The words spun in her head and she needed the support of his arm as he led her upstairs to his room. A grand room overlooking the splendour of the rear grounds with a cosy area by the window, chairs and a small table grouped there. The big bed, covered with a tartan quilt, beckoned and she found her eyes drawn to it, nervous and excited.

'Ridiculous, isn't it?' he said, blessedly taking a moment to allow her to relax. 'I know we haven't known each other very long but I feel as if I've known you for ever.' He smiled, adorably intense now, his eyes greedily taking in every inch of her. 'I haven't felt like this since . . . well . . . since Lizzie.' He laughed his irritation. 'Damn, I'm sorry, I didn't mean to say that.'

She laughed too. A back-handed compliment, but she took it for what it was. He meant well. He was also desperately attractive and very male and it had been a helluva long time . . .

He only had to draw her close and trace his finger slowly down the entire length of her back and that was that.

She decided her confession could wait.

32

One of her opposite numbers had rung saying that he was worried about old Trevor. He had been off work for several days, unheard of, and nobody could get hold of him. Did she have any idea where the old so-and-so was?

Irritated that everyone seemed to assume she had some sort of special relationship with Trevor, probably guessing they were in the throes of a love affair, Jenny tried his home number, left a message on the answering machine before deciding she would visit him personally. She had a legitimate excuse to go down to London on business so it would not be so surprising if she popped in to see him. He had invited her often enough, for heaven's sake, but, amber lights blazing, she had always avoided it.

It occurred on the flight down just how worried she was about him. He was unpredictable, that's what. In all the years she had worked with him, she had never really known him. Funny that . . . she felt she knew Stephen so very very well, his moods, his hopes, his despairs, everything – and yet Trevor Cummings remained an enigma. She didn't really expect to find him slumped in his fume-filled car in the garage but it was upsetting that that thought should even have entered her mind. The feeling lurked. Uneasy.

She thought, just to cover herself, she'd better mention her intentions to someone else and so she told Trevor's long-suffering deputy, Brian Bailey.

'I'd have thought he's best left alone,' he said in surprise. 'He must be going through some mid-life crisis. Bloody pain in the neck, whatever it is. Can you shed any light on it? You seem to know him better than most of us. To be honest, he's driving everybody up the wall. Nobody can do anything right. They're all shit scared, Jenny – sorry – but they're all frightened he's going to give them the push. It's stress alley. I'm having a hard time to keep things together. There's going to be a revolution before long. There's only so much people can take.'

'As bad as that?' She wondered what to say, wondered if he was really in the dark about what was to happen or if he assumed she was. Either way, she had to be careful. 'It's just the way he works,' she said at last. 'You should know him by now.'

'I certainly do. Or at least as well as the next man. You can tell him from me that everything's running like clockwork here. We get on better without him but don't tell him that.' He smiled, a very able man who would probably not get the job he had been understudying so competently for so many years. 'On second thoughts, don't say anything about work. He'll expect the place to crack up without him. Sooner the better he retires, but knowing him, we'll be stuck with him until he's sixty-five at least. Not the retiring sort, is he?'

'Hardly.'

Jenny was relieved she had not given anything away. If there were just private consultations yet between Trevor and the board then she must not.

'I'll pop along to his place before I go to the hotel,' she said. 'It's on my way.'

'Of course, Jenny.'

There was something in his expression that caused her to frown. Surely he didn't think she was having an affair with Trevor, did he? She could understand rumours circulating amongst the lab staff for they had nothing better to do. She supposed she might have a bit of a glow about her that could be misconstrued.

It was difficult these days to concentrate on work, to smother the happy, dizzy feeling, but that was because she was in love with Stephen and he with her. She was, unashamedly, a romantic and for the moment she was happy to let things go on, unwilling to say anything that might spoil it, knowing it was a fool's paradise and that, sooner or later, she would have to tell him the truth. He had to know she had had a baby and, if that baby was Abby, then God help them.

Trevor answered at the third ring just when she was about to give up on him. He looked as if he'd hurriedly stepped into clothes, more so than usual, unshaven, bleary-eyed and smelling of cigarettes and booze. She was so relieved to see him alive that she very nearly kissed him as she almost fell through the door.

'You look terrible,' she said, taking a deep breath. 'Are you ill? Everybody's been so worried about you.'

He grunted, unconcerned, showing her into a really messy room. Somewhere, under the squalor, the former elegance showed through. 'Sorry about all this,' he said, scratching his body through the thin shirt. 'I was going to clean up.'

'Let me do that,' Jenny said briskly, taking off her jacket. 'Get yourself cleaned up,' she said, looking pointedly at him, 'and I'll tidy up. Have you eaten?'

'Eaten? Can't remember.' He smiled, a shadow of his former smile, and rather to her surprise, took her at her word and wandered upstairs, presumably to get himself smartened up.

It wasn't as bad as it looked. Just surface mess. She found a vacuum cleaner and duster and flew round, surprising herself with her endeavours. By the time he emerged, clean and shaved, the place was fairly shipshape and she was in the kitchen, cooking him a meal.

'I didn't know you were domestically inclined, Sweetman,' he said. 'My cleaner's taken the bloody huff. Walked out. God knows why.'

'You must have said something to her,' Jenny said, entirely unsurprised. 'Upset her,' her hesitation was minimal, 'as you seem to be upsetting everybody at work. I hope you don't mind me speaking frankly, Trevor . . .'

'Fire away,' he said, looking without enthusiasm at the fry-up she set before him.

'You're getting everybody's back up. I know why, of course, but they don't.' She let that thought sink in before continuing, 'Wouldn't it be better to be nice to them for a change? Before you go.'

'I am nice to them,' he said, thoroughly puzzled, 'as nice as I can be. They piss me off most of the time. The majority are chronically useless, but I try not to let that influence me. Under the circumstances, I'm bloody marvellous to them.'

• Patricia Fawcett

She let it pass, sitting opposite at the kitchen bench as, after a slow start, he began to wolf down the food, appetite obviously back in harness.

'Trevor, I wanted a word about work in fact. It's urgent.'

'And I thought you cared . . .' he said, with a grin. 'It's about Len, I suppose?'

She nodded. 'I have the report prepared for you. I've made my recommendation but . . .'

He pushed the plate away, sighed. 'Don't go soft, Jenny. You have the salary, the perks *and* the bloody responsibility. You can't afford to go soft. Go soft once and they'll nail you to the wall. Do you understand?'

'Yes.' She stared down at her hands, knew he was right.

'I've accepted the retirement package you'll probably be glad to know. News breaks next week if not before. Thanks for keeping mum. The official line is I'm retiring to spend more time with my cat. Fat cheque to follow.'

'What are you going to do? Did you work out a plan?'

'As a matter of fact I have.' He lit a cigarette, waited a moment. 'And the bloody cat's not included. Me and Hugh had a helluva natter last night and downed a few beers . . . more than a few,' he groaned, 'that's why I'm a bit knackered. Hugh's a great guy.'

'Someone I know?'

'My son. Didn't I mention him?'

'No you did not,' she said, allowing her surprise to show. 'I didn't know you had any children.'

'I haven't seen much of him. He lived with my first wife and only visited me now and then. I was always too bloody busy. Fancy a coffee?' he asked abruptly, turning his back on her and reaching for the pot. 'I've neglected him, I suppose,' he went on, still not looking at her, his voice rather subdued. 'Surprised he's still speaking to me as a matter of fact. My retiring means we can finally get together.' He spun round, and it was as if a great weight had been lifted from him. 'Know what we're going to do, me and my son? We're going off. Backpacking. Wherever takes our fancy.'

She laughed. Couldn't help it.

'Backpacking? You?'

'You heard. I know I'm more used to four-star hotels, the

works, but this will be something completely different. Hugh's a real outdoorsy type, God knows where he gets it from. His mother felt faint in fresh air. Anyway, we'll be roughing it, maybe even camping out under the stars if it takes our fancy. Time I got a bit fitter.' He drew on his cigarette, coughed heartily, as if to confirm the fact.

She let that go too. She couldn't imagine Trevor lasting five minutes without his room service and someone to attend to his every need but she wasn't going to spoil the dream.

'We're going to get to know each other. Quality time, all that sort of crap. Hugh's a bit mixed up and I'm going to help him find himself and vice versa, I suppose. His mother's delighted. Gets him out of her hair for a while. Thinks it's bloody hilarious, in fact. Thinks I can't do it. She never had any faith in me.' He poured the coffee, took his black. 'We're going to write a book. Father/son travels, rediscovering our identities. My thoughts. His thoughts. What do you think, Jenny? To tell the truth, I'm bloody excited about it.'

'What about your cat?' she asked as the animal, a sleek ginger puss, appeared and wrapped itself round her legs. She bent down to stroke it. 'The cat can't come with you.'

'She'll have to go to a cat's home or whatever,' he said with a shrug, the casual statement not fooling her for a moment. She'd heard him talk about his cat often. 'Unless . . . ?'

'I don't like cats particularly,' she said, knowing as she said it that the die was cast. 'But if you're stuck . . .'

'She's yours,' he said simply. 'I'd like you to have something of mine, Sweetman. I've always had a soft spot for you.' His glance was shrewd. 'What's brought all this on? All this motherly concern?'

'No reason. Does there have to be a reason for everything?'

'Absolutely. Know something? I can't make you out at all. You've always been cool towards me, towards everybody, but I get the feeling there's more to you than meets the eye. What are you hiding, Jenny?'

'Nothing that concerns you,' she said, whipping his plate from under him and smiling. She could say this sort of thing now. 'Do you know something, Trevor? Someone once told me, someone at work, that I was a hard-faced bitch,' she said. 'I laughed it off but, believe me, it hurt. Sometimes there's a conflict between being a good manager and being a woman. Of course you don't understand that but take this thing with Len. I've never had to do it before and I can't help wondering if there's some way round it, room for compassion. A second chance.'

'Second chance then third and fourth. Think about it. Think about the damage he might have done, would have done but for sheer good fortune. CWC could have been sued out of existence in the present climate.' The stubbing out of his cigarette, the pushing away of the ashtray had a very definite air of finality. 'Thanks anyway for hearing me when I was down. It was just a way of clearing my thoughts. You're a damn good listener.'

'I hate it when people say that.'

'Why? It's true. We must keep in touch.'

She smiled. 'Drop me a postcard when you can. Let me know how things are.'

'Will do.'

Trevor backpacking? She was inclined to agree with his ex-wife, it was hilarious. But it was also, in a strange way, hopeful.

Fancy him having a son.

She had never known that.

But then, he had never known about her daughter either.

33

Stephen was worried about Abby. It was quite ridiculous because he ought to be feeling on top of the world these days, for he and Jenny were getting on like a house on fire. Yes . . . it did feel like that, bloody good and hot and vital. No half-measures with her. She was one hundred per cent woman, was Jenny, more than happy to leave her sharp-fired independence in the workplace and become soft and feminine and a complete delight for him. It was like it had been in the old days with Lizzie before her sheer cussedness took over and poured cold water on their passion.

What was wrong with Abby? He knew this adoption thing was getting her down, that she was agonising about what to do, whether or not to start the ball rolling, trying to trace her natural mother and he couldn't help any more. He had to stand back and let her make the decision for herself. He was trying to be as neutral as possible, given Lizzie's opposition. That way he couldn't be accused later of persuading her to take one line of action in preference to another.

Or was she worried about something else? What in heaven's name would an eighteen-year-old girl be worried about? She wasn't pregnant, was she? Bloody hell! He cringed as the thought hit him. He'd tried to be a modern-day father, tried to acknowledge that these days young girls did this sort of thing, had a sexual relationship, so it would do no damned good to get on a high horse now. That arrogant sod Ben Chambers! It had to be him because there hadn't been anybody else since then as far as Stephen knew.

If she *was* pregnant then they'd just have to get on with it. He'd have to try to tell her somehow that it would be OK. Lizzie would

243 •

be very cross because, for all her so-called modern attitudes, she remained at heart pinchingly narrow-minded when it came to him and the girls.

Emotionally punch-drunk, wanting to tell the world and particularly Lizzie about his new love, he wandered into the kitchen where Abby was making lunch. It promised to be a long weekend with Jenny away on business so he was going to do nothing much. He was contemplating ringing Lizzie sometime over the weekend to tell her about Jenny. Not to gloat of course, merely to keep her up to date. Oh all right . . . maybe to gloat a little!

As well as his powerful sexual feelings for Jenny, he felt an enormous fondness for her. He enjoyed and was enthused by her presence and wanted to look after her, care for her, although he was wary of harping on too much about that. He had to remember she was an independent lady.

One in the eye for Lizzie that!

'Are you all right these days, darling?' he asked Abby as they ate. Emily was nowhere to be seen, still in bed, her music thumping from above. 'I don't want to pry but . . . have you got over that thing with Ben?'

He watched her closely, trying to gauge her reaction. If she was pregnant, then now would be as good a time as any to tell him. The door was open . . .

'I'm over it,' she said quietly, shutting him out, and he knew she would not tell him.

'Is there anything you want to tell me?' he persisted, letting the question hang in the air but she did not reach for it, merely shook her head.

'Have you thought any more about trying to trace your mother then?' he asked instead, needing to know how that was progressing, if at all.

She nodded, looking down at the table. 'I've started things off, been in preliminary touch with the agency,' she said. 'I hope you don't mind, Dad. It's not too late to pull back if I feel I have to. Either of us can do that.' She managed a tight smile. 'Are you sure you're not upset?'

'No,' he said quickly, 'not at all. If that's what you want then you must do it. I'd just like to be sure that you've thought it through, considered all the implications. It's not a decision to take lightly.'

'I know that. I've thought about it a lot. Please let me do it. It's important to me.'

'If you need any help – transport or anything – just ask,' he said, feeling a little helpless. Now was not the right moment to tell her about Jenny. Time enough for that. He couldn't rush the lady. He was going to ask a lot of her when he proposed marriage. Like it or not, she was going to become very much involved with his daughters. Lizzie would hate that as well but Lizzie would have to lump it.

'It's nice of you, Dad, but I want to make all the arrangements myself,' she told him, and he saw her eyes were deeply troubled. Poor darling! Sometimes, irrationally, he wished they'd never told her she was adopted, kept it secret. A dreadful thing to do but a lot easier in the end. It would have saved her all this heartache for one thing.

During the afternoon, as he was out walking in the gardens, he heard a car approach the house, the sound of voices. Dammit, a visitor? He wasn't expecting anybody and he suspected it would be someone for Emily. One of her string of boyfriends. Oh the joys of having a beautiful daughter!

'Dad . . .' Abby's voice, loud and insistent, from the back entrance. 'Dad, you'll never guess.'

He caught her excitement, hurried indoors and there, standing amongst a set of matching grey suitcases, was Lizzie.

'Stephen, darling . . .' she beamed at him. 'Pay the cab, would you? I have no change at all. It seems like foreign money to me these days. I was going to ring from the airport and then I thought, What the hell! I'll surprise them. Sorry, darling, the fare will be absolutely horrendous. You didn't tell me it was so *far*. I thought we were never going to get here. The cab driver has been a darling. We've had a very interesting conversation about California. The poor dear is morbidly fascinated by earthquakes. I sang for him too. We had to do something to pass the time. Tip him well.'

Hotly perfumed. Dark as ever. Eyes flashing. Bright red lipstick. Wearing a yellow fitted jacket over a black figure-hugging dress. Dripping with gold chains and bracelets. Expensive stuff. Smiling

• Patricia Fawcett

at him as she hugged Abby to her once more. The same damned smile. Aimed squarely at him. She gently dislodged Abby from her grasp and came towards him, as he fished for some notes and passed them to Abby, asking her to pay the taxi.

'He can keep the change.' He never took his eyes off Lizzie, that old fascination bubbling anew.

'Well . . .' Lizzie stood inches away, looking up at him. 'Hi . . . I can see I've managed to surprise you well and truly, you big baby.' She somehow managed to insinuate herself into his arms, and he bent to kiss her. Very lightly.

Emily, hearing the racket, suddenly burst onto the landing, leaning over the stairs, all smiles, squealing with excitement before thudding downstairs in her pyjamas, leaping onto Lizzie.

Stephen watched the reunion with a wry smile.

What did she want? Why had she come back?

And why did it give him a distinctly uneasy feeling?

34

'Tell Auntie Christine you are sorry,' Janice thundered. She had Shane in some sort of arm lock, or so it seemed. He was wriggling but not getting anywhere. 'Tell Auntie Christine you are sorry,' she repeated, punching out the words in a dangerously quiet tone, 'or else . . .'

'It doesn't matter,' Christine said with an attempt at a laugh. 'Don't go on at him, Janice. He didn't mean it. He couldn't help it.'

'Shane,' Janice warned, her eyes never leaving him, ignoring Christine. 'I shall count to ten. One, two, three . . .'

'Sorry,' he mumbled with a shuffling movement, Janice's grip on him dislodging his glasses. 'Sorry, Auntie Christine.'

'That's all right, love.'

Janice shot her an irritated glance. 'He hasn't finished yet. Now the rest of it. "I am sorry, Auntie Christine, that I broke your lovely . . ."' she looked at Christine for help. 'What was it exactly?'

'A claret jug,' Christine said, her smile glued. It was no use crying over spilled milk, as they say, or in this case a claret jug. Harold would go spare. 'It just slipped out of his little hands,' she went on, not knowing why she was defending him but he still looked quite shocked, poor lad. She had made the mistake of letting him take some toys into the front room and he had of course discovered the boxes of car boot stuff. And well . . . boys will be boys . . .

Shane obligingly repeated the words, rubbing his arm as his grandmother reluctantly let him go. Christine, trying to make amends, asked if he would like a glass of Ribena and a chocolate biscuit. Bless him, he was trying hard not to cry, lower lip fair trembling with the effort.

Janice followed her into the kitchen as Shane started on the piano. A somewhat subdued solo.

'I feel awful,' Janice said, taking off her glasses and rubbing at her eyes. Suspiciously moist eyes. 'Telling him off like that. Do you know, I very nearly hit him and that's not me at all. It's fair shook me up. It's just that – well, I'm worried to death, Christine. Can you keep a secret?'

Christine nodded. 'What's wrong?' she asked briskly, knowing that was far the best way with Janice. 'Out with it. Is it Catherine?'

'And Len.' Janice came closer, lowered her voice. 'He's in some trouble at work. Strictly between ourselves of course.'

Christine put Shane's glass on the tray, put him a little wrapped chocolate biscuit beside it, and prepared a pot of strong tea for them. She needed a brandy really but that was only for very special occasions and she did not think this quite warranted it. She dare not look at the bits of glass in the dustpan. It would be just like Harold to find out that the thing was worth a fortune.

'Trouble? What sort of trouble?' she asked Janice. 'Serious?'

Janice was quite pale and even her drop earrings seemed to have lost their glitter. They swung dully against her neck. 'Our Catherine's at her wits' end, what with her expecting. God knows what will happen if he loses his job. They're up to their eyes in expense. Between you and me,' she cast a sly glance through to the living room but Shane was still soberly playing a melancholy tune of sorts, 'I've always had my doubts about him but can you tell them, daughters, when they think they've met the right man? Will they be told? He's too slick for my taste, always an answer for everything. And I never could stand the way he has his hair and the way he doesn't shave enough.'

'What's he been up to then?'

She carried the tray through as Shane finished with a flurry, sat him in front of the television with his juice and biscuit and waited for Janice to tell her.

'Oh . . . it's technical,' Janice said vaguely. 'Something he hasn't done that he should have done. Taking time off when he was supposed to be at work or at one of them other places he goes to. I thought it was funny because he was supposed to have a bad back and you know as well as me, Christine, that if you have a bad back proper, you can't move for pain.'

They exchanged a sympathetic look, both having had their share of pulled ligaments and the like.

'It was all right when the old boss was there,' Janice continued, 'but now your Jenny's tightened everything up, had a word with him about it. The thing is, he thinks he's for the chop.'

Shane was not listening, patiently trying to open the wrapper on the biscuit as a cartoon flickered on the screen.

'What I wondered is . . . could you have a word with her? Would you talk to her?'

Christine drew a sharp breath. 'Don't ask,' she said. 'How can I have a word when we don't speak, Janice. Talk sense for goodness' sake.'

'But you could explain about Len,' Janice said, 'say that he's not himself, worried about Catherine.'

'I can't interfere,' Christine said, not liking to upset Janice, who'd been such a good friend over the years. She glanced anxiously at the clock and wished Harold would get a move on. He was cock-a-hoop because he had a buyer for his house. First person to view it. A cash buyer at that. A hefty wad of notes indeed. Would you believe his luck?

'Surely you can put in a good word? That's all I'm asking.'

'You don't put much of a good word in for him and you're his mother-in-law,' Christine said. 'I'm sorry, love, but I can't. Even if we did make it up . . .' she sighed.

'Well I've asked. I thought it was worth a try. Do what you can,' Janice said, resigned and mercifully not seeming to hold it against her. 'Come on, Shane, finish up your biscuit, there's a little sweetheart, and we'll leave Auntie Christine in peace.'

Not for long. Harold arrived just as Janice left, hardly in the room before he was telling her the news.

'It was made in about 1870 and, because we've got the glasses as well, that makes a set. It's worth about three hundred and fifty pounds in mint condition, and it is, isn't it? Right bonny jug that. I knew as soon as I saw it. What did I tell you? He'd have made a tidy profit, wouldn't he, that chap who wanted to buy it if I'd have parted with it for fifteen?'

Christine decided she would tell him later. No point in upsetting him just now. 'What about your house?' she asked instead. 'Any nearer?'

'Not yet but I am confident that everything will proceed according to plan. I have been in communication in the meantime with an agency that specialises in properties abroad.'

Christine ignored him. There was no stopping him once he got started.

'Janice next door has put me in a right old pickle,' she said, as she prepared hot buttered crumpets.

'Nothing to do with that Wayne, is it?'

'Shane. No, not him, his dad. He's . . .' she bit her lip, 'it's supposed to be a secret, just me and Janice, and you know what they say – three may keep a secret if two of them are dead.'

'Your secret is safe with me,' Harold said a little indignantly. 'The number of times I have been asked to keep secrets. Some people are very indiscreet when there's a death in the family – loosens their tongue. Their secrets will die with me. Me and a thousand secrets in that coffin.'

Christine told him. Asked what she ought to do. She wasn't surprised when he agreed that she should do nothing. Janice had a cheek asking but then she was very worried about Catherine so you could understand it. Jenny could not be bribed into doing something underhand. Not for Len. Not for nobody.

'She always had a mind of her own,' Christine said thoughtfully, passing him a cloth to wipe his buttery fingers. 'I've a mind to speak to her. Phone her or something. You didn't tell her about me going that day, did you?'

He shook his head. 'You asked me not to,' he said simply.

She smiled her thanks. Deliberated a moment.

'You're right, it's gone on too long. Reg will understand, won't he?'

'He hasn't much option. Oh by the way, can you come for tea on Wednesday? I thought I might try my hand at baking a nice cake. You're always baking for me.'

'All right.' She nodded, pleased to be asked, smiling as she washed up, listening to Harold singing. He could hold a note for ever such a long time, Harold.

'So what about these buyers of yours?' she asked when she had finished.

'They require a further look. They are talking of an extension.'

'Extension? What do they want an extension for? It's like a barracks, that house, with all them rooms.'

'I wonder about that,' Harold said with a frown. 'I trust the house will be safe in their hands. They are from Yorkshire.'

Christine laughed. 'It's nothing to do with you what they do once they buy it. They'll probably demolish that lean-to,' she said wickedly. 'And your vegetable plot is sure to go.'

'Lean-to?' he repeated, in a flurry at the word. 'They call it a conservatory now. It's a solid construction, Christine. Why would they want to demolish it?'

'Folks have their own ideas. Especially folks from Yorkshire.'

He smiled a little. 'You're trying to put me off and it's going to take more than that. Now, let's have another look at that claret jug. Is it in the front room in one of the boxes?'

'It was,' Christine said, facing the moment of truth.

She'd swing for that Shane one of these days.

35

'Just like Mum to surprise us like that,' Emily said, sprawling on the bed in Abby's room. 'Wasn't it sweet of her?'

Abby nodded. Since Mum's arrival, it had been one long dizzy whirl. No wonder Dad had looked so dazed. She couldn't be sure but she thought he had brought forward his trip to the Middle East for he was now due to leave next week for an unspecified time. Mum was very miffed about that.

'You're a real misery these days, Abby,' Emily said, perceptive as usual. 'You're not still worried about that business of finding your mother, are you? Have you talked to Mum about it?'

'I've tried,' Abby muttered.

Time and time again. There was always something of pressing importance Mum had to do, somewhere she had to disappear to, if Abby so much as breathed a mention of her adoption. It had been like that all her life: Mum had never wanted to talk about it, to discuss it, not after she had got over the initial telling. She would really have preferred it not be mentioned ever again.

'Well, try once more. You're so defeatist,' Emily said with a big sigh. 'What a life, eh! Exams. Exams. I've got my eye on this fantastic guy at school. He wants to be a vet. That has a certain glamour, don't you think? Do you see me as a vet's wife?'

'I thought you weren't going to get married,' Abby reminded her with a smile. 'Weren't you going to have this wonderful career?'

'Well . . . that depends on the bloody exams.' Her second sigh was loud. 'I could murder a cigarette but I'm trying to give up. I can't afford them, not them and clothes and make-up as well, and I can hardly ask Dad for an extra sub, can I? And they do

253 •

• Patricia Fawcett

say you put weight on once you stop smoking.' She raised herself on one elbow and eyed herself in the mirror. 'Am I?'

'You're as thin as a rake.' Abby glanced at her watch. 'Aren't you supposed to be going out?'

'Jesus! I forgot . . . why didn't you remind me?' Emily said, slipping her shoes on. 'I've got to catch that stupid bus. I'll have to ask Mum for some money. Do you know what sort of mood she's in?'

Abby shook her head, rooted in her own purse for some cash instead. Dad was at work and Mum was downstairs. She'd give it one more try. She ached for Mum's approval, otherwise doing it would reek of behind-the-back negotiating. She wanted both of them fully behind her in this, Mum as well as Dad.

She made sure she looked nice, applying a bit of make-up and doing her hair before she confronted her.

'Mum?'

'There you are, darling, looking very pale and interesting. That look's all the rage, sort of ethereal. You need to be a tiny touch slimmer, of course. Emily's quite a nice weight.'

Her mother was in the drawing room, wearing a mustard jumpsuit with a broad leather belt and lots of shiny silver chains. She smiled and patted the sofa beside her. 'Come and sit down, we haven't talked in ages.'

Abby did as she was told, perched on the sofa, tense as a wire.

'Mum . . . ?'

'Isn't this cosy?' Lizzie beamed. 'And this house is lovely. Very English. If only I could have this house in California. The views there can be so spectacular, darling. Here, I have to admit I'm not exactly wild about the village. So dreary. However . . .' she stopped, looked closely at Abby. 'Aren't you happy? Is work getting you down?'

'No, I like my work.' Abby wondered how best to approach this. She wanted to explain to her mother just why she had decided she was going to do this. She wanted to explain that it was nothing to do with how she felt about them, Mum and Dad and Emily. Nothing could change that. They were her family. Simple. No, she wanted to explain . . .

'So do I, darling. I adore my work,' Lizzie said, eyes glowing with the thought. 'Unless you've been on stage, I can't begin to explain how it feels. The audience out there, hushed, waiting for you to sing. Sometimes it's as if my voice isn't part of me, it's on its own, soaring to every corner of the auditorium. And then that moment's silence before the applause. Ah, the applause!'

'Mum . . . ?' Abby attempted to bring her down to earth. 'Can we talk about me a minute?'

Lizzie looked at her in astonishment. 'Aren't you interested in my singing? Your father was never interested either, not properly. He pretended to be but he never was. He's not very good at hiding his feelings.'

'Of course I'm interested,' Abby told her, speaking quite sharply and getting a corresponding aggrieved look as a result. 'Sorry, but, Mum, please can we talk about me? It's so important to me that I have your approval for this.'

'What is?' She snatched another look at her daughter. 'Oh God, Abby, why didn't you say? I know . . . I know what it is you want to talk about. Your father mentioned it.' She waggled a finger. 'You should have spoken to me about it first, darling. He's hopeless with things like this. Men always are.'

'He's been quite understanding,' Abby said. 'He says that I must do what I want. That it's up to me.'

'That's big of him. Typical. Of course it's up to you.'

'Well, I do worry about it a lot,' Abby told her, pleased that at last she seemed to be prepared to discuss it. 'I've started making enquiries—'

'Leave the details to me. I know an excellent surgeon,' her mother said, patting her hand. 'Don't worry about the cost. I will attend to that personally. I'm very well off for funds just now. Simon had a fit of conscience, settled a considerable amount on me as a present. Actually I think he was frightened of adverse publicity, kiss-and-tell, you know. He's petrified of anyone finding out he wears a corset. Despite his weight problem, he is doing very well with records and personal appearances. As long as he keeps still on stage, he's fine.'

'Surgeon?' At a complete loss, Abby stared at her.

'Yes, plastic surgeon. What is the matter with you, Abby? Sometimes you can be extraordinarily obtuse. You mustn't get yourself in a tizzy about it. There's nothing to it.' Lizzie crossed her legs in a graceful movement. She wore expensive-looking spiky-heeled shoes in black patent leather with a mustard trim. 'Once it's done, you can hide away somewhere discreet for a while to convalesce. Until the bruises fade, you do rather look as if you've gone ten rounds with a heavyweight boxer. You have no need to worry at all. Actually, darling,' she touched her cheeks, 'haven't you noticed?' She ran her fingers over her face. 'I suppose it's a compliment that none of you has noticed.'

'You've had a face-lift?' Abby asked, aware only now of the peculiarly smooth surface, the tightness of the cheekbones.

'It was barely necessary at my age,' her mother said with a smile, 'but I had the money available so I thought, why not? It's so important how I look. I can still take on the younger roles without anyone quibbling.' She leaned over, patted Abby's hand. 'You *shall* have your nose job, darling. Take no notice of what your father says. Men are hopeless about things like this. They have no idea how a woman feels when she is less than perfect.'

A nose job?

'I don't want a nose job,' she heard herself saying, 'I'm OK about it now.' She touched it, the implied criticism hurtful. 'It's not that bad, is it?'

'You don't? Even if I pay?' The amazement was doubly hurtful. 'Then what is this conversation about? Really, Abby, I don't know what to make of you sometimes.'

Abby couldn't tell her.

It was a waste of time trying to explain how she felt about this. Unlike Dad, her mother had never ever thought about the woman who had given Abby birth, other than in a dismissive way.

She was incapable of understanding how important the subject was.

'Do let me know, darling, if you change your mind.' Lizzie relaxed against the cushions, breathing deeply. 'I'm thinking I might possibly do something about my breasts next. I've become a bit flat.'

Abby managed a smile.

Mum flat? She was never that. She was so in tune it was near perfect.

Let her get on with her singing.

'For God's sake, Stephen, anyone would think you were avoiding me,' Lizzie said, cornering him as he came downstairs, having spent an hour working in his study. 'Working every minute God sends and then you're off next week. It's most inconsiderate.'

'It's a long-standing arrangement,' he said with a smile, 'organised a while since. I have to go myself, Lizzie. They will be terribly insulted if I send a replacement. Status matters a lot out there.'

'I suppose you're right,' she said sulkily. 'How is work, Stephen? You seem to be coining it in these days.' The glance round the room said it all. 'Who would have thought you'd have been able to afford something like this?'

'I've worked for it,' he said, not at all uncomfortable with his success. 'Our new clients are very excited by our designs. We've had to make adjustments of course because of the climate and so on, but money's no problem with them, thank God, so we don't have to worry about cutting costs. Yes, Lizzie, work's pretty good just now, exciting and fulfilling.'

'Good. I'm pleased for you.'

She didn't look it, shining like a beacon in the understated room in a brilliant red dress. The skirt had ridden up, drawing attention to her legs, lovely legs silkily clad. Scarlet backless sandals with a high heel swung on her tiny feet, a mass of gold bracelets jingled on her arm, a Californian tanned arm.

'Abby had a heart-to-heart with me,' she told him, 'yesterday. She was in her usual self-effacing mood. The poor darling can't get round to admitting it but she quite obviously wants a nose job so can I leave you to make the arrangements for it? Someone reputable. You can send me the bill if you wish. I ought to pay for my daughters' little luxuries.'

'Are you sure she still wants that?' he asked in surprise. Abby had seemed to be over that little problem, happy now with her looks. A tiny imperfection added character. He liked Abby's nose. He also liked the way Jenny's eyes were a little too widely spaced for perfect beauty. He looked at the perfectly symmetrical face of his beautiful Lizzie. She had aged well, unlined, the eyes bright. She looked just as good now as she had at twenty-six.

• Patricia Fawcett

'Quite sure but you know her, she can be so awkward. She feels it, you know, being a little in Emily's shadow. Emily's so like me, isn't she?'

'I'll have a word with Abby when I get back,' he said. 'If it's what she wants, then of course she shall have it.'

'Let's not talk about Abby. Talk to me, darling,' she said. 'You've never talked to me since I got back, not properly.'

'I thought we'd said all there was to be said, Lizzie.'

'That was before. A lot of things have happened since then. I want to explain about Simon,' she said. 'It was a ghastly mistake. I was caught out by his charm, missing you and the girls, and before I knew what was what, it was too late. Serious. Divorce and everything. I never meant that. I never meant to hurt you, you big baby. I always loved you, Stephen. For me it was love at first sight.' There was a significant pause. 'When did you fall in love with me? The exact moment.'

He took his cue as if hearing it from the wings.

'The first moment I saw you . . .' He turned away, went over to the window, looked out. Storm clouds battled overhead, the distant hills dark and forbidding this morning, and a stiff wind battered the flowers in the beds. He wasn't really seeing them, he was seeing Lizzie in a white gown with a red rose pinned to the shoulder. Standing there in that crowded room looking at him. Singing.

'And . . . ?' she prompted. 'Tell me again. Who were you with? What was I wearing? What did you think the very first moment you saw me? Did you really fall in love at first sight?'

'Lizzie . . .' The vision faded and he turned to look at her. 'Before we go any further, I have to tell you something. I've met someone else and I love her.'

'Love her?' The laugh was short.

'Yes. I hope we're going to get married. I haven't asked her yet, in fact with one thing and another I haven't seen her in days but—'

'Good God, you can't mean Clare?' she said. 'Emily said that was all over. The woman's hopeless, darling. She always was. Frankly, I'm amazed Roger stayed with her as long as he did. Talk about mismatch. Roger had such vitality, such wit. Clare is so wishy-washy. A grey lady, darling. Not your style at all.'

He felt, not triumph, not revenge, but a sort of guilty satisfaction. 'It's not Clare,' he said with a dismissive shake of his head. 'That fizzled out. It might have come to something if it had been up to her but—'

'Someone else?' She stared at him through an amazed silence. Then she recovered and laughed although her eyes remained amazed. 'My, we have been painting the town red! Or village rather. How you can live in this godforsaken place is beyond me. It's the woman from here, from that cute little white cottage, I suppose, this Jenny woman? Emily told me all about her.' She rearranged her dress, her hands with their red-tipped nails, bare of rings. 'Don't tell me you're sleeping together? She's years younger. Are you cradle-snatching now?'

He looked at her, decided gallantly not to say it.

'I know. It was different for me,' she said, flushing. 'Simon and I fell in love.'

'And so have I,' he said patiently. 'I know it's happened fast but that's the way it is sometimes.' For a minute the vision blurred – the white gown, the red rose. 'We don't need any more time, Jenny and me. She's a bit like you and sometimes she reminds me of Abby too. She's quite earnest and sincere, hard-working, a little serious, and . . . just nice, I suppose.'

'Sounds utterly dreary,' Lizzie said, eyes now angry. 'Do you mean I've come all the way here to this . . .' she waved her hand towards the window, 'to this lousy climate, probably missed out on something terrific in the way of work over there – if you're not instantly available, you might as well be dead – just to have you stand there and have the cheek to tell me it's all over? That there's no hope of us getting back together? Not even for the sake of our daughters? I thought you'd take me back if only for their sake. Do you realise, Stephen, what I've done for you? I've deliberately reneged on my current contract just to be here. I probably won't be offered work ever again.' Her lip trembled in true Lizzie fashion. 'How can you upset me like this, darling? You know it affects my voice if I get upset.' Tears flooded the dark beauty of her eyes, spilled gently over. A little sob of perfect pitch accompanied them.

If Stephen had any shadowy doubts, it was in that moment that they were dispelled. Finally, he had got her out of his system, fallen out of love. And the impact was just as shattering as falling *in* love had been.

'I'm sorry,' he said, as a crack of thunder sounded, accompanied by a flash of lightning that momentarily lit up the room, showed up her startled features, the utter disbelief. 'We can still be friends, can't we?' he added awkwardly. 'For the sake of the girls?'

'Hah!' She rose in a single graceful movement, casting him a tortured glance for all the world as if she were on stage and this were one of the more dramatic moments in the opera. Ridiculously, he half expected her to burst into song. Something poignant, of course, rippled with meaning. 'I might have known it was a waste of time,' she said, the voice flat and expressionless. 'And while we're at it, what the hell are you doing condoning this mad idea of Abby's? I won't talk about it to her. It's absurd of her to be thinking of tracing her mother. As well as unwise. We know nothing about the woman. God knows what she'll turn out to be like. It will devastate poor Abby. You know how sensitive she is.'

'She'll be just an ordinary woman,' he said mildly, 'just getting on with her life. Now and then she might wonder about her daughter, wonder how she's getting on, what she looks like. In fact, Lizzie, the more I think about it, the more I agree with Abby. She won't be complete until she finds her.'

'Rubbish! I'm her mother. I'm her mother just as much as Emily's,' Lizzie protested, starting as another huge clap of thunder sounded overhead followed immediately by a flash. 'God, I hate thunderstorms.' She shivered, moved closer. She had that look on her face; she had not completely given up on him, she was still under the illusion that she could win him round with her charm. 'Abby's very ungrateful. I'm the one who cared for her when she was little. I'm the one who read to her, tucked her in, told her how to handle boyfriends when she was older, that sort of thing. Aren't I? I'm her mother, not some woman who's never set eyes on her for eighteen years, who abandoned her when she was a baby. Got rid of her.' She noticed his expression, softened her own. 'I'm afraid it's true, harsh but true. No matter how you wrap fancy words round it, it's what she did, Stephen. What sort of woman could do that?

I couldn't. I couldn't have got rid of darling Emily, not even if I was offered the chance of singing principal at Covent Garden if I did.'

She was very close, inches away, very aware of the power she could exert over him – the power she could once exert over him but not any more. '*I'm* Abby's mother,' she repeated, and for once the agonised expression in her eyes was genuine. 'Aren't I, darling?'

Stephen thought of the stream of nannies and au pairs, himself, the times the girls had called out for her and she wasn't there.

He pulled her close, merely to pat her shoulder, to tell her what she needed to hear.

'Of course you are,' he said sadly.

36

Jenny parked her car in the special slot reserved for her, reached for her briefcase and stepped out into a pleasant sunshine, rapidly drying out the effects of the downpour. She skirted the puddles and headed indoors.

Hardly a word from Stephen since his ex-wife had arrived back and she was ready for him when he deigned to put in an appearance. How dare he treat her in such a cavalier way as this? She had glimpsed the woman a few times. Flamboyant sort. Being an opera singer would suit her very well!

'Good morning, Rose,' she said as she went through the laboratory, bracing herself for the usual chilly reception. She was picking her way barefoot through pine needles with her staff. She might have thought twice about taking the job if she'd known it was going to be such an uphill struggle.

'Good morning, Miss Sweetman.' Rose smiled, straightened the telephone, fussed a moment. 'Gorgeous day, isn't it? It makes you think of holidays. Have you any plans?' she asked as she followed Jenny into her office.

'Not yet.' Jenny hung up her coat, slipped behind the desk, confronted the day's workload.

Damn Stephen Finch! Just when she'd thought she'd met the man of her dreams, dammit to hell, that ex-wife of his turns up and reclaims him. That's what it felt like anyway . . . Serve her right, she supposed, for going off at a tangent into some sort of romantic stupor. She ought to know by now. Thirty-five and she still hadn't sussed men out. She was still looking for Mr Right. It would be amusing if it wasn't so pathetic.

'Everything's ready for your trip next week,' Rose said,

• Patricia Fawcett

whistling up an envelope out of nowhere. 'All in here. First class. And I've booked you in at your favourite hotel. OK?'

'OK.' It took a moment, preoccupied as she was, for it to dawn that Rose was being exceptionally nice today. And today was the first day that Len would be absent. She had some explaining to do.

'Sit down a moment, Rose,' she said.

Rose obliged, slipping her spectacles on, poising a pen over her notepad.

'No . . . not that.' Jenny sighed, smiled. 'I know rumours have been circulating, this business with Len, and I think I should make it clear—'

'Sorry to interrupt. But before you start, can I just say something, Miss Sweetman?'

'Of course.' She had asked the girl to call her Jenny but she stubbornly resisted so Jenny let it pass. It wasn't important after all.

'Len's been getting away with murder for ages,' she began. 'Everybody thinks so but he and Mr Harding were like that – played golf together, you know . . . Well, he turned a blind eye, didn't he?'

'I don't think we should be discussing Mr Harding,' Jenny reminded her gently. 'But go on, I'm listening.'

'That's it really. That's all I wanted to say. We didn't think you'd have the . . .' She hesitated. 'What I mean is . . .' She gestured helplessly towards a heap of files. 'Do you want me to get rid of them? Everything's on the computer now.'

'I'd better glance through them first.'

'No need.' Rose picked them up, held them lovingly against her bosom. 'They're just Mr Harding's stuff. Not important. He was a bit of a hoarder. I know I shouldn't say it but he wasn't half a ditherer too.'

'Rose . . .' Jenny said warningly.

'A lovely man, don't get me wrong, Miss Sweetman. He always bought me a beautiful big box of chocolates at Christmas.' She blushed, carried on. 'But he couldn't make a decision if his life depended on it. We never knew where we were with him. It's different with you. We know where we stand now . . . with you. Even the smokers have got to accept it. They know it's not your fault. It's the same everywhere nowadays. We're all behind you, and Len got what he deserved. Now, if there's anything urgent you want done, just give me a buzz.'

Bemused, Jenny asked her to send Alan in for a quick word.

He appeared, looking serious.

Jenny informed him officially of Len's departure and her plans for filling the vacancy. She thanked him in advance for the extra work he and his staff would be involved in.

He shrugged. 'I feel sorry for him, I can't pretend otherwise,' he said, 'but it was on the cards. He underestimated you,' his glance was shrewd, 'more fool him.'

'Let's put it behind us,' Jenny said, half rising from her chair. 'From now on, this department's going to run like clockwork, Alan. No dead wood.'

He shook her hand. Smiled.

'Well done,' he said.

She was invited to Uncle Harold's for tea. It felt a bit strange going to the old house now that it was up for sale. She would be sorry to see it sold and especially sorry to see him go. If he ever went, that was. She had grave doubts. Uncle Harold's roots were firmly embedded in Preston soil. He was devious and she sensed he was up to something.

She went there straight from work, still in her smart suit, parking her car in the quiet cul-de-sac where he lived, a pleasant leafy avenue off Watling Street Road. They had often walked here from their home in Hargreaves Street when she was little and she had loved playing in the big garden, the rear completely private with its border of trees. How she would miss it!

She clicked the gate open and went up the path, seeing him peering through the window at her and waving to him.

'Jenny, love. In you go,' he said, taking her jacket and briefcase. 'Good day?'

'A lot better, thanks,' she said. 'Things are starting to settle down at last. They're finally forgetting how Mr Harding did things.'

'Folks are cautious,' he said, 'don't like anything new. Your mother's like that. If it was up to her, we'd still be driving round in horse-drawn carriages. Suspicious of change, she is.'

'How is she?'

'All right. Lost her job at the supermarket. Spoke her mind, you know. It was all on account of baked beans. On the lookout for something else but she's all right. She won't take any harm. Your father left her provided for.'

'I know he did.'

Jenny felt uncomfortable discussing it. If she ever thought for a moment that her mother was struggling financially she would do something to help – if she would let her, that is.

She sat in the front room while he made the tea. It was exactly the same. The same furniture. Surely the same curtains? Heavy and dark. Brown gloss paintwork. A busy darkish wallpaper that shrunk the room. She supposed the new people, when they came in, would brighten it up and it would be unrecognisable.

The garden was terraced, rockery and heathers, with big old hedges framing it. The hedges cast a big shadow and she supposed the new people would prune them back, let in more light, scrub out the heathers, put in a lawn maybe. It just wouldn't be the same. Once he had gone, she would never be able to come up this avenue again. She loved him, she realised, as she had never quite loved her father. Funny that . . .

'Are you sure I can't help?' she asked as he started on the second verse of 'Praise to the Holiest in the height'.

'All in hand,' he called back. 'Oh, did I remember to tell you your mother was coming for tea?'

'What?'

She was through the door to the kitchen in a flash. 'No you did not,' she said. 'Does she know I'm coming?'

'No.' He finished laying things on plates. Sandwiches. A squidgy chocolate cake. Barm cakes. Cheese. Pickles. Celery sticks in a glass. 'No, she doesn't know, Jenny, or she wouldn't be coming, would she?' His glance was shrewd. 'I've taken it on myself to do something about it. I'm fed up with you two. I've had enough. It's gone on too long. There . . .' the doorbell rang, 'that will be her now. Do you want to get it or shall I?' he asked, slicing the breadknife through the air as he spoke. It could have been viewed as a threat but short of making an escape through the rear and over the high wall, Jenny was well and truly stuck. She whistled her annoyance at him before stamping off. She paused at the door, took a deep breath, and opened it.

'Jenny . . .' Her mother was there, wearing trousers of all things, something she never used to wear. Softly shaped olive-green trousers and a silky spotty blouse. Her hair glinted red and she was made up prettily. Flushed now.

'Mum . . .' She stood aside, let her in. 'It's Uncle Harold's fault,' she said. 'He's done it. I didn't know you were coming.'

'I didn't know *you* were coming either,' her mother said with a tight smile. 'You don't look any different.'

'Nor do you. Well, not really different.' Jenny saw the anxiety in the eyes, remembered the last words she had uttered all those years ago. They came screaming back at her, echoing off the narrow walls of the hall, like a snake spitting venom.

Now, after all this time, she didn't know what to say. It wasn't like this in the dream she sometimes had. In the dream, they just rushed into each other's arms.

'These are out of the catalogue,' her mother said, pointing down at her clothes. 'Janice runs one and I buy something now and then. I like to help with her commission. You remember Mrs Middlebrook, don't you? Janice next door? She has a little grandson now. Right little so-and-so called Shane.' Her voice was bright and brittle as she called out to her brother, 'And you can stop that singing, our Harold. Pulling a trick like this. He's going to live in France, so he says,' she said, turning back to Jenny. 'Has he told you?'

Jenny nodded. She still didn't know what to say. She had forgotten how strong the accent was, stronger even than Harold's. Comforting though, her mother's voice. Poking at her memory, slicing through to the very early days.

'It'll leave me in a merry pickle I can tell you. We go car booting, you know. Every Sunday. It gets you out, you meet people. When you live on your own . . .' Her eyes were suspiciously bright as Harold clattered through, pushing the tea trolley. 'Are you stopping then, our Jenny?' she asked, somewhat aggressively. 'For your tea?'

'Mum . . .' Jenny felt her own tears bubbling up. Despite what she'd said about her not looking much different, her mother *was* older. Eighteen years older. It showed somehow. 'I'm sorry.'

• Patricia Fawcett

Christine sniffed. 'I hope that tea's properly brewed, Harold,' she called out to him as he went into the dining room. 'He makes tea like dishwater,' she said and then, her voice a whisper, turned half away so that Jenny could hardly hear, 'I'm sorry too. Daft we've been, the pair of us.' She finally looked properly at Jenny, smiled a sort of smile. 'Well, don't just stand there like a tailor's dummy. Come here.'

Jenny moved towards her, and they paused, a long moment, before simultaneously shaking their heads and settling into an embrace. Her mother patted her, muttered something about it being all right now. Jenny had forgotten what it felt like to be held by her. The warm feeling was very nearly too much for her to bear. She felt suddenly like a little girl again. 'Oh Mum, I wish it hadn't happened like that.' She struggled to make some sense. 'I wish—'

'I wish too but there's no point in it,' her mother said, holding her away, blue eyes aglow. 'Come on, buck yourself up. Look at you. All messed up. Go and wash your hands, brush your hair and then come and have your tea. And be quick. If your Uncle Harold runs true to form, that tea will be stone cold in five minutes.'

Jenny laughed.

And went to do what she was told.

'You've a nerve,' Jenny told Stephen, before he had the chance to open his mouth. 'Now that Lizzie's gone, you decide to come to see me. I never saw hide nor hair of you whilst she was here. I was beginning to think it had never happened, you and me. I was beginning to think it was a dream, our being together.'

'Please . . .' he smiled, 'please Jenny, I can explain.'

'You'd better come in, I suppose.'

She stood aside, childishly dipping her head so that his kiss landed in mid-air, moving quickly before he had the chance to take her in his arms. She wanted him to. Oh how she wanted him to.

'I tried to ring you, even tried you at work but all I got was your secretary. I called a couple of times but you were never in,' he said, standing huge and awkward and boyishly embarrassed just inside the sitting-room door. 'And now I have to shoot off to the

Middle East on business. There's just never been the time. One thing and another . . .' he shrugged. 'I've never stopped thinking about you, my love. It was pretty special, wasn't it?'

'Sit down. You don't need to hover there. Do you want a drink?'

'Coffee would be nice.'

'I meant something stronger,' she said, rather enjoying this. Let him stew a while! 'A whisky?'

He nodded. 'You look terrific. Hell, I've missed you so much.'

She felt the slightest weakening of her resolve to give him a hard time.

'I've missed you too,' she acknowledged, 'but I want you to be honest with me, Stephen. You can't mess me about like this. You've got to make your mind up. Do you still love her?'

'Lizzie?'

'Of course, Lizzie. Who else? You act like you're still infatuated with your wife, Stephen. Are you?'

'My ex-wife,' he corrected her, 'and you're wrong, Jenny. To be honest, I've needed time to sort out my feelings and yes, I suppose I did wonder how I would feel if she were to come back. Would it rekindle things? Set us off again? We had some good times together. We were very happy together once.' He caught her expression. 'For God's sake, Jenny, listen to me. We have the girls to consider, me and Lizzie. It would have been nice for them if we could have got it together again. But . . .' He came across to her, pulled her a little roughly, because she was resisting, into his arms. 'Dammit, she meant nothing to me. It was a shock when I realised but that's the honest truth. She wanted to try again but I told her I'd met you and fallen in love with you. So,' he smiled as she wriggled in his arms, 'how about it? Will you marry me? Or are you still mad as hell at me?'

'Marry you? It's a bit sudden. We haven't discussed marriage at all.'

'We're not youngsters, we don't have to suffer a long engagement. What's the problem?'

'Can you give me time?'

He let her go, managed a smile.

'Of course. All the time you need. I realise it's a big decision.

• Patricia Fawcett

You're not just taking me on, there's the girls as well. Teenage tantrums and everything. It's asking a lot of you.'

She knew he wanted to stay with her, sleep with her tonight, but she dragged up an excuse because she needed to think and she couldn't do that if he were around. She didn't know what to do. It would make no difference to him that she'd once had a baby. It was a long time ago and it wouldn't matter at all. But it would matter if that baby turned out to be Abby. It produced awkward knots that might never be unravelled. For her. For him. And for Abby.

At first, she had told herself it was just too much of a coincidence. Coincidences like this just do not happen in real life. But lately . . . she had to face up to it. Abby looked like the man who was the father of her child.

There was no way she was going to risk spoiling what was a close father-daughter relationship. She had seen the fond looks they exchanged, more so with Abby than Emily, for Emily was very much her mother's child. She was not going to ruin it for them. What they had was precious. Lizzie might be part of his past now but she would still be around from time to time and Lizzie would never accept the situation. Never.

Giving him up would damn well break her heart, and his maybe, but this way, Abby would be safe. There was still some protection. The agency would not divulge her name to Abby until they got the go-ahead from her. She could still block Abby finding out.

She did not know how she was going to tell him no. It wasn't her first proposal of marriage but she had not lost any sleep over saying no to the other.

But this time it was different.

This time she wanted to say yes.

This time, she loved him.

37

Jenny was watering the hanging baskets when Abby walked past.

'Hello, Jenny. They look great.'

Jenny smiled. 'Thank you. I'm making a big effort to be kind to all my plants. Are you coming in a minute?'

'I was just having a walk,' Abby said, smiling but a little subdued. 'I've been stuck in the office all day and I need some fresh air.'

'I'll come with you if that's all right,' Jenny said, not knowing quite why she was throwing herself on the child. It would be better all round if she stood back now especially when she turned Stephen down. They would have to learn to live with it as she and Ben had done. Stephen would never move from Curwin Hall because he loved it so and she would not move either. So it was stalemate. She hadn't yet worked out how she would cope with being so near to Abby and yet she couldn't move away, leave her again.

They climbed the stile and took the public footpath skirting the fields over to the next village. The path was very dry and dusty, edged with tall spiky grass and dried mud. A softly summer evening, one of those sort of evenings you remember in the thick of winter. Crickets sang. Scurries underfoot. Birds rustling. A sort of silence.

'I'm going ahead with it, trying to trace her,' Abby told Jenny.

There was just room for them to walk side by side. Abby was wearing shorts and a loose linen top, her hair newly trimmed. 'I thought you'd like to know. I've been in touch with The

Children's Society, spoken with the counsellor by telephone and I've an appointment to see her soon. We've got a lot to talk about.'

'Don't be upset if you come up against a brick wall,' Jenny said, trying to make it easier. 'At least you will have tried.'

Abby nodded. They had walked through to the next village and strolled over to the green, sitting on a bench. There was a pub here and a few people sat at tables outside, taking advantage of the summer sun. Jenny glanced at Abby, feeling wonderfully comfortable and at ease with her.

'Would you like an ice cream?' she asked, seeing some hikers coming out of the little shop. 'They do wonderful ice cream there.'

'Thank you.'

Jenny went across, returned with them, sat down beside her, started to lick the creamy mixture.

'Is something else bothering you, Abby?' she asked. 'Is there something you want to talk about? You can tell me. I won't tell your father if it's something you'd rather he didn't know.'

'It's a bit delicate. I'm not sure about this, so I didn't want to upset him before he flew off. He was a bit preoccupied with the business, sorting out the designs and everything,' Abby said, the cream beginning to melt on her fingers. She seemed so distracted that Jenny was suddenly very worried. A worried eighteen-year-old? The truth hit her with a thump. Why hadn't she thought of it before? Abby was pregnant. It was perfectly obvious. That's what Stephen had been on about, although he had so gone round the houses that in the end she wasn't entirely sure that's what he meant. He must have suspected it too. Abby was pregnant by Ben. Oh God!

'How long have you known?' she asked softly.

'Suspected,' Abby said, looking at her with some surprise. 'I don't know for sure. Have you been thinking it too?'

'It isn't the end of the world, you know,' she said gently, putting her arm round her shoulders. They were alone. Above them, the branches of a tree sagged heavy with broad green leaves. At the pub, the outdoor benches had emptied suddenly.

'Years ago when I was your age,' Jenny began, 'a bit younger than you in fact, I had a baby too. A little girl.' She heard her voice shake. It still did that to her, dammit. 'My parents . . . well, they found it difficult. I had her adopted. You won't have to do that. I'm sure your father – and your mother – will let you keep it. It really doesn't matter. As for Ben . . .'

Abby turned, stared a minute, smiled. 'I'm not pregnant,' she said. 'Is that what you think?'

'Oh . . . well . . .' Acutely embarrassed, Jenny took refuge in licking her ice cream. 'I'm very sorry. I don't know what made me think that. Your—' she nearly blurted out Stephen's fears on the very subject, stopped herself in time.

'What it is,' Abby took a deep breath. 'I need to talk to someone. I'm worried about Emily, actually. She's behaving very strangely.'

'Strangely?'

They exchanged a small smile.

'Worse than usual,' Abby said. 'I don't think she's eating. I forgot about it when Mum was here but I've started watching her again. You don't think she could be starting to be, you know, anorexic?'

'Goodness no,' Jenny said firmly. 'She was round at my house the other evening tucking into biscuits like there was no tomorrow. She is thin but she's OK.' She smiled away Abby's fears. 'How nice of you to be concerned. She's often concerned about you too.'

'Is she? Then you really think I've been worrying about nothing?' The relief and surprise showed, followed by curiosity. 'Did you really have a baby? And they made you give her up? How awful!'

'It was.' She felt a great lump in her throat. 'It was awful, Abby.'

They sat a moment, finishing off the ice creams.

Abby broke the silence at last. 'What a coincidence!' she said. 'Here I am looking for my mother and your daughter might be looking for you. Wouldn't it be wonderful if you turned out to be my mother? I wish you were.'

'It would be a miracle,' Jenny said with a quick laugh. 'Coincidences like that do not happen.'

Abby laughed too, dismissing it.

They strolled back, talking of other things.

38

In view of the lovely day, Harold was sporting his panama hat.

'You look a right twerp in that,' Christine remarked with a smile. 'You'll be wearing your shorts next.'

He made room for the mobile phone on top of the table, edged into the space beside her. Humming another favourite, 'I Know that my Redeemer Liveth'.

'Don't start singing,' Christine warned him, checking that nobody was looking their way. He had this knack of showing her up, Harold.

'Grand day,' he said happily. 'More days like this and I could see me staying. We could be in for warmer summers. They call it the ozone theory, Christine love. Melting icecap. Greenhouse effect.'

'Never heard anything so barmy as that. I don't know who comes up with these far-fetched notions. Pity they haven't a proper job to do.'

She was wearing a new outfit for the occasion, cotton skirt and matching top in what they called wild sage from C & A. New sandals too, pinching her feet they were. It promised to be a good day and they'd already sold some pieces. Harold had finally forgiven her about the claret jug but it still annoyed her that that little devil Shane had put paid to a few hundred pounds.

Still, what was money? Her and Jenny had been fools, the both of them. True, the last words took some forgetting, never would be forgotten, but they both understood now what the other had been feeling at the time. Reg going so suddenly like that had unhinged her a bit and she'd not been herself for a few months

• Patricia Fawcett

after. And she had to recognise that Jenny was serious about her career and would probably not get married and have children. It was her life, her choice. She would never understand it properly but she had to respect it.

Friends again then, wary and anxious not to offend each other, but friends. They were going shopping together tomorrow and Christine looked forward to that. Jenny was going to take her somewhere posh for lunch so she would wear that dress and jacket she'd worn for Shane's christening. She'd only worn it twice.

Thinking of Shane, reminded her.

'That little grandson of Janice, he got his finger stuck in a half-opened can of tomato soup,' she told Harold. 'Catherine called the fire brigade. She was frightened to death that he'd lose his finger if she tried to pull it off. The fuss . . .' She clicked her tongue as Harold smiled.

'I've got some particulars of houses in France,' he said, 'old stone houses with roses. Grand-looking. I shall start going to the local market when I get settled. They say French markets are different.'

'Countryside is for countryfolk,' Christine said, 'not for the likes of us. Townees. You'll never get used to it. It's pongy and mucky and there's all that quiet. Fair gets on your nerves, that quiet. I sat in that church at Hazelburn while I was waiting for Jenny and it was stone-cold quiet. Made me shiver.'

'I am an old man,' he said, 'and when you're old, you like quiet.'

'Quiet makes you think too much,' she said. 'What you need is a bit of something going on. A bit of life. Come and live with me,' she added recklessly. 'It'll be the best thing for both of us. We can get ourselves properly organised, Harold. We can have days about with the cooking.' She smiled fiercely at a couple of lads who were eyeing up the wares, dirty hands hovering, cotton sleeves trailing. 'Don't touch, lovies,' she said. 'You might break one of the glasses.'

Harold muttered something she didn't quite catch before adjusting his hat to a rakish angle.

'Did I hear you asking me to come to live with you?'

She nodded irritably. 'Anything to stop you going over there, you big daft thing. I've never heard such a crackpot idea for a long time.'

'Let me think about it,' he said. 'There are factors to consider.'

'Don't start getting awkward. You either want to come or you don't.'

She watched as he wandered off to get a cup of tea. He stooped a little now and he was very thin. His jacket hung on his bony shoulders. She smiled at his retreating back, recalling for a moment how he used to be. Straight-backed and proud, a credit to his profession. An undertaker of distinction.

Sisterly love suddenly flooded her, taking her by surprise, something she hadn't felt for a long time. It mattered, this family thing. Thank God, she and Jenny had squared it up. She hadn't visited the cemetery recently but when she did, it would be to take some flowers. She wouldn't see the grave neglected, dear me no, but there would be no more soul-searching. Reg was gone. Give him his eternal rest, for God's sake.

The woman on the next table top had a display of homemade quilted and embroidered cushions. Very nice. She might get one for the front room if she could get a bit knocked off the price.

Christine smiled at the woman.

'My brother,' she explained, indicating Harold's disappearing back. 'Him with the straw hat.'

'Come here often?' The woman put down the stitching she was working on and returned Christine's smile. 'First time I've been. I feel a bit embarrassed sitting here.'

'You get used to it,' Christine told her. 'We're regulars. If it was up to me, I'd pack it in tomorrow but he likes it, my brother. He used to be in funerals. Taylor & Walmsley, out at Ribbleton. Remember them? Do you come from Preston?'

'Broughton,' the woman replied. 'I'm Sheila.'

'I'm Christine. Prestonian and proud of it. I've always lived here. I lost my husband Reg eighteen years back. Brain haemorrhage.' She nodded her acknowledgement of the sympathetic response. 'My daughter, Jenny, works at CWC, the chemical firm. She has a senior job there – head of quality control.' She let that sink in and carried on, 'She's done marvellous. She's only just coming up thirty-six and that's very young to be in charge. She has a university degree, you know. In that Chemistry.'

'She must be very clever.' Sheila was suitably impressed. 'I don't have any children myself. Wish I had sometimes. We used to run a shop in town and we were always too busy. Do you have any grandchildren?'

'Oh no,' Christine said with a short laugh, 'she hasn't time for that. She's a career woman, devoted to her job. You have to admire that, don't you? If I had my time over again . . .'

'Looks like you've got a customer,' Sheila said as a lady reached for a sugar bowl.

Without pausing for breath, Christine launched into the sales patter, remarking that it was a lovely bowl that, cut glass, came from a house up at Clitheroe, she thought. They'd bought a job lot but that was one of the special items. A rare treat.

39

Stephen was away and the weekend promised to be so boring. He had telephoned before he went, made no reference to his wife, had not pressed her further on the proposal.

Jenny met her mother in town for lunch, drove her home, resisted the invitation to stay, saying she had some work to catch up on.

She needed to get used to her mother again in small doses. Easy does it. Her mother was cautious too and so far it was all going very well. A gentle getting to know each other again and, after eighteen years, there was so much to catch up on.

She was immensely irritated at herself that she had told Abby about her baby. Stupidly misinterpreting the situation was bad enough but to go and blurt that out as well was beyond belief.

Ben was lounging against his garden wall, some pretence of gardening, when she got back, coming over when he saw her. Smiling. The snake!

'I like the car,' he said. 'Suits you. New job, I hear tell?'

She nodded. Lifted out her purchases, refusing his offer to help.

'You're not still seeing that Finch bloke, are you?' he asked, following her to the door of the cottage whereupon she had to straddle the doorway with her bags and belongings to prevent him entering. 'I didn't take to him at all.'

He was not, absolutely not, coming in. Jenny dropped everything at her feet, smiled at him. 'It matters not one iota what you think,' she told him sweetly. 'Yes I am seeing him and I happen to like him. And his daughters,' she added, 'particularly

Abby.' She looked at him as she said it, making quite sure he understood that she knew all about that.

'Wasn't my fault, that Abby business,' he muttered. 'She was secretive. I like a woman to be open and honest.'

'As you are? Did you actually want something?' she asked. 'Or are you simply being a nuisance?'

His eyes narrowed, but the smile was there.

'I just wanted to offer the hand of friendship,' he said easily. 'What's wrong with that? Just because you put a stop to our relationship there's no need for us to be awkward with each other. After all, Hazelburn's only a small place and we should try to be one big happy family. This cold shoulder business is a bit boring.'

'It was you who put the brakes on things, Ben,' she reminded him, 'not me.'

'Ah . . . so that's what you think, darling. A complete misunderstanding,' he said, putting his hand against the doorframe, wedging her in. 'How about . . . how about you and me trying again?'

'What is it with you?' she asked. 'Are you trying to humiliate Stephen now? God, you make me sick.'

'I admire your fire. I admire the way you've clawed your way up in life. Got to the top. Mother likes that too. But most of all, Jenny—'

'If you don't move your hand from that doorpost, I will slam the door and trap your fingers in it,' Jenny told him, cold as cold. 'How dare you come slithering to me with this cock-and-bull story about admiring me. I wouldn't resume our relationship if you were the last man left on the planet. I know your game. And I won't stand for it. Upset me, yes, but not Abby. I will never forgive you for that.'

'I don't understand you. What is it with you and her?' he asked, the smile on the wane. 'You've really taken her under your wing, haven't you? Abby this, Abby that – taking on your stepmotherly duties a bit early, aren't you? I assume that's the reason. He has asked you to marry him, the Finch guy?'

'That is none of your business,' she told him, her attempt at slamming the door rather spoiled by trapping the grocery bag in it.

As she retrieved the broken eggs, she found herself annoyed once more at her reaction. Ben, an outsider to the immediate problem, had hit the nail on the head. She *was* behaving like a mother hen towards Abby and she had better stop it before it dawned on Abby too.

Sunday afternoon she spent packing for a trip away.

At one of the regular monthly meetings of the company Quality Assurance Managers' Committee, QAMC, she had come up with a suggestion for a strategy for minimising ongoing costs. Trying to show them she was worthy of the appointment, that's what it had been, but as a result, intended or not, she had really got herself landed in it.

Her idea to create 'centres of excellence' at three of the eight sites where they would use special and expensive techniques to do sample testing on behalf of the other sites would cost in the region of one and a half million pounds and had to be seen to generate a saving of at least half a million per annum to be worthwhile.

She was to present her detailed report on Monday at the meeting that they were holding in London and she was determined to try to swing opinion her way. The report was damned good and, although she was nervous, being the new girl on the team, she was also excited. It would work. Trevor, before he left, had OKed it with his customary cautious stamp of approval but he wasn't here any longer and it was other people she had to convince now. There was a lot of money involved and some of them were incredibly tight-fisted about spending it. Technically they wouldn't be able to fault it but that didn't necessarily mean it would get the green light. She had her work cut out.

She would not be driving herself so she was being collected at six o'clock Monday morning and driven to Manchester Airport. All she needed now was to make sure she got a good night's sleep so that she would be bright and breezy.

It was a very warm night, stuffy, with the prospect of another thunderstorm not altogether unwelcome. It would clear the air. Jenny went to bed early, a mistake of course, because it took ages to get off to sleep, even with the window wide open and the covers flung back. Summer scents drifted in from outside and somewhere an owl hooted. Tomorrow night it would be London traffic and constant sirens no doubt and the hum of air conditioning.

She must have dozed off, waking suddenly to hear the sound of a car driving past. Ben's by the sound of it. Irritated, because the disturbance had probably knocked any idea of getting a good night's sleep on the head, Jenny pounded her pillow and lay back. A few moments later, as she began to drift off, came the sound of running feet and a hammering at the door.

Ben! What the hell did he want now? If he persisted in bothering her like this, she would make a complaint against him.

'All right, I'm coming,' she yelled, even though the caller probably could not hear her. She reached for her satin wrap, decided it was altogether too sexy and would give him ideas, and slipped her mackintosh over her nightgown instead. Very fetching!

'Jenny!'

Even before she opened the door, she realised she had been mistaken. It was Abby not Ben. Wild and tousled, also wearing an outer jacket over what looked like pyjamas.

'It's Emily,' she said, tumbling inside. 'She's taken the car and she's not back and I don't know where on earth—'

'Calm down,' Jenny soothed her. 'Take it easy and tell me slowly.'

'Well,' Abby allowed herself to be led into the living room, sat down and tried to compose herself, 'you know Dad's away?'

'Yes, he did mention it,' Jenny said, feeling a tightness at the mention of his name.

'He wasn't sure he should leave us alone but I said, "Honestly, I'm eighteen . . . of course you can leave us. We'll be fine." And then,' she bit her lip, sighed, 'Emily tells me she's off to an all-night party at a friend's. Would you believe that? She's got an exam, several exams, next week. I wasn't very happy but she called me one of her snotty names,' a faint smile passed over her face, 'and said she was going anyway and I couldn't stop her.'

'And you're worried because she hasn't arrived back yet?' Jenny asked, pulling the mackintosh nearer as it threatened to show off the rather pretty slinky nightgown she was wearing underneath. Abby's pink striped pyjamas looked altogether more wholesome. 'But if it was an all-night party then she won't be back until tomorrow, will she?'

'She wanted to take the car,' Abby went on, 'and of course I said she couldn't because she can't drive yet. Well, she's had a few lessons with Dad but that's about it. She knows how to drive a bit.'

'And you say she has taken it? Your car or your father's?' Jenny caught the worry. That was serious. Apart from the fact that she might be in grave danger of crashing it, she would be in awful trouble in any case if she was found out.

'Oh mine. She wouldn't dare take the Mercedes. She pinched the keys. They were in my handbag and I've only just realised. I couldn't sleep . . .'

'Nor could I. It's so hot.' Jenny was happy to give her a moment to compose herself.

'And you know how it is – something preys on your mind. I couldn't remember whether or not I'd locked the back door and, with Dad being away . . . So I got up and got the key from my bag and then I saw that my car keys weren't there. I looked all over the house for them and then something made me check the garage. And the car's missing.'

'Oh God . . .'

'Perhaps her boyfriend's driving. At least I hope he is,' Abby said. 'Oh Jenny, what on earth are we going to do?'

'Right.' Jenny stood up, not knowing why, but it seemed a first step anyway. 'Let's phone round. Where is this party?' She sighed as she saw Abby's expression. 'You don't know? She didn't tell you?'

Abby shook her head. 'If it wasn't for the car disappearing, I wouldn't be so bothered. After all, she's supposed to be able to look after herself.'

'We'll ring the police, ask if there have been any accidents.'

'No. She'll get in trouble then,' Abby said. 'Perhaps we could try the hospitals.'

'Have you her friends' telephone numbers? The party must be at one of their houses surely?'

'Some of them. I don't know them all. I'll have to look through the phone book.'

'I'll come with you,' Jenny said. 'Give me five minutes to put some clothes on. It'll be best if we're at Curwin Hall in case Emily tries to ring home.'

It was three thirty in the morning and she was due to be up in two hours, dressed impeccably ready for her trip. God . . .

'If anything happens to Emily,' Abby said, her face quite pale, 'I don't know what I'll do. It will be my fault, Jenny. I should have stopped her going.'

'How? Nothing will happen,' Jenny said quietly with more confidence than she felt. 'There's probably a perfectly reasonable explanation.'

'For her taking my car?' Abby raised her eyebrows. 'I can't think of one offhand. She's not got a licence, she's had about four driving lessons and she'll probably be drinking under age. Is that reasonable?'

From Curwin Hall, they tried a few numbers. Her friends from school. To Jenny's relief, none of the parents she spoke to was angry for being wakened in the middle of the night, but instead anxious rather on their behalf. Nobody knew anything about an all-night party. It began to look increasingly as though Emily had made that up. In that case, where the hell was she?

'Should we tell Dad?' Abby asked as she replaced the receiver. 'I have a number for him.'

'No. We mustn't worry him yet,' Jenny said, looking at the clock. Four thirty. Where had the last hour gone? 'So, we seem to have established there wasn't a party. Where else might she go?'

'To her boyfriend's, I expect,' Abby said. 'I'm surprised but it's quite likely, isn't it?' She shrugged. 'I always felt she was making it up, all this stuff about boyfriends and what they get up to – although I certainly wasn't behaving like that at her age,' she added, indignantly comic as if she were aeons old herself.

'And we don't know the name of the current boyfriend?' Jenny asked wearily, running fingers through her hair. She felt exhausted now, from tiredness and worry. Emily was so bright and eager and beautiful and Jenny couldn't bear it if anything had happened to her either. Stephen would never recover if it had.

Abby made them coffee while they considered what to do next.

Not the police. Not yet.

Hospitals then.

Reluctantly, Abby nodded.

They tried Preston and Lancaster. No luck. Although, as the voices on the other end said, they were very busy tonight and it was possible someone had been brought in and not yet processed.

Processed?

'I can't believe she could be so thoughtless,' Jenny said, a vision of Emily dead in a crashed car bolting into her head.

'Suppose she's dead,' Abby said, reading her mind, and even more colour drained from her face. 'I feel it in my bones, Jenny. She's done something really really stupid and she's dead. She's crashed the car. That will be it. She can't drive.' Her eyes filled with tears and, with a great shudder, they began to overspill. 'It's my fault. I should have stopped her. Hidden the keys when she first asked.'

'Hey, stop that.' Jenny spoke sharply. 'Where on earth have you got that idea from? Of course she's not dead. She's irresponsible and she needs a helluva good talking to when she finally gets in but she's not dead, Abby.'

'Are you sure?'

'Absolutely.' Jenny looked round helplessly for some tissues. 'Dry your eyes and go and have a wash,' she said. 'Brush your hair. It'll make you feel better.'

She sank down onto one of the huge sofas when Abby was upstairs, finally, now she was alone, able to let her own great dread show. She had a worse fear. That Emily was fool enough to experiment with drugs. Drink. Drugs. Driving. It could hardly be worse . . . Stephen would be furious if he were here. Why wasn't he here? She needed him beside her at this very moment, consoling her and his daughter. She was trying damned hard to be strong for Abby but she needed someone to be strong for her.

The clock ticked on and still there was no sign of Emily. Abby reappeared, freshened up and a bit happier.

'Emily never wanted me to find my mother,' she said, sitting down and speaking quite calmly. 'She didn't want me to do it because she didn't want me to find another sister. It's always been just the two of us, ever since I can remember. She's my baby sister, you see.' The doubt surfaced again and a frown crossed her face. 'I don't know what I'll do if she is dead. Mum will go daft – blame me.'

'For God's sake, don't start that again. She isn't. Look, we're doing no good sitting here. Let's try ringing round some more . . .' Jenny glanced at the clock. Five twenty. God in heaven, she had to be up in ten minutes. The taxi would be here at six and she had to pack and get her documents together. She couldn't get out of it at this stage. There would be no time to arrange a replacement to do the presentation, for, at a pinch, Alan could have deputised for her.

'Blackpool!' Abby said suddenly. 'She might have gone there with the boyfriend. Try the hospital there.'

They tried. No luck.

'That's encouraging, I suppose,' Jenny said. 'She's not in intensive care, Abby, so she's not been in an accident. The worse thing is that she's stopped the night somewhere with her boyfriend. Bad enough with her exams coming up and everything, inexcusable in fact, but not the end of the world.'

'I'll kill her,' Abby said, eyes flashing now with annoyance, 'and I shall tell Dad. I keep all sorts of things from him just to keep the peace.'

'I could go out to look for her,' Jenny said, realising the stupidity of the remark as soon as she uttered it. 'But where?'

'I'm sorry.' Abby yawned, dressed now in jeans and shirt, pale-faced from lack of sleep. 'I shouldn't have bothered you. Keeping you up all night. Look at the time . . . six o'clock.'

Six o'clock!

'Excuse me a moment.' Jenny attempted a smile. 'I've got a car coming for me to take me to the airport. I'll just have a word with the driver.'

'You're not going, are you?' The question was edged with panic at the thought of being left alone to cope. Abby, it seemed, despite her general air of being older than she was, was not handling this particular crisis very well. 'You're not leaving me?'

Jenny thought of the meeting, the amount of time she had put into her presentation, the boost to her own reputation, the anger that her absence would cause, the grovelling she would have to do as a result.

Oh God!

'You will stay?'

She looked at Abby, saw the anxiety she was now trying hard to mask, and hesitated no longer.

'You bet,' she said.

They heard the car first and then a door slamming. And then the scratch of the key in the lock and Emily sneaking in.

'Hold on . . .' Jenny was through into the hall in an instant, revelling in the surprise it caused Emily. 'Where the hell have you been?'

'I beg your pardon,' Emily said coolly, smiling at Abby as she came to stand just behind Jenny. 'Abby knows. I've been to a party. I told her I would be late.'

'Late! *Late!*' Jenny screamed, temper on full power now. 'Nine o'clock in the morning. We've had our breakfast, for God's sake.'

'Good. Did you enjoy it?'

'Emily, don't you dare talk to Jenny like that,' Abby said quickly. 'I've been worried sick and so has she. You took the car.'

'Ah yes . . . sorry about that. It's OK. No harm's come to it.'

'Where have you been?' Jenny asked in a quieter tone, anger abating a little as she realised Emily was all right. No outward signs of anything badly amiss. 'We've been ringing hospitals, ringing your friends' parents . . .'

'Jesus, you didn't?' Emily gasped her horror before turning on her sister, ignoring Jenny. 'Why did you let her do that? Talk about overreacting? I told you I was at a party. I told you.' She was wearing tight black velvet trousers and a violet satin blouse, evening wear that looked vaguely tarty at this time of day. It also looked as if she'd slept in them.

'There wasn't a party, was there?' Abby said. 'Nobody knows of one so you might as well be honest now.'

'What is this,' Emily looked from one to the other, 'the Spanish Inquisition? OK . . . so I lied but it was only because you'd have gone grotto if I'd told you I was going out with Robert to a very grown-up nightclub. Naughty cabaret.' She grinned, unrepentant. 'It didn't finish until four o'clock.'

'Why didn't you ring? Pick up a phone? God, is it too much to ask? And another thing, young lady,' Jenny said, bustling in front of Abby, 'in future, you will tell us where you are going and what time you'll be in. Are you sure the car's in one piece?'

'Of course it is.' Emily shrugged. She was dishevelled and sleepy and irritatingly unconcerned. 'Robert drove most of the time. OK, so I drove to Garstang to pick him up but there was no traffic on the road and I was very careful. It wasn't far.'

'Careful!' Jenny shrieked. 'You have *no* licence. What would happen if your father found out about this?'

'You won't tell him, will you? Nothing happened. Robert's mum was in the house,' she added with a sigh. 'I slept in the spare room and he slept on the sofa. That's all.' The shrug was explicit. 'And this morning his mother insisted we put L plates on and she sat beside me and Robert drove her car so it was all legal. They've just gone. I was going to ask them in for a cup of tea but it's just as well I didn't, isn't it? I don't know what all the fuss is about. Honestly,' her eyes suddenly blazed, 'who the hell are you to tell me off anyway? You're not my mum.'

True.

And there was really no answer to that.

Abby saw her to the door.

'No harm done,' Jenny said, subdued and thoughtful. 'I did go on a bit I suppose but she asked for it. God, I could kill her for worrying us like that.'

'Thanks,' Abby said, hesitating a moment before kissing her on the cheek. 'You've been fantastic. I don't know what I would have done without you.'

'That's OK.'

She might have added, 'That's what mothers are for,' but of course she didn't.

40

The counsellor at the adoption agency was quite a young woman, curly-haired, wearing a longish scarlet skirt, white embroidered blouse and ankle boots. She was called Sue and had a gentle quiet voice and a wonderfully sympathetic smile.

There was no pressure to talk, even better no pressure to make her rush things, and so, at a leisurely pace, it dribbled out. Abby's life over the last eighteen years. Her mum and dad and Emily. The happy moments that outweighed the sad. She even talked about boyfriends and Jenny. Her concerns for trying to contact her natural mother. Sue listened patiently, prompting occasionally with a question.

'You're right to be concerned,' Sue said when Abby had at last finished. 'Some people I see never seem to have thought things through at all. I'm glad you're doing this with the full co-operation of your adoptive parents. Doing it in secret leads to problems, believe me.'

'I wouldn't say full co-operation,' Abby reminded her. 'As I've already said, Mum's not too keen.'

'No, but she's come round a little. It's not an uncommon reaction. You see, she's worried about you. Worried that it might be stressful for you and worried for herself too, that you might exclude her from the new relationship, particularly as things have been difficult since your parents' divorce. Guilt really.'

Abby agreed. She felt Mum was more complex than that, impossible to categorise, but she saw what Sue was getting at.

'Have you thought how you might feel if you're rejected?'

• Patricia Fawcett

'Rejected? By whom?'

'By your birth mother. It happens sometimes.'

But it would not happen to her. Abby just knew. She smiled complacently. Didn't she dream sometimes of her mother and wasn't she just wonderful? Someone about Jenny's age, a tall slender lady with blonde hair and her own blue eyes. That's how she saw her.

'I'll risk that,' she said, putting it aside.

'I'll help all I can,' Sue said, suddenly brisk. 'Don't raise your hopes too much at this stage. We have records to look through. Sometimes people have moved and it proves to be quite impossible to find them, especially if they don't want to be found.'

'That's what my sister says. She doesn't believe I will find her.'

'We can't make any promises but we'll do our very best. We may be able to trace your father although that can be even more difficult. Often he isn't recorded on the original birth certificate.'

Strangely, she hadn't thought much about her father, her real father. She wasn't entirely sure she wanted to know about him. However she had come this far and she wasn't stepping back now.

'Leave it with me,' Sue said cheerfully. 'I need to make some phone calls. Despite what I've said, Abby, sometimes it can be incredibly easy. Until we start, we have no idea.'

When Trevor went, his deputy had, to everyone's surprise, been promoted and it had given him a new lease of life. Trevor had, also to everyone's surprise, departed in a frantic final flurry, hanging grimly onto his responsibilities until the very last second before casting himself into retirement. He had been solidly determined to avoid any fuss, or worse, as he had said, any bloody presentations and fond farewells. It was said that he could be seen sticking two fingers in the air as he made his way to his car.

Jenny had duly congratulated Brian Bailey on his appointment before facing his wrath. God, what a way to start with a new boss.

'What the hell were you thinking of, Jenny? It was very inconvenient, you crying off at the last minute. Inconvenient for everybody. It was an extra meeting we'd slotted in as you know and there'd been a lot of rescheduling appointments as a result. Somebody stepped in, filled your spot, but you'd better have a good excuse. Were you ill?'

Jenny felt herself flush. Being ill would be OK. It would only be a white lie.

'Well . . . ?' His impatience was obvious. 'Were you ill? Simple enough question.'

'No,' she said quietly, not able to do it, 'not exactly.'

'Not exactly? You either were or weren't.'

She stared at him. God, he'd taken to the job like a duck to water. Sitting in Trevor's desk in Trevor's office. Suddenly she longed for the smoke and the red tie and the battered face. She could have explained to Trevor.

'I couldn't help it. Something cropped up suddenly. A family crisis.'

'Oh . . .'

The expectant pause meant it required a longer explanation. Impulsively, she decided it would be better to be a little short on the actual truth. Family crisis meant 'family'.

'My . . . um . . . fiancé's daughter . . . well, we thought she'd had an accident and I had to phone the hospitals and everything and by the time we'd done that, it was too late. I had to stay with his other daughter because her father . . .' She was growing ever hotter round the collar of her laboratory jacket. Dammit, she sounded half-baked. She should have left it at just 'family'. Or, gone the whole hog, lied and said she was ill. Sometimes she suspected she had a touch of her father in her for he had sometimes got himself into trouble with his boss because of his honesty.

'Are they very young? The daughters of your fiancé?' The tone was a little more sympathetic and she wished they *were* little. A missing three-year-old would sound so much more important.

'We were very worried,' she said, not actually answering the question. 'We thought she'd had an accident.'

'Yes, you've said that.'

She knew from the tone it was borderline, that he was hard pushed to think it a good enough reason.

'I am sorry. It won't happen again,' she said briskly. 'I'll be happy to do the presentation again whenever it's convenient to you, Mr Bailey.'

'Brian, please. Remember, you got this job because Trevor pushed you, Jenny. There are a helluva lot of people just waiting for you to fall down on it. This sort of thing doesn't help at all.'

He looked at her, grim-faced. He would be just as hard as Trevor to deal with except there would be no sexual eyeings-up, not from him. It was pure business, thank God.

She felt herself flush, infuriated because she had let herself down as well as the company. He obviously noted her evident distress, blessedly cut short the reprimand.

'Very well. We'll leave it at that,' he said. 'I think I've made my point.'

No smile.

He agreed to arrange an alternative date for her presentation but she was left with the definite impression that there would be hell to pay if she cried off again with another pathetic excuse.

After all that, had it been worth it?

She didn't know but there had been no damned choice. It was simply something she had to do and, thinking about it now, she savoured those quiet moments together. A bond had been forged that night. She wished she could have talked to her mother like that but her mother had always been in the shadow of her father, so much a part of him that often she didn't seem to have a separate identity.

Maybe they could get to know each other now, now that he was gone.

She told her mother everything that evening. Face to face. She had to tell someone, for God's sake, and her mother was there, sitting in the front room in Hargreaves Street. The house was in a state of disarray prior to Harold's expected arrival next week. He was bringing some of his favourite pieces of furniture with him although how they were going to get them upstairs Christine had no idea. He was to be installed in Jenny's old room, a room that had been stripped and bare for years. A room whose door had been kept firmly closed.

Jenny hadn't really intended to tell all but her mother had watched her closely all through the meal she had prepared for them and wasn't letting her get away with it.

'Now then, lady,' she said, her feet tucked into well-worn slippers that took the edge off the pretty shirtdress she was wearing. 'Let's have it. Boyfriend trouble, is it?'

Jenny laughed.

'Mum, I'll be thirty-six in October. I don't have boyfriend trouble any more.'

'Well, man trouble then?'

'All right. It's a man in the village if you must know. His name's Stephen. Stephen Finch,' she said. 'He lives at Curwin Hall.'

'Does he now? That's the posh place with the balls on the gate?'

'That's the one.' Jenny smiled. 'He's an architect, divorced, has two daughters.'

'Ah . . . I met this woman on the bus and she was telling me about him. Little girls?'

'No. One's eighteen, the other seventeen. Nice girls.'

'Well then, that sounds all right. Do they like you?'

She nodded. 'I think so. Although it's not going to be easy. The seventeen-year-old – Emily – she's going through a difficult phase. Rebellious, you know.'

'I know.' Her mother smiled a little. 'Bad age that.'

Jenny smiled too. 'The point is, Mum . . .' she struggled to come out with it, 'Abby's the eighteen-year-old and she's adopted. She doesn't know who her mother is, her natural mother, but she was born in Wales and her birthday's in April,' she added quietly. 'And she looks a bit . . . well . . . she's got . . .' she hesitated, unwilling to say it because it seemed so silly.

'So that's it. You've got it into your head that she might be our Helen.' Christine smiled gently. 'Oh love, that's only wishful thinking. Surely you can see that? It's funny the ideas you can get into your head if you set your mind to it. You haven't got a degree in common sense and that's for sure.'

There might have been a time when she'd have reacted angrily to that but that time was past.

'I know it's stupid, irrational and I know it's impossible but ... something tells me she is. Something.'

'A feeling?'

'I know it's a coincidence,' Jenny said desperately, anxious not to admit that her mother was being sane and sensible. 'But, you see, she does look like him. Like her dad. Only I could know that. And she's like me too in a lot of ways. Do you know, I've just realised who she reminds me of. You. She walks just like you, Mum. Shortish steps. Quick.'

'That's the shoes. You can't walk any other way in high heels.' Her mother was unconvinced. 'I see what's upsetting you though. It puts you in a merry pickle if you and this dad of hers were getting together. Were you?'

'You could say that. He wants to marry me.'

'Does he? And do you want to marry him?'

'Yes, if it wasn't for Abby. If she is Helen, don't you see how complicated it gets?'

'It's only complicated if you bother to tell him. Have you told him you had a baby?'

'No. Not yet,' she said defensively, 'but I will. I'm not going to keep it a secret. I'm not trying to hide it from him.'

'Truth lies at the bottom of a well,' Christine said, folding her hands demurely in her lap.

'Oh Mum, I don't know where you get all these sayings from,' Jenny said with a slight smile. 'What does it mean, for God's sake?'

'It means that if I were you, love, I'd keep it there. Best hidden. There were some things your dad didn't know about me.'

'You're saying I should keep quiet?' Jenny said, shaking her head doubtfully. 'I don't see how I can. I do want to marry him, Mum. You'll like him.'

'Then do it. All the rest can be sorted out.'

Jenny looked at her.

'Then you're saying I should say yes?'

'Yes. That's exactly what I'm saying.' She sniffed and sat upright. 'Whether or not you'll take any notice is another matter. You always did have a mind of your own, madam.'

The words, thank God, this time, were accompanied by a smile.

41

The phone call, expected for so long, came out of the blue.

'Yes, speaking . . .'

The counsellor from the adoption agency introduced herself and, before she had even got the words out, Jenny had to sit down, folded rather onto the chair beside the telephone.

The gist of it was, and it needed to be repeated, the gist of it was that her daughter, Helen, had been in touch with them, purely a preliminary enquiry, you understand. She had provided proof of identification and her sealed file had been opened and the letter in her file passed to her. The counsellor was really ringing to enquire if there would be a problem. If Helen wanted to go on to the next stage after reading the letter and taking more time to consider things, would there be a problem? Did she, Jenny, still wish to meet her, talk to her, write to her? Did she want to be contacted by phone or would she prefer a letter?

'I . . .' She couldn't think straight. 'Can I get back to you? If you'll give me your number? I need some time to think about it. I wasn't expecting this.'

She realised she hadn't expected it. Hoped for it. Prayed for it even on occasions. But never really expected it.

The girl gave her a name and number.

'I hope you don't mind me contacting you,' she said, a smile in her voice. 'I never know how people are going to react. Sometimes my calls are welcome, sometimes not. But I do need to know how you feel. The wish to communicate between you and your daughter has to be mutual.'

Jenny thanked her and replaced the phone tenderly.

So . . . Abby had the letter.

The letter to Helen.

42

'I couldn't interfere,' Christine said, watching Janice closely. 'It wouldn't have been right. She had to do what she had to do.'

'It's all right,' Janice said. 'It's no more than he deserved, the lazy so-and-so.'

Christine fussed around her a moment, relieved that Janice seemed to be taking it so well. She had thought she was for the high jump when Janice told her that Len had been sacked. Well, not exactly sacked – they didn't call it that nowadays but it amounted to the same thing when you got down to it.

'No, I can't say I'm surprised,' Janice went on, glancing at Shane to check he wasn't up to mischief. 'Catherine's sick of him. In fact,' she leaned forward, lowered her voice, 'I think it'll be the end of that marriage. It was shaky enough before. I blame it on that do-it-yourself. It gets you down, all that dust, and Catherine's so particular about the house, like me and you.'

'They all have their little peculiarities, men. We have to make allowances. Let's hope you're wrong, Janice. Adversity brings people back together.'

'Who says? Is that one of your daft sayings?'

'I don't know where I've heard it. Reg used to say it although I can't say it brought him and me close when we had our spot of bother. I should have took Jenny's side. I should have told him we were bringing that baby home and he could like it or lump it.' She sighed, bit her lip, momentarily overcome. 'I'm only trying to help, Janice. I don't like to think Jenny could have been responsible for splitting them up.'

'It's not her fault. It's his. Not going to work when he should have been. Is that a way to carry on? I'm saying nothing,' she said. 'It's up to them to sort it out.'

'But she can't leave him now. What about the new baby? And what will she do for money?'

'What *about* the new baby?' Janice asked with a sniff. 'It'll take no harm, not with me and Catherine looking after it. As for money – I've a bit put by, as you know, and Catherine's talking of going back to work after it's born. She's going to move in with me like your Harold's moving in with you. Her and the two little ones. We'll be all right together.'

'Oh I see.' Christine decided not to pursue it further. Thank goodness Janice wasn't going to hold it against her. She didn't want to lose Janice as a friend. She needed someone to talk to although, these days, she had Jenny as well. She hoped Jenny would get married to that nice-sounding Stephen. Architect! She'd brag about that and no mistake.

But she mustn't interfere. She had to leave Jenny to make her own decisions, her own mistakes. Perhaps if she and Reg had let her make the decision, all them years ago, she might have decided to keep the baby, and Christine wouldn't be worrying her head about her now, and she'd have had a lovely granddaughter.

'He's growing, isn't he?' she said, changing the subject and managing a fond look at Shane. 'He looks different.'

'New glasses,' Janice said proudly. 'Show Auntie Christine your new glasses, sweetheart. Big boys' glasses. He's going to be ever so careful with them this time.'

They admired the new glasses, sparklingly clean as yet, found him something to occupy himself with, and sat down with their coffee.

'Harold's signed the papers for his house,' she told Janice. 'Cash sale. Would you believe it? He always was a jammy so-and-so. He's moving in tomorrow.' She ignored Janice's look. 'It will be the best thing. I've made up my mind that I'm going to look after him when the time comes. After all, he is family.'

'Sly one, that brother of yours. He never intended to go to France, not in a month of Sundays. Can't you see how he conned you? He always meant to move in here with you.

Didn't I tell you he'd get round you in the end by some means or other?'

'I'm all for a quiet life,' Christine said, even though the thought had not occurred to her. It had been her idea, hadn't it?

'I'm glad you and Jenny are speaking again,' Janice said, smiling at last. 'Catherine worked it out, mind, who Jenny was. It's the name, Sweetman. Asked me point-blank if she was your Jenny. Not that she put any pressure on me to ask you to speak up for him. I did that off my own bat. Not for Len – dear me no, I wouldn't lift a blade of grass for him – no, on account of the little ones, Shane and Jordan.'

'Who's Jordan?'

'The new baby, of course.'

'Oh . . . very nice.' Christine smiled politely. 'I haven't given up yet,' she said, 'on having a grandchild myself. I think there's every chance she'll get married, our Jenny. There's a lovely man in that Hazelburn, an architect – ever so clever, he runs a business in Winckley Square – who thinks the world of her. And even if they decide to live together instead, well, I'm broad-minded, Janice.'

'So am I. You have to be these days. The things they put on that television, makes your eyes pop out, doesn't it? Your Reg wouldn't have liked it though, her living in sin.'

Christine refrained from further comment. It didn't do. She didn't give a toss what Reg thought but she shouldn't talk about him behind his back even if he was dead.

'Will she carry on working?'

'What? Jenny? Oh yes. I shall look after it,' she said, confident that Jenny's baby that was now developing into a real possibility would be a little treasure. A little girl, of course, with a nice traditional name. What had she said his name was? Finch? Something to go with Finch then. She'd have to think about that so that she could offer suggestions when the time came. She had a little christening gown put by, the one Jenny had worn. Wrapped in tissue all these years. She hoped Harold would still be around, bless him.

'It's the least you can do, help them out,' Janice said wearily. 'I just hope Jordan will turn out quieter, bless his little heart.'

'So do I,' Christine said as Shane abandoned his quiet game

• Patricia Fawcett

and began a very noisy overture on the piano, chubby grubby fingers moving over the keys nineteen to the dozen.

'Would you listen to that? There's a tune there, isn't there? He's got a musical ear. Definitely. If they come to live with me, he'll be able to pop round anytime, keep you company. If he learns proper, he can give you a tune. You like your Auntie Christine, don't you precious?' she challenged over the racket.

Christine pinned a smile on her face, not trusting herself with a suitable reply.

He had some verve, that child.

Stuff Reg.

It was going was that piano.

The sooner, the better.

43

The call from the counsellor saying she had news, although expected, nevertheless caught Abby by surprise. It left her feeling excited and optimistic although the counsellor had said very little, in fact. It was better, she felt, if they talked face to face. Abby agreed to go to see her, having to ask for yet another day off.

She had started to dream more and more of the reunion. They would rush immediately into each other's arms, recognising each other at once. She was prepared for it to be a bit stilted and embarrassing at first until they got to know each other, but they would have all the time in the world. No rush.

Sue greeted her like an old friend.

'Have you found her?' Abby asked at once, her mouth suddenly dry, trying to see something in the other girl's expression. Sue had been terribly discreet over the telephone, not actually admitting anything. The suspense was driving Abby mad. Not a dreaded suspense like the night Emily had failed to come home, not like that. More of a suppressed excitement like in the days before Christmas when you were a child. Fit to burst, as a matter of fact. Within minutes, she would know.

Sue had a folder on her desk. Her hand trailed over it but it remained closed. Something in her manner warned Abby that all was not well.

She felt the excitement fizzle.

'There is a problem,' she said, and it was a statement, not a question. 'Are you trying to tell me she's dead?'

Sue shook her head. 'No. She's very much alive. I've spoken to her on the phone. She sounds very nice. She lives in Sussex.

• Patricia Fawcett

By the sea. She's married and has other children. I'm afraid we have no joy about your father, name not divulged. There was a note and a letter in your file. She worried that you might want to get in touch when you were eighteen. The letter was updated as recently as last year so that there would be no misunderstanding. I checked with her just to make sure it still stood.'

'May I have it?'

'Of course.' Sue slipped an envelope across the desk. Abby did not read it. She held on to it instead.

'She called you Jacqueline, by the way,' Sue said, her slight sigh just decipherable. 'You mustn't feel it's personal, Abby, her not wanting to contact you. She's rejecting the situation in a way. Remember . . .' she paused whilst Abby collected herself together, 'it arouses a lot of memories for her, memories that she wants to forget. She has not told her husband or her other children and she's frightened of the consequences. She really doesn't want them to know.'

'Then she doesn't want to see me?' Abby said, the words a whisper as it finally dawned. The envelope rustled between her fingers. 'She doesn't want me?'

'Not at the moment,' Sue said, trying to be kind. 'She may change her mind when she's had time to think about it. She was very upset when I phoned. She says to tell you she's very pleased you're well and happy and that she is too. When she got married, she had a baby as soon as possible, but it wasn't a replacement she says. She could never replace you. She has three sons now. She loves you and she hopes you will understand. The rest is in the letter . . .'

'Can you tell me her name?'

'Deborah.' Sue, for all her professionalism, looked tearful too. 'As I say, she sounded awfully nice.'

Silence.

And then a deep sigh from Abby.

Against the window, behind Sue's desk, a huge bee banged angrily several times before darting off. It was a lovely morning, an optimistic sort of morning. The sun shone straight in and Abby put a hand up to shade her eyes.

'This sun . . .' she muttered.

Sue rose and came round the desk, putting her arm round Abby's shoulders.

'I'm fine,' Abby said, 'honestly.'

Her Finch upbringing surfaced and she remembered her manners. 'Thank you very much for trying. You've been very kind. It isn't your fault that it's turned out this way.'

Sue's grip on her shoulder tightened as the tears began.

44

Jenny was asleep in the hotel bed. Deeply asleep. Somewhere, in the dream, a phone was ringing. Ringing.

Oh no ... She surfaced, struggled to the top of the dream, and waggled a hand towards the phone, managed to hook the receiver off.

'Yes?' She wiggled to a half-sitting position, fell back against the pillows with a yawn.

'Jenny, it's me, Stephen. Sorry to ring so late. Were you asleep?'

The clock's features unblurred. 'It's one thirty. Of course I was asleep. What's wrong?' Anxiety caught at her. One of the girls. There was something wrong with one of the girls.

'Nothing's wrong. I couldn't sleep.'

'Oh, thanks a lot. I could,' she muttered. 'I was dead to the world.'

'You've been avoiding me,' he said. 'I know it's been hellish difficult with first me and now you being away from home but I just haven't managed to catch you at all. You've never been in when I've popped round, you haven't returned my calls. I know I said I'd give you time to think but enough is enough. I want an answer.'

'Oh you do, do you? You're going about it the right way, ringing me at this time.' She frowned, catching sight of her grumpy reflection in the mirror opposite the bed. He didn't know her very well if he thought he could get any sense out of her at this time. She was a day person.

'Look, what's the problem, Jenny? I know it's been quick, you and me, but that's how I operate. I know instantly. I knew with

• Patricia Fawcett

Lizzie ... oh damn it, sorry. I don't love her any more, darling, I love you and you love me. I want to be with you. Simple.'

'No it's not. It's not simple at all.'

'It is to me.' He sighed. 'OK. How much more time do you need?'

'I'll talk to you tomorrow. I can't tell you what I have to tell you over the phone. Not at one thirty in the morning.'

'God, you're not going to turn me down, are you?' He paused and then, when she made no reply. 'I shan't be going off again for a while. I'm going to make sure I'm home-based for as long as it takes.' A short hesitation and then, 'Did something happen when I was away? With the girls? They've both got this look on their faces. Similar to the one they used to have when they were little and had been up to no good.'

She tried a Finch trick. Did not answer the question.

'How are the girls?'

'Fine. Well ... more or less. Emily's in the thick of exams. She's been down in the dumps ever since Lizzie went back but she's getting herself back together again now. As for Abby – it's all happening with poor Abby.'

'Why? What's the matter?'

'It's the adoption thing The poor darling went to see this counsellor at the adoption agency and they traced her original birth certificate. She insisted on doing everything on her own. Drove down herself. Wouldn't let me help one little bit. When she got back, she wouldn't tell me for days what had happened. Then it came out bit by bit. Apparently, there was a letter from her mother. She brought it back with her.'

'And?' She felt her breath catch.

'You're not going to believe this but she didn't want to know. All I can get out of Abby is that her mother's called Deborah and she lives in Sussex. She's shattered, Jenny. Perhaps you'll have a word. It might help.'

The shock spun the room a moment and she gripped the telephone tight as things dizzily returned to normal.

'Will you have a word with the girls? Both of them? They like you, Jenny. As a matter of fact, and don't think I'm pushing you,' his voice was gentle and she loved him for his tenderness, 'you're almost like a mother to them already.'

'Lizzie won't like that,' she said. 'I can't take Lizzie's place, Stephen, and I mustn't ever try.'

How stupid! How very stupid. The disappointment that Abby was not her daughter loomed large, overshadowing everything. It wasn't fair. She wanted Abby to be her daughter. She liked Abby.

'Lizzie is not here, nor will she be,' he said simply. 'We'll get along just fine, the four of us. I know we haven't known each other long but . . . oh God, trying to say this sort of thing on the phone is hopeless. It sounds like third-rate movie stuff.'

She laughed to spare his embarrassment.

There were going to be problems. Heaps of them. For a start, she had to go a bit easier where Emily was concerned. Losing her temper with her was not the best way to tackle the difficulties. She would not make that mistake again.

'So, leaving the girls aside, let's think about us. Surely that's all that really matters. Me and you. I love you, Jenny. I can't wait to be with you again.'

'I know. Save the romance for tomorrow,' she told him, regretting her rather brusque attitude but not able to cope with it any other way just now. If he was here, with her, it would be different. 'I'll be home tomorrow,' she added, softening her tone.

'Come for dinner,' he said. 'I'll fix us something special. You won't mind if the girls join us, will you, at least for part of the time?'

'No, I won't mind. Oh . . . by the way, Stephen, you don't have an allergy to cats, do you?'

'No. Why?'

'I've inherited one,' she told him. 'I'll tell you about it tomorrow.'

'Good night, my darling.'

Sleep would not come. There was too much on her mind. What was it that Mum had said? Something about truth lying deep in the well. Wise advice maybe but she wasn't going to take it. She would tell him about the baby. But now of course there was no connection with Abby. Not much anyway. When she married Stephen, she would be Abby's mother in a way, her stepmother, and that was better than nothing. It would take some time to accept the truth. Her own daughter, not Abby, had the letter and was, even at this moment, deciding what to do about it.

Deborah!

She remembered Deborah.

She remembered her with a sudden intensity. The chirpy walk. The tilt of her head. The clear, childlike voice. The determined jaw and the strong nose. The blue eyes. The buttermilk colour of her hair.

Abby!

EPILOGUE

Some day it won't matter at all, this sort of thing. Perhaps by the time you're eighteen and reading this, it won't matter at all. You'll wonder what all the fuss was about.
 I love you so much, little love, it hurts.
 I wish I could keep you.
 I wish I could.
 Tomorrow will be the saddest day of my life.
 With all my love,
 Your mother.

She finished reading the letter again and sighed. She tugged and twisted the long strands of her brown hair, her dark blue eyes clear and bright and without tears.

She looked at her own letter. Tore it up. Threw it into the bin with the others. It still wasn't right. She couldn't get it right.

She was hopeless at English and this was proving to be the hardest letter she had ever written.

With renewed determination, she pulled another sheet of paper towards her and began once more.

'Dear Mother . . .